Books by Holly Chamberlin

LIVING SINGLE

THE SUMMER OF US

BABYLAND

BACK IN THE GAME

THE FRIENDS WE KEEP

TUSCAN HOLIDAY

ONE WEEK IN DECEMBER

THE FAMILY BEACH HOUSE

SUMMER FRIENDS

LAST SUMMER

THE SUMMER EVERYTHING CHANGED

THE BEACH QUILT

SUMMER WITH MY SISTERS

SEASHELL SEASON

THE SEASON OF US

HOME FOR THE SUMMER

HOME FOR CHRISTMAS

THE SUMMER NANNY

A WEDDING ON THE BEACH

Published by Kensington Publishing Corporation

A
Wedding
on the
Beach

Holly Chamberlin

KENSINGTON BOOKS
www.kensingtonbooks.com

KENSINGTON BOOKS are published by

Kensington Publishing Corp.
119 West 40th Street
New York, NY 10018

All Kensington titles, imprints, and distributed lines are available at special quantity discounts for bulk purchases for sales promotion, premiums, fund-raising, educational, or institutional use.

Special book excerpts or customized printings can also be created to fit specific needs. For details, write or phone the office of the Kensington Sales Manager: Kensington Publishing Corp., 119 West 40th Street, New York, NY 10018. Attn. Sales Department. Phone: 1-800-221-2647.

Kensington and the K logo Reg. U.S. Pat. & TM Off.

ISBN-13: 978-1-4967-1921-8 (ebook)
ISBN-10: 1-4967-1921-2 (ebook)
Kensington Electronic Edition: July 2019

ISBN-13: 978-1-4967-1920-1
ISBN-10: 1-4967-1920-4
First Kensington Trade Paperback Edition: July 2019

10 9 8 7 6 5 4 3 2 1

Printed in the United States of America

As always, for Stephen
And this time also for Amy

Acknowledgments

Once again, thanks and gratitude to John Scognamiglio. And to my father, now in a far better place, the most thanks and gratitude of all. A man among men.

When friendships are real, they are not glass threads or frost work, but the solidest things we can know.
—Ralph Waldo Emerson

Chapter 1

Bess Culpepper steered her white Subaru wagon past the First Congregational Church at the crossroads of North Street and Log Cabin Road, noting with pleasure the pristine whiteness of the stately old building. Just beyond the church was the serenely charming Arundel Cemetery with its well-tended stone grave markers. Not many moments later Bess turned left onto Main Street, making a right onto Western Avenue at the Village Baptist Church.

She didn't need to drive through Kennebunkport—a town founded in 1653—in order to reach her destination, but she so loved the quaint town with its charming boutiques, beautiful homes, and the famous, though unassuming, bridge over the Kennebunk River that she chose to do so, patiently inching her way through the heavy summer traffic. Kennebunkport's year-round community was small—only a few thousand people made their homes there through winter—but in summer the population swelled to much larger numbers.

As Bess drove through Dock Square—at an even slower pace; cars vied with heavy foot traffic—she recalled the many delicious dinners she had eaten at Hurricane Restaurant, and the excellent local musicians she had heard there as well. She vowed to stop into Abacus Gallery before long; there was always something special and absolutely essential to be found there. Bess loved to shop.

Once out of the center of town, she made a left and began the final leg of her journey to Birmingham Beach along roads that were shady with the dark green leaves of trees and bordered by charming Colonial-style homes, their lawns colorful with blooming rhododendrons, their gardens bright with peonies and roses.

Summer had always been Bess's favorite time of the year. Winters in Maine were long and more often than not, brutal. Fall was gorgeous but too short, and many years spring came almost too late to be properly appreciated. But summer! Now there was a season to be cherished. The sun in the sky until nearly eight o'clock; temperatures that didn't call for layers of fleece and wool; the sound of local bands playing rock and blues at the restaurants with decks and patios. Summer provided an excuse (as if there needed to be one) to eat ice cream whenever the mood struck and to wear bright and happy colors with pretty names like Mint Froth and Petunia Pink, and to visit the beach without the risk of frostbite.

And this summer would be the most special of them all because this summer forty-two-year-old Bess would be getting married. Like many women, she had dreamed of her wedding day since she was a little girl, long before she had any conception of the real meaning behind the pomp and ceremony. She had pored over magazines and websites, and had spent just as many hours imagining scenarios based on the classic fairy tales she had read and the movies she had watched throughout her childhood and adolescence. The magnificent wedding scene in *The Sound of Music*. Audrey Hepburn wearing Givenchy in *Funny Face*. Queen Victoria marrying her beloved Albert. Sigh.

The details of a wedding—from the veil, to the dress to the flowers to the bouquet—had been easy to conjure, even as she progressed through varying moods and fancies. At twelve Bess had thought Princess Diana's frothy confection by David and Elizabeth Emanuel was the model for the perfect wedding gown. At twenty, she had considered the possibility of getting married at the top of Cadillac Mountain, a location that seemed to call for a lacy, prairie-style dress, like something a Bohemian bride might have worn back in the 1960s. At thirty, a sleek frock like the one by Narciso Rodriguez that Carolyn Bessette had worn on her wedding day had seemed just the thing.

What had been more difficult to imagine through the years was the groom, that necessary figure who would make a wedding possible. But Bess hadn't been worried. Prince Charming would make an appearance at the right time as all romantic heroes did. He might come in an initially off-putting packaging like The Beast or in an all-around glossy form like—well, like Prince Charming—or somewhere in between the two, a Mr. Darcy complete with a bit too much pride or prejudice but an otherwise stellar character and on sound financial footing to boot. Bess had dated enough deadbeat guys to appreciate the value of financial health.

But as she approached her fortieth birthday Bess had begun, just a little, to doubt that her very own Knight in Shining Armor would ever show up to walk side by side with her through life. She needn't have worried. Less than a year later, Nathan Creek, a widower for the past twenty odd years, had spotted her across a crowd of party-goers, introduced himself, and asked if he might take her to dinner one evening. Bess had said yes; three months later, Nathan had proposed; in about two weeks' time they would be married.

For the past eleven years, Bess had owned a party and event planning company called Joie de Vivre. The business continued to flourish even in years when the economy was not as robust as anyone would like it to be. People needed to honor loved ones and to acknowledge milestones no matter how much or how little money they had. Bess strove tirelessly to create special occasions tailored for each client; she loved what she did and could think of no career for which she was better suited.

So, when it came time to plan her own wedding, Bess was in the perfect position to make her dream a reality. A wedding on the beach. That was what she wanted, and that was what she was going to have. And an essential component of that wedding was a charming vacation house from which Bess could hold court prior to the big day.

Her amazing assistant, Kara, had found just such a place. Driftwood House had cost Bess a fortune, as the owners quite wisely preferred to rent for a four-week minimum, Maine's short summer being prime time for discriminating vacationers. But nothing was too good for her wedding or, perhaps even more importantly, for her friends. And not just any friends. The friends she had made in college and had kept and cherished all the years since. Marta Kennedy, long married to Mike MacIntosh, another of the old gang. Chuck Fortunato, now husband to Dean Williams. And Allison and Chris Montague.

There was only one dark spot in the sunny scenario. Two of those dear friends, a couple since freshman year of college, were nearing the finalization of a divorce. Bess and the others were deeply puzzled. No explanation or excuse had been offered. Questions had been deflected or met with silence. Endless hours had been spent guessing at reasons why the seemingly golden marriage of two such perfectly matched people as Allison and Chris was about to be so decidedly broken.

The upsetting fact of the impending divorce hadn't put Bess off from wanting—indeed—from needing—both Allison and Chris at her wedding. Even the fact, recently uncovered by Mike through an unprofessionally chatty colleague in the law, that Chris had been the leader in the divorce proceedings hadn't put Bess off inviting him.

Marta, however, had strongly suggested that before extending Chris an invitation Bess ask Allison how she felt about her soon-to-be former husband attending the wedding. So, Bess had called Allison one evening and after a few minutes of small talk had broached the delicate subject. "I'm thinking of asking Chris to the wedding," she said. "But I wanted to check with you first. It's totally fine if you say you'd rather I didn't. The decision is yours."

After a long moment of silence Allison had given her permission if not exactly her blessing. "Of course, you should ask him if that's what you really want. It's your day, Bess. It's all about the bride."

For a split second Bess had wondered if Allison had meant something snide by that last remark but dismissed her suspicion as ridiculous. Allison was never snide. Still, Bess had gone on to extract a promise from her old friend that she was one hundred percent sure that she was okay with Chris attending the wedding. "It's just that

it would be a shame for him not to be there," she said. "Even knowing . . . even knowing that it was Chris who initiated the divorce."

Allison had laughed then, an unhappy laugh. "I suppose I should
have known it would come out sooner or later," she said.

But she had offered no further information and ended the call
quickly after that. Bess sent the wedding invitations the very next
morning. Before a full week had passed Chris had returned the reply card with the WILL NOT ATTEND box firmly checked off and a
brief note scrawled on the back of the card. *I wish you and Nathan
the best*, it read.

"I'm sure he'd like to come to the wedding," Bess told Marta
on the phone that night. "He probably just thinks that it would be
awkward seeing Allison. I'll tell him that Allison is fine with his being there. He'll change his mind. You'll see." Marta had not been
so sure.

Bess had gone on to pursue Chris with a vengeance, first with
texts and e-mails and when they went unanswered, with a hand-
written letter. When after two weeks Bess had received no reply
to this missive, she had called his cell phone; the call had gone to
voice mail and Bess had left a carefully rehearsed message in a determinedly chipper voice.

Still, Chris did not respond and finally, with both Marta and
Nathan urging she back off, Bess agreed to leave the matter alone.
But in spite of Marta's telling her that she was being dangerously
naïve in thinking that by bringing Allison and Chris together under the same roof she would work a miracle of reconciliation—and
that was indeed Bess's fond hope—Bess wasn't sure she had done
the right thing by ending her campaign to get Chris to join his old
friends at her wedding this summer.

Driftwood House! There it was just ahead. Bess turned into the
drive and parked outside the three-car garage. The house really was
lovely. Built about ten years earlier, the cedar shingles had softened
to silver. Gables, a traditional aspect of the Shingle Style home, gave
a soaring aspect to the two-story structure. A back porch looked out
over a lawn that rolled gently down to a set of wooden stairs that led
directly onto Birmingham Beach. There could be no more perfect
setting for Bess's perfect wedding.

Bess got out of her car, pushed her wavy light brown hair from her face, and smiled up at the house. It was certainly large enough to accommodate her friends comfortably. Mike and Marta were due to arrive first, followed by Allison, and then by Chuck, Dean, and baby Thomas. He would be the only child in Driftwood House until the day of the wedding when Bess's nieces and nephews, all seven of them, would make their boisterous appearance. Though it would embarrass Bess to admit this, it always took her a moment to recall the children's names and to remember which child belonged to which of her two sisters. Dennis, Alan, and Gus Jr. belonged to Mae and her husband. Lily, Tildy, Jacob, and Little Owen belonged to Ann and Walt. Bess kept meaning to come up with a trick to help her keep straight her family members, but she never got around to it.

Bess had included Marta's three kids in her invitation to the wedding, but Marta had told Bess that she could use a vacation from her brood. It was the first time Bess had ever heard Marta say such a thing. In fact, imagining Marta without her children gathered around her was almost impossible to do. But everyone needed a bit of a break from responsibility, even a Super Mom.

The car unloaded, Bess brought her travel bags inside and stowed them in the largest of the three bedrooms on the second floor. Then she returned to the car and began hauling the boxes she had packed at her office into the den, the room she had designated as her command center. A laptop and printer; charges for both of her cell phones; notebooks and pens; a framed photo of Nathan taken on the first long weekend they had spent together. In this pleasant room, *the* wedding of the year would take its final form.

Bess was no stranger to the fact that an outdoor wedding was a fairly big risk—even in the summer bad weather could be an issue—but she was prepared for all eventualities. Her backup plans had backup plans, and she had taken out insurance against every imaginable disaster that might disturb the perfection of her big day. She had even hired a children's performer to help keep her sisters' offspring occupied. Bored children could mean trouble.

Bess opened one of the boxes she had brought to the den and removed a handcrafted leather folio, a gift from an admiring colleague who would be out of the country at the time of the wedding. Indeed, many of the vendors and clients with whom Bess worked had sent her incredible gifts. The owner of a high-end boutique in Ogunquit had given her a gorgeous John Hardy bracelet. A new corporate client in Portland had sent a large cut crystal dish from Tiffany's. There seemed no end to the arrival of baskets filled with caviar, pâtés, and cheeses, or those crammed with cookies, candies, and jams. One vendor who had been working with Bess for years had given her two tickets to the Boston Symphony Orchestra; Bess had passed them on to Kara, who loved classical music. She had, however, kept the gift certificate for dinner at The White Barn Inn right here in Kennebunkport; Nathan had never been to the venerable Maine institution and was sure to love it. Everyone did.

Bess's phone alerted her to a call from her fiancé. She smiled as she heard Nathan's familiar voice greet her. The proverbial "everyone" said that the initial excitement of a romantic relationship wore off, but Bess didn't believe that it had to. Ten, twenty, even thirty years from now she fully expected to find a smile on her face when she heard Nathan's voice on the other end of the line. Romance didn't have to fade and die. It just didn't.

"So, does the house measure up to your impossible standards?" he asked when Bess got through telling him how much she loved him and he had returned the sentiment.

"Pretty much," Bess admitted. "Though I haven't made a full inspection yet."

"You know your friends will love it, flaws and all."

"I know but . . ."

Nathan laughed. "But you won't be happy unless every tiny detail is perfect. Well, just be careful not to lift anything too heavy. I'll be there before you know it."

"And you're Mr. Universe!"

Nathan, while fit, was in fact fifty-three years old. He laughed. "No, but I do own a monster of a hand truck and a pretty heavy-duty dolly."

"Good. And be sure to bring bungee cords, too. And a screwdriver. Never go anywhere without a screwdriver. My father told me that once and he was right."

Nathan promised to bring a screwdriver and with another protestation of love he signed off.

Bess sighed in contentment. She felt so very lucky to have finally found The One. Even her family liked Nathan and they had never liked anyone she had dated, not that they had ever said as much. They were far too reticent a bunch to speak freely about tricky things like emotions. Bess had grown up in rural Green Lakes, Maine, as had generations of Culpeppers before her. Introducing the cosmopolitan Nathan to Owen Culpepper, a man who had never traveled farther north than the paper mill town of Madawaska on the Canadian border or farther south than the amusement park in Old Orchard Beach, and to Matilda (née Wade) Culpepper, a woman who had dropped out of high school in her junior year to help care for the first of several elderly relatives she was to care for in her life, was bound to be tricky. But Nathan had very quickly won over Bess's parents with his sincerity and good humor. Even Bess's sisters and their husbands had given him the thumbs-up.

The raucous caws of a seagull caused Bess to frown. She went out to the back porch and eyed with suspicion the giant bird staring at her from the lawn. Hmm. How to keep seagulls from swooping in on the food at the reception? It was a problem she hadn't considered. Maybe she could enlist her brothers-in-law to be on seagull patrol. They could shout and wave their arms when one of the birds came too close for comfort. But that could prove dangerous. What if the bird was made angry by loud noise and vigorous movement?

Still, the image of Gus and Walt shouting and waving made Bess smile as she turned back into the house. Both were good men, though decidedly lacking in anything remotely akin to glamour. Like Bess's sisters, Ann and Mae, neither had gone to college. Neither earned much money in spite of working long and arduous hours. Gus could not afford to replace two front teeth he had lost in a hockey accident back when he was a teen. Walt suffered from a degenerative disc issue that caused almost constant pain. But as far as Bess knew, neither man had ever expressed dissatisfaction with his life; neither man allowed personal hardship to get in the way of his being a dutiful husband and father. And not once had either Ann or Mae complained to their big sister about her husband;

both women seemed full of genuine affection for their spouses. But would Bess's sisters, each other's BFFs, ever confide in her about anything vital? That was a question that possibly muddied the waters when looking for a clear vision of Mae's and Ann's married lives. Even assuming that neither of Bess's sisters were lying about their happiness, and taking into consideration all of the stellar qualities Bess's brothers-in-law exhibited, Bess still had never been able to identify the passion or romance in her sisters' marriages. Unlike the passion and romance at the heart of what was going to be *her* special marriage.

But Mae's and Ann's domestic bliss or lack thereof was of little concern at the moment. No doubt about it, there was a layer of dust on the living room's baseboards. Kara had ensured that the house was stocked with cleaning supplies; Bess located a duster and briskly went about the task of chasing dust. Not one little thing was allowed to mar what Bess was sure would be the best wedding ever.

Chapter 2

"Remember not to use this outlet by the toaster," Marta called in the direction of her two older children. They were in the front hall, arms folded, leaning against the wall, just barely tolerating their mother's last-minute fussing.

"How can we forget?" twelve-year-old Leo called back dryly. "You put a layer of duct tape approximately three inches thick over the broken plate."

Marta came from the kitchen into the hall and looked from Leo to his sister. "It doesn't hurt to be sure," she pointed out.

Sam, Marta's seventeen-year-old daughter, exchanged a weary look with her brother before pushing herself off the wall and heaving a dramatic sigh.

"Your grandmother will be here in half an hour. Are you all packed?" Even as she asked the question Marta realized that she had asked it at least twice within the past several minutes.

"Yes!" Sam and Leo intoned.

"You don't want to get to your grandparents' house and realize you forgot to bring something you need," she went on. Marta's mother, Estelle Kennedy, was only in her early sixties and still had the vigor of a much younger woman. Still, Marta thought, there was no need to tax either of her parents unnecessarily.

Sam rolled her eyes. "Mom, we'll be fine and if we did forget something vital, it's only, like, a twenty-minute drive back to the house from Grandma's. Relax!"

"You should be checking your own stuff," Leo said. "If you forgot something important one of us would have to send it to you overnight delivery and that would be expensive and you know how careful you are with money. And it would be kind of annoying for us by the way."

Marta looked at her middle child. His eyes were his father's, as was his dark brown hair, but his tendency to direct others and point out the obvious flaws in their thinking had come from his mother. There was no point in denying it.

Sam, however, while she had inherited her mother's medium stature, dark blue eyes, and auburn hair, had not inherited her mother's clear and decisive habits of thought. She had complained about being sent to her grandparents' house, insisting that she was old enough to stay alone in the house while her parents were vacationing in Kennebunkport, but Marta had not relented. Sam wasn't a bad kid, but she could be a bit flighty and needed to be reminded that the world didn't revolve around her. "And remember," Marta had warned when alone with her daughter, "no sneaking back here with Adam. I mean it, Sam." Adam was Sam's boyfriend of five months. Sam had taken offense at this and accused her mother of not trusting her. There had been times enough when Marta had been right not to trust her daughter but in truth, never when it came to boys. Sam was too much a part of the current generation of "woke" young people to be ignorant about the dangers of casual sex and of overt as well as subtle manipulation by men. At least, Marta hoped that she was.

When Leo was given the news that he and his siblings were being shipped off to their grandparents' house for two weeks he was unmoved; he was an expert at rolling with the punches, and before long in any new situation he was somehow in charge of it. Besides, he would still be attending a day camp for young technology geeks.

Troy, his grandparents' darling, was thrilled to be staying where he knew he would be pampered and get to play with Roger, his grandfather's Dachshund, who was notoriously fond only of Troy Sr. and his youngest grandchild. But a seven-year-old was still a baby in some ways and Marta expected a few teary moments once her youngest child was tucked into his bed at Grandma and Grandpa's that night and truly realized that he wouldn't see his parents for days and days. Marta and Mike had never left the kids alone for two weeks at a time, but this occasion—the long-awaited wedding of their friend Bess Culpepper—was special.

Suddenly Marta realized she couldn't remember where she had put the pen she had been using only a few moments earlier. She patted the pockets of her cargo pants. There was something in the pocket on her right thigh. Marta reached in and out came the stylus she used to text. It fell to the floor. "Damn it!" Marta bent to retrieve the stylus. It was unlike her to be clumsy. It was unlike her to forget something so trivial as where she had stashed a pen. "Sorry," she mumbled.

"Does 'damn it' qualify as a swear?" Leo wondered. "I'm not sure we ever clarified that point. If it does qualify, you need to put a quarter in the swear jar before you go. Otherwise, you might forget. I'd remind you, of course, upon your return, but it would be much easier for you to pay your dues right away."

Marta frowned. Could you legitimately complain about your child being a reasonable and logical thinker? Probably not. Too bad. Marta fished in another pocket and found a quarter. "Here," she said, handing it to Leo, "put it in for me."

Sam frowned. "Are you okay, Mom? You seem kind of nervous. I mean, more than you usually are when you leave us on our own. Which is, like, hardly ever, because you're such a helicopter parent."

"I'm not a helicopter parent and I'm not nervous," Marta snapped. "I'm just . . . I'm fine." Were hormones already playing their nasty tricks on her? It had been only weeks since she had verified her pregnancy, only weeks since she had unwittingly conceived this fourth child. Entirely without design.

Marta liked babies. She wasn't opposed to them in fact or in theory. She was looking forward to meeting Thomas, Chuck and Dean's six-month-old adopted son. And babies that weren't your own were the best kind of all. Parents usually didn't expect another adult to handle the messier aspects of caretaking; no one would dream of asking Bess, for example, to change a diaper. Marta frowned. But they *would* ask *Marta* to change a diaper and to wipe away spit-up and to soothe a screaming infant because that's who Marta was. A mother. A mother of three, before long to be a mother of four.

Sam and Leo didn't seem to have noticed her sudden silence, or the fact that she was frowning. When the front door opened behind them, they turned to see their father coming into the house, hand in hand with Troy. They had been packing the car with the travel bags, a cooler, beach chairs, and other necessities for two weeks of fun in the sun.

"Come on, Marta," Mike said. "Let's get this show on the road. We've got a long drive ahead of us."

He lifted Troy in his arms and gave him a big kiss on the forehead. Troy giggled and then squirmed to be let down; Marta scooped him up. Leo stuck out a hand and gave his father a manly nod. Mike stuck out his own hand and grimly shook. Sam slipped her arm through her father's and whispered in his ear. Marta hid a frown. What request was Sam making of her father that she didn't want her mother to hear? Use of the house for a party while her parents were gone? An extra hundred dollars to spend at the mall?

In spite of Sam's claim to be a feminist, a claim she backed up by attending the yearly Women's March and by supporting the #MeToo movement and every other related cause that popped up on social media, she was also a spoiled daddy's girl. Marta had done what she could to counter Mike's preferential treatment of his female child. Sometimes she wondered if she had gone too far in the direction of the harsh parent. A girl needed her mother's indulgence, too. It was a constant struggle; Marta suspected she was doing a better job raising her sons than she was raising her daughter. She wondered how often that was the case. Her relationship with her own mother was sometimes tense, but not half as tense as it had been before Marta had married and had her kids. Maybe one day she and Sam would be friends of a sort, the earlier power struggles forgotten, common ground discovered in the trials of adulthood. Maybe.

"Ready?" Mike asked with a smile.

Marta nodded, kissed Troy on each chubby cheek, told him to be good for his grandparents, and handed him off to Sam. Mike strode down to the car, a bounce in his step. Marta followed more slowly.

She wasn't really looking forward to this two-week venture, though she was acutely aware that it was Allison who would have the truly difficult time. At least Chris wouldn't be present, though not for lack of Bess's urging him to come. *Harassing* might be a more accurate word than *urging*, Marta thought now. Luckily, she had managed to convince Bess to leave Chris alone, if not for his sake then for Allison's.

What had happened between Allison and Chris to cause a rift deep enough to compel Chris to seek a divorce? Marta wondered if either would ever share the truth with their college friends. She, for one, didn't feel the same way about the others as she had felt back when they were in school. It wasn't that her love for them had diminished as much as it had altered so that now, she was less inclined to turn to Bess or to Allison when something important was on her mind, and more inclined to turn to one of her newer friends, women whose children went to school with her own, whose husbands knew one another, whose daily lives were less of a mystery to Marta. She wouldn't be surprised if this was the case with every other member of the old gang with the notable exception of Bess. Bess's need for her college besties seemed, as far as Marta could tell, just as intense as it had been all those years ago when they had been cramming for finals, rooting for the home team, and bingeing on pints of double-fudge ice cream while watching eighties rom-coms until late into the night.

Marta was almost at the end of the driveway when suddenly she whirled around. Only Sam stood at the door now. "I almost forgot to remind you—" Marta called, taking a step back up the drive.

"Go!" Sam commanded with a shout. And then she shut the door firmly against her mother.

Marta shrugged. She would send Sam a text reminding her to lock the basement windows before they left the house with their grandmother. She turned back toward the car. Mike sat behind the wheel. Two long weeks with her dearest friends lay waiting for her. Now to muster a mask of enthusiasm.

Chapter 3

"Flight attendants, prepare for arrival."

Allison automatically felt for her seat belt; it was fastened low and tight as it was supposed to be. Her tray table was stowed and her seat was in the full upright position. Allison liked to play by the rules. Not that she believed a stowed tray or a fastened seat belt was going to save her life should the plane decide to dive into Boston Harbor rather than land safely at Logan Airport. Still.

In spite of Bess's generous offer to pick her up, Allison had rented a car for the drive to Kennebunkport. She didn't want to be without her own means of transportation—i.e., escape—once in Maine. She suspected that being in the presence of her oldest and dearest friends for the first time since Chuck's wedding almost two years ago might at times be difficult. It was so soon after that happy occasion that everything had fallen apart so horribly. Two years. At moments Allison felt it had been more like a lifetime since she had last looked at herself in the mirror and seen the face of a happily married person, a person who knew without a doubt who she was, a person so sure of the love and devotion of the man she had married twenty years earlier that life seemed almost *too* good.

Allison squirmed. She was romanticizing the past again. There had been plenty of times in the last few years of her marriage when she had seriously wondered if Chris was even aware that she existed as Allison Montague, a professional photographer, a painter, a person other than the vehicle through which he could achieve his dearest dream—a family.

The woman in the aisle seat next to Allison shifted. Her comfortable bulk and all-around pleasant appearance made Allison that much more aware of her own strained looks. Pale and interesting, indeed. She wondered what the others would think when they saw her. She had lost weight. She ate when she remembered to eat, which wasn't often. At least twice a week her wonderful assistant, Greg, made it a point to tempt her appetite with warm croissants from the pâtisserie next door to the building in which Allison had her studio. To please him she usually managed to swallow part of the pastry before abandoning it to the side of her desk, where it sat until Greg retrieved it for the trash.

Sleepless nights were also to blame for Allison looking worn and wasted, but there wasn't much she could do about her appearance in the short term. Piling makeup on a face ravaged by sadness only served to accentuate that sadness. Wearing bulky clothing only called attention to the thinness beneath. Not that strangers seemed put off by her haggard appearance. There were still plenty of men who saw only the long blond hair, the height, and the model-thin frame, ignoring entirely the pain emanating from the wide blue eyes, the lines at the corner of the mouth, the shoulders that might have been held straighter if she had had any energy to do so.

Allison glanced at the overhead compartment in which she had stored a bag containing her two favorite cameras and other essential photographic equipment. Bess had hired a professional event photographer, but Allison would be documenting the wedding in her own way as a gift for the happy couple. There was a bonus to this. Being an official observer allowed one to limit one's participation in the social whirl, and social whirls had never been Allison's natural environment. It wasn't that she was particularly shy; it was just that she preferred small, intimate gatherings to large, boisterous parties. Like weddings. Especially weddings.

Allison glanced out of the window; buildings, backyards, roadways were becoming more distinguished by the minute. And with every foot the plane descended, this Kennebunkport wedding was becoming more of a reality as well. Allison was genuinely happy for Bess; for so long Bess had wanted to be married to a man who would love and respect her entirely. Well, who didn't want that from a spouse? And yet, so many people married wrongly, sometimes spectacularly so, and in spite of the good advice and warnings of friends and family. Human nature, Allison thought. The most complex puzzle there was and a puzzle with no ultimate solution.

It was going to require a large amount of emotional energy for Allison to be an attentive friend to Bess these next two weeks. Luckily, Chris would not be at the wedding. Allison had been shocked by Bess's request for permission to invite him, though on later reflection she had realized that it was not such an outrageous idea after all. Of course, Bess wanted her dearest friends around her on her wedding day. Of course, she had the right to invite whomever she pleased.

Still, Allison had been relieved when Bess told her that Chris had declined the invitation—and also, surprisingly, a tiny bit disappointed. If Chris was at the wedding Allison might be able to get him alone and . . . And what? Chris had made it abundantly clear that he had no further use for the woman who "murdered their child." Allison flinched at the memory of Chris speaking those very words, the harshest, most vile, and worst of all, the truest words anyone had ever spoken to her.

Boston was assuming its full shape below her. Allison felt a stab of nostalgia. She had grown up in a lovely suburb of the city, in a lovely home with two lovely parents. So how had such a happy, even an idyllic, childhood come to this state of miserable adulthood? If only the whole mess wasn't shrouded in secrecy. And that secrecy had been Chris's idea. She was to tell no one about the pregnancy or the miscarriage or how the miscarriage had come about. He could not, he said, handle the scrutiny and did not want to be viewed in a pitying light by anyone, old or new friends, family or colleagues. Allison had wanted to argue her husband's mandate—the unfairness of it to both of them struck her immediately—but when she opened her mouth to protest she hadn't known what to say. Finally, she had simply nodded, said "okay" or maybe "all right." So much of that awful time between the miscarriage and Chris's moving out of their home was foggy in her memory. At times this seemed like a blessing. At other times, it was unbearably frustrating.

It had, of course, occurred to Allison that Chris's demand for silence was a form of punishment; in effect, he had sentenced her to solitary confinement and had appointed her own sense of guilt and shame as jailors. If that was cruel on his part, well, she could understand and forgive that cruelty. Most of the time.

According to Bess, Allison's friends had learned through the grapevine that Chris had been the one to seek the divorce. They must be going mad with speculation! Truth be told, once or twice since Bess had admitted to this knowledge, Allison had been tempted to break her promise of silence and reach out to Bess or Marta or Chuck with an outpouring of her grief. But those excellent jailors, guilt and shame, had prevented her from reaching for her phone and seeking solace. Some people didn't deserve solace. Allison Montague was one of them. At least, she might be.

The plane shook as it descended farther, and Allison gripped the armrests. She had never been afraid of flying before, but in the last two years so much about her old familiar self had altered. So much about her world was now unfamiliar.

"You okay?" the woman seated next to Allison asked kindly.

Allison managed a nod of thanks. When the plane touched down moments later, she gathered her belongings. She yawned, not as much from tiredness as from anxiety. Still, if she wasn't going to crash the rental car into a tree she had better take a few deep breaths and calm her tumultuous mind. Maybe she should get a cup of strong black coffee, unless that would result in trembling hands and an acidic stomach. That was one of the annoying things about adulthood. You realized that every action caused a reaction, every decision had a consequence, often both good and bad.

Adulthood, Allison thought, as she inched her way to the exit door of the plane, carry-on bag in tow, was exhausting. You were responsible for everything you did and said and thought. There was rarely anyone else to blame for the bad or merely stupid things that happened to you. Allison had never been the type of person to blame the victim, not until now, not until she had been forced to accept full responsibility for the tragedy that had destroyed her marriage.

Allison decided against the coffee. There was an energy bar stashed in her carry-on; she would try to remember to eat it before starting out on the drive. There was a long trip ahead of her, the worst of which would be getting beyond Boston's notoriously insane traffic. Once out of New Hampshire and over the state line into Maine she would be able to breathe a bit more easily in spite of the fact that she would be that much closer to her destination, the house in which she would be spending the next two weeks under the direct and questioning gaze of her dearest friends. Driftwood House. The name conjured images of fallen trees, barren stretches of sand, and neglected gardens. Gloomily, Allison wondered if the house was situated precariously on a rocky cliff under perpetually stormy skies. It was a scenario that would fit her current mood nicely, though it was highly unlikely that cheery Bess Culpepper would have chosen a setting anything less than completely joyful for her wedding celebrations.

Allison retrieved her bag from the luggage carousel, deftly avoiding the unwanted help of a slick-looking middle-aged man who had been eyeing her. Allison had never been the sort of woman who tarred all men with the same brush. Now, she found herself lumping them all—with very few exceptions—into the categories of shallow deceivers, egomaniacal jerks, and unbearably self-centered moralists. The negative thoughts were unproductive, though Allison felt helpless to combat them and had finally given herself permission to let them come as they would. What did it matter what she thought of men? It wasn't as if she was ever going to date again, let alone remarry, not after the man she had adored for so many years had walked out on her in her moment of need. No, she was finished with romance. Yes, she had done wrong, but romance had betrayed her in a stunningly harsh way and she was not stupid enough to repeat a very bad mistake.

Wearily, one bag slung over her shoulder, the other trundling along behind her, Allison made her way to the shuttle bus that stood waiting at the curb outside the terminal; it would take her to the rental car lot and then . . . Well, then she would be on her way to Maine and Bess's long-awaited wedding. And there would be no turning back.

Chapter 4

It was late evening and in the dying light of day a strange and compelling shape at the bottom of the yard caught Bess's attention. She skipped down the short flight of steps that led from the back porch and made her way to what she could eventually see was the fantastically warped remains of a dead tree. Funny she hadn't noticed it before now, as it was the only object of any height between Driftwood House and the ocean.

In spite of having grown up in rural Maine, Bess was no naturalist and couldn't identify the type of tree that stood before her. Whatever it had been when alive, what remained was—well, was just a dead tree. Bess frowned. There was something undeniably beautiful about the form—about five feet tall with a trunk about two feet in circumference and reaching, arching, odd-angled branches. But the tree was dead. Bess wondered why the owners of Driftwood House hadn't had it removed. True, it posed no danger that Bess could see—it looked solid enough—but it seemed odd to allow a reminder of decay to remain in the midst of flourishing life.

Bess shrugged and returned to the house, where her betrothed waited. She liked that word—*betrothed*. It had a romantic ring. And the manner of her meeting her betrothed was also, she thought, romantic, because it had come about in an entirely accidental way.

Lisa and Howard Fanshaw were probably Bess's all-time favorite clients. She had organized their daughter's sweet sixteen party and college graduation party, Lisa's mother's eightieth birthday bash, and a ball to benefit the charity for which Lisa worked so tirelessly. So, when the Fanshaws' twenty-fifth wedding anniversary was approaching, of course they had turned to Bess to create a magical day for them.

About an hour into the festivities, held at the Fanshaws' expansive home on twenty acres of land, Bess had suddenly felt someone's eyes upon her. She looked up from the clipboard in her hand to see one of the guests looking directly at her. He smiled. She smiled back. One of the servers needed Bess's attention. When she looked back to where the man had been standing he was no longer there. A similar incident occurred about an hour later. And an hour after that. Bess was intrigued.

Finally, when the crowd had thinned considerably, Bess's hired staff had begun to quietly clear away empty plates and glasses, and the band was already halfway packed up, the man Bess had been exchanging smiles with all afternoon appeared at her side.

"Hello," he said.

"Hi," Bess said.

"I'm Nathan Creek."

"Bess Culpepper. How do you do?"

They shook hands. Bess liked the feel of Nathan's hand in hers.

"I know this is going to sound bold," he said, "but would you like to have dinner with me? I'm not a jerk," he added hastily. "Lisa can vouch for me and I've known Howard since college. I'm staying with them for a few days before I go back home to Boston. I'll be fifty-three years old next February. I think I'm a Pisces. I'm the senior vice president of communications and marketing for a company called Winter International. You can check their website to verify that I am who I say I am." Suddenly, a look of vivid embarrassment crossed his face. "I'm babbling, aren't I?"

Bess had laughed. "A little. But yes. I'd like to have dinner with you." She handed him her business card. "Call," she said. "Don't text or e-mail."

So, he had called. Thus had begun a whirlwind affair. Bess and Nathan were engaged not long after their first meeting. For the foreseeable future, Nathan would keep his condo in Boston's South End and Bess would keep hers in Portland's West End. Eventually they would sell both properties and buy one larger place, possibly somewhere between Boston and Portland, possibly in one of the cities. They were in no rush to finalize the details. In the meantime, once or twice a month Nathan would continue to travel to Stockholm, his company's European headquarters.

A honeymoon would have to wait as Nathan was due to return to Stockholm in mid-July and Bess had several big parties and events to plan and stage through the end of the year, including a major costume charity event at Halloween; no less than two weddings the week before Thanksgiving; and a New Year's Eve event in Québec City, where part of her generous compensation would be a suite in the Hôtel Palace Royal Centre-ville for two nights. In February or March, when winter in New England was at its ugliest and most depressing, Bess and Nathan would fly off to a tropical destination for a few days or maybe even a week. It was all good.

Bess climbed the stairs to the back porch and went inside the house. Nathan was peering at the books on a set of shelves to one side of the fireplace. He turned when Bess entered.

"Nice selection of reading material," he noted. "Everything from beach reads to some pretty heavy nonfiction. And, of course, a good selection of the classics."

Bess nodded. "It was one of the details about this house that drew me. Something for everyone. Not that people won't be bringing their own books." She glanced around the spacious first floor, from the well-appointed kitchen to the long, pinewood dining table, to the living area with its selection of comfortable seating options. "I just know this reunion of the old gang will be perfect," she said. "Well, as perfect as it can be without Chris. But that's all right. I'll make sure the rest have a fantastic time."

"Hmmm," Nathan said meaningfully.

"Hmmm, what?"

"You do know that the more you build up an event the more likely it is to feel like a letdown when it actually takes place?"

Bess laughed. "I'm an incurable optimist. I usually find something to be glad about in even the most disastrous situations."

"That is true," Nathan admitted. "Okay, no more trying to get you to curb your enthusiasm for the weeks ahead. I don't know why I even bothered in the first place."

"Because you don't want to see me hurt or disappointed and I love you for that."

Bess *was* an incurable optimist. Still, every once in a blue moon a disturbing thought snuck across the corner of her mind. Was she, Bess Culpepper, the only one keeping this group of friends together? If she were to give up contacting the old gang on a regular basis, would it all be over? What if she died? Would any of the others ever see one another again after her funeral? Was this entire friendship dynamic all down to the force of her will?

What if, what if? What if they were all to meet for the first time now, at the age of forty-two and -three, at a hotel bar say, thrown together while stranded by a snowstorm or a citywide power outage? Would they take to one another the way they had back in college? Bess was afraid they might not. They were different now, maybe not entirely, but they were older, more themselves than they had been as teenagers. Or, was it that they were in fact *less* themselves? The self was always changing, at least within parameters . . . Bess's head would begin to ache at this point. Philosophical exploration wasn't her strong point.

Being optimistic was.

"Where did this come from?" Nathan asked, pointing to a large aloe plant on one of the kitchen counters. "Does it belong to the owners? Only I didn't see it before."

"I brought it in this morning," Bess explained. "It's for treating sunburns. I don't want anyone suffering because they missed a spot with the sunblock."

"You really are the hostess with the most-est," Nathan noted.

"Making people happy makes me happy," Bess admitted. "Marta calls me a people-pleaser and I guess she's right about that. But I don't let people walk all over me," she added hastily, remembering with embarrassment the times she had indeed allowed that very thing. Should she tell Nathan about those times? He was, after all, soon to be her husband, and you weren't supposed to keep things from your husband.

"It can be a difficult balance to strike, serving others without letting it slip into servitude." Nathan ran a finger along one of the aloe plant's thick leaves. "I have to admit I'm nervous about meeting the rest of your old gang," he said.

"Don't be," Bess said firmly. "If Marta gave her approval, and she did, the others will love you as well. I know they will."

"Still, you've built them up as a pretty hard act to follow. I might have to ask Dean for tips on how to fit into the inner circle. Secret handshakes, passwords, that sort of thing."

"Don't be silly," Bess scolded. "Just be yourself and they'll adore you as much as I do." Though in truth Bess *was* a bit nervous about her friends' opinions of Nathan. She had made so many gruesome mistakes in the past. There was, for example, the guy who was training to be a circus clown. A few months into their relationship, he decided his career would be better advanced if he dressed the part 24/7. Things between them had gone rapidly downhill after that.

"Well, I'll just have to wait and see, won't I?" Nathan said. "In the meantime, put me to work. I've got the dolly and the hand truck out back."

Bess put her hands on her hips—such as they were. She was a small woman with a boyish figure that belied her physical strength. "The big credenza needs to be moved. It looked just right in the pictures Kara sent, but now that I see it in person I'm convinced it would look so much better against the opposite wall. The love seat will have to be repositioned and we might have to move that rug out of the way first. What do you think?"

Nathan grimaced. "I think I'm sorry I asked. But just a bit," he added hurriedly. "Let me get my back brace first. It won't do to have the groom in traction."

Chapter 5

Mike turned his attention from the road for a half a second to look meaningfully at his wife.

"How are you feeling?" he asked.

Marta smiled brightly. "Fine," she said. "You?"

Eyes on the road again, Mike laughed. "I'm fine. I'm not the one who's—"

"Not sick," Marta said a bit testily. When would Mike get it through his head that pregnancy was not an illness? He meant well, of course, but his archaic attitude could be infuriating.

Mike began to hum along with the radio. When Marta was the driver she preferred silence; no music, no conversation. She and Mike were so different in so many ways that at times it made for those ridiculous conflicts that could all too easily escalate into a full-blown argument resulting in hurt feelings. You would think that after twenty-five years in a relationship a person would no longer fall prey to minor irritations like the other person's habit of eating his coffee cake in two phases—crumb topping first, followed by the plain cake underneath—or a person's habit of putting ketchup on her scrambled eggs. But Marta and Mike did fall prey to these irritations. Thankfully, they were almost always entirely in sympathy regarding the topics that really mattered. Almost always.

Marta let her thoughts drift. Unsurprisingly, they made shore on the subject of Bess's wedding. With the bride's okay, Marta had chosen to wear a dress she already owned. And as she was still far from showing there had been no need to pay for alterations. If she could find a skilled tailor, that is. In a throwaway culture, tailors and shoemakers and anyone who could salvage a broken household appliance were a dying breed. It was a pity.

More important than what Marta was going to wear to the event was what she was going to say. She had begun to write her maid of honor speech weeks ago. She was used to public speaking; being chairwoman of endless committees had made her an expert at grabbing the attention of a crowd and holding on to it. But this was different. She had never stood before a group of friends and family eagerly awaiting a heartfelt, slightly humorous, and ultimately tear-jerking tribute to a person they loved. Marta was still tinkering with the speech and suspected she would be crossing out lines and inserting catchy phrases until the very last minute before she was called to raise her glass.

A glass that would belong to a set of Riedel glassware provided by the exorbitantly expensive caterer Bess was sure to have hired. Marta, priding herself on budgeting down to the last penny, was often critical of Bess's extravagance and had to remind herself that Bess had every right to spend whatever amount of money she cared to spend. She earned it, after all, and she wasn't burdened with three children and another on the way.

Marta frowned. An interesting choice of words. Burdened. She was certain she had never chosen that word before to describe her domestic situation. Marta glanced at her husband. He certainly didn't look like a man who felt burdened by his family. In fact, at that moment he looked a picture of contentment, tooling along the open road, listening to popular songs.

The man Marta had chosen to marry. Her soul mate?

Truth be told, there had been times when Marta had wished that Bess would abandon her belief in a soul mate. Adhering to the idea that there was one perfect someone out there hadn't helped Bess when it came to discriminating between the eminently unsuitable (there had been a white-collar criminal) and the potentially desirous (until that one was revealed as a bigamist). But she had never said as much to Bess because Marta knew she had been lucky. She and Mike had virtually stumbled upon each other. Were they soul mates? Did it matter? And what did Marta know about the beliefs that sustained a person yet to meet someone compatible enough with whom she could build a rich and satisfying life? She knew nothing.

At least things had come right in the end. Nathan Creek was the real deal. Elected by Mike, Chuck, and Allison to check him out, Marta had flown to Boston to spend a day with the happy couple. Everything about the visit had been a success. Nathan, who had lost his first wife to cancer when they were both in their early thirties, was charming and intelligent. He looked attentively at Bess when she spoke, and his responses to her statements or questions revealed that unlike so many men he actually listened to what his partner was saying.

Try as she might, Marta could find nothing wrong with him and she had taken her leave with hugs and kind words. Once back in her hotel room she had texted Chuck, Allison, and Mike the following message: *He's the one.*

Marta's cell phone jangled. It was the ringtone she had chosen for Leo. He was a jangling sort of kid.

"Hi," she said. "What's up?"

"I just got a call from camp," he said matter-of-factly. "You should expect a text soon. There's been an outbreak of some sort of virus among the counselors and the place is shutting down for at least a week. Frankly, it doesn't matter one way or the other to me—I can learn more on my own—but I thought you might like to be informed."

"Thanks, I do like to be informed when one of my offspring is cut loose for a week. And why didn't the camp contact me or your father before you?" Marta rubbed her eyes. "Might I make a suggestion?"

"Of course."

"Don't spend the entire week holed up with your phone and computer. Get some fresh air. Run around a bit. Play catch with Troy. Go to the golf course with your grandfather."

"I'll take your suggestions under consideration," Leo said flatly.

"Tell Dad to pay attention to the road. He gets too distracted by the radio."

Leo signed off and Marta sighed. "I know he's my own flesh and blood, but I swear sometimes he freaks me out. Was he born an adult?"

"Not when he's forbidden seconds of ice cream after dinner." Mike smiled. "Leo is an unusual kid, but you handle him so well. You really are Super Mom."

"Hmmm," Marta said, looking out the passenger side window at the passing landscape.

"Hey, did I tell you that Stan's wife is in Japan for two months?" Mike went on. "She's taking an advanced course in Ikebana. Stan is beside himself. Marcia left everything in tip-top shape, of course, you know what she's like, super organized, but not a day goes by when he doesn't show up to work with a major trauma to report, like not being able to find the milk—how do you lose a bottle of milk!— or not being able to figure out the TV remote. I don't know, Marta. I chuckle when he goes on about his sorry life, but I know I'd be the same way if you ever decided to go away for a week. That one night you spent in Boston a few months ago was tough enough!"

Marta managed a smile. Mike meant his words as a compliment and a sincere one at that, but in truth she felt annoyed. She would prefer to be missed for the passion she evoked in her husband's breast, not for her efficiency. But she *was* an efficient person, and proud of it. When Mike was called away on business Marta managed just fine without him. Okay, a week wasn't a lifetime, but there was no doubt in Marta's mind that she was more than competent to handle the world on her own.

Well, if not *the* world, then *her* world, the one that involved managing the family's finances, supervising the day-to-day running of the household, seeing to the kids' education and after-school activities, keeping her involvement in the community alive, assuring that Mike was in a state of decent dress, and . . . And what? What did she organize or handle or assure for *herself*, only herself? Nothing. Nothing at all.

Marta frowned. Sometimes it felt like being a wife and mother had served to erase the person beneath—below? behind?—those social roles. And the unexpected fourth child would seriously damage, if not destroy, her nascent plans to build a life of her own that had nothing to do with the domestic duties that had come to feel so deadly dull, even stupifying.

"Oh, I love this song!" Mike cried.

Mike began to warble what he thought were the words to the bouncy tune. Mike didn't listen to lyrics all that closely. Sort of like how he didn't listen all that closely to what his wife was saying.

"Wait, you used to love this one!" Mike now exclaimed as the opening bars of Sheryl Crow's "Everyday Is a Winding Road" sounded through the car.

Marta leaned her head against the headrest and wondered. Had she once loved this song? She couldn't remember. Odd. But maybe not so odd. So much had happened since college; her life had become weighed down by a million little details and distractions and disturbances and responsibilities . . . And all had served to dim memories of the time when Marta Kennedy existed on her own, beholden to nobody but herself.

Those were the days, Marta thought, of freedom and happiness. Sometimes—but only sometimes—she missed them.

"How are you feeling?" Mike asked again.

Only sometimes.

Chapter 6

The rental car was a bit larger than what Allison liked to drive, but better she supposed than being cramped. She didn't like to feel cramped. And the air-conditioning worked, something you couldn't always be sure of in a rental car, in spite of assurances. All in all, she felt comfortable behind the wheel as she made her way north to Maine.

For the thousandth time, Allison mentally reviewed the contents of her travel bags, stowed in the trunk of the car. She didn't think she had forgotten anything vital and even if she had, southern Maine was hardly the end of the world. And there was always Amazon. One thing Allison had not brought with her on the flight from Chicago was a special gift for Bess. In addition to the photo documentation of the festivities she would put together after the wedding, Allison had made Bess a painting. She had wanted to give her something more personal than a contribution to one of her favorite charities, though it could be argued that such a donation was a highly personal gift indeed.

The idea for the painting had come to Allison not long before when she had come across a photo of herself and Bess taken in Salem, Massachusetts, in their junior year. (A fellow tourist had obligingly taken the shot, this being before the time of selfies.) The highlight of their day trip was a tour of the famed House of Seven

Gables, a timber-framed mansion built in 1668 and made famous by Nathaniel Hawthorne in the novel by that name. The building was said to be haunted, though, as their guide pointed out before the tour began, only the most highly attuned people were able to sense the otherworldly presences. It turned out that Allison and Bess were highly attuned people. Bess had gotten seriously dizzy on the staircase to the attic, home, it was said, to the ghost of a young boy; her hands were shaking badly by the time they reached the top of the stairs, where Allison had been overcome by a sense of cold and sickness. Ghosts. No doubt about it. They had been glad to get away, but the experience had fascinated them and been the topic of much conversation for a long time to come. Conversation between Allison and Bess. Neither had told their friends about their supernatural experience. They knew an unreceptive audience when they saw one.

Allison half smiled as she passed a car loaded with canoes and bicycles; a family heading to Maine, the Vacation State, where life was the way it should be. If she had driven all the way from Chicago she would have brought the painting along; as it was she had sent it on ahead to Driftwood House. And if a portrait of The House of Seven Gables seemed an odd one for a wedding present, no doubt Allison's emotional distress could be blamed. She remembered now the images she had conjured of Driftwood House as a place of almost Gothic gloominess. Another haunted house? Not likely.

Not for Bess Culpepper's long-awaited wedding day. Allison frowned. The very last thought that would cross Bess's mind as she joined hands with Nathan was that the man she was marrying before the eyes of friends, family, and God might one day be divorcing her. But it could happen. It did happen.

And in Allison's case it was all because of Chris's obsessive desire for a child to replace the brother he had lost so long ago.

They had been trying the good old-fashioned way to have a child for several years before Chris suggested they investigate Assisted Reproductive Technology. Allison, eager to start a family, had agreed.

What they had learned was sobering.

While there was no denying the importance of ART, there was also no denying the many risks involved. Egg retrieval could result in bleeding or infection, or even damage to the bladder or bowel. And there was the chance of multiple pregnancies and the attendant moral and economic issues that raised.

Allison and Chris had been made to realize the significant financial, physical, and emotional commitment involved in undertaking a course of ART. One round of IVF could cost up to $17,000. And ART did not guarantee results. In the United States, the live birth rate for each IVF cycle started for a woman between the age of thirty-eight and forty—the category into which Allison fell during the final round she had undertaken—was a mere twenty-three to twenty-seven percent. And the rate of miscarriage was similar to that of an unassisted conception; in both situations, the risk of a miscarriage increased with the age of the mother. Chris knew that. They had been told often enough.

But nothing seemed to matter to Chris after the miscarriage, only the fact that—as he saw it—Allison had destroyed his attempt to bring his brother back to life.

As she often did, Allison glanced at her wedding ring. Her engagement ring, a two-carat asscher cut diamond set in platinum, was in a private safe deposit box. She wasn't afraid of Chris's taking the ring from her. Not really. At least, the old Chris would never have dreamed of doing such a thing. Then again, the old Chris would never have dreamed of divorcing his grieving wife.

The last time she saw Chris—the day he had moved out of their home and back in with his parents—he hadn't been wearing his wedding ring. Sometimes she wondered what he did with it. Sometimes she told herself she didn't care, not even about what Chris felt about his soon-to-be ex-wife attending Bess's wedding with the other members of their tribe. For all Allison knew Chris could be dating someone, even planning to propose after the divorce became final. Maybe this woman had already proved her fertility; maybe Chris was poised to be a stepfather as well as a father of his own biological child before long.

The driver to her right leaned on his horn. "Damn it," Allison muttered. She had drifted. She hadn't been paying full attention. Maybe she should have had that cup of coffee before leaving the airport after all. She felt a wave of exhaustion overcome her, and gripped the steering wheel more tightly. Why was she doing this to herself? *Who* was she doing this for? Who among the old college gang did she genuinely still feel close to? Was remembered affection as valuable as current affection? Did it matter in the end?

Allison's head began to hurt. Maybe, she thought, she should turn the car around and drive back to the airport. She could be in Chicago in a matter of hours. Bess would understand. It was too much to ask of Allison to participate in a friend's joyous moment when her own heart was broken beyond repair.

But then Allison thought of all the times when Bess had been there for her. When Allison's computer had died while she was writing her end-of-term papers, Bess had worked into the night to retrieve the important files. When her wallet had been stolen and with it the cash she had budgeted for the month, Bess, never flush herself, had loaned her enough money to get through. And when Allison had broken an arm while Chris was on a business trip in Poland, Bess had flown to Chicago to help Allison around the house before she was able to go back to work. Both Allison and Chris had been so grateful.

You could count on Bess Culpepper. *And she can count on me,* Allison told herself, sitting straighter behind the wheel. With grim determination, Allison continued north to Maine.

Chapter 7

"You're glowing!" Mike announced the moment Bess opened the door.

Bess laughed. "I think a bride is supposed to blush and an expectant mother to glow."

Mike looked well, if tired. He was still a handsome guy, though a bit on the pudgy side, no doubt due to long hours stuck at a desk. Marta looked tense, but she often looked tense. Nothing new there.

"Well," Marta said when she had hugged Bess. "Let me see the ring."

"It's an antique cushion cut diamond," Bess explained. "I had it set in a custom rose gold design. Do you love it?"

Marta laughed. "Yes, Bess," she said, "I love it." Marta's own engagement ring was comprised of a small, but good, round, brilliant diamond set on a plain yellow gold band; the wedding band matched. "Hey," Bess had heard Marta say on more than one occasion, "I have more important things on which to spend my money than diamond upgrades." Bess assumed, of course, that by "things" Marta meant her children and their education.

Nathan, who had been on the phone with his office, now emerged from the den, hand outstretched to greet Mike and Marta. "I'm so glad you're here," he said. "Bess isn't the most patient person when it comes to waiting for her guests."

Bess shrugged. "I get worried," she said. "But you're here now and the festivities can begin. Your bedroom is on the second floor; you'll be sharing a bathroom with Allison. I've stocked the house with everyone's favorites, but if there's anything you need or want that I've forgotten just let me know. If I can't get it locally I'll ask Kara to hunt it out in Portland and drive down with it."

"Stop fussing, Bess," Marta commanded.

Nathan smiled. "You know she can't. Fussing is in her blood." He turned to Bess. "I've got the list for the fish market. Mike, want to come along?"

Mike agreed. "I'll bring the bags up when I get back," he told Marta.

"I'll take them up," Marta said quickly. "There's no need to wait on me."

Bess thought Mike was about to argue, but he didn't.

"Don't forget the oysters," she instructed as the men walked toward the door. "A lot of them. You still love oysters, right?" Bess asked Marta when they had gone.

"I don't know about love them," Marta said. "They're okay. Mike will eat what I don't, no worries there."

"I could call Nathan and have him pick up something else for you, whatever you'd like. Mussels? Clams? I could make clams casino or—"

"Bess! Enough. You're not entertaining royalty. It's just us. Good ole Mike and Marta."

Bess smiled warmly. "My best friends in the world."

"Look, I'm sorry if I sounded short-tempered," Marta said. "It was the drive. My back is hurting, that's all."

"Back pain is the worst! Would you like a heating pad or an ice pack?" Bess asked. "I have ibuprofen and Tylenol, and I'm almost certain there's a brand-new tube of one of those creams you rub into sore muscles. I can't remember if it's the kind that turns hot or cold, but I can get it for you."

"I'm fine, thanks," Marta insisted. "I don't need anything. Really. The house is beautiful, by the way. How did you get it? Don't these places usually book years in advance?"

"They do. It's a miracle that it was available." Bess suddenly frowned. "I just hope it won't be too tight once everyone is here."

Marta laughed. "It's not as if a person couldn't escape to the beach if she needed some time on her own. You've really outdone yourself this time, Bess."

"A girl only gets married once." Bess winced. "God, I'm glad Allison isn't here. What I mean is that I intend to marry only once."

"I don't think many people intend to marry multiple times," Marta pointed out. "Things just turn out that way."

"They won't for me," Bess insisted. "I know it. Only death will part me from Nathan and Nathan from me."

"You know, when your Pollyanna attitude isn't annoying me it's striking me as being oddly admirable."

Bess smiled. "Thank you."

"But could we lighten up a bit, please?" Marta asked. "There's no need to bring death into things."

"Sorry. But we're having death in the ceremony. What I mean is the minister is saying 'til death do you part' or something like that."

"You're taking this very seriously, aren't you?" Marta said in a considering tone.

Bess frowned. "Of course, I am," she said. "How could I not?"

Marta put her arm around Bess's shoulders. "Don't mind me. Like I said, my back hurts and pain makes me grumpy."

"How about a glass of champagne?" Bess suggested. "I know you don't usually drink but champagne is pretty much the antidote to anything unpleasant."

"No, thanks," Marta said. "But that shouldn't stop you. I'll have a glass of whatever juice you've got on hand and we'll toast. To Bess and Nathan and the most perfect wedding ever."

Bess fetched the drinks. After taking a sip of her champagne, she said, "I'm looking forward to seeing Allison, but I'm also a bit nervous. I mean, are we not supposed to ask about the divorce? All Allison will tell me is that things weren't working anymore. What does that even mean? It's so ridiculously vague."

"She's hiding something, all right," Marta said. "They're probably claiming irreconcilable differences as the cause for the divorce, which is just a convenient way of saying to others, butt out. Bad stuff happened and it's none of your business."

"Yeah, maybe, but—"

"Leave Allison alone, Bess. Let her just enjoy this beautiful house on the beach."

But Bess couldn't leave it alone. "I just can't understand why neither one of them came to us for support. We're all so close."

"We *were* close," Marta replied. "Once upon a time. But we've changed, Bess. Everything has changed. Everything is always changing. That's the only constant in life, change."

Bess knew the horror she felt at Marta's words showed; she did not have what was known as a poker face. "Surely not *everything* changes," she cried. "Because if nothing is sure and solid, then why am I bothering to get married?"

Marta sighed. "Oh, come on, Bess! You can't really be telling me that at the age of forty-two you're not well aware of the fact that nothing stays the same for very long."

"All right," Bess conceded. "Of course, I know that *most* things don't stay the same for long, sometimes not even from one moment to the next. But that doesn't mean I can't believe that *love* never dies or that *friendship* can survive any manner of traumas."

"Bess, your firm belief in the fundamental goodness of people and in the fairness of the world is one of the primary reasons we all love you."

Did she detect something insincere behind Marta's words? No, Bess thought. That was craziness.

"Thanks, Marta," she said. "I'm so glad you're here."

Chapter 8

Marta looked around the room Bess had selected for her and Mike. The semi-sheer curtains were a sparkling white. The sheets on the bed were high count cotton. The pillows were perfectly plumped. A vase of fresh flowers lent the room a pleasant but not overwhelming scent of early summer. A stack of fresh white towels sat on a bench next to the painted dresser.

Mike's favorite bit of the room was the massive welcome basket. It contained all sorts of goodies. There was a bottle of sunblock and a tube of lip balm. There were two sun visors, one navy, one pink, on which was printed: BESS LOVES NATHAN. There were two pairs of red plastic sunglasses with frames shaped like hearts. There was a box of truffles from Harbor Candy in Ogunquit. Mike loved truffles. A plastic-coated folding map of the attractions in the area would come in handy; it highlighted historic homes and museums; shops and galleries; nature preserves and beaches. A bottle of wine, a jar of caviar, a box of crackers—was there nothing Bess had not thought of?

With her attention to the details of comfort, and her warm and giving nature, Bess would have made a very good mother, which was why Marta found it odd that Bess had never wanted children. But no one ever knew what went on in another person's psyche, Marta thought as she stretched out on the comfortable bed. Bess's sisters had certainly provided their older sibling with plenty of kids to spend time with if she chose to.

Marta reviewed what she knew of Bess's sisters. Neither Ann nor Mae Culpepper had gone to college. Each had married soon after graduating from high school. Ann had four children and was pregnant with her fifth. Mae had three children, the oldest of whom was ten. Neither woman worked outside of the home. For money, that is. Bess had intimated that Ann and Mae were active in the Green Lakes community. It was where they had been born and raised.

How much, then, did Marta have in common with Bess's younger sisters, especially Ann? More than most people knew.

"My deep, dark secret," Marta whispered. Well, one of them. The other would remain forever veiled. . . .

Marta had often wondered what would compel a person to write an autobiography. (Apart from a huge advance, of course.) Whenever she tried to trace the route her life had taken, she met with so many obstacles to memory. Facts blurred. Fictions seemed real. Timing got mixed up; what had she done and when had she done it? Lately, this exercise had been driving her a little mad.

There were a few irrefutable facts, however. Mike had gone on to law school after graduation from college. Marta had not. Her decision had come as a surprise to just about everyone who knew her. Her grades were excellent. Her LSAT scores near perfect. Her extracurricular activities, including important internships, outstanding. Then why, people wanted to know, wasn't Marta going on to obtain a degree in the law as she had planned?

Why indeed.

If Marta's memory served her—and that was debatable—the decision had developed slowly but surely during the course of her junior and senior years. The more she read about the emotional and intellectual benefits to a child of growing up with a parent (or grandparent) tending the home fires, the more she thought about how much she appreciated having grown up with a stay-at-home parent, the more certain she became. What she really wanted for her life was to be a full-time mother, to raise a family without having to divide her time between the demands of a career and the demands of the home. There would be time and space for other things in the future.

Marta frowned. Here was where things had gotten odd. Smart women like Marta Kennedy didn't put a stop to their careers before they had begun to stay at home and raise kids. They just didn't. Strong, intelligent, nobody's fool Marta, though convinced of the rightness of her chosen path, had yet been too embarrassed to admit the reason behind her decision to forgo law school. "I've changed my mind," she told inquirers loftily. "I believe I'm allowed to do that." To herself she said: "I can go back to school anytime I want. School will always be there."

But that sort of thinking was naïve. Yes, school was always there, but as an adult with a busy life raising children and running a home, how could she ever be a student in the fullest sense? Even if she enrolled part-time in a degree program, how would she manage the day-to-day stuff like driving Leo to debate society and getting Troy ready for school each morning and helping Sam with her history homework while attending classes and writing papers, studying for exams, and meeting with fellow students to argue legal points and hone her writing skills? It was ridiculous to think that Mike and the kids would step in to take over part of her household responsibilities—ridiculous and unfair. Marta often recalled something her paternal grandfather was fond of intoning when one of his grandchildren complained of life's unfairness: "Tough luck, kiddo," he would say. "You made your bed, now you've got to lie in it." Her paternal grandfather was not the warmest fellow; his grandchildren seemed more of a source of annoyance to him than of joy. Still, he had a point. Most troubles in life were brought on by one's poor choices, and to complain about those choices after the fact was totally unproductive. Human, understandable, but unproductive.

Marta twisted onto her side. She had often wondered why her parents of all people hadn't urged her to continue her studies. They had always been proud of their daughter's intelligence and work ethic. But even if Marta's parents had protested, would she have changed her mind and gone on to law school? Unlikely. At the time, she had been thoroughly committed to her domestic goal.

At the time?

Marta sighed. Blushing bride-to-be. Glowing mother-to-be. She was sorry she had been so out of sorts with Bess earlier, but Bess was the sort of person who dug at any little thing she saw as worrying until she unearthed its cause. The problem was that Bess often imagined trouble in the first place, so concerned was she with the well-being of the ones she loved, so that in some crazy way she wound up creating a problem that hadn't existed in the first place. She could drive you mad but for the fact that her heart was truly in the right place.

"She's here!"

This shout was followed by the crunch of a car's tires on gravel. Allison had arrived. Marta got up from the bed and went downstairs to join her friends. They were gathered in the front hall.

Allison had always been thin—she was one of those people who lost a pound if she skipped a meal—but now she looked almost skeletal. The skin around her eyes was taut and her hands were trembling ever so slightly. For a split second, Marta wondered if Allison was physically ill, recovering from something that could be dangerous to a pregnant woman and her unborn child. Then she scolded herself for succumbing to paranoid nonsense. Allison wasn't careless. If she was carrying a contagious bug she wouldn't have inflicted herself on her friends, especially at so special a time.

No, Allison's malady was one of the spirit. This visit must be costing her greatly. Marta felt a flash of annoyance when she recalled how Bess had pursued Chris. His presence at the house would have killed Allison.

Mike leaned toward Marta. "Poor Allison," he whispered. "She looks awful. Why didn't she just come for the wedding itself rather than the full two weeks ahead of time? It would have been easier on her I'm sure."

"I have no idea," Marta whispered back. She moved forward and greeted Allison, whose hug was quick and light.

"This is truly the most gorgeous beach house I've ever seen," Allison cried, turning to Bess. "Truly. *The* most gorgeous!"

Marta blinked. Allison's enthusiasm was almost manic.

"Did my package arrive yet?" Allison asked. "The one marked Do Not Open."

"Yes," Bess said, "and I'm dying to see what's inside. Can't I—"

Allison shook her finger at Bess. "No, you have to wait until your wedding day."

Nathan lifted Allison's bags and headed for the stairs. Mike fidgeted, clearly awkward in Allison's presence. Bess fussed.

And Marta watched.

Chapter 9

Allison hefted one of her travel bags onto the bed and opened it. She could still feel the eyes of her friends upon her. She was aware she had been acting a bit over the top, extolling the beauties of Driftwood House, being so mock stern with Bess about her not sneaking a look at the painting. It had been a poor effort to avert attention away from her appearance; no doubt her unusual animation had had just the opposite effect.

Thankfully, Allison thought, Bess had given her a room clearly meant for one. The bed was a queen; there was one set of pillows on it; there was one armchair in the corner; there was one dresser against the wall. There was nothing within these four walls to emphasize the fact that she was on her own, unlike what had greeted her downstairs. The pitying looks from Bess. Marta's eagle-eyed glance of concern. Mike had been awkward with her, making it all the more obvious that something was amiss. If only he had grabbed her in a bear hug like he always had, said simply, "It's good to see you, Allie," instead of mumbling a greeting, avoiding her eye, and patting her on the shoulder much as he would pat a dog of whom he was unsure. Gently. Cautiously.

Thank God for Nathan, Allison thought as she brought her bras, underwear, and nightgowns to the dresser. Of course, he only knew of her through the others, but Allison had the feeling that even if he had been greeting an old friend who had gone through a traumatic time his manner would be more natural than Mike's, less pitying than Bess's, less sharp-eyed than Marta's. Maybe she was being unfair to her old friends. So be it.

Allison opened the closet to find padded hangers and a sweet-smelling sachet tied to the rack. Chuck would great her normally and naturally, she thought as she slipped a linen blouse onto one of the hangers. And it would be nice to see Dean again. She had enjoyed getting to know him during the three-day festivities that marked his wedding to Chuck. And the baby . . .

Meeting Thomas would be a challenge. Since the miscarriage, the sight of babies and toddlers could cause Allison actual physical discomfort in addition to the expected emotional pain. But she could not let the others see any sign of her discomfort. She could not let slip any clue as to the weighty secret she held.

Allison closed her travel bag and stowed it at the back of the closet. She dreaded dinner that evening. She would join her friends, eat what she could, and escape as soon as possible without giving rise to too much comment once she was gone. Once back in her room she could collapse into her own misery until she had to face her friends again in the morning.

With a sigh, Allison sank into the high-backed rocking chair and carefully removed her wedding ring. The inscription inside the ring Chris had given her, worn now by constant wear, read: ALWAYS MINE. The inscription inside the ring Allison had given Chris read: ALWAYS YOURS. Only in the past few months had these sentiments struck her as problematic. Chris had claimed her as eternally his. She had pledged to belong to him eternally. There was a disparity there.

Had she given away all of her agency when she promised to belong to Chris forever? Perhaps it hadn't been the wisest promise to make, but she had been so in love there had seemed no sacrifice too large.

"I knew from the very moment I first saw you," Chris had told Allison early in their relationship, "that you were the one I was meant to marry. It was as if there was a shining light over you, a halo around your head." Allison had laughed. "The halo was probably just the sun on my hair. Surely you don't see me as a saint?" Chris had smiled. "To me, you are perfect and if that makes you a saint, then so be it."

Ominous words if only she had known it then. Adoration could not coexist with equality in a relationship. No one could live up to a reputation for saintliness (especially one based on nothing more than the worshipper's fantasy), and it was wrong of anyone to expect a person to conform to an ideal. Still, there was no getting around the fact that she had failed Chris, the only man she had ever loved, when she had insisted on going to work that fateful day. . . .

Allison returned the ring to her finger, got up, and quickly changed for dinner. Clothes worn on a plane always seemed in need of an immediate and thorough washing; maybe after dinner she would toss a small load into the machine Bess had told her was located in a room off the kitchen.

Allison's pedestrian musings were interrupted by a knock at the door. She opened it to find Bess.

"I just want you to know something," she said, coming into the room. "I wanted both you and Marta to stand up for me at the wedding, but Nathan pointed out that given the situation it might be too difficult for you. I mean, it's probably going to be painful enough for you to smile your way through a wedding ceremony as a guest. To ask you to stand by my side in front of a whole bunch of people you mostly don't even know—Well, it seemed unfair of me to ask."

Allison smiled. "I'm grateful," she admitted. "I suspect that if I had a big role to play I might ruin your celebration by being a sobbing mess."

"I got you a special posy to carry, only slightly different from Marta's bouquet. Now, let's go down to dinner." Bess linked her arm through Allison's and Allison thought she felt her friend recoil from the boniness of Allison's arm through her lightweight blouse.

But maybe that was her imagination.

Chapter 10

Bess was pleased to note that Allison was wearing her wedding ring. It must be a sign of hope, a sign that all was not necessarily lost, a sign that . . .

Or maybe it was just habit. Interestingly, on their way downstairs to dinner Allison had asked to take a close look at Bess's engagement ring. Her enthusiasm had seemed genuine if a bit much, as had been her praise of Driftwood House. Poor Allison, Bess thought.

Now they were gathered at the large table in the dining area. The windows were open and an ocean breeze wafted through.

"The hostess with the most-est," Mike said, patting his stomach. "But where's the barbeque sauce?"

Bess began to rise. "I could run out and—"

"No!" her friends chorused. "I was only kidding," Mike added. "You've provided us with a fantastic Welcome-to-Maine spread."

That had been the point. Bess had ordered fish and chips from a popular local restaurant. It was a simple meal that could go horribly wrong if you didn't have the right equipment at home for frying, but the Harbor House Clam Shack always nailed it. The fish was sweet and flaky, and the fries were crisp on the outside and tender within. Another night there would be lobsters for dinner, and one morning they would visit a restaurant where Nathan could order Lobster Benedict, one of his all-time favorite indulgences (he had several), and Mike, whose taste in food was distinctly basic, could be happy with the blueberry pancakes. (If the blueberries came from out of state—it was a bit early for the Maine season—Mike wouldn't be the wiser.) One of the keys to a successful party, Bess had learned early on, was food and plenty of it.

Though there was always one person at an event who for some reason couldn't be tempted by the delicacies provided. Tonight, it was Allison; she barely touched her meal, though she had drunk two glasses of red wine in rapid succession, resulting in her cheeks flushing and an artificial spark appearing in her eyes.

"So," Bess announced. "I have a surprise for everyone. Remember when we had that fondue party back in senior year?"

Mike frowned. "Yeah, it took months for that burn on my wrist to heal. I've never understood the point of fondue. I like to eat my dinner without the risk of being engulfed in flames while doing so."

"The cheese sauce was good," Marta commented. "What was in that, anyway?"

"Gruyère and sherry," Bess told her. "Very cheap sherry."

"The meat was pretty much inedible," Allison said, one of her first verbal contributions of the evening. "It was like the proverbial shoe leather."

"Well, we're having a fondue party two nights before the wedding," Bess went on, undeterred.

"Do you have asbestos gloves?" Mike inquired.

"Come on, it'll be fun. And I've bought really good sherry and the meat will be an excellent cut, I promise."

Several conversations began to take place at once. Bess focused a bit of her attention on each, pleased with how things were going. Mike was thrilled with the truffles from Harbor Candy. Marta had pronounced the bed in their room perfect for a back sore from a long car ride. Allison seemed happy with everything, if not with her dinner.

"I was reading an article in the *New York Times* the other day about that new museum being built in Detroit," Bess heard Nathan say to Mike. "It's supposed to be revolutionary in the way it will show contemporary art in relation to the Old Masters."

Mike nodded. "I read that article, too. I thought Chris's father's firm might be one of the architects, but there was no mention of them. I mean, Montague and Montague has a strong reputation in buildings related to the arts. Allison?"

Bess's stomach flipped.

Allison looked up from her plate. "I don't know what the firm is up to these days," she replied flatly. "You'd have to ask Chris."

"No need to do that," Mike said quickly. "It doesn't really matter. Just wondering."

Allison put her fork across her plate. "It's okay," she said. "You can talk about him. He does still exist."

"I'm sorry," Nathan said. "I shouldn't have brought it up in the first place. I wasn't thinking."

Bess felt a bit sick. "Really, Allison, we're all—"

"Please!" Allison cried. "Please stop apologizing. All of you." Allison shook her head. "I'm sorry." Then she laughed. "Now I'm doing it, apologizing. Can we please just all stop saying how sorry we are for being human and move on? Do you enjoy the travel aspect of your job, Nathan?" Allison asked, turning deliberately to her host.

"I do," Nathan said promptly. "I've made friends in Stockholm, and Sweden is a beautiful country."

"I can't wait to go there with Nathan," Bess said. "While he works, I'll play tourist. Did you know that Stockholm is actually made up of fourteen islands?"

"I'm afraid I know little of that part of the world," Mike admitted. "Sweden is on the Baltic Sea, isn't it?"

"Yes," Bess told him. "And there's so much history! You can take sightseeing ferries to the different islands. The Old Town—it's called the Gamia Stan—is one of the best preserved medieval city centers in all of Europe."

"And don't forget the ABBA Museum," Marta said.

Bess laughed. "Like I would! But I'm really psyched to visit the sites of the Viking settlements. Ancient history is so . . . It's so . . ."

"Ancient?" Nathan suggested with a smile.

"You know what I mean. We just don't have much of it in the US. What remains of native cultures here is so sparse. Such a shame."

"What's the food like in Sweden?" Mike asked.

Marta raised an eyebrow. "The most important question for Mike."

"Their cinnamon buns are the best in the world, hands down," Nathan declared.

"And he says there's lingonberry jam served with just about every dish," Bess added, "including meatballs."

"And let's not forget anchovies and herrings grilled and pickled," Nathan went on. "It's hearty fare and good for you."

Mike wrinkled his nose. "I'm not sure how I feel about the herrings," he admitted. "But I'm all for meatballs. By the way, what's for dessert tonight?"

"Strawberry shortcakes," Bess told him. "Pretty American I think."

"Fantastic," Mike enthused. "I love strawberry shortcake!"

Marta gave her husband a meaningful look. "Are you planning on a run tomorrow morning?" she asked.

"You know," Mike replied, his eyes wide, "I realized just before we sat down to dinner that I forgot to pack my running shoes!"

"You did forget," Marta told him. "I packed them for you."

Mike looked dejected. "I guess I am going for a run tomorrow."

"Aren't you going to thank me for having your heart health in mind?" Marta asked with a broad smile.

"Yeah," Mike mumbled. "Thanks. You're such a devoted wife."

Everyone but Allison laughed at this dry remark.

"I'll go with you," Nathan offered suddenly. "Sometimes having a buddy along makes working out easier."

"I don't know about easier," Mike said, snagging a final fry from his plate before Marta could protest. "More tolerable, maybe. Thanks, Nathan."

Suddenly, Allison folded her napkin and stood up from the table. "I don't know what it is about flying that wears me out so," she said, stifling a yawn as if to prove her exhaustion.

Bess smiled sympathetically. "Plus, you had that long drive from Boston. I wish you had let me pick you up."

"I didn't want you to." Allison's abrupt response was met with silence. "Good night," she said.

When she was gone, to a chorus of softly spoken farewells, Mike shook his head. "I could strangle Chris," he said. "Look what he's done to her."

"We'll never know all that went on between Allison and Chris, so we can't judge or point the finger and say this one or that one is to blame," Marta argued. "The fact is that what had been a good marriage for a long time ended. And that's sad. But we should be celebrating Bess and Nathan's union. Always look forward. It's sound advice, and you can thank my mother for it."

Bess shook her head. "We're never really free of the past."

"True," Nathan replied, "but we don't have to stare over our shoulder at it."

"Okay, so don't stare," Mike said. "But you'd better at least take a quick look. Forewarned is forearmed. Know the past and you have a pretty good chance at guessing what might be coming at you in the future."

Bess stood. "Time for dessert," she announced. Marta joined her in helping to clear the table. And as they brought empty plates to the kitchen and returned with the strawberry shortcakes, Bess found herself wondering if Allison missed the routine aspects of married life, the daily duties freely undertaken, the little sacrifices happily made, the sweet liberties one was allowed to take with each other, like halfheartedly scolding one's spouse for gaining weight. *She must,* Bess thought, as she placed a dessert in front of Nathan. *Allison must miss it all so much.*

Chapter 11

Mike and Nathan were on the back porch. Marta heard the low murmur of masculine voices and the occasional laugh, subdued in deference to those already in bed. Or those, like Marta, who were still preparing for bed, hanging up the blouse and pair of pants she had been wearing, placing underwear and ankle socks in a laundry bag. She had already washed her face and brushed her teeth and gotten into her cozy lightweight flannel nightgown.

Marta removed her earrings (she always wore a pair of small gold studs); her wedding rings had already been carefully stowed in the little padded jewelry pouch she used while traveling. She had noticed at dinner that Allison was wearing her wedding ring. It was a dangerous thing, Marta thought, to cling to a past that hadn't moved along with you into the present. Always look forward, but be sure to understand what you've left behind.

What a tall order for any mere mortal!

Marta checked to see that there was a box of tissues within reach of the bed. Of course, there was. This was Bess's house, at least for the next two weeks. Marta was sure that Allison was finding her own room as well supplied as she and Mike had found theirs.

Poor Allison. Marta wanted to help, but she believed that sometimes it was best not to inquire too closely about a person's unhappiness; sometimes unhappiness needed to be guarded. This philosophy got complicated when the unhappy person was a child. But Allison was no one's child, not any longer. Who was there to take care of Allison now that both her parents and her husband were gone? Self-sufficiency was all well and good, but how far could it be asked to go?

Marta decided that she would watch and wait. She would take her cues from Allison and act accordingly. Leave it to Bess to stumble in where she might not be wanted or needed.

No doubt Chuck would agree with Marta's decision regarding Allison. He and Dean were due to arrive the next day. They would be full of the determined energy of all first-time parents. The very thought made Marta yawn. Did she have what it took to be a Super Mom all over again? All those years ago she had chosen to be the dominant, hands-on parent, allowing Mike to sleep through the night so that he could go off to work in the morning rested and refreshed. She had chosen to be the one who took the children to the doctor at the slightest sign of illness; the one who religiously attended every play, concert, soccer game, and parent/teacher meeting. But near-sleepless nights and seemingly endless days took their toll when one was forty-two, more so than they did when one was thirty-five, the age Marta had been when Troy was born.

Suddenly, Marta was visited by an image of her mother tucking Troy into bed. What would Estelle Kennedy think if she knew her daughter didn't want the baby she had just conceived? Marta felt like a small child, caught out attempting something naughty. She shook her head clear of the thought, only to find another slightly embarrassing thought creeping in.

For some unaccountable reason, Marta, a three-time mother, had mistaken this pregnancy for symptoms of perimenopause. Only after almost a week had gone by did she decide to take an at-home pregnancy test. It was positive. But she was not a person prone to panic. She disdained that sort of person. Calmly, she made an appointment to see her ob-gyn.

The ob-gyn confirmed the pregnancy. She spoke to Marta for some time about the risks inherent in a later-in-life pregnancy; she gave Marta pamphlets about tests for Down syndrome, neonatal nutrition, and exercise. "Congratulations," Dr. Smith said finally. "You can book your next appointment on the way out."

"Thank you, Doctor," Marta said. She shook the doctor's hand. She made another appointment.

But once in her car, she had put her head on the steering wheel in despair. "Shit," she said. And then again, this time louder: "Shit."

She reached home without incident. Mike arrived at his usual time, just before seven. When the kids were in bed or at least pretending to be, Marta was finally alone with her husband. Now was the time to tell him that he was going to be a father again, but she could not open her mouth. Being silent didn't erase the fact that she was carrying the tiny beginnings of a new life. But she could not open her mouth.

That night she lay in bed and realized that never in her adult life had she acted so childishly. An adult might ask: Don't I have a right to act childishly once in a blue moon? But the answer to that question was always no. You might have a right to feel a certain way in a certain situation—hurt, angry, annoyed—and even that was debatable, Marta thought, but you didn't have a right to act on those feelings. Not as a responsible adult. And you couldn't check in and out of being a responsible adult, not if you wanted to maintain any degree of self-respect in the eyes of others. In your own eyes.

She said nothing the next day. The silence wasn't a decision. It was a state of inertia.

She said nothing the day after that.

On the fourth day, the words finally just came out. Mike was elated and Marta knew immediately that she would have to lie to him, pretend that she, too, was happy to welcome a fourth child. So, she had said things she had not meant, told him she was thrilled about the pregnancy, determined to suck up her distress as a responsible adult should do.

But faking it was taking its toll. She had never lied to Mike about anything of importance and only resorted to white lies for his benefit, like when he made his infamous meatloaf for dinner each year on her birthday. It was horrid; none of the kids could tolerate even a bite, but Marta ate it with a smile. True, there was that one old secret she had never told anyone, that she never, ever would tell anyone. But there was only that one.

Marta glanced toward the window. She hoped Mike lingered over the whiskey and conversation. She wanted to be dead to the world by the time he came to bed. She wanted to be utterly and blissfully alone. Like in the days before she had fallen in love with Mike. Like in the days when she was truly Marta Kennedy, a daughter, yes, but only a daughter, not a wife and a mother as well. There had been a freedom in that, one Marta barely remembered; there was a person she barely recognized deep inside herself, buried under layers of service to others, service that had largely shaped who she was today—a habit of service she had enjoyed and relied on to define herself. The question now was, did she still need this habit, at least, to the extent that she had?

It would be nice if only for a very brief time to be a child again, not to care about anyone or anything but her own contentment. A child's love was selfish; a child loved her parents for what they did for her. It took years of learning before love began to mean something unselfish, or at least partly so, to understand that to be healthy, love had to be about giving as well as about taking.

Marta got into bed. She was annoyed with herself. She was not a child. She was an adult.

Chapter 12

Allison sat in one of the comfortable armchairs in the living area, pretending to be interested in one of the many wedding-related magazines to be found around the house. Here was an article about how to incorporate stepchildren into your wedding party. Lots of ink was spilled on how to ensure stepchildren felt comfortable at family celebrations. Was as much ink spilled on how to ensure adopted children felt as comfortable?

When Allison was eighteen her parents told her that if she decided to locate her birth parents they would support her decision, but she had never had any interest in doing so. Now, however, being an orphan (if also an adult), about to be divorced from her one and only love, Allison thought it might—just might—prove helpful to uncover her roots. She might discover a stronger sense of belonging in the world. She might discover another loving family to replace the one she had lost.

Allison tossed the wedding magazine onto one of the little tables that dotted the room. But what if what she found instead were badly damaged people, a mother who had been a teenaged runaway forced into a life of prostitution, or a father who had been a drug addict? What if she discovered that both were long dead? What if she discovered that while both were alive, neither wanted anything to do with a mistake made long ago? What if her birth mother couldn't

identify her birth father? What if, in the end, Allison was left feeling more isolated than ever? What if, what if! No decision carefully
undertaken after the age of about thirty was without its share of
what-ifs.

"That's them," Bess announced, suddenly throwing open the
front door and racing out to the drive.

Allison got to her feet and joined the others as Bess led the
Fortunato-Williams family into the house.

Dean, a few years younger than the others, was about five foot
six inches tall, burly and muscular. He wore his head shaved. He
was famous for his collection of designer eyeglass frames; indeed,
the ones he was wearing now were, Allison thought, fantastic. They
shared a hug and a kiss. Dean didn't tell her how wonderful she
looked, which would have been an outright lie. Neither did Chuck.

Allison didn't wait to be asked if she wanted to hold the baby.
Better to be proactive, she thought. Dean carefully placed his son
in Allison's arms. She felt a slight buzzing in her head, and it took
every ounce of her strength to keep a hold on the bouncing baby
boy. It wouldn't do to drop her friends' child, a child chosen as
she had been chosen, in a conscious and deliberate act of love and
faith. She lightly kissed his smooth forehead and willed herself not
to cry. Only after a long moment did Allison relinquish Thomas to
Dean.

While Mike and Marta exclaimed over the baby, Chuck dis-
creetly took Allison aside.

"Have you talked to him?" he whispered.

"No," Allison said simply.

Chuck frowned. "I'm sorry, Allison. I can't tell you how sorry
I am."

"How can you be sorry?" Allison replied. "You don't even know
what happened." And then she put a hand to her head. "Forgive me.
I'm . . . I'm not myself."

"Understandable. Look, we'll talk whenever you want to, okay?"

Chuck turned back to the group, and Allison thought: *Even if I
want to talk I won't let myself because I promised my husband I wouldn't.
I'm being held prisoner by guilt and shame, those strongest of internal
guards.*

"How about it, Bess?" Dean was saying. "Want to hold Thomas?"

Bess hurriedly, though politely refused Dean's offer. "Babies kind of scare me," she said. "In fact, until children can drive and maybe even vote I'm kind of at a loss."

Chuck laughed. "I told you, Dean. He thought that even Bess would melt at the sight of our perfect prince of a son!"

"Oh, I love him, of course," Bess said. "As long as I don't have to be responsible for his welfare before he can legally drink."

Mike tickled the baby's plump cheek with his forefinger. "No worries, guys. When you need a break from being parents, Marta will take over."

Allison noted that Marta's expression contracted into something approaching a frown.

The crunch of wheels on the gravel drive announced that Nathan had returned from the grocery store. Introductions were made and Nathan grabbed two of the men's many bags. "I'll show you to your room," he said. "It's on the first floor, just down this hall. Bess didn't want you to have to lug all the baby stuff up to the second floor. Let alone the baby. He looks like a fine, hefty fellow."

Allison twitched. A fine, hefty fellow. What her child might have been if he or she had lived.

"You must be pretty darn special to have convinced our Bess to take the plunge," Chuck said to Nathan when they had returned to the front hall. "We thought her Knight in Shining Armor had gotten permanently stuck in a Dungeon of Despair or a Mire of Misery."

Nathan laughed and looked to Bess. "It did take me until I was over fifty to spot her across a crowded room. Well, across a crowded backyard. I'm sure Bess told you we met at a party she had organized for old friends of mine who just happened to be her favorite clients."

Bess laughed. "A coincidence made in heaven!"

"And you somehow managed to notice her as she dashed around behind the scenes making sure that the flowers weren't wilting and the icing on the cakes wasn't melting," Dean suggested.

"Pretty much! And she really does dash about!" Nathan put his arm around Bess's shoulder.

It was so very obvious to Allison that Nathan was head over heels in love with Bess. She was happy for her friend, of course, she was, but she also felt a tiny sliver of jealousy snake through her.

Suddenly, Bess broke away from her fiancé. "I forgot to take the fruit salad out of the fridge! Right back." And she dashed off, proving Nathan's observation.

"So," Dean asked, "is your wedding song going to be 'Some Enchanted Evening'?"

"I think Bess has something else picked out." Nathan shrugged. "Music doesn't play a big part in our relationship, so whatever song she chooses is fine by me."

"Even if it's 'Bohemian Rhapsody'?" Chuck asked with a twinkle in his eye.

"I love that song!" Nathan enthused. "Anything by Queen would be cool."

"You know that's not going to happen," Chuck said. "If I know Bess, she's chosen something from *The Great American Songbook* or maybe even a sickly-sweet pop ballad. God, I hope it's not that. I might not be able to refrain from keeling over."

Mike announced that he would fetch the rest of the baby equipment and luggage still outside and Nathan went with him to help. Chuck suggested he and Dean take the baby for a stroll down to the beach. "His first glimpse of the famous Maine coastline," he explained. "We'll be back within half an hour."

Allison and Marta joined Bess in the kitchen, where she was slicing a loaf of hearty wheat bread. The aforementioned fruit salad sat on the island counter.

"They look wonderful," Bess said, beaming. "Parenthood agrees with them."

"So far," Marta added. "Just that I've seen that look of slightly stunned bliss wear off at about the ninth month when total exhaustion has set in."

"I wonder if Dean has help during the day," Allison mused. "I mean, I hope he gets some time to himself, other than when the baby is sleeping, and that's not really time alone, is it? It's not like a parent can go for a stroll and leave the baby alone at home." She and Chris had talked about such things in anticipation of their own family. They had talked so many times.

"I certainly hope they've made some provision for Dean's mental sanity!" Marta said robustly. "Chuck gets to go to work most every day and yeah, it's work, but he does something he loves and he's around human beings who speak in more than a coo and a gurgle."

"You didn't have help, did you, Marta?" Bess asked. "I mean, nobody professional, like a nanny."

"No, I didn't." Marta laughed a bit wildly. "I guess I never thought much about . . . about me. I wanted to do it all on my own and I did."

"Well, with Troy already seven it won't be too much longer until you've got some solid you time on your hands," Allison said. "Any thought about what you might want to do then?"

Marta waved a hand dismissively. "Oh, I've got years before I need to plan my future. Years. Anyway, I'm more than happy to help out with Thomas," Marta went on, "but I hope Mike doesn't overcommit me. I mean, I did come here to relax, at least in part. It's why I chose to leave the kids at home. Day after day, night after night. Sometimes I—"

Marta stopped mid-sentence, as if she was only then aware of what she was saying.

"Don't you love how men volunteer our services without first checking with us?" Allison said quickly. "My dad used to do that all the time, though my mom never seemed to mind it."

"I'm sure Mike didn't mean any harm when he said you'd help out," Bess said with a note of distress in her voice. That was Bess, Allison thought. Always afraid of offending; always ready to apologize for someone else's wrongs.

"Of course not," Marta said quickly. "Anyway, babies are a breeze. Now, let's get lunch going. The guys will be hungry after the ride from the Cape." She strode to the fridge and gathered plastic bottles of mustard and mayonnaise.

Allison had never heard Marta admit even for a moment that the duties of parenthood wore on her. There had been times when Allison felt that Marta was invested in appearing untouched by the usual annoyances of life. Maybe it was an unfair assessment; maybe it was an assessment rooted in jealousy. Though her own life had been good, it had not been as good as Marta's life; Marta was the proud mother of three happy and healthy children. Certainly Allison would take no satisfaction in knowing that her friend's life wasn't as perfect as she made it out to be . . . or as perfect as Allison chose to see it as being.

"Allison," Bess said, breaking into her musings. "You're in charge of salad."

Chapter 13

Bess's friends had spent the afternoon in a variety of ways: Chuck, Dean, and the baby napping; Marta on the back porch, scrolling through something or other on her iPad (when Bess had inquired what it was that was holding Marta's attention, Marta had replied, "Nothing much"); Mike and Nathan taking an exploratory excursion to the HoneyMaker Mead Room in town.

Allison had gone down to the old gnarled tree at the base of the yard and spent what seemed hours circling it, then sitting on the grass with her sketch pad and pencil making drawings. When Allison finally returned to the house Bess had asked her what she thought of the thing. "It's very beautiful," Allison said. "One of the most beautiful natural objects I've seen in a long time. It makes me think about the lightning-struck chestnut tree in *Jane Eyre*." Allison had smiled. "I just hope it's not a sign of turmoil to come."

Mike had been present at this exchange. He had laughed. "Beautiful? It reminds me of a weird little creature in one of Leo's sci-fi comic books."

"Beauty is in the eye of the beholder," Allison replied before going upstairs to her room, sketch pad under her arm.

So far, Bess thought, the reunion was a success. She was sure that every one of them felt Chris's absence but surprisingly, it didn't seem to be creating an atmosphere of gloom. Bess was glad.

For dinner that evening Bess had served clam chowder, crab rolls, salad, and of course, dessert. Again, much of the meal had been ordered in; Bess had no intention of spending hours in the kitchen, even with help from her friends.

The baby had been put to bed before the adults sat down to eat, though his presence in the house was indicated by the baby monitor on the kitchen counter. "He's got a set of lungs all right," Dean had informed them. "It's not like we won't hear him if he bellows. But the monitors pick up the smaller signs of distress you could otherwise easily miss."

Bess had not lied to her friends earlier when she said that babies scared her. In spite of—because of?—her early life experience taking care of her much younger sisters, she really *wasn't* comfortable around little ones. She eyed the monitor with trepidation, half expecting alarms to suddenly begin screeching dire warnings of impending disaster. If such a thing occurred she would dial 911 immediately and ask questions later. Better safe than sorry, especially with someone's child. Sometimes, a burp was more than just a burp.

"So, Chuck, how do you like living in La La Land?" Nathan asked when everyone had tucked into the meal.

"It's taken some real doing on my part," Chuck admitted, scraping his bowl of chowder clean. "As a kid from a working-class neighborhood of Boston, life in Los Angeles is seriously alien. I mean, what happened to being able to run down to the corner store for a quart of milk? Now I've got to get into my car and get on a highway before I come across a grocery store."

"Poor you," Dean said.

"You must appreciate the good weather," Mike pointed out. "No shoveling out from under mountains of snow!"

"Oh yeah," Chuck said. "The weather is fabulous. I think the biggest thing I had to get used to was the amount of time and energy people spend on their personal appearance. I grew up thinking a Red Sox sweatshirt was couture. I had to buy an entirely new wardrobe when I moved to the west coast! And what's with the constantly changing fads in food? Can I please just stick with sausage subs every Tuesday and roast chicken every Saturday like my mother served?"

"Chuck, you sound like an old man!" Marta cried. "In my day, everything was better and we were smarter and kids these days have no respect."

Chuck laughed. "I'm not that bad yet."

"Do you still call your sisters The Nina, The Pinta, and The Santa Maria?" Bess asked.

"When I can get away with it." Chuck looked to Nathan. "Their names are Maria, Theresa, and Christina, but it's a brother's job to be obnoxious."

Dean, who had consumed two crab rolls, turned to Bess. "So," he asked, "any pre-wedding jitters?"

"I'm actually pretty calm," she stated. "As long as we don't get a totally random hurricane, everything will be perfect."

"You know," Marta said, "even if the caterer goes out of business at the last minute and the band all come down with the flu, the day will be perfect."

"Of course, it will," Bess said, waving her hand dismissively. "I've got a backup caterer on call and a second band on retainer!"

This was met with general laughter. "That's my bride-to-be," Nathan added. "Nothing escapes her attention, even highly improbable catastrophes."

Dean looked to Nathan. "No last-minute reservations for the groom?"

"None whatsoever," Nathan said robustly. "I'm marrying the woman I want to be marrying and not a day too soon."

Mike raised his glass and the others followed his lead. "I propose a toast. To marriage!"

Bess shot a look around the table. For a moment, there was dead silence. Mike looked as if he wanted to slide under the table and never emerge. Marta put her hand on his and squeezed.

"To marriage," Allison said in a clear, if somewhat thin voice. "Long may it live."

"Hear, hear," Dean added quickly.

Bess stared down at her half-empty plate. With an unpleasant start, she realized that she resented the fact that the most important event in her life was being strained by the looming idea of divorce.

How much worse it would have been if Chris had been there with them! Thank God, he had declined her invitation to the wedding. But as quickly as it had come, the resentment passed and Bess felt ashamed. Poor Allison. She was the one truly suffering.

"Bess?"

"Hmm?" she said to Dean.

Dean raised the bottle he was holding. "I asked if you'd like more wine?"

Bess managed a smile. "Sure, thanks. The white was recommended by one of my beverage vendors. I hope everyone likes it."

Mike chuckled. "I'd know rot gut if I tasted it, but other than that my palate is wasted on good wine. Now beer, that I can tell you about."

"There are several good craft brew pubs we could check out while you're here," Nathan said enthusiastically. "We could spend an afternoon in Portland and do a pub crawl. And when we've had our fill of beer and burgers we could stop for coffee at one of the local shops that roast on-site."

"Chuck hasn't had a beer since one memorable night after acing his boards," Dean said, failing to restrain a smile.

Chuck grimaced. "Even thinking about it makes me woozy. I'll let you guys do the pub crawl without me."

Mike met Nathan's suggestion with enthusiasm and the two men were quickly involved in a discussion about the relative merits of popular trends in craft brewing, a subject about which Bess was surprised to find her fiancé knew anything at all.

Bess glanced at the rest of the group in turn. Allison's face wore a look of distraction. And there was something—different—about Marta, though for the life of her Bess couldn't say what. Chuck seemed his usual phlegmatic self. Dean—

"Oh!" Bess cried.

Out of nowhere a big wind slammed the house; shutters banged and windows rattled.

"Are we in for a storm?" Chuck asked.

Dean shrugged and Marta pulled out her iPhone, no doubt to check the forecast.

Bess glanced toward the back porch and thought of the shattered tree at the edge of the yard. What force would it take to uproot such a thing, when it had already survived death?

"The sea is a mysterious force," Allison intoned. "The moon, too, unpredictable in spite of what the scientists say. Maybe together they've conspired to cause a storm to shake up our complacency, that random hurricane you mentioned, Bess."

Dean laughed, though Bess was sure Allison had not meant her words as a joke.

Suddenly, the wind died as abruptly as it had come. Bess felt a hand on her arm. It was Nathan's.

"Bess," he was saying. "Should I put on a pot of coffee?"

"Not for me," Mike said. "I'll be up all night."

"Nor for me," Marta added. "But I wouldn't say no to whatever sweet you might be serving."

"I think I could be tempted as well," Dean added.

Bess beamed and hurriedly got to her feet. All was well. The storm—if it had been a storm—had passed and there were brownies for dessert. "I'll be right back," she assured her friends. "You won't be disappointed."

Chapter 14

The day had dawned warm but not unpleasantly so. Chuck had taken Thomas with him to the outlets in Kittery. (Bargain hunting was a skill that couldn't be learned at too young an age.) Dean, Nathan, and Mike had gone into Kennebunkport. There was a baseball game they wanted to watch, and Nathan had ascertained that a local Mexican restaurant doubled as a sports bar.

Marta, at the beach with Bess and Allison, wasn't sure if she was happy or not about being alone with the other females of the group. Women were smart. They sensed things. Would either Bess or Allison suddenly discern Marta's secret? No, Marta told herself, more firmly than she believed. Why would anyone think she was pregnant again? Weren't three kids enough? A perfect odd number, great for placement in photos, even when the parents were added to the picture, making another perfect odd number.

"So, are your mom and sisters helping with the wedding preparations?" Allison asked Bess. Allison was wearing a linen sheath in a pretty shade of peach; her straw sun hat and large, Jackie O–style sunglasses hid a good deal of her face.

Bess was wearing a T-shirt and cutoff jean shorts, and looked about twelve years old. "I didn't ask for any help," she said. "They mentioned giving me a shower back home, but they didn't press the idea so that was good."

Marta, long interested in the Culpepper family dynamic, strongly suspected that Bess's family might be intimidated by Bess's party-giving expertise and relieved they hadn't had to attempt to meet her high standards.

"Why?" Allison asked. "Didn't you want to celebrate with the people from Green Lakes who've known you since you were little?"

"I didn't really have the time," Bess said dismissively. "It's a three-hour journey each way. Besides, it's not like Nathan and I need anything. Everyone would have been wasting their money buying me stuff I already have."

"But your colleagues threw you a shower, didn't they?" Marta said. In an oversized shirt and baggy Bermuda shorts she was definitely The Frumpy Friend. It didn't bother her. Much.

Bess laughed. "I could hardly say no to my colleagues! Anyway, it wasn't a traditional shower. It was a cocktail reception at the Top of the East in the Westin." Bess paused. "Though my mother and sisters were there. One of my colleagues invited them. It was a total surprise."

So, Marta thought, Bess's family had made the effort to travel three hours south to Portland and three hours back north to Green Lakes.

"How did they get along with your crowd?" Marta asked. She knew it might prove to be a loaded question.

Bess shrugged. "All right. My sisters wondered why there were no traditional party games, like the one where everyone writes some bit of wisdom—real or ironic or humorous—and the papers get all mixed up in a bowl and the bride has to guess who wrote what. And they were a bit wary of the food. If it isn't a casserole heavy on the processed cheese and canned onion strings they don't have much interest. Of course, everyone was super nice to my mom and sisters," she added hastily.

"Why wouldn't they be?" Allison asked, hugging her knees to her chest.

Bess shrugged. "Just saying. You know how my family is."

"How, exactly, are they?" Marta asked. For Bess, of all people, to be critical of her own flesh and blood had always seemed very odd. Okay, Bess was ten years older than Mae and eleven years older than Ann, an age gap that had made it difficult for Bess to be close to them, or even to know them well; the younger girls were only nine and eight, respectively, when Bess had gone off to college. But surely Bess knew that her parents were thoroughly good and respectable people?

Bess's face flushed. "Well, you know. They're different from me. I'm different from them."

"They seemed very nice the one time I met them," Allison said. "At our graduation. They were all so excited for you."

"Oh, they *are* very nice," Bess said quickly. "They're probably some of the nicest people you'll ever meet."

"So?" Marta pressed. "What's the problem?"

"There's no problem." Bess stretched out her legs and buried her heels in the sand. "Except that my mom insisted on making my bag for the wedding."

Marta laughed. "My mom can't sew on a button. My father handles any task that requires manual dexterity."

"Why so grim, Bess?" Allison asked.

Bess sighed. "My mom made my sisters' wedding dresses. And Mae's headpiece. They were all pretty awful. Well-made, but awful. My sisters don't really have an interest in style. Actually, Mae does but what she thinks is style, well, isn't."

"But surely your mother will make something stylish for you," Allison said.

"I'm not so sure she'll pay any attention to the materials and sketches I've sent her as guidance."

"But why wouldn't she pay attention?" Allison pressed.

"Bess doesn't give her mother credit for seeing her as an individual," Marta said.

"Oh, it's not that!" Bess cried. "It's just—never mind."

"So, your father's not walking you down the aisle?" Marta was aware she was still being provocative and didn't much care.

Bess looked downright horrified. "I think it's a bit late for that! Besides, there isn't going to be an aisle. The ceremony is on the beach, remember?"

"I was only kidding, Bess," Marta assured her.

"Anyway, no one's going to notice your bag," Allison said consolingly. "You don't even have to carry it around the whole time. As long as your mom knows you've got it somewhere with you she'll be happy. Remember, a wedding ceremony and the reception are largely about the families and friends, not the bride and groom."

"At my wedding my mother insisted on there being a cheeseball at the cocktail hour," Marta added. "Why? Because she had wanted a cheeseball at her own cocktail hour and her mother had nixed the idea."

"It was pretty tasty," Bess pointed out.

"Nevertheless."

"My parents were so happy on my wedding day," Allison said quietly. "I miss them so much, though I'm glad they didn't live to see me divorced. It would have broken their hearts. They always wanted the best for me. Well, of course they did; any good parent would. But somehow, I felt they were extra grateful for having me in their lives. I guess I'm a poster child for the beauty of adoption."

Marta reached out and gently squeezed Allison's hand. The hand was bony. *Poor Allison*, Marta thought. *This all must be so terribly hard for her.*

"But if they had lived they would have been here to help you in your time of need." Bess grimaced. "Sorry. Like you wanted that pointed out."

Allison sighed. "There you go again, apologizing. Look, there's no way around the fact that my life is pretty unhappy right now. It's just the way it is. Why pretend otherwise? I don't."

"Maybe pretending that everything is rosy isn't the right thing to do," Marta said. "But maybe you should try not to focus entirely on what's gone wrong." Marta winced. "How obnoxiously know-it-all was that?"

"But it's still good advice." Allison smiled. "And I thank you for it, really. I pay good money for similar counsel."

Marta stuck a finger in the sand. If only she could practice what she preached. But being positive and counting one's blessings *was* far easier said than done. It was so easy to slide into a pit of self-pity and from there, into an even deeper pit of despair, and that most often led to a crushing feeling of self-loathing.

Whoa. Marta straightened her shoulders. Things were not that bad. She was pregnant, that was all.

"I knew there was something I wanted to tell you," Bess said suddenly. "I saw on Facebook the other day that our old roommate Honor passed away. I asked around a bit and learned that she'd committed suicide. I can't say I'm surprised, but it was still so sad to hear."

Sheesh, Marta thought. *Could this conversation get any jollier?*

"I used to get annoyed with her, like when she wouldn't come out of her room for days except to use the bathroom, no matter how often I knocked and asked if she was okay." Allison shook her head. "I was trying to be helpful, but I guess I just didn't understand depression and how it paralyzes a person."

"Did anyone ever understand her, I wonder?" Bess mused. "Her parents, a therapist, a friend, a lover? In her entire life, as short as it was, I wonder if she ever was able to really connect with another person, or if the depression always stood in the way."

"Mental illness is so dreadfully isolating," Allison said quietly. "And it can so badly affect the people around the sick person. Well, I suppose that all illness is isolating to the sick person and a drain on others."

Marta nodded. "One of Sam's classmates was briefly hospitalized with anorexia. I can't help but wonder how her parents are going to handle her leaving for college next year. I know the girl applied to several schools out of state—she's a super student—and I also know she's been healthy for some time. But it's going to be tough to let her go, knowing that her illness could be triggered again and possibly not noticed soon enough to be of help."

"We were so young when we started college," Allison said, musingly, "so inexperienced. Somehow, we were supposed to know how to regulate our daily lives all on our own in a brand-new environment, surrounded by brand-new people and brand-new routines." Allison paused. "No wonder so many kids have breakdowns their freshman year, gain fifteen pounds, drink to excess, fail courses they should have been able to ace."

"But *we* made it through," Bess pointed out.

"And," Allison noted, "we've managed to stay friends. That might even be more remarkable."

Marta nodded. "True. In spite of the different paths our lives have taken. Sometimes I wonder what really keeps us all together. Habit? Laziness?"

"Nostalgia for simpler, more innocent times?" Allison wondered. "We met when we were kids."

"It's not habit or laziness or even nostalgia that keeps us together," Bess said firmly. "It's love, pure and simple. We're true friends."

Marta supposed that was true. Still, she often wondered how comfortable she would feel socializing with Allison's colleagues in the world of art and commercial photography, or with Chuck and Dean's L.A. circle that included people in the medical profession as well as those in education. What about with Bess's eclectic circle of wealthy party-givers and successful businesspeople? And would Marta's old college friends be bored with her circle of suburban moms and dads? Would Allison think them dull and uninformed? Would Chuck and Dean find them hopelessly frumpy and behind the times? Would Bess decide she would rather spend time with her provincial sisters than with Marta's friends?

Allison's voice interrupted Marta's grim reverie. "Remember when we learned that Rosalie, the suitemate we had in sophomore year, was harboring a sick squirrel in her room?"

"Yeah, only after I went to the campus nurse complaining of this horrible itch and was told I had fleas!" Bess shuddered.

"The squirrel was taken away and the suite was fumigated," Allison pointed out. "No real harm in the end."

"Does anyone know what became of her?" Marta asked.

"I came across information on LinkedIn," Bess said. "She's a veterinarian, no surprise there. She has a clinic in Tucson."

"There's someone who knew her passion right from the start," Allison said. "I remember her telling me how when she was a little girl she would bring home all sorts of injured birds and animals, including once the neighbor's Great Dane. She thought he looked pale. Can a dog look pale?"

Marta wished she was wearing a big, floppy hat and large sunglasses like Allison was wearing. She was pretty sure there was a pained expression on her face. *Her* passion had been her husband and her kids. Hadn't it? Was it still? Was anything?

"I'm starved," Bess announced. "I'll head back to the house and start lunch."

Allison rose from her blanket. "I'll join you," she said.

"Me too." Marta got up from her beach chair and began to gather her belongings. At the moment, the idea of being alone with her thoughts didn't feel like a very smart one.

Chapter 15

Allison had gone back to the beach after lunch, this time with her camera. A few seagulls were standing about on one leg; others sat like Aladdin's lamps at the water's edge. She snapped a few shots of the birds. They might be a nuisance at times, but they were beautiful.

As she turned away from the birds and began to stroll, she thought about the sound advice Marta had shared earlier, that she focus on what had gone right in her life rather than on what had gone wrong. And what had undeniably gone right was her work and her friendships, and together they might very well be enough to see her through the remaining years of her life. Why shouldn't they be? Both brought purpose, challenge, and comfort to one's life.

Allison noted a couple walking slowly toward her over the firmer sand near the water's edge. They were arm in arm, wore matching sun hats, and those large wraparound sunglasses that helped to protect against the sneaky rays of the sun. The woman had a cane in her left hand. The man's shoulders were significantly bent, forcing his head to hang forward at what must be an uncomfortable angle. Had he gotten used to the pain? Allison had once been told that a person could get used to anything. She didn't agree. There were some things a person simply could not learn to live with.

She wondered how long the couple had been together. Maybe

they had come together in their youth, or maybe they had only come together as middle-aged adults. For that matter, maybe the man and woman were brother and sister. Whatever the case, they strongly illustrated the value of companionship. Allison had never known loneliness until it had finally become clear to her that Chris was not coming back, that her marriage was indeed over.

It was so hard to accept the fact that she and Chris wouldn't grow old together. It was something Allison had taken for granted, that one day they would walk arm and arm along a quiet shoreline, reminiscing about the early days of their relationship, proud of having weathered so many storms and come through with their marriage intact and perhaps stronger than ever before.

But that was not to be. Two anniversaries had come and gone since Chris had moved out. That first anniversary had been torture. Allison had purposefully avoided looking at her phone or her e-mail all that day. When she did finally check her personal messages a little after midnight, she found only a call from Bess. Bess meant well. She did.

The second anniversary, only a month before Allison had gotten on the plane for Boston, had gone unnoticed. No word from Chris. No well-intended messages from her friends. Nothing.

Time healed. It brought oblivion. It wore down the acuteness of both pain and pleasure.

"Allison!"

There was no mistaking that ebullient voice. Allison felt annoyed. To be fair the beach did not belong to her alone and Bess, who was paying for the house and everything that went with it, had every right to enjoy the sun and the sand whenever she pleased. This Kennebunkport gathering was about Bess and her long-awaited wedding, not about her friend's impending divorce.

"How are you?" Bess asked when she joined Allison, with that look of intense, caring scrutiny that could be so annoying.

"Fine," Allison said brightly. Would it make Bess feel better if she collapsed in sobs and admitted that she had never been so miserable in her entire life? "The light is perfect. I've been getting some great shots."

"I saw you alone down here and I thought—"

"Look at that cloud formation." Allison lifted her camera to her eye. When she had fired off several shots she turned back to her friend. "So, have you had any additional ideas about the wedding day photos?" she asked.

Bess's expression brightened. "I have!" She went on enthusiastically to share her ideas, most of them quite good if also ideas Allison had already planned to execute.

When Bess had run out of steam her expression instantly sobered. "You do really like Nathan, don't you?" she asked.

"I do," Allison said. "He seems kind and intelligent. But it doesn't matter what any of us think."

"Yes, it does!" Bess cried. "It truly does. If even one of you thought I was making a mistake I would—Well, I would have to give the whole thing more thought."

"The whole *thing*?" Allison said, more sharply than she had intended. "Nathan is a *person*, Bess. If you love him and he loves you, that's all that matters. Sure, listen to opinions from people who really know you, but in the end this is your decision to make, not ours."

Bess sighed. "I know. It's just that I can't believe my luck after all those years of dating the wrong men. I keep thinking that something bad is going to happen to spoil the wedding. I don't know what I'd do, I really don't!"

"Nothing bad will happen to ruin your wedding," Allison said with what she hoped was a reassuring tone. She had never seen Bess so agitated. "Not if you concentrate on what really matters, meaning every single word of your wedding vows."

"You're right," Bess admitted after a moment. "And I'm sorry. I know this is difficult for you and here I am complaining when I have nothing to complain about!"

"No worries." Allison forced a bright smile. "I'd say you have a case of pre-wedding jitters. Perfectly normal. Now, come on. Let's head back to the house."

"Is that Chuck I see on the porch? And is he pouring cocktails?" Bess waved wildly and Chuck, after putting the cocktail shaker he was holding onto the table, waved back. "I'm so happy for them, aren't you?" Bess said. "A perfect little family of three."

Allison flinched. A perfect little family of three. How different things had turned out for Chuck and Dean than they had for herself and Chris.

Bess seemed not to have realized her comment had been tactless and really, why should she have held her tongue? Just because Allison had no children didn't mean she should be protected from the presence of other people's familial happiness. She didn't want to be one of those people around whom others felt it necessary to tiptoe so as not to remind her of what she had suffered. If she didn't learn to look her situation in the eye and face it down she would be lost.

But it was all so very hard.

"Yes," she said, with a genuine effort at sounding pleased. "I'm happy for Chuck and Dean. I truly am."

Chapter 16

I've attached a few pix of the balloons in action. I think you'll see how charming they are in situ. Give me a call and we'll get an order placed right away!

Bess frowned at the screen. A third-rate party supply company located in Biddeford was always trying to get her business in spite of the fact she had told the sales rep in no uncertain terms that their products did not meet the needs and desires of her clients. Period. Ten-foot-tall blow-ups of a bride and groom, over-long arms waving wildly? Nope. She dashed off a firm but polite rejection and scanned the rest of the e-mails that had come in that day.

Though she was focused on the task at hand, her mind was also roaming. The e-mail from the party supply company had served in a roundabout way to remind her of how far she had come from Green Lakes, from a childhood spent wearing her cousin's hand-me-down clothes, shunning waste in any form (turnip tops could be cooked and eaten, and coffee grounds were a valuable bit of compost for the vegetable garden), and doing without Christmas gifts in lean years, to an adulthood in which she was able to afford this beautiful house on the beach, where she could treat her dearest friends to a vacation.

And Bess associated those friends with the time in her life when she had begun to blossom into a full person. That was why the reunions meant so much to her. These people—Mike and Marta, Chuck, Chris and Allison—had been witnesses to her coming of age as she had been to theirs.

And what a coming of age Bess's had been. She was the first in her immediate family to go to college; the first and so far, the only one. While her parents had been supportive they had also been wary, especially when Bess announced her intention of accepting an offer from a school in Massachusetts. Without her own car—and that was out of the question—Bess would be able to afford few visits home. This prospect didn't worry Bess; summers in Green Lakes would be quite enough for her what with two much younger, rambunctious sisters underfoot.

Although Bess had begun to put out feelers for jobs at the start of her senior year, nothing had come through by June and she had been forced to return home after graduation while she continued the search. Several members of her family had expressed the hope that she would settle down in Green Lakes, marry, have kids, and maybe find a job at the mini-mall out on the highway. To this, Bess had argued (if silently): "What was the point of my going to college if all I was going to do is come back here and be someone I never was in the first place?" But she had simply smiled and said meaningless, noncommittal things like, "We'll see," and "That's an idea."

After a depressing summer spent earning what money she could locally while continuing to hunt for jobs in Portland, and somewhat sadly realizing how little she knew of her newly adolescent sisters, who only wanted to spend time with their friends, Bess finally landed a gig working as a waitress for a caterer on Exchange Street in the Old Port. She could barely contain her excitement the day she left home for what she swore would be forever.

Six months later, Bess was promoted to assistant manager. A year after that, Bess was manager. Two years on, she was working for another, bigger and more successful catering company that also did some event planning. Bess Culpepper was on her way.

Still, those early years in Portland were tough. Her parents had no money with which to help her make ends meet (not that she would have accepted it if they had) and worried constantly about her safety, calling daily and sending care packages of homemade cookies, jams, and deer jerky. The few times Bess had suggested that Ann and Mae visit for a day—they had never been to big, bad Portland—her parents had firmly nixed the idea; Bess had later learned that her sisters hadn't wanted to visit. Green Lakes offered all they wanted, except, maybe, for a few better shops selling cool hair ornaments and pre-made friendship bracelets.

But Bess survived those lean years living in awful little apartments shared with unsuitable roommates. She never doubted that she was where she was meant to be, doing what she was meant to do, which would one day lead to her establishing her own successful event and party-planning business. It had taken her less than ten years to achieve that goal.

Bess knew that her native idealism and optimism had served her well. Allison had once compared Bess to the infamous Sarah Bernhardt, who kept on going in spite of a series of outrageous setbacks and who had had fun in doing so. "Her catchphrase," Allison had told Bess, "was *quand-même*. Roughly translated it means even though, or anyway, all the same, *malgré tout*, nevertheless. As in: *J'avais peur, mais je l'ai fait quand-même.* I'm afraid, but I'll do it anyway." "That's me, all right," Bess had said. "For better or worse I keep on going!" Mike had likened her to the Energizer Bunny, a less happy comparison that was nevertheless accurate.

Nothing else in Bess's e-mail folder needed immediate attention, so she closed her laptop and left the den. She found Allison and Marta relaxing on the back porch, a pitcher of lemonade on one of the side tables.

"Can I get you anything?" Bess asked.

"Nothing," Marta said, indicating the lemonade. "We helped ourselves."

"So, tell us about your dress," Marta asked.

Bess shook her head and sat in one of the white wicker armchairs. "Nope, it's a surprise. But I will tell you that my something old is a gold brooch that once belonged to Nathan's grandmother. Her name was Betty Creek. What luck, right, that we have the same initials! It's a beautiful piece."

"The something new is the bag your mother is making," Marta said. "And we know how you feel about that."

Bess restrained a frown. Marta really could be annoying. Bess would not mention that her original something borrowed was the fussy garter her sister Mae had worn at her own wedding. It was made of a cheap acrylic-like material and was a ghastly shade of pink. Bess had no intention of wearing it.

"My something borrowed," she went on, "is from my assistant, Kara. It's a Victorian silver filigree bangle. As for my something blue . . . Wait, I'll go and get it."

She returned a few moments later, clutching a black velvet ring box in one hand. "I splurged," she said.

Marta laughed. "No! You?"

For a moment, Bess hesitated to show her treasure. She thought of what her thrifty parents would say if they knew how much this wedding was costing; if they knew she had spent several thousands of dollars on her something blue; if they . . .

"It was worth it," Bess said stoutly. And, she thought, she could well afford it. "Remember when Meghan got married last year?"

"Who?" Allison asked.

"Meghan. Meghan Markle, Duchess of Sussex."

Allison raised her eyebrows. "Oh, that Meghan! How could I have forgotten?"

"And Harry gave her his mother's aquamarine cocktail ring and she wore it to the evening reception. Well, since then I've been searching for a perfect aquamarine cocktail ring of my own to wear on my big day and voilà!"

Bess opened the box to reveal a six-carat emerald cut aquamarine in a retro-era yellow gold setting.

"It's stunning," Marta admitted. "Way too glamorous for me, but it suits you, Bess."

"Where did you get it?" Allison asked.

"Market Square Jewelers, in Portland. There's a shop in Portsmouth, too, if you guys want to do some fun browsing. We could drive down one afternoon."

"No, thanks," Marta said sharply. "When you have three kids you don't have the luxury of buying yourself gifts."

Bess looked at Allison, who smiled kindly. "I could be persuaded to spend an hour or two window-shopping," she told Bess. "I remember all the time you and I spent browsing those vintage shops in Cambridge. I still have a silk Hermès scarf I found for ten dollars!"

Marta put her empty glass of lemonade on the table at her side. "I guess I could go along and keep you two out of trouble."

"Wonderful!" Bess pronounced. She wouldn't mention it at the moment, but she had her eye on a ring from MSJ's Elizabeth Henry collection. "Are you sure I can't get anyone anything? A snack? Maybe a sandwich?"

Marta rolled her eyes.

"No, thank you, Bess," Allison said with a hint of a smile.

Chapter 17

Allison had gone out early that morning, telling none of them where she was headed. Not that she was under any obligation to do so, but Bess had seemed a bit hurt by Allison's discretion. Nathan and Dean had taken the baby to the Seashore Trolley Museum, leaving Marta, Chuck, Bess, and Mike lounging on the back porch with second and third cups of coffee. Once again, the conversation had drifted to the subject of their friends' divorce.

"Even though Chris was the one to file for divorce, he might not be totally innocent in whatever went on," Marta pointed out.

"Of course. Rarely is one person entirely to blame," Chuck said. "Or, better put, rarely is an issue that becomes problematic created and sustained by only one partner."

"I just wish we knew what happened," Bess complained. "I know we could bring them back together."

"Their marriage is not your business," Marta argued.

"In some ways, it is my business. Yours, too. That's why we're all talking about it. We're friends. We have each other's backs."

"Stay out of it, Bess," Chuck said firmly. "If Allison or Chris want to tell us what went on behind closed doors they will."

Mike shook his head. "The last thing I ever thought Chris would do was leave Allison. She's so pretty and sweet-natured, she just couldn't have done anything so bad."

Marta frowned. She wasn't jealous; she knew Mike was devoted to her, but his typical male stereotyping annoyed her. This sort of archaic thinking—that pretty women were morally pristine, above temptation and yet, paradoxically, in need of protecting—had resulted in his spoiling his own daughter. And spoiling was not protecting; if only the spoilers could understand that! Sam would be in for a rude awakening once she was at college and realized that Daddy was no longer around to smooth every bump in the road.

"Nothing against Allison," Chuck commented dryly, "but a pretty face and a sweet personality doesn't necessitate an innocent soul. Come on, Mike. Get with the twenty-first century. And it's dangerous to put people on pedestals. Chris is only human. He shouldn't be unduly punished for taking a step he felt was necessary to his happiness, even if that step hurt someone else."

Marta drained the last of her decaf coffee and rose from her chair. "I'm off to take a shower," she announced. *Only human*, she thought as she climbed the stairs to the second floor. Chuck was right. It was because they were only human that she and Chris had indulged in a one-night stand in college while she was dating Mike and he was dating Allison.

Marta grabbed her robe from her room and went down the hall to the bathroom. It had taken some brutally honest thinking the night before to realize that her current discomfort about this old crime was closely linked to the unsettling knowledge that the person she was most angry with about the unwanted pregnancy was *herself*, not Mike. To keep the acknowledgment of one's own culpability firmly centered on oneself and not to shuffle the blame onto someone else required Herculean effort. It was so much easier to point the finger—at Chris; at Mike—than to admit that *you* were the cause of your own calamity.

Once back in her room, Marta impulsively reached for her phone.

"Why are you calling?" her mother asked bluntly. "We spoke last evening."

Immediately, Marta regretted having made the call. "No reason," she said.

"I don't believe that," Mrs. Kennedy said. "You never have 'no reason' for doing something. Spontaneity isn't your strong point."

Marta wondered about that. Was her mother saying she was a calculating person? "Fine then," she said, trying to hide her annoyance. "I called to see if everything was all right this morning. Are the kids wearing you out? I know Leo can be a know-it-all and—"

"Marta," her mother interrupted, "you worry too much. Leo is fine. Sam and Troy are fine. Your father and I are fine. And if we weren't all fine, I'd have let you know."

"Fine," Marta said, then winced. The most overused word in the English language. One of them, anyway.

"Oh, there's something I've been meaning to tell you," Mrs. Kennedy went on animatedly. "Guess who I ran into the other day in the mall? Olivine Kaye. Do you remember? You were in Girl Scouts together for a few years. Then she went to that private high school so you stopped spending time with each other."

Marta vaguely remembered Olivine. The girl had been one of those forgettable people you came across on occasion—and promptly forgot. "What's she up to?" Marta asked, not caring in the least.

"Well, now that both of her children are in college, Olivine's gone into business for herself. She opened a classic English tea shop and it's just what the town needed. It's doing fantastically well and she's already thinking of expanding!"

"How nice for her," Marta said woodenly. There was an uncomfortable, mean-spirited feeling in her gut. So, Olivine had turned out to be not so forgettable after all.

"You'll be looking to fill your time now that the kids are growing up," her mother went on. "Sam will be off to college next year and once Leo gets his driver's license he'll be gone most of the time and then there's only Troy. Before long you'll be your own woman again."

Marta frowned. Her own woman again? Whose woman had she been these past seventeen years? Fill her time? As if she would just be marking off empty days on a calendar until the moment of her death? She said as much.

"I meant no such thing," her mother replied placidly. "I just meant that as your responsibilities toward the children fall away, you'll have more time to spend pursuing your own interests and passions. Like how once you were in high school I had more time to devote to my gardening."

That question again! Interests. Passions. What *were* they? What brand of cold cereal had the most nutritional value for the dollar? Making sure Sam had filled the tank with gas whenever she returned her mother's car? What fertilizer was most eco-friendly so that Leo wouldn't start in again on how irresponsible his mother was when it came to caring for the planet? Trying to convince Troy that pajamas were never appropriate school clothing?

Anyway, what did it matter if she had no real interests or passions? She was pregnant. Again.

"I often wondered," her mother went on, "if you were one hundred percent sure about your decision not to go on to law school but at the time I didn't like to ask."

Marta was stunned. "Why didn't you like to ask?" she demanded.

"Well, you were very fierce about it being your right to choose not to pursue another degree," her mother explained. "Frankly, I didn't think I'd get anywhere if I questioned your motives. But look at how nice your life has turned out. Three lovely children, a wonderful husband. How could you have any regrets?"

"I couldn't," Marta snapped. "I mean, I don't have any regrets."

Marta ended the call as soon as was compatible with decency and found herself standing before the closet she was sharing with Mike, unable to select a pair of pants and a blouse. She had been very fierce about her choice not to go to law school? Maybe that was only her mother's take on things. But if she had been fierce, had her defiance served to mask an insecurity, a deep-down fear that her decision to focus on a family was in some way misguided? Would it have made a difference if her mother had quizzed her? And what did it all matter now?

Marta rubbed her temples. She was convinced this soul-searching in relation to her lost career wouldn't be half as upsetting if she hadn't gotten pregnant. The whole mess had begun in a very ordinary way. After almost twenty years on the birth control pill, Marta and her doctor decided that enough was enough. There were too many health risks for someone with heart disease in the family (two maternal aunts) and twice in seven months she had developed a benign ovarian cyst. Benign or not, cysts were no fun. Her doctor had outlined the alternatives, none of which were terribly attractive, until she had mentioned a vasectomy. The procedure was common and safe, and the results were pretty much foolproof. Sexual function was not negatively affected. In short, it was a fantastic option with only one potential drawback—getting Mike to agree to it.

The conversation in which Marta had told Mike she was going off the pill was still crystal clear in her mind.

"Oh," he said, a look of abject panic on his face. "So, uh, what do you have in mind instead?"

"That should be a mutual decision," she replied. "I've been carrying that burden on my own since we met."

Mike nodded. "Right. Absolutely. So . . ."

"Condoms are an option, though not a fabulous idea on their own."

"Right," Mike said hastily. "Not a fabulous idea. What else?"

"You could get a vasectomy," she had gone on. "It would take care of the problem once and for all and would also make good economic sense. We decided after Troy there would be no more children. Right? It's not an outrageous idea, Mike," she went on reasonably. "Lots of men get vasectomies and it would be doing me an enormous favor."

But Mike balked. He was not a bad or an uninformed guy, just a *regular* guy, and the idea of having his "manhood" snipped away made him badly nervous. Marta got that. She didn't like it, but she got it. So, she let him off the hook. She agreed—as a temporary measure only—to get fitted for a diaphragm. Mike had been relieved. He promised he would give serious thought to getting a vasectomy.

After a few weeks, Marta again approached Mike. "I've gotten the name of a highly respected proctologist," she told him. "I can call first thing tomorrow to make an appointment. I'll be with you, Mike. We're in this together."

But Mike had no spare time, not in the foreseeable future. "It's this case I'm working on," he explained. "It requires all of my time and attention."

Marta had wondered. Was Mike aggrandizing his workload in

order to avoid having to make a decision? But nagging never helped. Time went on. Day-to-day stuff happened. They used the diaphragm; Mike wasn't too busy with work to forget about sex.

Then, after about two months, Marta discovered that she was pregnant. She had been scrupulous about following the directions provided by the manufacturer as well as by her ob-gyn, but the fact was that with "average use" there was a failure rate of twenty to forty percent after childbirth. Marta had known that all along. But she was devastated nonetheless. She did not want to be pregnant, not again.

She was angry with Mike for not having taken the idea of a vasectomy more seriously. Then again, she was the one who had let him off the hook. They were both to blame for the pregnancy, but Marta was the one who felt like a fool.

"Hey, Marta?" It was Mike, his voice startling her out of her reverie. "We're going to meet up with Dean and Nathan and the baby. Are you coming?"

"Yes," she called back, snatching a pair of chinos and a cotton blouse from the closet. "I'm coming."

Chapter 18

Allison had taken a long and leisurely drive along back roads in Kittery Point. The sightseeing was unbeatable. Charming, well-kept homes, many dating to the eighteenth and nineteenth centuries; little red schoolhouses neatly restored; big white churches—Baptist, Methodist, Congregationalist, Episcopal. Art galleries in old barns. Farms stands. Yard sales. She really did love New England; even in the dead of winter its appeal was strong. But there had never been any discussion about where she and Chris would live after college. Chicago. Close to Chris's parents—and to his brother, Robby Montague, who was buried in the family's plot in an old and well-known cemetery in a leafy suburb of the city.

Chuck was in the kitchen making a cup of tea when Allison got back to Driftwood House. "There are no fewer than seven kinds of tea in this kitchen," he said by way of greeting. "I'm surprised Bess hasn't supplied seven kinds of honey, as well."

"She is determined to make this reunion special," Allison agreed. She went to the fridge and removed a pitcher of lemonade.

"Want to tell me anything?" Chuck asked when Allison had joined him at the kitchen island.

"No," she said quickly. "Yes, I don't know. Don't ask me, Chuck." Chuck nodded. "Okay."

They sipped their tea and lemonade in companionable silence

for a few minutes until Allison asked a rhetorical question. "Back in college," she said, "did any of us have any real idea of who or what we would be in our forties?"

"Of course, we didn't," Chuck answered, "and thank goodness for that. Who among us could go on living knowing exactly what the future held? In this one case, ignorance is bliss."

"I suppose you're right. Chuck? Has being a father changed you?" Allison shook her head. "What a ridiculous question."

"Being a father is forcing me to be the best version of me there is," Chuck said promptly. "It's showing me how precious life really is. You'd think as a doctor I'd know that, but too often that truth gets buried under a barrage of facts and figures. And fatherhood is making me appreciate my parents in an entirely new way." Chuck paused. "Is this too difficult for you to be hearing?" he asked. "After all the years you and Chris spent trying to get pregnant?"

"No," Allison told him truthfully. "I wouldn't have asked if I didn't want to know your answer. I don't begrudge my friends their lives."

"Good. Begrudging is a waste of time and energy."

Chuck brought his empty teacup to the dishwasher and excused himself. "Nap time," he said.

A few minutes later Marta and Bess joined Allison, Marta from upstairs and Bess from the den. Bess took a bowl of green grapes from the fridge and poured herself a glass of water.

"Men can be so insanely infuriating," Marta stated.

"And you're making that observation why?" Allison asked.

"I just got off the phone with one of the guys on my neighborhood watch committee. He floated a few ideas for changes to our community website and I found them badly presented. All I did was ask a few clarifying questions and he went immediately on the defensive, as if I was criticizing and not just trying to understand. So not helpful."

Allison nodded. "Men see every conversation as a contest. Someone wins, someone loses. Completely unproductive."

"Mars and Venus," Marta added. "Never the twain shall meet."

Bess waved her hand dismissively. "Oh, come on. Men and women aren't that different from each other."

"No matter the similarities," Marta said, "the division of the sexes is real. Men made the rules and they're still enforcing the ones they can get away with enforcing without being eviscerated in the media or hauled into court. They don't want to give up any of the power base they created and in a way, you can't blame them. Power is good."

"Yeah, okay, but *our* guys aren't power-hungry men holding us down," Bess argued. "And we've never fought along gender lines, not once."

"Yes, we have," Allison said, feeling slightly guilty for revealing the secret. "We just never told you."

Bess looked stunned. "What do you mean?"

Marta shot a look at Allison before speaking. "Do you remember back in college when Garth Simmons was accused of date rape?"

"Of course, I remember. The scandal rocked the campus. No one could believe that Garth of all people could do such a thing."

"Why?" Marta challenged. "Because he was smart and good-looking and everyone from teachers to cleaning crews to students found him funny and charming?"

Bess shrugged. "Well, yeah."

"Bess, you're badly naïve. I knew a darker side of Garth and so did others. There was a complacency about him, an assumed superiority. At the time of this 'incident' he was only nineteen, but he was as full of self-importance as a power-hungry man of thirty-five."

"Garth? I can't believe it."

"Believe it," Allison said sternly.

Marta went on. "When the woman who accused him—her first name was Sarah, but I suddenly can't remember her last name; doesn't that say it all about how we treat the victims!—anyway, when she reported him to the campus authorities, almost the entire school divided up along sex lines. Even Mike, Chris, and Chuck couldn't believe that Garth was guilty. They were as in awe of him as most of the campus. Which is not to say that all women backed Sarah. There will always be the sort of women who find it expedient to cozy up to the enemy, hoping for a prize, like a convenient marriage to a billionaire." Marta frowned. "I didn't talk to our guys for weeks until they came around or pretended to. I'm ashamed to admit it, but by then I was so tired of being angry I was willing to 'believe' they'd had a change of heart."

"What about you, Allison?" Bess asked. "Did you refuse to talk to the guys, as well? Even to Chris?"

Allison hesitated. "The rape," she said finally, "happened a few months after I'd gone to the memorial rally for that poor young local teen who'd been killed by homophobic bullies in his own class. Chris had been so upset about my going. We were still in a state of partial reconciliation so I . . . I capitulated." *Again*, she added silently. "I wanted to make things right between us. I'm ashamed to say I told Chris that I respected his opinion about what had happened between Garth and Sarah and that I wouldn't argue with him any longer."

"But you still believed Sarah?" Marta pressed.

"Yes," said Allison. "I always believed her. I just failed to show that support when I gave in to Chris."

Bess shook her head. "How could I not have been aware of such controversy in our own group of friends?"

"We kept it from you as best we could," Allison explained. "We knew how upset you got whenever there was the slightest bit of dissension among us. Besides, at the time you were knee-deep in the theater department's spring production of whatever musical they were mounting, some Gilbert and Sullivan thing. You were always running off to vintage shops or flea markets in search of old-fashioned corsets or stuffed sofas or whatever else it was you were in charge of finding."

"You're right," Bess admitted. "That was an incredibly busy time. I hardly slept for weeks, trying to keep up with my classes and not let the set designer down." Bess paused for a moment. "But I do remember how the whole thing turned out, the date rape case I mean. The girl who accused Garth took her case to the police when the school didn't take her claims seriously. I can't remember if there was a trial, but he was thrown out of school, wasn't he?"

Marta nodded. "Good riddance to bad rubbish."

"But was he ever proved guilty?" Bess asked.

"All I know is that there was sufficient evidence against him for the school to finally act," Allison said. "And that's what matters."

"But what if he was innocent?" Bess pressed. "What if it all came down to miscommunication, or what if the girl regretted having had sex with Garth and was trying to shift the blame for her own mistake onto him? Garth's entire life is now tainted by that scandal and that seems unfair."

"As unfair as it would be if no one had believed the victim and she spent the rest of her life battling debilitating shame and anger?" Marta's face was alarmingly red. "And why would a young woman choose to subject herself to the humiliation of going public with a claim of rape when it wasn't true? Okay, yeah, one in a million women might be warped enough to claim to be a victim of a crime that never took place, but not Sarah—Metz! That was her name! I knew it would come to me. She was as levelheaded and as upright as they come."

"Besides," Allison went on, "Garth's daddy owns half of Manhattan. You can be sure Garth hasn't suffered one iota due to that annoying little episode, as I'm sure he thinks of it now."

Bess shook her head. "I think I have to process all this."

"While you do that I'm going to drive to Goose Rocks Beach. Allison?"

Allison declined Marta's invitation and went upstairs to her room to rest. If Bess had to process what had happened in the past, so did Allison. Why had she always been so ready to sacrifice her own firm beliefs for the sake of harmony with Chris? Was love to blame? Fidelity? Loyalty? Well, then, all three could be bad for your soul when they compelled you to deny your instincts and your better nature. Lesson learned.

Allison stretched out on the bed and folded her hands across her stomach. And she said a prayer that Sarah Metz was living a truly wonderful life.

Chapter 19

"How did sand get into my pockets when I haven't even been to the beach today?" Nathan held his cargo shorts over the wastepaper basket and shook.

Bess was barely aware of her fiancé. She was still wrapping her head around the fact that her friends had kept a secret from her. What else about the group did she not know, the reason for Allison's divorce aside? What else had they hidden from her? Bess thought of the charms she was going to present to her friends the night of the wedding, special gifts she had chosen for the people she knew she could trust the most. Trust did not go hand in hand with secrets.

Bess glanced around the room as if someone might be lurking behind the long curtains or under the four-poster bed. Of course, no one was there. But the dramatist in her had felt compelled to check.

"What's up?" Nathan asked, stepping into a fresh pair of chinos. "Why are you looking around like that?"

"I feel an atmosphere," she whispered. An image of the blighted tree came to her mind, that one stark reminder of imperfection at Driftwood House. "Something's wrong."

"In this room?" Nathan asked, lowering his own voice.

"No, in general."

Nathan put an arm into a linen shirt and then the other arm. "What do you mean, in general?"

"I don't know, exactly."

Nathan frowned. "You're not helping me understand, Bess."

"Sorry," Bess said. "Marta, for one. She seems—harder—than ever, ready to fight at a moment's notice."

"Maybe she's just missing her children. Didn't you tell me she pretty much never leaves them for more than a few days at a time?"

"Yeah," she said, sinking onto the edge of the bed. "But I don't know . . ."

Nathan came to sit next to her. "I won't say you're imagining things," he began, "because that would be condescending. But maybe you're being a bit too sensitive. You've put a lot of pressure on yourself to make this reunion—and the wedding—perfect. Could the strain be causing you to sense trouble where there is none?"

Bess shrugged. "It's possible. I know I can be a bit—nosy. Everybody tells me so."

"Everybody loves and appreciates your big heart." Nathan took her hand in his and squeezed it gently.

Bess frowned. "Except when I'm interfering."

"Maybe you're just picking up on Allison's unhappiness," Nathan suggested.

Bess nodded. "Yes, I wish there was something I could do for her. . . ."

"There is. Give her the space to grieve. She'll talk when she wants to. And if she doesn't, that's her choice, too. Just love her."

Bess leaned into Nathan and kissed his cheek. "You're very smart."

Nathan shrugged. "I'm all right for a guy, or so I've been told."

"Who told you?"

"My mother, of course!"

Bess laughed.

"Ready? I'm starved. Maybe it's the salt air. Whatever it is, I've been as hungry as the proverbial horse since I got here."

Bess and Nathan were greeted enthusiastically as they came into the dining area on the first floor.

"There they are," Dean announced, raising his glass of wine. "The couple of the moment."

"The beautiful bride," Mike added.

"And the handsome groom!" That was Allison; she was smiling.

"Hear, hear!" Chuck said.

"Mazel tov!" Marta added.

Bess squeezed Nathan's hand and she looked upon her friends with fondness. Nathan was right. She was probably being hypersensitive, imagining trouble where there was none.

Chapter 20

Mike was already sound asleep. Marta, sitting up in bed beside him, had tried to read, but thoughts of the conversations that had taken place at dinner kept intruding. Allison had mentioned that the lease on her studio was coming to an end; she feared a big hike in the rent. Bess told an amusing story about a client. Nathan shared a complaint about the airline he routinely used to travel to and from his office in Stockholm. Chuck asked Mike a general legal question; in turn, Mike asked Chuck to take a look at a mark on the palm of his hand. "You know I'm a heart specialist," Chuck had pointed out while peering at Mike's hand. "But you're here," Mike had replied. Chuck had proclaimed the mark harmless. Even Dean, though on a hiatus from work, had contributed an anecdote from a recent teachers' conference he had attended.

And what had Marta contributed? Nothing. She could have talked about what was going on with Sam or Leo or Troy, but she didn't. Why? Marta thought about what her mother had told her regarding her old friend Olivine's apotheosis. If Olivine could restructure her life . . .

Marta rubbed her eyes with her fingertips. Chuck had his passion for medicine. Allison had her passion for art. Every one of her friends believed he or she was doing what he or she was meant to be doing. Of course, some people came late to their talents. Others exhausted one talent and then moved on to another. There were plenty of people who at the end of their lives could claim several careers and could boast of having successfully shouldered through a succession of challenging phases during which they mastered new skills and conquered hitherto unconquered territory. Why couldn't she be one of those people? What was stopping her but for the usual things that stopped so many people from achieving their dreams—fear and a lack of self-confidence? She really couldn't claim the more prosaic obstacles like time and money; sure, both were limited, but not to a debilitating extent like they were for some people.

Marta adjusted the pillows behind her back, careful not to wake her husband. What *had* her younger self been thinking when she chose to forgo a career and be the stay-at-home parent in her family? Had she been so idealistic that she had simply ignored all thoughts of life post children in the house? Or, Marta wondered, had she blithely assumed that once her kids were raised and on their own she could easily pick up where she had left off? Which was where? She had no career to which she could return. And how had she been so naïve—so willfully naïve—as to assume that she wouldn't have to face what countless other women had to face, almost insurmountable obstacles to reentering the workforce in any meaningful and financially significant way? How could Marta Kennedy, always a top student, president of her high school's student council, Phi Beta Kappa, how could she of all people have been so careless and disrespectful of her future? But it was human nature to put off until the next day or the day after that what one assumed could be put off without dire repercussion. The here and now, the present moment required so much focus and energy, who could be blamed for pushing aside the making of plans, especially when everyone knew that The Future, no matter how carefully mapped, was at root an unknown thing?

Like any intelligent, self-aware person, Marta knew that one got nowhere by self-blaming, but in this case she found it impossible not to indulge in scolding her younger self. Who else could she blame for choices freely made? And they had been made freely.

Marta glanced over at her husband. She recalled his surprise when she told him she had decided not to go to law school. "But you're smarter than I am and a way better student," he had argued. "And you've been talking about law school since we first met. I don't understand."

Marta had explained that her focus had changed, that her goal had morphed into something she regarded as higher and better. Being a mother to their children. Full-time. Always. Every minute of day and night. Mike was surprised but pleased. They agreed upon a plan. He would earn the money and provide the health insurance for their family while she ran things at home—in Mike's opinion, the far more difficult task. He had always been vocal about that opinion, too, eager to give Marta credit where credit was due and then some, grateful for her and proud of her.

But now Marta wondered. Had Mike ever resented his wife for not contributing to the family's finances? He had never even hinted at feeling dissatisfied or put-upon. But Mike was a good guy. Maybe he had been hiding his discontent so as not to hurt her. Maybe he'd had second thoughts along the way, after Troy's birth, for example, when Marta's energy level had hit an all-time low and he had been compelled (he would not have said forced) to help out more at home; even with Marta's mother stopping by every other day to do some light housekeeping, Mike had been strained.

Maybe, Marta thought, he had even talked about his unhappiness to the colleagues with whom he worked such long and exhausting hours. Maybe he wasn't alone in his situation, either. Maybe one or more of the other men or women at the firm were in a similar position, stuck in a deal made long ago, a deal that no longer worked as well for the breadwinners as it did for the stay-at-home partners.

Marta frowned. There was no way she could ask such questions of Mike and expect to receive an honest answer. Mike was no liar, but above all his concern was to protect his wife and his children from any undue stress, and telling Marta that he was unhappy would absolutely cause her stress. Which in turn would cause Mike stress. What a ridiculous nightmare of a situation, Marta thought angrily.

And there were still the children to tell about the pregnancy. Marta suspected that Sam would be the most displeased. Sam was mature enough (wasn't she?) to have sensed that her mother hadn't been pining for the presence of an infant. She might very well guess that her mother's pregnancy was an accident (unpleasant word; better to say unintentional). Maybe, Marta thought, she should come right out and tell Sam the whole truth. On the one hand, why not? Sam was a young woman and needed to understand the complexities of an active sexual life. On the other hand, did Sam need to hear details of her *parents'* sexual life? Most definitely not.

Here was another thing. Sam had always enjoyed being the only girl. If Marta should give birth to a second daughter, would Sam be mature enough to share the spotlight? Being a successful adult was largely about knowing when to let the spotlight shine on someone more deserving—like your kids or your spouse or your aging parent or your baby sibling. Marta frowned. Adulthood was exhausting, no doubt about it. Selfishness was so much less taxing. Too bad she didn't have a talent for selfishness.

What about Leo? Of all three kids, Leo, with his roll with the punches attitude, would best adapt to a new member of the household. No, Marta wasn't worried about Leo.

As for Troy, it would take some skillful parenting to ensure that he didn't feel ignored, while at the same time making him understand that the *new* baby was as important as he was.

Marta sighed. What a mess. And who was she kidding? Her nascent plans for her future had been more fantasies than anything. All they had consisted of was the thought of one day making enough money on her own through her as yet to be determined career to buy herself presents without guilt (she thought of Bess's vintage aquamarine ring), to feel independent, to spend time on her own or with other women in business, to grab back a part of the person she had been before becoming a wife and a mother.

But those days of "me time" were now so very far away. . . .

A deeply unpleasant thought occurred to Marta as she sat in bed next to her lightly snoring husband. Could she have, on some unconscious level, *wanted* to get pregnant again? Could she have been so fearful of the state of independence she had envisioned that she had taken steps to ensure it wouldn't come about? Marta shivered. No. Sometimes things just happened. And there was never any wisdom in blaming the victim.

She had sex and got pregnant, so let her suffer.

He smoked and got lung cancer, so no pity for him.

She met her friends for cocktails one night and was raped on the way home. What did she expect?

That sort of attitude was smug and cowardly, and Marta had always loathed and despised such shabby thinking.

Suddenly, Mike tossed wildly in his sleep. The light must be disturbing him, Marta thought. She reached for the cord on the bedside lamp and then slid down under the covers. Sleep would come eventually.

Chapter 21

Allison sat crossed-legged on the lawn a few feet from the gnarled tree, her sketch pad balanced on her knees. The tree was proving a great source of inspiration and comfort to Allison on this visit to Maine. In a way, it was a perfect companion, comfortably silent but always listening. Sympathetic without being curious.

The poor dead tree did not question why she had followed Chris to Chicago after graduation, even though it had meant leaving her beloved parents. It accepted the fact that at the time only Chris's desires had mattered. It did not scold her for having wanted what she had wanted, which was to be with the person she loved more than anyone else. It did not give her false hope when she wondered if it was too late to begin a life based on her own needs and wants.

The side door of the house opened. (It was unmistakable, the only door that squeaked.) Allison looked over her shoulder to see Nathan striding toward the drive. A moment or two later she heard a car crunching toward the road. She turned back to the gnarled tree.

In Nathan, Bess had found her Prince Charming. In Chris, Allison had found hers. At least, she thought she had. But maybe she had been wrong about Chris from the start. She had always believed that together they could see any of life's many challenges through to the end. Hadn't they made vows at the altar? While it was true they had married in a church more as a matter of form than one of belief, didn't it still mean something that God's name had been invoked as they were joined as husband and wife? Maybe the belief of others was enough to sanctify her own union.

But maybe not. Chris had left her to bear the pain of their loss all alone. Such an action was unprecedented in their relationship. He had always been so solicitous of her feelings, so tender and caring. More like a father at times than a husband. The thought was disturbing.

Allison quickly got to her feet, stowed her pencil in its case and the sketch book under her arm, and joined Bess and Marta on the porch. There was a stack of paperback romances on one of the small side tables; on another sat a book of crossword puzzles. She sank into one of the white wicker chairs and stretched her legs before her.

"I just made the lemonade," Bess told her, indicating a frosty pitcher on another of the small tables scattered across the porch. "It doesn't have much sugar so it should be nice and tart. But if you want more sugar I could—"

"I'm sure it's fine," Allison said quickly.

"Nathan went to buy a few bottles of Prosecco," Marta noted. "He suggested we start tonight's festivities with Prosecco and yet more oysters. You're a lucky woman, Bess Culpepper."

Bess laughed. "Don't I know it!"

"I'm not really surprised that you're marrying someone significantly older than you," Allison said, after a sip of the lemonade. It was very refreshing.

"Why?" Bess asked. "Frankly, I haven't given our age difference any thought."

Allison shrugged. "It's just a feeling I have that the age difference will work for you. I can't explain it. But what do I know? You've dated older guys in the past and some of them were just downright bad for you."

"Bess doesn't need to be reminded of her mistakes," Marta said. "Like that sixty-something fitness instructor who turned out to be suffering from an eating disorder. Didn't he dump you, Bess, because you refused to stick to some weird starvation diet he swore would halt the aging process?"

"Hey!" Bess cried. "I thought you said I don't need to be reminded of my past—um, experiences. Anyway, Nathan is as active as I am and his parents were healthy until well into their eighties, so I'm fully expecting us to celebrate at least thirty years of marriage."

"Ever the optimist," Allison said, with an abrupt laugh. "How nice for you."

Bess looked as if she had been struck across the face.

Allison put her glass down and leaned over to put a hand briefly on Bess's arm. "I'm so sorry, Bess, really."

Bess managed a smile but said nothing.

Allison, ashamed, rose from her chair. "I'll see you later," she said. As she climbed the stairs to her room she felt a great sense of weariness overtake her. Sometimes lately she didn't recognize the person she had become, mean-spirited and jealous. It would not do. She would get herself in hand immediately so as not to ruin Bess's wedding. That would be unforgivable.

Chapter 22

Poor Allison, Bess thought, sitting at her desk in the den, scanning her e-mail in-box. She was clearly so unhappy and though her sarcastic remark had hurt Bess, it had hurt for only a moment. After all, Bess was the lucky one. In less than two weeks she would be married to the man of her dreams.

Her cell phone beeped. Bess glanced at the screen; the call was from her sister Ann. Bess looked away. She wasn't in the mood to talk to Ann—to any of her family—at the moment. She let the call go unanswered and then played the message Ann had left on voice mail.

It's me, Ann. Your sister. Just calling to see if there's anything I can do for you now that the wedding is almost here. I hope you're not having jitters but if you are, call me. Maybe I can help. Bye.

Sweet, generous Ann. If this was the first time she had reached out to her oldest sister in this way, it was still a nice gesture. Bess wondered. Was it really too late to involve her family in the wedding? Maybe not, but the truth was that she didn't want to give any of them a significant role. It wasn't that she didn't love her family— she did!—it was just that she had never felt all that *close* to them, particularly her sisters. It was no big surprise why, really. Bess had been ten when Mae came along; eleven when Ann was born. With Mrs. Culpepper burdened with the full-time care of two sick and elderly relatives who lived a few miles down the road, Bess was required to be more of a nanny than a sibling. It had been Bess who changed diapers and gave bottles and baths after school, who put the babies to bed when Mrs. Culpepper had to be gone, who soothed the girls when they were teething and rocked them back to sleep when they woke with a bad dream. There was little doubt in Bess's adult mind that those few years of maternal duties, undertaken when she herself was still a child, had largely decided her against having children of her own one day. If she pretended incompetence when it came to child-rearing, so be it. In the end, it was easier than trying to explain her reasons for keeping her distance from children.

There was something else, as well, that had contributed to the growing distance between Bess and her younger sisters. With Ann and Mae not quite a year apart they had behaved almost like twins, content with each other to the exclusion of Bess, as well as of other children their age. By the time Mrs. Culpepper's duties to the elderly relatives had come to an end, and Bess was relieved of most of her duties, Ann and Mae were inseparable. By the time Bess was in high school, her sisters had come to feel almost like strangers.

Almost like strangers. Bess frowned as memories of the shower her colleagues had given her at the Top of the East came back to her. Finding her mother and sisters there had been a total surprise, and not an entirely pleasant one. They had never, not once, visited her in Portland. An uncomfortable thought had occurred to Bess. Was it only because she was becoming one of them—a Married Woman, someone who mattered—that her family was finally ready to show some real interest in her?

Not that Bess needed their interest. She wasn't jealous of the close bond Ann and Mae shared with each other and with their mother. She wasn't. At least, she hadn't been jealous for a long time.

Bess had pasted on a smile and welcomed her family along with the rest of the guests. Mrs. Culpepper had been dressed plainly if respectably. Ann had worn a dress she had bought at least ten years and twenty odd pounds earlier; the fabric was strained across her middle and there was a small but obvious stain on the collar. Money was an issue for Ann, but not a drastic issue; it was more that Ann just didn't spend any time or energy on her appearance. Bess often wished that she did.

Mae, who was proud of her pretensions to style, was dressed in a black skirt that was far too short and a red sequined sleeveless top too heavy for the season. Mae kept yanking on the hem of the skirt and wriggling inside the top as if the lining was scratching at her. Her nails were painted a truly awful green. Most disturbing to Bess was the fact that Mae didn't seem in the least self-conscious.

Bess remembered thinking that Mae *should* feel self-conscious, as should Ann. She remembered being embarrassed by her sisters.

What sort of person was embarrassed by family members whose only fault—if it could be called a fault—was a poor sartorial choice? A lousy person, Bess thought, snapping closed the lid of her laptop.

Bess had come home from the party with a crashing headache that had only gotten worse when Mae sent her a text saying what a great time she had had and wanting to know when she could come back into Portland and hang out with Bess and her girlfriends. (This, too, was a shocking first.) Her mother had then called to say she hoped Bess had gotten enough to eat at the party. (Not a surprise. For Mrs. Culpepper, food equaled love.) Finally, there had been an e-mail from Ann in which she had so profusely thanked Bess for having been included in the festivities that if Bess hadn't known better she would have suspected her sweet sister of bitter irony.

The headache—the guilt—had gotten much worse before it finally subsided.

At least Bess had done her duty by her sisters when they married. Nevertheless, she squirmed as she remembered feeling huge relief that neither had asked her to be maid of honor. The last thing she had wanted was to help orchestrate the weddings back in Green Lakes, only partly because she didn't know either of her sisters well enough to plan a proper shower. Who were her sisters' friends? What was Ann's favorite song, her favorite color? What was Mae's favorite flower or TV show? Shouldn't a big sister know these things? But the three Culpepper girls hadn't lived under the same roof for more than a few months in over ten years.

Still, Bess had twice accepted the role of bridesmaid, had uncomplainingly worn the unflattering, ill-fitting dresses, stood at attention as the minister blessed the union of man and wife, and posed for endless pictures with the other bridesmaids as well as with the groomsman with whom she had been partnered, in each case the same young man with sweaty palms whose attentions she had been dodging since puberty.

Disaster of a sort had struck at Mae's wedding when Bess accidentally caught the bouquet. She was horrified as all eyes turned on her; though she identified as a romantic she did not believe a sign of such importance would come to her at an event at which one of the desserts was a gelatin mold studded with sliced bananas and canned pineapple chunks. For the remainder of the reception she had endured good-natured teasing from the guests. An elderly woman who was a member of the church the Culpeppers attended had asked Bess if the lucky young man had already appeared in her life, to which Bess had replied, "No, I'm waiting for my soul mate." The woman had chuckled so heartily her false teeth had almost popped out of her mouth. When she had recovered her breath, and adjusted her teeth, the woman had said, "Oh, dear child, then you'll be waiting a very long time indeed!"

Well, Bess thought now, the long wait had been worth it. She could have done without some of the interesting interludes along the way—like the aging fitness nut—but maybe those experiences had helped train her to spot the real soul mate when he finally came along.

The door to the den opened behind her. Only one other person used this room.

"I was just thinking of you!" Bess said brightly, turning to face her fiancé. All unhappy thoughts fled.

"In what way?" Nathan asked.

"I was thinking," she said, rising to greet him, "that you were well worth the wait."

Chapter 23

Marta opened the bedroom door, towel over her shoulder, her lightweight robe belted tightly around her waist. No visible bump yet; just the usual tummy Marta had been carrying around for years. Should any of her friends see her before the door closed behind her, they would be none the wiser.

"You're up," Marta said to her husband, who was sitting in the comfortable high-backed chair in one corner of the room, reading something on his phone. Why did people feel the need to note the obvious, she wondered? It was a mystery for the ages.

Mike immediately put his phone in his pocket and smiled at her. "I've been thinking," he began.

Marta, used to hearing this opening line from her husband to refer to anything from what kind of pizza he was going to order that evening to what bank account he was considering moving some money into, smiled back at him. "And?" she asked, running the towel over her damp hair one last time before reaching for the comb on the top of the dresser.

"And I was wondering if this isn't the perfect time to share our big news. I know Bess wouldn't mind if we stole a bit of the limelight. What do you think?"

"No," Marta said flatly. She did not turn from the mirror over the dresser. She had not meant to sound harsh, but she was pretty sure that she had.

"Oh," Mike said. "It's just that . . . You're sure?"

Marta turned to face her husband. "I'm sure," she said.

Mike rose from the chair and came over to where Marta stood in her robe, the comb still in one hand. When he spoke, his voice was softer than it had been; he sounded almost cajoling. "I know you're worried that because of your age . . ." he began. "But these are our dearest friends, after all. If we learn something bad or we lose this child, at least we'll have the support of those closest to us to help us through."

With great effort Marta controlled an impulse to—to what? To shout, stamp her foot, scream. "I said I'm sure." There was a trembling in her voice. "I'm not ready to tell anyone. Please, Mike, don't press me on this."

Mike reached out and placed his hands on her arms. "Do you feel okay?" he asked, a note of concern in his voice. "Do you have a sense that something's wrong? A sixth sense, women's intuition?"

"No!" Marta clenched her fingers around the comb so tightly that her fingers prickled with pain. "Sorry," she said. "I didn't mean to raise my voice. Just, please, Mike, let me . . . Let me alone with this for a bit longer."

Mike took his hands from her arms. "Of course," he said. "Whatever you want. You know best."

Did she? Marta managed to say, "Thank you." She turned to the mirror over the dresser and stared unseeingly at her reflection.

"I'm going to take a shower." Mike took his robe from the hook behind the door and left the room. When he was gone, Marta moved away from the mirror and sat heavily on the edge of the bed. She knew he didn't understand. How could he when she was being so uncommunicative? The poor guy probably just chalked up her strange behavior to a particularly aggressive assault of hormones. Those mysterious Female Troubles. That infamous unbalanced state of mind that made women unfit for high political office or for holding down major corporate appointments. Marta felt like hitting something, and not because her emotions were out of control. Her emotions were very much in her control and what she wanted to do with them at that moment was to destroy. The feminine destructive force was as real and as strong as the feminine creative force. And the sooner men understood that, the better.

Marta got up from the bed, hurriedly dressed, and headed for the kitchen before Mike could return to their bedroom. She was not eager to be alone with him right then. She found Allison and Bess in the kitchen, leafing through the local papers. A bouquet of flowers from the garden sat on the island counter.

"Do either of you have journals or diaries from years ago?" Marta asked when she had poured a cup of decaf coffee. "Like, from our college days?"

Allison looked up from the newspaper. "Mine are in a storage unit," she said. "When my parents died, I had to empty their house before selling it, so what remains of my childhood came back into my possession. Not that I have any plans on reading those old diaries," she added. "I suspect the experience would be both painful and cringe-worthy. Anyway, why the question?"

Marta took a sip of coffee and shrugged.

"My stuff is still in my parents' attic, where I stashed it years ago," Bess said. "Until they sell the house—if they ever do—that's where everything from my childhood will remain."

Allison smiled. "We hang on to the relics of our past, as if throwing them out would somehow—What? Blot out who we once were? Aren't memories enough?"

"Relics help trigger memories," Bess said, "especially ones we might not otherwise recall so easily."

"Maybe we don't need those particular memories triggered," Marta pointed out.

"What about your old things?" Allison asked Marta.

"I never kept a diary or a journal. And I donated or threw out most everything else ages ago. I'm not the most sentimental person, but you know that." Marta paused before going on in what she hoped was a nonchalant tone. "I was wondering. What did you guys feel about my not going to law school like I had planned?"

"It was your decision," Bess said after a moment. "I don't think I felt anything about it."

"I was surprised," Allison told her. "I always saw you as a lawyer in the making, maybe because that's how you introduced yourself when we first met. Hi, I'm Marta and I'm pre-law. I wondered if you'd be bored not going on for a higher degree, but then I figured you'd never allow yourself to be bored. You'd find something else challenging to do."

Marta laughed; she was afraid it was bitterly. "And then I became a mom."

Allison smiled kindly. "See? I was right."

"You're not having regrets, are you?" Bess asked.

Marta laughed. "Like I'd welcome that sort of debt on top of what Mike accrued during his law school days? And for what? Long hours and difficult clients? Every Tom, Dick, and Harry you meet at a party asking for free legal advice? Being the butt of stupid anti-lawyer jokes? No, I have no regrets."

Marta put her empty cup of coffee in the sink.

"Don't you want any breakfast?" Bess asked.

"No, thanks," she said. "I'm not hungry." She made her way to the back porch and from there down to the lawn. What a liar she had become. She couldn't even tell the truth about something as minor as a desire for one of the raspberry muffins sitting prettily on a platter.

Let alone the truth about an unwanted pregnancy.

Chapter 24

"Do you think she *does* regret not going to law school?" Bess asked when Marta had gone.

"I don't know," Allison admitted. "It's hard to tell what Marta feels or doesn't feel. She keeps so much to herself and when she does talk she so often resorts to exaggerations or flippant remarks." More so recently, Allison thought.

Bess shook her head. "It's just that she's such a great mother. And even if she does feel the need for a change, she's got all that mom experience to use toward building a career."

"The situation might not seem so positive to her," Allison pointed out. Naïve, simplistic Bess. "And not all 'mom experience' as you call it is readily marketable, at least not without a lot of spin and convincing. Not that Marta doesn't have it in her to elbow her way into public notice, I believe she does, but *she* might not think so, not after so many years on the sidelines as it were."

"Mike would help her," Bess said firmly. "I know he would. He must have tons of contacts, and not only in the law."

"Maybe Marta doesn't want his help—assuming, of course, she's thinking about making a change. His support, sure, but knowing Marta, I think she'd want to do whatever it is she wants to do on her own. Remember how in college she was the only one of us who never joined a study group? She always went her own way."

"I remember," Bess said. She glanced at her watch. "Almost eight thirty. I have to call Kara in a moment. Don't forget to have one of those muffins," she added as she dashed in the direction of the den. "They're awesome."

Allison did help herself to a muffin, though she was unable to eat all of it, then headed down to the beach. She didn't see Marta on her journey; who knew where she had gone? Marta wasn't the type to wander aimlessly; at least, she hadn't been in the past.

Allison had been at the water's edge for only a minute or two when a young man holding the hand of a toddler came into her line of vision. She watched as the man bent down so that he was face-to-face with the child as he spoke. The child squatted and splashed the water with his free hand. Allison's heart contracted painfully.

That day. That dreadful day. Chris had gotten to the hospital before the ambulance that had brought Allison. Tears coursing down his face, he insisted on holding her hand in the ER while doctors examined and nurses tended. It wasn't long before it was confirmed that the baby had been lost. Within hours, Chris went from excessively solicitous behavior to an inability even to meet Allison's eye, let alone hold her hand.

One of the nurses, noticing Chris's behavior, had tried to comfort Allison. "Men feel just as deeply as we do," she had said, "but they have a hell of a time admitting what they feel, even to themselves." She had smiled and patted Allison's shoulder. "He'll come around once you're both home. You'll see."

Allison was grateful for the nurse's efforts at comfort, but the woman didn't know that Chris was still grieving the loss of his younger brother, a death that had taken place over thirty years earlier but that in some ways felt as new and raw to Chris as if it had happened the day before.

So, the following morning Allison and Chris went home. Allison, mourning her own loss, vowed to help Chris deal with his. In time, she believed, they would begin to heal and together, they would emerge from the darkness as they had once been, a deeply devoted husband and wife.

Things did not go well. When Allison reached out to Chris he flinched before accepting her touch. He went from sleeping with his back turned to her, to staying up very late into the night so that even at two or three in the morning Allison, half-waking from a troubled sleep, would find herself alone. Come morning she would discover him on the couch in the living room, his face a mask of tension, his eyes screwed shut, as if in his sleep he was battling a very great enemy.

Chris went back to work immediately. He turned down all invitations to meet with well-meaning friends. Allison could only imagine how Chris and his father were behaving with each other at the office. They had always been rather formal. Now, they must be downright frigid.

Allison returned to her studio. Answering clients' calls, meeting the demands of a deadline, all of it was better than sitting alone at home, worrying about the state of her marriage, worrying about the state of her mind.

The days dragged on. More often than not Chris claimed he didn't want dinner. Allison found herself eating most of her meals alone. Gradually, she stopped eating any sort of regular meal.

One afternoon, while cleaning out her desk, Allison came across a photo she had taken three years earlier when she and Chris had spent a week in San Francisco. It occurred to her, as she looked at their smiling faces, that maybe a vacation was what they needed. Getting away wouldn't erase what had happened, it wouldn't even cause them to forget, but it might give them the time and space to acknowledge *together* what had happened to them. It might allow them to bridge the dizzying gap that had opened so suddenly between them, a gap that seemed to be getting wider and deeper with each passing day.

When Chris got home from work that evening Allison broached the subject. "It's just that everything here is such a reminder of what we've lost. If we could just go somewhere new together and be on our own, maybe then we could . . . Maybe then we could talk and begin to heal. What do you think?"

Chris had looked at her, stunned. When he spoke, his voice was almost unrecognizable, so filled was it with outrage. "How shallow and coldhearted can you be?" he asked. "You want to take a vacation? As if you deserved a treat after what you did!"

Deserved? What did deserving have to do with healing? After what she had done? As if she had callously set out to put the life of their unborn child at risk?

Allison could find nothing to say. There was much that could and maybe even that should be said, but she was incapable of accessing it.

A few days after that dismal exchange Chris announced that he wanted a divorce. More, that he had already hired an attorney. Maybe the news shouldn't have come as a surprise, given the domestic atmosphere of raw misery that had taken hold in the month since the accident, but it did. When the words had sunk in, Allison made the mistake—if an excusable one—of asking Chris why he wanted a divorce.

"Because," he said, his tone flat and cold, "I can't get it out of my mind that not long before you got pregnant you told me you wanted to abandon our efforts. I can't help but wonder if you didn't get into your car that morning wishing there would be an accident that would solve your little problem."

It was the cruelest, most brutal thing anyone had ever said to Allison. "No," she cried. "You can't believe . . . I never . . ."

But Chris went ruthlessly on. "I'm moving into my parents' place for the time being. You can stay here. I can't bear it one more minute."

Those words. *I can't bear it one more minute.* Allison used the toe of her sneaker to dig a pretty white shell from where it was half buried in the sand. The bit that had been hidden was mottled with a greenish growth. Allison took a step away from the shell. As if *she* could have born for another moment the atmosphere of alienation that had come over their home?

For almost two weeks she had absolutely refused to believe that Chris really wanted a divorce. She had gone through the motions of her days and nights, expecting a call from her husband, expecting him to appear at the door to their home, expecting a miracle.

One afternoon the landline in the condo rang. Allison remembered wondering why they still had a landline. She answered the call.

"Good afternoon," a woman said. She spoke with a practiced

professional voice. "My name is Meryl Moss and I'm an agent with Leafy Bough Realty. With whom am I speaking?"

Allison told her, wondering how quickly she could end the call without being rude. She did not need a Realtor.

"Good afternoon, Ms. Montague," the woman went on. "The reason I'm calling is to enquire if you've chosen an agent to handle the sale of your property at Market Avenue."

"But the condo isn't for sale," Allison had replied promptly.

"I don't understand," the Realtor went on. "I was informed that the property *was* for sale but that it hadn't yet been listed with a broker."

Allison's hand tightened on the phone. "Where did you hear that?" she demanded.

"The property was discussed at our meeting this morning," Ms. Moss said. "We were told the owners are divorcing and looking to move the property quickly. If I may—"

"No," Allison spat. "You may not." With a satisfying slam, she replaced the receiver. Good old landline.

She could no longer deny the inevitable. Chris was serious about a divorce.

Allison turned away from the sight of the ocean and headed back to Driftwood House. How much longer could she remain silent, plagued by these loud and insistent memories, bound by that promise to Chris he had so unfairly forced her to make? For better or worse, she thought, not much longer.

Not much longer.

Chapter 25

Bess had brought in dinner from Molly's Family Pizza that evening. An easy meal with virtually no cleanup meant that by seven thirty everyone was gathered on the back porch to enjoy the sunset. Bess felt content and thought the others might be feeling the same, even Allison. But maybe that was her optimistic nature at work. She looked more closely at her friends. What was she missing about them all? What were they hiding?

"We've had our share of adventures, and not all of them pleasant," Chuck was saying to Nathan.

Marta raised an eyebrow. "Who could forget the time Mike got lost in Mexico City!"

"I did not get lost! We were all together at the Metropolitan Cathedral," Mike said, looking to Nathan and to Dean, "and the plan was for Allison, Chris, and Marta to go to The Dolores Olmedo Museum to see the Frida Kahlo and Diego Rivera collections, while Chuck and Bess went back to the Palacio de Bellas Artes to see some temporary folk art exhibit they'd somehow missed the day before, and then for us all to meet up after for lunch."

"And where were you going to be while the others were soaking up culture?" Dean asked, restraining a grin.

"I was just going to wander around, see the sights. The problem came when I set out later to meet everyone where we'd planned to meet . . ." Mike put meaningful emphasis on those last few words.

"And he wasn't there when we arrived," Chuck went on. "So, we sat down anyway and ordered lunch and still no Mike. And he wasn't answering his cell phone—"

"Turns out I'd left it at the hotel," Mike said with a shrug. "But I was on my way to—"

"The wrong restaurant!" Marta said with a laugh. "He thought we'd agreed to meet at some place called Casa Tito by the Palacio."

"That *is* what we said!" Mike insisted. "I remember it distinctly."

"When in fact," Bess went on, "we'd said we'd meet at the Café Teatro!"

Mike rolled his eyes, put up his hands, and surrendered.

"By the time we all hooked up again," Marta said, "none of us was in a very good mood."

"We had been worried," Bess explained. "For a while we thought that maybe Mike had been mugged and his ID had been stolen and he had a head injury and was wandering around the streets not knowing who or where he was."

"*You* thought those things," Marta corrected. "The rest of us weren't worried, just annoyed."

"Thanks a lot," Mike said. "I *might* have been in trouble, you know!"

"Sensibly," Bess said, "Chris suggested we go back to the hotel and wait for Mike there. So, we did and that's when Marta found Mike's cell phone in their room. That solved one part of the puzzle."

"And finally," Marta went on, "Mike showed up, looking all grimy and sweaty."

"I did not look grimy and sweaty," Mike protested.

"Didn't it ever occur to you that maybe you'd gone to the wrong restaurant?" Nathan asked Mike. "Or that maybe something dire had happened to one of the others?"

"Eventually. But without my cell phone I had no choice but to go back to the hotel and wait for word."

"Next time we're putting a homing device on him," Marta said, with a jerk of her thumb in Mike's direction.

Nobody laughed or made a comment. Bess thought Marta was being pretty harsh with Mike, bringing up the incident in the first place and then belaboring the story.

"And who could forget the time Marta went into labor during our ski holiday in Colorado," Allison said. "Thinking about it still gives me chills!"

"I wasn't due for almost three weeks," Marta told Dean and Nathan. "Luckily, we weren't far from civilization."

"I panicked," Bess admitted. "I was a total wreck, like that character from *Gone With the Wind*, the one who cries out something like, 'I don't know nothin' 'bout birthin' no babies.'"

Mike shook his head. "I never should have allowed you to leave home," he said gravely.

Marta's face turned red. "Allowed me?" she demanded.

"I'm sure he—" Bess began.

"I mean," Mike corrected, "I should have more strongly suggested you not travel."

Marta did not reply, just looked away from her husband.

"At least Chuck was there," Allison pointed out. "If Marta hadn't been able to get to the hospital in time he could have delivered Leo."

"Hey," Chuck said. "I deal with the heart. I'm no obstetrician."

"But aren't you required by law to help someone in physical distress, even if what's required isn't your specialty?" Bess asked. "Isn't that part of the Hippocratic Oath or something?"

Chuck laughed. "That's not exactly how it works. And nowadays the original Hippocratic Oath is taken more as a rite of passage. It's been replaced by continually updated codes of ethical conduct, and that's a good thing. People will sue for malpractice on the shakiest grounds. Those of us in the medical profession live in absolute fear not so much of making a mistake but of being thought we did so purposely or due to negligence." Chuck shuddered. "That said, I'm not in the least bit eager to deliver babies without a full operating theater of sterile instruments and specialists to back me up!"

"As much as I love and trust you, Chuck," Marta said, "I'm very glad you weren't called upon to bring Leo into the world."

"Knowing Leo, he probably would have fixed me with one of

those critical stares he seems to have mastered in utero and begun to lecture me on exactly what I did wrong."

"He does seem to know an awful lot of stuff the average twelve-year-old doesn't know," Bess added. "Well, there's your answer. Leo isn't average. Which is not to say that Sam and Troy are below average!" Bess added hastily.

"I have no need to equate one of my children to the other, Bess," Marta said sharply. "Each is an individual and that's fine by me."

"This is the best reunion we've had so far," Bess blurted, and immediately felt awash in embarrassment. What a ridiculous thing to say! Why did she insist on ignoring painful truths, like the fact that Chris wasn't with them? Like that fact that Marta had just spoken sharply to her and had taken offense at something Mike had said in all innocence?

No one commented on the statement. Nathan gave her a small smile. Bess wondered if her friends had suddenly become so used to her spouting inane statements they no longer cared to remark on them.

"Remember one of the times we went into Boston to that great French bistro we loved?" Chuck said suddenly. "They had the best brunch and the prices were doable for broke college kids." Chuck looked to Nathan. "That particular day there was an anti-nukes protest rally going on—Pakistan had just staged five nuclear tests in response to India's staging three—and a reporter from one of the local news stations was stopping people on Boylston Street to get their opinion of the situation. Anyway, Chris managed to get himself noticed—"

"He basically put himself face-to-face with the reporter!" Mike interrupted with a laugh.

"Yeah, and . . ." Chuck looked to Allison and then shrugged. "Never mind," he said. "It's not a particularly interesting story."

"Go on, Chuck," Allison urged. "It is a good story, even if it does show Chris in less than a flattering light."

Chuck shrugged elaborately. "I can't really remember any more . . ."

"I can." Allison turned to Dean and Nathan. "Chris has always liked to hear himself talk. The reporter asked his question and before he knew what hit him Chris unleashed a veritable dissertation on nuclear disarmament. We had to drag Chris away. He was so excited to see himself on TV that night, though he was pretending it was no big deal. At a little before six o'clock we gathered in the common room. Chris was so keyed up he was trembling." Allison smiled. "And it all amounted to nothing. The clip was less than a heartbeat long. All that was left of Chris's learned lecture were the words 'I don't know.' He was so disappointed. We all thought it was hysterical. What did he expect, the station's editors to air his entire speech and the phone to start ringing with offers of a TV presenter's contract?"

Allison's final words were delivered in an unmistakably mocking tone. Bess felt a bit sick. She remembered that long-ago evening. At the time, Allison had been very solicitous of Chris; she had not laughed.

"You're right," Dean said after a moment. "It is a good story, if somewhat . . ."

"Pitiful," Allison said firmly. "It illustrates Chris's need for attention. And," she added more softly, "his need for a devoted audience, a dedicated fan, someone to worship him." Allison stood abruptly. "I'm off to bed," she said.

The others soon followed, leaving Bess alone on the back porch with Nathan. They sat quietly. Bess's mind was whirling.

It had been unpleasant to hear Allison speak negatively about Chris. Shouldn't loyalty function in retrospect? Did the impending divorce negate the wonderful years of Allison and Chris's relationship? How would Chris feel if he knew his soon-to-be ex-wife was mocking him to his friends?

How did Mike feel about the way in which Marta had mocked *him* that evening?

"You okay?" Nathan said, taking her hand in his.

"Yes," Bess said automatically. "No, I don't know."

"How about a stroll on the beach?" Nathan suggested. "It's a clear night and we can count the stars."

Bess smiled gratefully. She really loved this man. She took his hand and together they went out into the night.

Chapter 26

Just saw the most amaze sandals. One pair in my size. Sale ends to-morrow.

This message was followed by three heart emojis.

Marta frowned. She wondered why Sam hadn't contacted her father. Maybe she had and for once Mike had said no to her indirect request for money. Well, Mom was saying no, too.

As Marta dressed for the day in a pair of chinos and a striped Breton top, she wondered (not for the first time) what sort of role model had she been for her daughter. She had tried to act according to what she believed she was—a feminist. A woman who made her own choices consciously; a woman who kept informed about politics and social issues and who acted on her informed views by voting and by being an active member of her local community; a woman who embraced and owned her power from her home base and who believed that good parenting was key to a successful adult life; a woman who respected the choices of other women. A person who believed that men were equally as valuable as women who were equally as valuable as men. End of story.

But how had Sam seen her mother? Recently she had been talking about going on to law school "like Dad," about having a career "like Dad," about earning lots of money "like Dad." Did Sam see her mother's role in the family as less important than her father's role? Would she view her mother as merely a broodmare when Marta announced her fourth pregnancy at the age of forty-two?

Forty-two. Marta peered into the small mirror over the dresser. Did men other than Mike still consider her attractive? (Assuming he considered her attractive and not just convenient.) She hadn't thought about that question in years—if ever. The fact was that Marta wasn't particularly interested in sex and never had been; while she enjoyed sex with Mike, she was rarely the one to initiate an encounter and could probably give it all up right then and there without a backward glance of longing.

Marta frowned and turned away from the mirror. Given the fact that she had never identified closely with her sexuality, she found it a bit disturbing that because of her three children she was seen by most people (she assumed) as someone whose sexual function had determined her role in life. She became pregnant. She gave birth to children. She raised children. She would see them off into the world and then she would . . . She would what? What then would be her function? How would the world define her? How would she define herself? How *had* she been defining herself all these years?

The unpleasant truth was that Marta needed sympathy. She couldn't remember ever feeling quite so isolated. And it bothered her. She *wasn't* alone, not really, she *knew* that, but she *was* alone all the same. Bess didn't need a bombshell dropped on her just days before her wedding. And she certainly couldn't tell Allison and expect sympathy. As for Chuck, he had enough on his plate getting used to life with a new baby. Marta believed her complaint was valid—every person's pain was real—but she was very aware that not everyone would see it that way. And too often women could be harshest to other women, which was another reason Marta was dreading telling her at-home friends about the pregnancy. She had no doubt that at least a few of them would have something snippy to say about it; though the remarks probably would not be made to her face, she would hear them secondhand and thirdhand.

"How could she be so careless? I'm sure it was unplanned."

"Why on earth does she want to go through another pregnancy at forty-two?"

"She'll never get her body back, such as it is."

Marta had never let other people's small-mindedness bother her. Wasn't one supposed to grow surer of oneself as one aged, to care less about the ill-informed and prejudiced opinions of others, to disregard the merely curious and uncaring scrutiny of one's neighbors? Clearly, Marta thought, she hadn't yet reached the point of real independence and self-confidence. More was the pity.

The room was beginning to feel claustrophobic. Marta headed downstairs. She found Bess and Allison in the kitchen, breakfast things spread out on the counter.

"Did I tell you guys I'll be hyphenating my name?" Bess said when Marta had joined them. "Bess Culpepper-Creek. I think it has a ring to it."

Marta shrugged. "I never felt very strongly one way or the other about Kennedy. And I got tired of people asking if I was related to *the* Kennedys. Exchanging it for MacIntosh was an easy decision."

Bess turned to Allison. "Do you think that after the divorce you'll go back to using your maiden name?"

"The idea never occurred to me," Allison admitted. "I was Allison Longfellow for the first twenty-one years of my life—even though Longfellow wasn't the name of my birth parents—and I've been Allison Montague for just about as long. I . . . I don't know who I am now."

"Maybe it's time for a new Allison to emerge," Bess suggested. "Phase three. The next twenty-one years, after which time you can move on again."

Marta rolled her eyes. In spite of being a loving person, Bess could be so dense at times. One look at Allison was all it took for a person—even a stranger—to see that the last thing she was prepared for was the start of a jaunty new phase. Marta refrained from making a withering comment and changed the subject. "The guys are planning a night out," she told her friends, "ever so thoughtfully leaving us in charge of the baby."

"Oh, I don't mind," Bess said.

"Of course, you don't. Because you'll leave the actual babysitting to me."

Bess laughed. "I can't deny that," she said.

Maybe, Marta thought, she should open a day care center. That was probably all she was seen as good for these days, corralling young children, changing diapers, cleaning up vomit, doling out snacks, soothing teething toddlers.

"Marta? Bess asked if you wanted some coffee?"

Marta faked a smile for her friends. "No, thanks," she said. "I'm fine."

Chapter 27

The town of Kennebunkport was teeming with young honeymooning couples. The women, neatly dressed and perfectly coiffed, spent an extraordinary amount of time staring down at their left hands. The men, just as neatly dressed and perfectly coiffed, stood tall, shoulders back and chests out, guiding their wives along with a firm hand. Good thing, Allison thought. Those young women were bound to trip and fall if they kept gazing at their engagement rings instead of paying attention to where they were going. Still, in Allison's eyes the couples were sweet, heartbreakingly naïve, and charmingly optimistic.

And they were getting on her nerves.

Allison ducked into Abacus; she had been to the Portland branch of the gallery but never to the one in Kennebunkport. It was a wonderful place with a wonderful selection of fine arts and crafts, but haunted by the images of those happy young couples on honeymoon, Allison found that all she could really see as she looked into glass cases filled with the work of contemporary fine jewelry designers was an image of her soon-to-be ex-husband.

She wondered if Chris ever thought with fondness of their early days together, or if he was still totally enmeshed in anger, unable to cut through the ever-tightening bands of bitterness and blame. And if that were the case, how had he *managed* to kill all warm, compassionate feeling for the woman who had been his companion for over twenty-one years? Was it an ongoing struggle to keep those warm, compassionate feelings from reviving at the most unexpected times? Did Chris find himself suddenly thinking kindly of his wife, reminded of her by the scent of lilac, Allison's favorite flower, or a song heard in passing? Did he ever feel pity for her poor feet, plagued with bunions, or did he now think of her physical imperfections with a shudder of contempt? Did he wonder if she was still prey to those awful nightmares, the ones that woke her violently in the dead of night, the ones that compelled Chris to take Allison in his arms to quiet her?

Allison left the gallery. She would return another time when her mind was clearer. On her way back to the main street, a young couple just ahead of her stopped in the middle of the sidewalk to hug. *How blissfully ignorant they are*, Allison thought as she slid past them. They thought they were on top of the world. Well, maybe they were, but no one stayed there for long.

So, how *did* the death of love and affection come about? Did it really happen in a thunderclap moment? Was the decision made in that thunderclap moment legitimate? Or would the decision eventually show itself to be fatally flawed, a reaction instead of an action? Surely upon reflection any reasonable person would reconsider his sudden declaration of love or hate to see if it felt valid.

But that was the trouble, Allison thought, scanning the street for a quiet spot to rest. Chris was not a reasonable person. At least, he hadn't been a reasonable person when he had rejected her. He had been in the grip of a grief strong enough to distort every thought and feeling. Did that excuse the horrible things he had said to her? Allison didn't know.

She spotted a low stone bench in the small alley between a souvenir shop and an ice-cream parlor and made for it. At least there she might be somewhat safe from the rough sea of self-absorbed loving couples swarming the streets. But thoughts could be jostled one way or another, too, and now, perhaps inevitably, they turned to her assistant, Greg, a young man Allison considered as she might a brother, with affection and hopes for his future.

Just twenty-five, Greg had graduated with a degree in art history and was a darned good photographer in his own right. He had been with his girlfriend for over four years and they were planning to marry the following spring. Allison had observed them together on numerous occasions; they were clearly the best of friends, laughed often, and when one spoke, the other paid close attention. These were all clear signs of mutual love and respect.

Of course, Allison thought gloomily, that was how she and Chris had once been. At least, that was how Allison remembered them to have been in the old days, before the quest for a viable pregnancy had taken over their lives. Allison hoped that Greg's marriage to Elena would be a happy one, free of the taint of old sorrows that refused to die, full of warm—

Sudden shouts of laughter startled Allison. Coming down the little alley from the direction of the sidewalk was a bride and groom, a photographer, and a small wedding party. As they swarmed past her on their way to the waterfront that lay beyond the alley,

Allison sat rigidly. The bride's wide tulle skirt brushed her knees. One of the groomsmen stepped on her left foot. He did not seem to notice.

Finally, the group was out of sight if not out of hearing. Allison put her hand to her head. Why had she come into town in the first place? Why hadn't she stayed in her cozy bedroom or ventured only as far as a secluded section of the beach that lay virtually at the door of Driftwood House?

Allison got up from the stone bench and, walking with a slight limp, made her way toward her car.

Chapter 28

Allison had gone for a drive; Marta, Chuck, and Dean were all around somewhere, though Bess had no idea where; and Mike and Nathan were off exploring the Rachel Carson Wildlife Refuge in Wells.

Bess, alone in the den reviewing Kara's latest correspondence, realized that she felt a bit lonely. Clearly, having found her soul mate did not serve to negate moments of sadness or anxiety or, well, loneliness. Bess had always known that life with Nathan would go on much as it had been going on without him but still, at times the reality felt like a total surprise.

A cool breeze drifted through the room. Bess got up from her desk to stand at the open window. For so many years of her life she had been focused on—obsessed with?—the idea of finding that one person with whom she would be totally in sympathy. And she had found that person in Nathan. And he had found that person in her.

But had he felt the same way about his first wife? Maybe Maggie had been his soul mate for the time they had shared together. If that were true, did Maggie still exist for Nathan as someone of seminal importance? He had told Bess that his first marriage was a good one and that the experience had allowed him to be open to marrying again after Maggie's death. If that were true, then in some way Bess had Maggie to thank for bringing Nathan into her life.

Earlier, she had mentioned these musings to Marta. Marta had laughed. "All that matters," she said, "is how Nathan treats you in the here and now, not what happened with someone else years ago. Anyway, once you're married you won't have the time to overthink the big stuff. You'll be too busy negotiating the day to day."

Bess suspected that Marta was right. The closer she got to her wedding day the more she felt she knew so very little about what marriage entailed. She had never even lived with anyone for any length of time and now she wondered if she was starting the whole living together thing too late, sharing a bathroom, waiting dinner until the other got home from work, watching a movie you really didn't want to watch because everyone told you that spending too much time alone could be bad for a relationship.

Bess shook her head. Nonsense. It was never too late to embrace the sort of change she had chosen. It couldn't be. She turned away from the window and went out to the kitchen, where she found Dean and Thomas. Thomas was in his high chair. "Ba ba ba ba," he was saying, a big smile on his face.

"Where's Chuck?" Bess asked. "I thought everyone was out."

Dean took a bite of an apple and chewed it before answering. "He went down to the outlets in Kittery again."

"Your face looks like a thundercloud," Bess observed.

"It's nothing," Dean replied quickly. "Well, yeah, it's something. I wanted to go to a workshop today at a branch of the local historical society and Chuck knew it, but he either forgot my plan or he decided his was more important. After all, I'm just the stay-at-home daddy. My needs aren't half as important as . . ." Dean winced. "I'm sorry. I hate when one person in a couple complains about the other one to a mutual friend."

"You know, if it's not too late for you to make the workshop I could watch Thomas." Bess looked at the baby. He was now rubbing his fat little fingers over a section of a brightly colored, multi-textured cloth. "He's just going to sit there playing with that thing, right?"

Dean laughed. "Thanks, Bess, but I'm not shifting my responsibility onto your shoulders because I'm pissed at Chuck. The time I get to spend with my son is always important; it's hardly as if I'm suffering. No, I'll take it up with Chuck later. That's what happens in a relationship with this particular balance of duties. It's easy for the one who's out in the world to overlook the needs of the one who works from home."

"I'm sure Chuck doesn't mean anything by his negligence," Bess said worriedly.

Dean smiled. "Hey, don't look so freaked out! It's not the end of the world—or of our marriage! Negotiation never ends. Blame is the death knell of a relationship so you just keep on talking and tweaking."

"Sometimes I feel I have absolutely no idea what it really means to be married," Bess admitted.

"You don't. Well, not much. No one does until they're neck-deep in the relationship." Dean smiled again. "It's part of the excitement."

"I'm not really much on that sort of excitement," Bess mumbled.

Dean suddenly shot a look at his son. "He needs to be changed," he said. "Or he will in about a minute."

"How do you know?" Bess asked.

"See the way his nose is scrunched? That's the signal. I'm off."

Dean, baby in tow, headed for his room. Bess poured a glass of cold water and thought about what he had said. *Negotiation never ends. You just keep on talking and tweaking.* It didn't sound so terribly difficult, Bess thought, not if she called on her native courage and optimism. *Quand-même.* She would be okay. She would figure out this marriage thing and everything would be all right.

Bess rinsed her glass and put it in the drainer next to the sink. Everything would be all right.

Chapter 29

Why did people have to be slobs? It was a question that could plague Marta when she let it. Like the puddle of juice on the counter next to the sink. How hard would it have been for whoever had spilled the juice to reach for a paper towel and wipe it up? Laziness. That's what it was, Marta thought grimly, as she mopped up the spill. Sheer laziness. And a disregard for others. In fact, she wouldn't be surprised to learn it was Mike who had neglected to clean up after himself this morning. Some things never changed.

When Marta had first met Mike MacIntosh he was living off-campus, a bit of a tear about who kept wildly irregular hours and who seemed perfectly content to wallow in slovenly domestic conditions. Every few months, when he was having trouble making the rent, he would find himself an unsuspecting roommate but said roommate never lasted for long. For a short time, Marta had taken it upon herself to stuff his dirty clothes into the laundry bag, to squirt disinfectant into the toilet, to scrub sticky rings left by the bottom of soda and beer cans off the counter. Mike never asked for her help with the housekeeping and Marta didn't enjoy playing unpaid maid, but as long as she was going to be spending time in Mike's hovel she might as well make it tolerably clean. The turning point came when one morning, while straightening the sheets, Marta had found a desiccated mouse behind the bed, after which she had refused to spend the night in Mike's apartment ever again.

Mike's habits changed once they were out of college and living together in a place of their own. Marta saw to that and perhaps not surprisingly, Mike seemed to enjoy living in a clean and orderly environment. It meant he no longer had to waste half an hour each morning scrounging around for something clean to wear. It meant that the food he ingested wasn't riddled with mold, and that the toothbrushes in his medicine cabinet weren't encrusted with highly questionable goo. Mike had proved trainable, though Marta knew that if she loosened the leash even a little he would very quickly slide back into his native slovenly state. Hence, no doubt, the spilled juice she had just wiped up.

Marta put her hand to her head and took a deep breath. It was wrong to blame Mike for the spill. And even if he was responsible, it was hardly a crime not to clean up after one's self. And she shouldn't forget that even if her husband was a slob by nature, he was genuinely appreciative of her dedication to the running of the household and of her ability to do so seemingly without effort. "Beauty, brains, and an endless tolerance for me and my annoying habits," he would say to anyone who would listen. "How did I get so lucky in a wife?"

Marta dropped her hand from her head. But was that an innocent compliment or a condescending one?

Bess came bouncing into the kitchen. Well, not exactly bouncing, but with that jaunty step that sometimes drove Marta crazy.

"I am dying for a cup of tea," Bess declared, and she opened a cabinet and peered inside. After a moment she turned, holding a small yellow box. "This hasn't been opened. I thought you loved ginger tea."

"Oh, I went off that a while ago," Marta said more dismissively than she had meant to. In fact, almost since the moment she thought she might be pregnant her stomach had revolted at the thought of her once-favorite tea.

"I wish you had told me," Bess said. "There are six other varieties here, but if none of them appeal I'll have my assistant send a few others down from this great tea shop in Portland."

Marta felt her temper rise. "Stop fussing," she scolded. "Look,

I'm sorry, Bess. I'm in a bit of a bad mood. I got a call from Sam this morning." She had not gotten a call from Sam. She was lying. "She was whining for permission to go with some friends to a concert in Philly next weekend. I said no. Of course," Marta said, hurrying on, burying herself ever deeper into the untruth, "then she wanted to speak to Mike. I told her to call him but to expect the same answer."

"And did he say no?" Bess asked.

Marta smiled a bit queasily. What if Bess asked Mike about the nonexistent call? "He was sitting right by me when Sam called," she went on. "I had explained my position when Sam and I had finished talking and so when Sam called Mike a few minutes later he was well prepped to refuse her permission."

Bess smiled. "Sneaky."

Marta shrugged. "Welcome to parenthood." For some reason, she thought, it now involved lying.

"I don't know how you do it," Bess said. "A twenty-four/seven job."

"Sometimes," Marta said quietly, "neither do I."

It was about a quarter after seven. Mike was in the bedroom speaking with one of his colleagues. Nathan was in the den, doing the same. The others were seated around the living room. Notably, Dean's naked feet were resting in Chuck's lap.

"What did Dean do to deserve a foot rub?" Allison asked.

"I took unfair advantage of him earlier," Chuck explained. "I promised I'd take Thomas so that he could catch a workshop at the historical society and I totally spaced. So now I'm doing penance."

"A little more on the left arch, please," Dean directed.

Marta laughed. "If I had a nickel for every time that Mike accidentally on purpose left me in the lurch with the kids I'd be dining out at Harry's Bar in Venice once a month."

"But you forgive him, right?" Bess asked worriedly.

"Of course, I forgive him. But sometimes I make him earn that forgiveness. I mean, no one likes to be taken advantage of, even accidentally on purpose."

"I've forgiven Chuck for this latest little incident," Dean announced. "I'm nothing if not magnanimous in my ability to forgive and forget. Especially when there's a foot rub involved."

"Still, what's that old saw," Chuck said, "you always hurt the one you love?"

Dean frowned. "I think it's more, 'every man kills the thing he most loves.' And I think it was said memorably, if not in those exact words, by Oscar Wilde."

"What was it he said about truth?" Allison asked. "'The truth is rarely pure and never simple.'"

"Now there's a guy I'd love to have dinner with," Chuck said enthusiastically. "To hell with politicians and statesmen. Give me Oscar Wilde any day."

"Even though his life ended tragically?" Marta asked. "And largely as the result of his own choices, however innocently made?" *The same could be said for so many of us,* she thought.

Chuck nodded seriously. "Especially because it did. He was a brave man, and all brave people are to some degree foolish. It comes with the territory."

Marta thought about that. "Well," she said after a moment, "I wouldn't mind having dinner with Queen Elizabeth the first. Now there was a woman to be reckoned with. Though I'd seriously prefer not to have to eat some of those disgusting dishes so popular among the elite in Tudor times. Calf's head with oysters? Ugh."

"I'd like to sit down with Pippi Longstocking," Bess announced.

"You do know that Pippi Longstocking wasn't—isn't—real?" Chuck said gently.

"I know. But if you can talk about sharing a meal with someone who's been dead for hundreds of years, then I can talk about having a milk shake with a character in a book."

"Why a milk shake?" Allison asked.

"Don't you think Pippi would like milk shakes?" Bess asked. "I mean, where does she get her superhuman strength from? Her diet must be hugely full of protein."

"I can't say I know much, if anything, about Ms. Longstocking," Dean admitted. "I've never read the book."

"You haven't?" Bess said. "It's not only one book, there are lots of books. And movies, too. But maybe because you're male no one suggested you read stories about a girl, even one as awesome as Pippi Longstocking."

Dean bowed his head. "I hereby promise to introduce Thomas to your fictional friend as soon as he's old enough to read."

"Good. You won't regret it. Her father is a buccaneer captain, you know. There's lots of stuff about adventures on the high seas."

Nathan came out from the den. "Ready, guys?" he asked.

"As soon as Mike shows," Dean answered, removing his feet from Chuck's lap and reaching for his sandals.

Mike appeared a moment later. He was wearing a blue shirt open at the neck and a pair of jeans. His thick dark hair, still damp from a shower, was swept off his forehead. The same old Mike, but Marta went weak at the knees. It took every bit of responsible adulthood in her not to rush at him. Hormones? Or something more—like love?

"Sorry I kept you waiting," Mike said to Nathan, Chuck, and Dean. He went over to Marta and planted a kiss on her forehead. Marta reached for his hand and gave it a squeeze, glad for his nearness. That would have to do.

"We'll take good care of the baby," Bess promised when the men had said their farewells and headed toward the front door.

"Yes," Marta called after them. "*We* will."

Chapter 30

When the men had gone, Allison opened another bottle of wine and brought it to the large central coffee table in the living area. Marta had drawn her armchair closer to the table—and the cheese, crackers, fruit, and nuts laid out upon it. Bess was curled up in another of the comfortable armchairs. Allison chose to sit at one end of the love seat.

"Three middle-aged ladies in for a cozy night of gossip," Marta commented. "Is that what we are?"

"Not middle-aged, surely!" Bess protested. "But gossip is okay as long as it's not nasty." She turned to Allison. "Do you ever run into Chris?"

"No," Allison replied. She wasn't surprised the conversation had so quickly landed on this topic. And she wasn't upset that it had, either. "I go out of my way to avoid places I'm likely to see him. I suspect he does the same. Honestly, I dread the idea of coming across him waiting for a light on a street corner or on line at the grocery store. I don't know how I could handle such a shock. I really don't."

Bess shook her head. "This is just awful."

"So, what's going on with the condo?" Marta asked, selecting a piece of a locally made cheese.

"It's under contract—and empty. I couldn't bear to stay until the closing date so I moved into a rental a few months ago and put most of my possessions in storage with the childhood stuff I mentioned. I'm living with less material goods around me than ever in my life," she said with a small laugh. "The emptiness around me reflects the emptiness inside me."

"That doesn't sound very healthy," Marta said briskly.

"Maybe not, but it's the truth. If you don't want an honest answer, then don't ask the question."

Marta raised her glass of seltzer in acknowledgment.

"Allison," Bess asked after a moment, "I've been wondering if the infertility issue got too much for you guys to handle. I've read that the emotional aspects can be really destructive to a marriage, and I—"

"Bess," Marta said firmly. "Don't."

Allison sighed. "No, it's all right." And she remembered the question she had asked herself the other day on the beach. *How much longer could she remain silent, plagued by these loud and insistent memories, bound by that promise she had made to Chris?*

"For better or worse," Allison whispered as if to herself. "Not much longer."

"What did you say?" Bess asked.

It was time. "All right," Allison said, looking from one to the other of her friends. "You might as well know the whole story." So, she told them. How after years of ART she finally got pregnant. How her doctor suggested she consider a few days of bed rest. How she decided to finish an important assignment before taking a few days off at home.

"Chris wasn't happy about my finishing the job, but it wasn't as if I'd been told in no uncertain terms not to leave my bed for the remainder of the pregnancy or I'd risk losing the child," she explained. "I'd been given no warnings, just advice, which I fully planned to follow once the job was completed."

Allison paused. Her friends sat quietly, their eyes on her.

"It's funny," Allison finally said, "but the accident itself didn't feel like such a big deal. I knew I'd been hit, of course—the airbag deploying was only one obvious clue—but I didn't black out or even feel much physical discomfort. Later, at the hospital, it was discovered that two of my ribs had been fractured and my collarbone broken by the airbag. I looked like one massive bruise for weeks." Allison paused. "And I'd lost the baby. Or, if you prefer, the pregnancy had been terminated."

"Terminated is an ugly word," Bess muttered.

"I'm sorry," Marta said. Her voice was rough.

"Chris couldn't forgive me for taking such a risk with our child. He said that if I hadn't gotten into my car that morning I never would have miscarried."

"He couldn't have known that," Marta said angrily. "No one could have. You could have miscarried while watching TV with your feet up!"

"I know. But you can understand Chris's feelings, can't you? No one could fault me for watching TV with my feet up. But I could be faulted for . . ."

"Allison," Bess said, shaking her head, "don't! Just don't."

"Anyway, about a month after the accident he told me he was filing for divorce and he moved back into his parents' home."

"What a shit," Marta murmured.

"You don't know the whole story," Allison corrected. "See, I came to believe—no, I came to know—that a large part of the reason Chris wanted a child so badly was because he needed to replace Robby, the brother he lost in childhood. Chris is obsessed with the brother he lost when he was so young. He's so unhappy."

"I remember Chris mentioning his brother's death from a rare cancer once or twice back when we were in college, but I had no idea he was so broken up about it," Marta confessed.

"Me, neither," Bess said. "And I didn't like to ask for details. A child's death isn't a subject you just bring up casually."

"I think Chris talked to Chuck about Robby a few times," Allison told them, "but not openly enough for it to do any good."

"I wish I had known," Bess said. "Maybe I could have done something to help."

"Like what?" Marta said. "Get over your obsession, Chris, before it wrecks your marriage? No, I doubt there was anything any of us could have done." Marta looked to Allison. "What about Chris's parents? Where are they in all this?"

"Chris's parents were as good to me as they could be when Chris left, but their loyalty rightly lies with their son. His mother did tell me she also believes Chris's obsession was behind the collapse of our marriage. But what can she do about it other than apologize for the role she feels she played in allowing the obsession to take hold in the first place?"

"I still don't know why you didn't tell us any of this before now," Bess said.

Allison hesitated. She knew this bit of the story would not go down well. "Because Chris swore me to secrecy," she explained. "He said he didn't want to be the object of pity. He didn't want people scrutinizing his pain. Look, don't ever tell him I told you about any of this. Please."

"Your secrets are safe with us, but what right did he have to demand you keep silent?" Marta cried, half rising out of her chair. "That's absolutely outrageous!"

"Why did you agree, Allison?" Bess asked. "Marta is right. It's outrageous."

"Because I felt so terribly guilty, as if I owed Chris penance. I still feel that way. Mostly. And I miss him. Not like I did when he first moved out, or even before that, after the miscarriage when we were living side by side but a million miles away from each other. That was awful. But I do miss him."

"Of course, you do," Bess said softly. "After so many years together . . ."

"Don't tell me Chris wanted to name the baby after his brother?" Marta asked.

Allison nodded. "He did. Robert or Roberta."

"You had no choice about it?" Bess asked. "The mother should have a choice in her baby's name."

"I don't know. Maybe I could have insisted on a say in the matter, but I didn't. I wanted to give him that gift. It made him happy to think of a little namesake growing up under his protection." Allison shook her head.

"You've got to be so angry with Chris!" Marta said.

"I wasn't angry at first," Allison admitted. "Hurt, confused, bewildered, but not angry. But now, yeah, I am angry with Chris for walking away. He ignored my pain; he ignored me. But I still struggle with the idea that I might have no right to complain. I know Chris filed for divorce in order to save his own emotional sanity. I'm not saying that I understand his obsession with his brother, but I do acknowledge it. It's real to Chris. I can't change that. And if you love someone, doesn't that mean you accept him for who he is, good and bad?"

Marta shook her head. "There are limits. And love can die. It can be killed."

"Oh, don't say that. Please." Bess put her hands over her face.

"Why not?" Marta snapped. "It's true. If you don't know that by now you're in big trouble."

Allison went on. "On Robby's birthday Chris visits the cemetery where he's buried. At first, Chris didn't want me to go with him. Then, after three or four years, he changed his mind and asked me to join him. I was glad Chris wanted me by his side."

"What was it like being at the cemetery with him?" Bess asked.

"The first time was decidedly uncomfortable," Allison admitted. "There were no histrionics. Chris just stood there looking down at the headstone, his hands clasped in front of him. I had no idea what to say so I said nothing. I'm still not sure why he asked me along, but every year after that I was witness to the little ritual. Maybe he prays. Maybe he talks to his brother. I don't know."

"It's so sad. Did you ever ask his mother what exactly happened all those years ago?" Bess asked.

"Once. Agnes was pretty forthcoming about the troubles Chris had at the time of Robby's passing. She told me how Chris—he was nine at the time—thought his parents should have been able to prevent his brother's death. He went through a period of depression but somehow managed to fool—that was the word Agnes used—his therapist into thinking he was well on his way to recovery." Allison shook her head. "After that, Agnes said, her attempts at talking to Chris about Robby, about the grief they all were feeling as a family, failed outright."

"Chris can't still be angry with his parents, not if he's living with them again," Bess noted.

"No, he's not angry," Allison said. "He finally came to understand his parents' decision to reject a controversial treatment for Robby. It held enormous risks and they felt their son had suffered too much already. Still, Chris feels Robby's loss acutely."

Marta made a noise very close to a snort. "I'm not claiming to be the perfect parent but come on, these people fell down on the job with Chris!"

"We weren't there, Marta," Bess pointed out. "If Chris seemed to be functioning normally, what could his parents have done?"

"They meant well." Allison put up a hand to forestall whatever protest was about to pour from Marta's mouth. "The Montagues are good people. After Chris filed for divorce, and before Agnes and Jonathan cut ties with me in a gesture of loyalty to their son, Agnes wrote me a very sincere letter apologizing for what she called 'the state of things' in the family. It's clear Agnes feels she and her husband failed Chris all those years ago, and in failing him, they failed me in turn."

Marta frowned. "You're a better woman than I am even to consider forgiving those two. At the very least they should have warned you before the wedding that Chris was mentally unbalanced."

"Don't be ridiculous!" Allison cried. "Chris isn't dangerous. Anyway, there was nothing they could have said or done at the time to make me change my mind about marrying Chris. I was in love. And what would Chris have thought if he knew his parents had warned me against him? Loving him the way I did I would have told him everything."

"Allison is right," Bess noted. "There was nothing Mr. and Mrs. Montague could have said to warn Allison without totally alienating their only remaining child."

Marta frowned and stuffed a piece of cheddar in her mouth. Bess took a long drink of red wine. Allison poured herself another glass of the white.

"It's ironic," she went on, softly. "Just before we were scheduled to begin what was to be the last round of IVF treatment, I realized just how emotionally and physically wiped out I was. I told Chris I wanted to stop what seemed like an endless round of building our hopes up only to have them knocked down."

"And how did he take that?" Marta asked, raising an eyebrow.

"Not well," Allison admitted. "He said he knew that this time things would be different. He said he'd been having a recurring dream in which he saw himself pushing a stroller, playing with a child at the beach, singing a baby to sleep."

"Nothing more specific than that?" Marta asked. "Sounds like a fib to me."

"Whatever," Allison said. "The point is he begged me to go through with the program and I agreed. Not the first time I backed down when maybe I shouldn't have. Anyway, Chris was right. Not long after that I was pregnant."

Bess sighed and stared into her glass.

"There's one other thing . . ." Allison shook her head. "On second thought, I'd better not."

"Why?" Marta demanded. "No one *here* is forcing you to keep silent, or judging you for that matter."

"It's just that you might think I'm a bit looney."

"We most certainly will not," Bess replied hotly.

"All right. During the pregnancy—what little there was of it—I began to believe more than ever that Chris cared less for me and our unborn child than he did for the memory of his brother. There were times when he looked at me and I could have sworn he saw not me, his wife, but Robby, and it gave me a chill." Allison waved her hand dismissively. "Don't listen to me. I'm making it sound way scarier than it was, a freakish plot from a Gothic novel. It was only at moments that I felt strange and I might have been imagining the whole thing. You know," she said with a weak laugh, "hormones playing tricks on my mind."

"Don't apologize for what you felt or sensed," Marta said firmly. "I'm one of the most grounded-in-reality people you'll ever want to meet, but I firmly believe that when we feel that something is wrong, it is. Call it ESP, intuition, or downright common sense."

Bess nodded. "I'm with Marta. The heart knows what it knows."

Allison felt a tear spring to her eye. What good friends she had. She should have spoken to them sooner.

"Would you really have come to the wedding if Chris had accepted the invitation?" Bess asked.

"I don't know," Allison admitted. "I know I said that I was okay with your inviting him, but I think I might have been lying. I'm sorry."

"You have nothing for which to be sorry, not on my account," Bess assured her.

"Nor mine." Marta stood and stretched. "It's late. I'm going to check on Thomas and then help clear away our little feast. Then it's bed for me."

"Don't worry about clearing up," Bess told her. "I'm just grateful you're here to be in charge of the baby."

"Thank you for sharing everything with us," Marta said. She went over to Allison, bent down, and gave her a quick hug. Then, she was gone.

"Can I help you?" Allison asked Bess, rising from the love seat.

"You know the answer to that. Now, go to bed. This has been a big night for you."

Allison did as she was told.

Chapter 31

Bess sat hunched in the high-backed armchair in the room she was sharing with Nathan as wave upon wave of sadness engulfed her. She felt as if something essential had been stripped from her. Hope. Her grief threatened to choke her and yet the tears wouldn't come.

With something very like a moan Bess got up from the chair and began to pace. If Chris had really loved Allison he should have been able to forgive. After all, Allison hadn't caused the car accident. She hadn't been careless as much as she had been hopeful that her pregnancy would be successful. Why should she be punished so severely for one bad mistake that might not even be considered a mistake? It was terribly sad that Chris's brother had died so young, but that wasn't Allison's fault, either. Robby's death had been no one's fault, just Fate playing one of its cruel tricks, yet another reason for those who didn't believe in a benevolent God not to believe.

Bess heard the front door open and the four men enter as quietly as four grown men could enter a house in the middle of the night. Which wasn't very quietly.

A few moments later, Nathan opened the door to the bedroom. "What is it?" he asked immediately, closing the door behind him and striding over to Bess.

She took his hands in hers and told him. She could feel Nathan's body tense as she did.

"Can you imagine how deeply unfair it would be to burden a child with all that emotional pain and psychic baggage?" she said when the tale was complete. "How could the child ever grow to be his own person if he was intended merely as a replacement for someone long lost?"

Nathan frowned. "Still, better the child had lived than . . . Hell, I don't know what to think about any of it. Look, it's late. Let's try to get some sleep."

Lights off, Nathan at her side, Bess stared into the dark for a long, long time. Her heart felt broken, but her eyes remained dry.

Chapter 32

Marta had checked on Thomas before going to her room. She had felt a huge surge of tenderness as she looked down on his sleeping form. She wondered about his birth mother, who she was and why she had given him up for adoption. She thought of how very lucky he was, having been brought into such a stable and loving home. She thought then of little Robert or Roberta Montague and of what sort of home that child would have been born into. It didn't bear thinking about.

Now Marta found herself wandering her bedroom. The baby monitor was on her bedside table. She was angry.

She believed that Allison had the right to live her own life, to make her own decisions, and yes, she had the responsibility to accept the consequences of those decisions, both good and bad. Not that Allison deserved to have her marriage fall apart, or to lose her baby. And certainly, nothing excused Chris's supremely selfish, misogynistic behavior. But part of being an independent adult was acknowledging that to every action there was a reaction and sometimes that reaction was deeply unpleasant.

Miscarriage was far more common than many people realized. Every pregnant woman, even the healthiest, was aware of the possibility. Well, Marta thought, maybe not the women who were without proper medical care. In that case ignorance was certainly not bliss.

And speaking of ignorance . . . Could Chris really be one of those ridiculous throwbacks to the times when men blamed their wives for giving birth to girls instead of boys, ignorant of the fact that it was their own Y chromosome that determined a child's sex? When men punished women for getting pregnant; for not getting pregnant; for getting pregnant at an inconvenient time; for getting pregnant by a man other than themselves? When men punished women for not being men?

Marta quickened her pace around the bedroom. What really pissed her off about the whole mess was Chris's attempt—and a successful one at that—to silence Allison at the moment when she most needed to be heard. From time immemorial, men had been attempting to silence women. History—art—literature—folklore—religion—every bit of cultured life was full of examples of men wanting women to shut up and give up. Silence and shame went hand in hand; men knew that and they had used the knowledge to their advantage. They continued to use it, and they continued to successfully recruit enough women to buy into the patriarchal culture they had created to keep their power base unmolested.

Feeling slightly sweaty from her exertions, Marta sank onto the edge of the bed. The clues about Chris's sexism had been there in college, if only Allison—and Marta herself for that matter—had been astute enough to take them seriously. All that swathing Allison in cotton wool wasn't about protecting her at all, it was about immobilizing her. There was, of course, that memorable time when Chris tried to prevent Allison from attending a memorial rally for the gay student who had been horribly killed by haters from his own school. An incident that would forever be associated in Marta's mind with her one act of infidelity. But she would think about that later. If she had to.

Even insisting Allison wear gloves under her mittens when the weather threatened to fall below freezing! To suggest such a strategy was fine, even smart. But to insist upon it, to bring along a pair of wool gloves just in case Allison had forgotten (or chosen not to?)

wear them under the big fuzzy faux fur mittens Chris had bought her, that was going a bit far. At least, Marta had always thought as much. Allison and Allison alone had the information—and the right!—to decide how many layers of clothing to wear. She was not a child, but Chris so often treated her as one. A beloved child, to be sure, but a minor nonetheless.

The opening of a door, followed by a burst of male laughter, urgently hushed, alerted Marta to the return of the men. She waited. Butterflies suddenly swarmed in her stomach. Why should she be nervous?

Carefully, the door to the bedroom opened and Mike stepped inside.

"She told us everything," Marta blurted.

Mike's face drained of color and he sank into the armchair. "Tell me," he said.

Chapter 33

The room was very dark. Allison liked it that way. She felt safe and that was good because she also felt uncomfortable. She ever so slightly regretted having told Bess and Marta the whole story, but the emotions stirred up by Bess's upcoming wedding, being alone with her dear friends for the first time since the breakdown of her marriage, the presence of baby Thomas—all had forced her tongue. And she was lonely, she reminded herself. She needed her friends' support and had a right to claim it. There was nothing for which to feel regret. And, she was so very tired.

Bess and Marta had taken the news much as Allison had expected they would. She wondered what to expect from the men—unadulterated sympathy or a more complex reaction. Everyone brought his own experiences, prejudices, and opinions to a situation. Mike would feel differently than Marta did, no matter how tight-knit their relationship. Nathan, on the eve of his wedding, couldn't be expected to react to the news in the same way that Chuck, married for two years and a father, would react. And Dean, who hardly knew Chris at all, would have his own thoughts, though he might be hesitant to share them.

Allison pulled the covers up to her chin. There were a few things she hadn't told Bess and Marta. Like how most of her women friends in Chicago, without concrete facts to go on because of Allison's promise of silence, were left to believe that Chris was being a typical male asshole, discovering he was bored with his comfortable marriage and wanting to sow some wild oats before he had no more oats to sow. No doubt, they pronounced, he would soon marry again, choosing a younger version of Allison, and in two or three years find himself right back where he had been, bored with the routine of his life, regretting the divorce, and wondering if there was any chance at all that Allison could be persuaded to take him back. Assuming, of course, he could get out of his second marriage with even a dime to his name.

Maybe one day she would set the record straight. Maybe.

On her way upstairs to her bedroom, Allison had stopped to scan the shelves of books provided by the owners of Driftwood House. Luck was with her; there was a paperback copy of *Jane Eyre*, arguably her favorite novel. She had taken the book to her room and now reached for it, flipping to the section in which Jane was living with St. John and his sisters. She knew exactly what passage she wanted and found it readily. Jane speaks to the reader about Mr. Rochester.

> His idea was still with me, because it was not a vapour
> sunshine could disperse, nor a sand-traced effigy storms
> could wash away; it was a name graven on a tablet, fated
> to last as long as the marble it inscribed.

For better or worse, Allison knew this was how it was with her; she could never forget Chris no matter what he had done to hurt her. She might be angry with him, but she could never not love him; though the shape of that love might change, it could never be eradicated. Wiping a tear from her eye, Allison closed the book.

A car pulled onto the graveled drive. The men were back. Allison pulled the pillow against her ears to block out any voices that might wander into her room as Bess told Nathan and Marta told Mike the truth behind the divorce of their dear friends.

Who would break the news to Chuck and Dean come morning?

Chapter 34

Bess was alone in the kitchen the next morning when Allison appeared. Bess thought she looked remarkably well; maybe the unburdening of her secret had helped restore some of her native vitality. Or maybe Bess was imagining Allison's healthier demeanor. Wishful thinking.

"I'm sorry for ruining your wedding celebrations by telling you what happened between Chris and me," Allison said by way of greeting. "I should never have told you now. This should be a happy time for you."

"Please, Allison, don't apologize! I'm so not mad at you for telling me—for telling us—what happened. We've all been so worried . . . And curious. At least now we know the truth."

"My version of it," Allison corrected, pouring a cup of coffee. "No doubt Chris would have another tale to tell."

"But I believe you!" Bess said vehemently.

"Why? Because we're both women?" Allison smiled kindly. "Don't get me wrong, Bess. I appreciate your support. But to be absolutely fair, our friends should hear Chris's version of the story before choosing sides."

"I don't want to choose sides," Bess argued. "Anyway, Chris doesn't want to talk to us. It's obvious he doesn't feel the need to tell us his version of what happened, or to justify his actions, so why should I be eager to hear what he has to say?"

"I'm not sure he doesn't feel the need to talk," Allison said thoughtfully. "Remember, he said he didn't want the pity—or the scrutiny. But he might want the sympathy. Maybe he can't talk to one of the group because he's afraid of judgment or outright condemnation." Allison sighed heavily. "Oh, I don't know. The point is I'm sorry if I sullied your happiness and your optimism. I really am."

"I tried to get Chris to change his mind about not coming to the wedding," Bess blurted. "Marta says I harassed him but honestly, all I tried to do was to make sure he believed that my invitation was meant sincerely."

"But he still said no."

"Not exactly," Bess admitted. "The truth is he never answered any of my calls or messages after returning the reply card in the invitation. I'm sorry, Allison. If I had known then what I know now . . ."

Allison smiled. "You would have done the very same thing. You want everyone you love to be happy."

"That's not a bad thing to want," Bess protested. She thought there had been something critical in Allison's tone.

"Of course not. You just haven't learned that you don't have the power to make that happen."

Bess considered this for a moment. There had been times when she had been called pushy and interfering when all she had wanted was to help. She could hear the accusations in her head. "What gives you the right to think you know what's best for someone else? Just because X or Y is what *you* want for someone, just because it will make *you* feel better if X or Y happens, doesn't mean it's right for someone else."

"I'm sorry," Bess mumbled.

Allison didn't reply. She went to the fridge and took out two bottles of water. "I'm going down to the beach," she said.

Less than a minute after she was gone Chuck came into the kitchen, yawning.

"Dean has a bit of a headache," he said. "And you look as if you might have one, too. What's wrong?"

"Did you see Allison this morning?" she asked.

"From a distance. Why?"

Bess told him. "It's too horrible," she said when she had related the tale. "Allison's not wanting to go through another round of IVF, the accident, Chris's leaving. They were the perfect couple. If their marriage couldn't survive a tragedy, how can anyone's?"

Chuck shook his head. "This is awful but Bess, no couple is perfect. Nothing human comes anywhere near perfection. That said, Allison and Chris were a pretty great team. At least, they appeared to be."

"They were," Bess insisted.

"Look," Chuck said. "I feel awful for Allison, and for Chris, but we can't let this ruin your wedding celebrations. Besides, your being miserable won't do Allison or Chris any good."

"I know, but suddenly I feel so guilty for being happy when my friend is so sad."

"Of course, you do," Chuck said with a smile. "You're a good person. But your guilt isn't doing Allison any favors, either." Chuck picked up a mug. "I'd better bring Dean some coffee. We're both getting too old for late nights."

When Chuck had gone, Bess put her hand out to take a peach muffin off the platter she had laid out earlier. Then she let her hand fall. She had no appetite. In fact, she felt slightly sick to her stomach.

Chapter 35

Mike was still snoring when Marta quietly left their room and tip-toed down to the first floor. It was only six o'clock; she had been able to slip out of Driftwood House unseen and make her way to the beach, where she was blissfully alone but for one other early riser who seemed as disinclined as she was to socialize.

Marta went down to the water's edge and began to walk in the direction of a very exclusive beach club whose members paid for the privilege of a semi-famous chef in the restaurant, a full-service spa on-site, and marble-clad changing rooms.

That stupid one-night stand, her one instance of infidelity! No wonder she had felt nervous in the moments before Mike had come into their bedroom the night before. Might Chris have told Allison about the brief affair in a fit of anger, as an act of revenge? Would Allison spring her knowledge of the affair on Marta or on Mike? Was that the real reason she had come to this reunion before the wedding?

An especially bold seagull swooped down only feet away from Marta. He fixed her with a beady eye and began to walk closer. "Shoo!" Marta cried, waving her arm. The bird scurried off a few yards. A silly little incident, but it rattled Marta.

Nothing about the afterward of an affair was good, she thought gloomily. If you had even one moral bone in your body, any pleas-

ant memory was invariably tainted by shame and guilt. And to recall the feeble justifications you had constructed for doing what you
knew you shouldn't be doing!

Marta remembered the path to that fateful night all too well.

A founding member of the International Institute for Women's
Economic Empowerment was coming to Boston to give a talk.
Marta was keen to hear the woman speak, but none of her friends
was interested. In the end, Mike had agreed to be dragged along.

After the lecture, which Marta had found greatly inspiring,
Mike suggested they stop by a party before getting the bus back to
campus. Marta hadn't been in the mood—especially not after the
eye-opening and sobering content of the talk they had just listened
to—but Mike had been decent enough to accompany her to the
lecture so she felt that the least she could do was chat with a few of
his rowdy friends before calling it a night.

The party was in full swing when they arrived at Howard's
Allston Street apartment at around ten o'clock. Mike immediately
accepted a beer and a moment later Marta found herself on her own
amid the crowd of laughing and shouting guests, the majority of
whom she didn't know even by sight. It took close to fifteen minutes for her to locate Mike, what with being waylaid by the host,
who pressed upon her a clear plastic cup sloshing with a liquid that
smelled suspiciously of gasoline (Marta did not drink it) and who
felt it necessary to tell her in great and specific detail the story of
his visit to the doctor's that morning to have a "honking huge" boil
on his butt lanced. Finally, Marta found Mike in conversation with
a very striking girl with the sort of figure that would have made her
a successful pinup star in the 1950s. Mike's gaze was riveted to the
girl's perfectly made-up face, which was surrounded by an impres-
sive head of dark wavy hair; his mouth hung open slightly. Marta,
pulling herself to her full height of five foot five, joined her wayward
boyfriend and the Amazon.

The Amazon was complaining to Mike that she was constantly
compelled to reject the advances of wealthy men looking for a gorgeous young mistress. "It's seriously a drag," she said, placing a well-
manicured hand on Mike's arm. "All I want is to be taken seriously."

Marta refrained from pointing out to the Amazon that she had used "seriously" twice and that there were plenty of other words in the English language she might have chosen. "Mike?" she said.

Mike, whose eyes had not once left the eyes of the Amazon, said, "Whaa?"

"I'd like to go home now."

Mike's head turned a bit—just a bit—in Marta's direction. "In a minute," he said. Then he looked back to the Amazon. "Go on," he requested earnestly. "It must be seriously difficult for you being treated like you don't matter."

Seriously? Marta thought.

The Amazon smiled dazzlingly. "I'm so glad you understand," she said in a breathy tone of relief.

Marta rolled her eyes—not that either Mike or the Amazon was paying any attention to her—left the noisy party on her own, and got the last bus back to campus. Mike did not call that night. Marta knew in her gut that he had not gone to bed with the Amazon. But she would have appreciated a call.

Only at eleven the following morning had Mike finally rung to apologize for having "lost track" of her at the party. Marta felt the apology wasn't enough. He had been letting her down a lot; in the past three weeks he had forgotten an appointment they had made to hear a mutual friend play guitar at the opening of a new coffee-house; he had canceled a movie date at the last minute because a buddy who had graduated the year before was back in town for a night and Mike didn't want to miss hanging out with The Beer-meister; and most annoying, he had forgotten that he had promised to help Marta move a dresser she had bought at a local secondhand shop to her dorm room. Bess and Allison had come to the rescue.

Things hadn't been perfectly smooth between Chris and Allison, either. A week earlier Allison had gone to a memorial rally in support of a local boy who had been brutally beaten to death because he was gay. Chris had been worried things would get violent and had asked Allison not to go. "I didn't tell her she *couldn't* go," Chris explained to Marta as they sat at a dive bar in the next town over from school, sharing grievances two weeks after the incident with the Amazon. (Allison was visiting her parents that night; Mike was visiting his. Chuck was on a jaunt to New York City. Bess was spending the night in the room of a classmate who had recently become "expert" at reading the Tarot.) "I *asked* her. But she said no, anyway. Why couldn't she have done this one thing for me?"

Present-day Marta frowned at the rippling waves and battled a rush of shame. At the time beer and her hormones had gotten in the way of applauding Allison's very reasonable desire to live her own life. She remembered consoling Chris, agreeing that Allison had been wrong to go against his wishes. One thing had led to another . . .

Before sunrise the next morning Marta had jumped out of Chris's bed (he was still asleep), dressed, and scurried back to her own room, furiously regretting her lapse in judgment.

That afternoon, Chris called. They agreed that what they had done was wrong. Fun, but wrong. They agreed to never do "you know" again. They swore secrecy and it wasn't long before the one-night stand was pretty much forgotten.

Only once, on the weekend of his wedding, did Chris mention the incident. "Allison is my everything," he had said. "I don't know what I would do without her. I feel guilty almost every day about that one night you and I spent together."

Chris's confession had made Marta feel strange. Months went by without her being bothered by any conscious memory of the event. Either the "you know" had meant a lot more to Chris than it had to her, or his devotion to Allison came far closer to worship than hers did to Mike.

A high-pitched scream alerted Marta to the fact that she was no longer virtually alone on the beach. Marta turned to see two teen-aged girls leaping about in the shallow water. No doubt the scream was due to the fact that the water temperature was probably hovering at forty. She turned away and continued to think about Allison and Chris.

The problem with worshipping a person, she realized, was that you were likely to become possessive, to stop seeing the person as an individual and to regard her as a manifestation of your own desires. Could this dynamic have morphed into the hold Chris had developed over Allison, leading to his utter rejection of her when she "defied" his wishes by going to the photo shoot that fateful day?

Poor Allison, Marta thought. Twice betrayed by Chris and once by one of her best friends. Old sins cast long shadows. There was a menacing sound to that adage—that warning?—as well there should be. No bad deed went unpunished? Marta didn't believe that; all you had to do was glance at the nightly news and you could see evidence of all sorts of bad deeds being left not only unpunished but virtually unnoticed. Or nervously laughed at before being pushed aside.

Marta sighed. If she had known what trouble going to bed with Chris would cause in the future . . . Who was she kidding? To a young person, the future didn't really exist; long-term consequences were insignificant; trouble could be dealt with in a mythical "later"; there was always time to give up the bad habit, start over, change direction. Until there wasn't. Until what was done was done and you were left with coping with a deep and unending feeling of loss and bewilderment.

Marta glanced at her watch. She had been gone longer than she realized. She had better get back to the house or Bess would be sending out a search party.

Chapter 36

"A few months ago, Dean suggested that I fly to Chicago and confront Chris, demand to know what was going on."

Allison and Chuck were on the back porch. Bess had told him what she had learned the night before, but Chuck had had questions of his own. Allison had answered them as honestly as she could. Now, hearing this bit of information from Chuck, Allison felt her stomach sink. Finding himself the subject of an intervention—of the sort used when well-meaning but misguided people separated a troubled friend from his daily surroundings in the hopes of forcing him to get help and in the process, of making themselves feel morally superior—might very well do lasting damage to a sensitive man like Chris Montague.

"Don't worry," Chuck added quickly. "Dean meant well, but he doesn't know Chris the way we do. A direct confrontation would only further alienate him."

"Yes," Allison agreed with a sigh of relief. "It would. But it was nice of Dean to suggest you be proactive."

"He knows how much I miss Chris's friendship. It's not as if we spoke every day, but we had—we still have, I hope—a strong bond. I'll never cease to be grateful for the support he gave me back in college when for a few months I was being bullied by two vicious little frat boys for having the audacity to be gay. Anyway, I'm not going anywhere. If and when Chris is ready to reach out to me again, I'll be there."

"That's good of you, Chuck." Allison smiled ruefully. "I wish I could say the same. The truth is I'm just not sure. As much as I still love Chris, as much as I believe I always will love him, there are moments when I very much doubt I could forgive and forget enough to have him back in my life in any meaningful way."

"Sometimes choosing no communication whatsoever is the wisest choice. Difficult, but the most self-preserving." Chuck smiled. "But I hope it doesn't come to that."

No communication whatsoever, not even through lawyers. Was that what Allison wanted? Her blood chilled at the thought.

"Maybe I should have said something to him when we were in college," Chuck went on, "and he first told me about Robby. Not that a nineteen-year-old would have known what to say."

Allison smiled sadly. "I doubt he would have listened to you even if you'd been the wisest teenager ever. He didn't listen to his parents or to the therapist he saw after Robby's death. And any time I tried to make a suggestion that might lead toward Chris's letting go even the tiniest bit of his—well, his obsession—with his brother, he shut me down. Eventually, I stopped making the suggestions. After all, Chris's life is his own."

"As your life is your own. But being married complicates that truth. By taking that pledge of love and commitment, you've created a third being, the union, to which you each have a duty to contribute the best person you can be." Chuck sighed. "I think about this dynamic all the time. I try to talk to Dean, just to get things clearer in my head, but sometimes I drive him nuts. He says, just live and stop talking about living. As if that were easy!"

Allison smiled kindly. "Easier for some, surely."

Chuck rose and stretched. "I need to make a call to my office. And here comes the swing shift."

Bess and Marta came out to the porch. Each took a seat, Bess to Allison's left and Marta to her right.

"Do you like your lawyer?" Bess asked abruptly.

"It doesn't matter if she likes her lawyer," Marta said. "It matters that her lawyer knows what she's doing."

"It's just that I don't want Allison to be cheated of anything she deserves."

"Illinois is an equitable distribution state," Marta pointed out. "All marital property is divided fairly and equitably. And by marital property it's meant all property acquired by either party since the marriage."

Bess shivered. "It all sounds so . . . so sordid."

"The law isn't sordid. People make things sordid."

"And people make the law," Bess said, undeterred. "But the stuff that's yours alone," she said, turning to Allison, "like your cameras and clothes, that's all still yours, right? And what about the presents Chris gave you over the years, special things, like for an anniversary or a birthday?"

"He isn't asking for anything I need for my career or for a return of the gifts he gave me," Allison explained.

"Could he if he wanted to?" Bess pressed. "I mean, legally?"

Allison felt an unpleasant tingling run through her. "I don't know," she said, "and I don't want to know."

"You should know," Marta said firmly. "Ask your lawyer. You need to be fully informed. Is she refusing to answer your questions?"

"No, of course not," Allison replied irritably. "She's always giving me information, too much information. I can't keep track of it all."

"What do you think Chris is going to do with the gifts you've given him over the years?" Bess asked.

"Bess, for God's sake, what a thing to bring up!" Marta shook her head. "Sometimes you have no sense at all!"

"I don't know," Allison said shakily. She thought of the eighteenth-century Italian brass drawing instrument set she had given Chris for his thirty-fifth birthday; she had bought it online from an antique dealer in Paris. She thought of the cuff links made of genuine Roman glass and silver she had given Chris for their seventh anniversary; he had worn those cuff links often. Maybe he no longer wore them at all.

"Did you two ever consider adoption?" Bess asked.

Allison sighed. Bess could win an award for bluntness.

"I've wondered about that so often," Bess went on, "but never had the nerve to ask. Maybe I shouldn't have asked it now, but . . ."

"It's okay," Allison said. "It's a good question, and the answer is that *I* considered adoption. How could I not? It's an integral part of my identity. But Chris felt otherwise."

"So many men do," Marta said grimly. "Something about having another man's child under their roof, a cuckoo in the nest. It's a stupid macho thing."

"That wasn't Chris's objection," Allison argued. "I think it had something to do with keeping a bit of Robby's Montague DNA alive, even though adoption would have been so much easier on me. Chris wasn't the one who had to endure the transvaginal ultrasounds and endless blood tests, or the one who had to be taking the fertility meds and dealing with the side effects." Allison shook her head. "I don't think Chris meant to, but he insulted me by rejecting the idea of adoption. He made me feel like damaged goods."

The screen door slid open again and Chuck rejoined them. "Hope I'm not intruding," he said.

Bess smiled. "Never."

"I've been wondering if it might be a good idea for me to search for my birth parents," Allison told her friends. "But Massachusetts is a closed adoption state, or at least it was. I have no idea what hoops I'd have to jump through to find answers."

Bess clasped her hands to her chest. "You so should!"

Marta, with a critical glance at Bess, frowned. "I wouldn't advise doing something so risky in your state of mind," she said. "What does your therapist say about the idea?"

"I don't have to ask my therapist for permission to do something I want to do!" Allison replied testily.

"I didn't say ask for permission." Marta's tone was neutral. "Advice is more what I was thinking. Seeking out your birth parents is not exactly a little thing."

"I know, I know. Sorry."

"No, I'm sorry," Marta said quickly. "I'm being a downer. If locating your birth parents is something you really want to do you should do it with the support of your friends. You don't need our grim cautions."

"Did you ever mention the idea to Chris?" Chuck asked.

"I did. Not long after the start of our relationship my parents gave me a little bit of information about my birth mother. She was the one who had named me Allison. I mentioned to Chris that one day I might decide to search for my birth parents and he said he thought it would be a big mistake. He never really said why and I never pressed him for his reasons because I didn't really want to find my birth parents then, anyway."

Marta shook her head. "Chris and his control issues! He was afraid that if you found your birth parents there'd be two more people demanding your time. Bad enough you already had two adoptive parents on hand to steal you away."

"Oh, don't be silly, Marta," Bess scolded. "I'm sure Chris was just being protective of Allison. There's no guarantee of a happy ending when you go in search of the mother and father who gave you up."

"I wonder," Chuck said. "It's kind of a far-fetched idea but . . . I wonder if Chris somehow unconsciously confused his anger at his parents for abandoning Robby with anger at Allison's birth parents for abandoning her. Maybe he felt that Allison's birth parents didn't deserve to know their daughter. Maybe . . ." Chuck laughed self-consciously. "Okay, maybe that's all a lot of nonsense."

"I don't think so, given what we now know about Chris's obsession with Robby," Marta said musingly. "But I guess we'll never be certain. What do you think, Allison?"

"Hurts sustained in childhood can fester and warp the mind. That's not news. So maybe Chuck is on to something." Allison smiled ruefully. "But like Marta said, we'll probably never know for sure."

Chuck rubbed his hands together. "All this heavy emotional lifting has given me an appetite. Any of that corn salad left, Bess?"

As Bess hurried inside and Marta and Chuck got into a debate about celery of all things—if cooked, did it really constitute a daily serving of vegetables?—Allison wondered how Chris would feel if he knew she had broken her promise of silence, a promise made under duress but still a promise. At that moment, she didn't much care.

"I think I'll have some of that corn salad, too," she said, rising from her chair. "I'll go help Bess."

Chapter 37

"What do you think about it all, Mike?"

Bess knew Mike wasn't comfortable talking about touchy-feely stuff, but Mike was smart and he was tough. Her questions wouldn't do him any real damage.

"About what all?" he asked, beginning to fiddle with the salt cellar. And Mike was an avoider. A lot of men were.

"About Allison and Chris, of course."

"Oh," he said. "That. I can't believe Chris could be so cruel as to leave Allison in her time of need. She's so . . . She's so vulnerable."

Bess—like Marta—knew that Mike had always seen Allison as weaker than she in fact was, the delicate, pretty blond girl in need of a savior. Bess wasn't sure that Allison was aware of this prejudice, or, if she was, how she felt about it.

"Yes," Bess said. "But what do you think about Chris's being so upset with Allison for not doing what he wanted her to do, which was to abandon the project she was working on at the time?"

Mike looked decidedly uncomfortable. He picked up the pepper shaker and shook it. "I don't really know what happened," he pointed out. "I mean, I don't like to . . ." Mike rubbed the back of his neck with his other hand. "Look, I've been through three pregnancies with Marta and I have to admit there were times when I wanted her to do less or to do something differently. Like the time she was five months pregnant with Sam and got invited to a bachelorette party at an amusement park. She swore she wouldn't go on the roller coaster and I believed her, but I spent the entire afternoon in a state of near panic." Mike smiled ruefully. "I never quite learned how to stop worrying, even through the second and third pregnancies. But Marta's body is her own, and it's her right to act as she pleases. There were times when I failed to trust her and it was wrong of me."

Bess recalled Mike saying something the other night about how he shouldn't have allowed Marta to go on vacation with the gang while she was pregnant. Marta had not been pleased. "I'm sure she understood that your motives were good," Bess said. At least, she hoped that Marta had understood.

"Yeah," Mike said. Then he shook his head. "I'd do anything to protect my children. Any halfway decent father would. I suspect Chris felt guilty after the miscarriage, even if he didn't admit as much to Allison."

"But why would he feel guilty?" Bess asked. "He had nothing to do with the accident."

"He was the father. Parents feel guilty about everything, Bess, even about the things we can't control. I guarantee Chris beat himself up pretty badly about what happened, even as he was blaming Allison." Mike sighed. "If only he'd reached out to someone, me or Chuck, anyone. I'm not saying we could have worked a miracle and talked Chris out of a divorce, but I know we could have helped. I know it."

Poor Mike, Bess thought. Of course, he couldn't know that. But in his effort to get a handle on the tragedy Mike needed to believe that there was a way in which he could have helped avert it. Men like Mike needed to fix things. That was okay, except when they *couldn't* fix something, or find a solution to a loved one's problem, or make an irritation go away. Then they felt really, really bad.

"It's so terribly complicated," she said neutrally.

"I've got a question for you," Mike said suddenly. "Define this famous soul mate for me. I mean, all those years you talked about this mysterious figure, what did you really mean? This isn't a challenge," Mike added hurriedly. "I'm genuinely curious."

Bess wondered why he was asking this question now. Prompted by the upcoming wedding? Allison's divorce? Or maybe by some point of tension in his marriage to Marta?

"I guess what I mean is someone with whom you feel totally comfortable and safe," she said. "Someone who likes you for your quirks, not in spite of them. Sometimes you get fooled—at least, I got fooled—into thinking, okay, he's my soul mate, but then you see that no, he's not, and that's fine. Better to be alone than with the wrong person." Bess sighed. "I'm sorry, Mike. It's really hard to articulate. You just know when you know."

Mike looked thoughtful; a moment later, he nodded. "Well, then, Marta is my soul mate, no doubt about it." Then he half smiled. "I just hope she feels the same way about me."

"I know she does," Bess assured him. But did she? It was difficult to know what Marta thought or how she felt about the more esoteric aspects of life. That Marta loved Mike and was devoted to him, Bess had no doubt. But love and devotion were practical matters in many ways; at least, Bess had been taught that they usually were in a marriage. They didn't necessarily have anything to do with Romantic Ideals like Soul Mates and One True Loves.

"Hey, is there any more of that blueberry pie left?" Mike asked brightly.

Clearly, he was through talking about the intricacies of romantic relationships. "One slice," Bess told him, going over to the fridge to fetch it. "I'll pick up a few more pies when I'm out later."

"Blueberries are good for you," Mike said, greedily eyeing the generous slice of pie Bess placed on the counter. "Antioxidants."

Bess patted her friend on the shoulder and handed him a fork. "Enjoy," she said. Silently, she added: *And be quick about it. You don't want Marta catching you eating between meals.*

The gnarled old tree beckoned to Bess as she made her way down toward to beach. She stopped to observe it once again. The bark was worn away in places, revealing the mottled wood underneath. In other places the bark was peeling, creating what to Bess was a slightly fanciful appearance. No doubt about it, there was something compelling about this old, dead tree. Bess wondered how many winters it had survived, how many springs it had enjoyed, how many people had sat under the canopy of its branches in full bloom.

Time passed. Things changed. So did people. What it would take, Bess wondered, for Nathan to leave her? Would he walk away if she made a bad mistake like Allison had made? No, Bess corrected. Allison had *not* made a bad mistake. Something bad had happened to her. She was not to blame, even though Chris was convinced that she was.

Bess considered. Once she and Nathan were married, would she have to hide her less than perfect self from him? He already knew she had a habit of eating half a banana and leaving the other half to rot instead of putting it into the fridge, and that she wasn't the most careful recycler, and that she was a committed people-pleaser, sometimes to her detriment. But what if as the years passed she developed a tendency toward chronic crankiness (it seemed impossible, but you never knew), or what if her mind narrowed as a result of her being the victim of a violent crime and she became the reverse of the open-minded, big-hearted person Nathan had fallen in love with and married? You couldn't hide things like negative personality changes or newly acquired character flaws. One day Nathan might look closely at his wife and realize he no longer loved her, that in fact he no longer knew her. Then he would want to leave. He would need to leave. And where would Bess be then?

Bess folded her arms across her chest in an unconscious gesture of self-protection. How could a marriage ever work without full disclosure? How could it work *with* full disclosure? Did anyone know the answer to those questions?

Bess knew the basics of Nathan's past. That he had married at the age of twenty-three. That Maggie, his wife, had died young of cancer. That they had not had children.

Nathan knew the basics of Bess's past. That she had never been married. That she had never wanted children. That she had spent many years at a stretch being single.

There was not much more to tell, Bess realized, certainly nothing that would upset Nathan if he were to find out. She had no criminal record. She had never even shoplifted a candy bar as a kid.

She had never knowingly cheated anyone in business. She gave money to the homeless women she encountered on the streets of downtown Portland. Some of the homeless men frightened her. She felt bad about that but not bad enough to have conquered her fear. But would Nathan think less of her if she admitted she was afraid of the homeless men?

"What have you been doing out here on your own?" Marta asked.

Bess cried out. "You almost gave me a heart attack! For a second I thought this gnarled old tree was talking to me!"

Marta raised an eyebrow.

"Sorry we startled you," Allison said.

"It's okay." Bess took a deep breath and smiled. "I'm glad you're here. I've been thinking about all sorts of things and making myself slightly crazy."

"Be specific," Marta suggested.

"Okay. For one, I don't know if Nathan's first wife was ever pregnant. If she was, she must have had either a miscarriage or an abortion because there was no child. Which was it?"

"Did it occur to you to ask Nathan if his wife was ever pregnant?" Marta said.

"Of course, but I don't want to upset him."

Marta laughed. "The hell with upsetting him. You have a right to know."

"I'm not so sure she does," Allison argued. "It really has no bearing on Bess in the here and now."

Marta shrugged. "You have a point there. But I understand Bess's curiosity."

"Remember," Allison pointed out, "curiosity killed the cat."

"Poor cat," Marta noted. "Only doing what a cat is meant to do. Killed for fulfilling his nature." And then she put her hand to her heart. "Sheesh! Look, in the tree! Speak of the devil . . ."

Bess turned. A large gray cat was perched in the twisted, peeling branches of the tree, staring at them with unblinking yellow eyes.

"How did I not see him before?" Bess murmured. A shiver ran through her.

"Maybe he just materialized," Allison whispered. "Maybe he's the genius loci. He's certainly magnificent."

"Yeah, and I'm the Wicked Witch of the West," Marta remarked. "It's just a stray or maybe a neighbor's pet."

"I think we should leave him alone," Bess said, beginning to back away. "What if he's vicious?"

"He's not vicious," Allison stated firmly, taking a step closer to the tree.

"Well, we'll leave you to get your eyes scratched out," Marta said, taking Bess's arm and pulling her along toward the beach.

Bess took one last glance over her shoulder as she followed Marta. Allison and the cat were staring at each other. Odd. Allison had never been interested in animals.

"Come on, Lazy Bones!" Marta urged.

Bess stepped up her pace.

Chapter 38

After a half hour Bess had gone back to the house to tackle some chore or other, leaving Marta on her own, sitting on the sand, her knees drawn up to her chest, her arms wrapped around her legs. Marta loved the beach. She wondered why she didn't make it a priority to spend more time at the shore. She wouldn't have to take along the children. Sam would prefer to be with her friends, Leo wasn't big on the outdoors, and Troy always enjoyed spending time alone with his father.

It was something to think about, carving out time for herself.

Marta squinted. Down by the water's edge, Chuck and Dean were walking hand in hand. The happy couple. Marta had been surprised when Chuck had announced he was getting married. He had seemed the least likely to settle down, having no history of long-term relationships. But just before his wedding he had explained to Marta what had decided him on a life partnership. In Dean, Chuck had found a person of good character, amiable personality, physical attractiveness, and most importantly, someone who wanted a family as much as Chuck did. Marta believed that you could dearly love someone who wasn't your grand passion, and maybe that made for a better marriage in the end. Who could say?

Marta's knees were feeling stiff. She straightened her legs; the sand was pleasingly warm on her calves and she dug her feet in deep. And she wondered, If her marriage were to end before she had reached a very old age, would she be tempted to marry again? She didn't think it was likely. Mike and Marriage were almost entirely bound up in each other, the reality of Mike, the ideal of Marriage. But people did remarry when they were old, after divorce or the death of a longtime spouse. And when they were not so old, like Nathan. Why? For companionship alone? What relation did that sort of late-in-life marriage have to the sort of marriage Marta shared with Mike, in which the most important function of the union was to provide a safe and nurturing environment in which to raise children? How likely was it that a parenting marriage could morph into a truly successful marriage of a different kind once the kids were gone? Were parents ever truly able to rediscover each other as individuals, as the people they had been pre-parenthood?

No, Marta thought. Of course not. Those pre-parenthood people no longer existed. But what about the *post*-parenthood individual, if you could posit such a being?

Marta breathed a sigh of relief when she saw Allison approaching. Bess was right. Thinking could drive you crazy.

"That cat is amazing," Allison said, sitting to Marta's right. "I wish I knew if he has a home."

"Looking for a familiar?" Marta asked.

Allison shrugged. "Maybe." She paused and then went on. "All morning I've been thinking about the time I insisted on going to that memorial rally back in college. The one for the local teen killed by his classmates."

"I remember," Marta said. Her stomach knotted. Why, oh why, was Allison bringing up that dreaded weekend now? Did she in fact know that Chris and Marta had betrayed her only weeks later? Was Allison taunting her?

"Chris was sure things were going to get violent. He begged me not to go."

"I remember," Marta said again.

"It meant so much to me to show my support for that boy and his family, but Chris acted like my decision to attend the memorial was a personal insult or a betrayal of our relationship. It took so long before things were normal between us again, and they only got that way because I was so tired of feeling like the bad guy I apologized, but for what exactly I don't know. Following my conscience?" Allison shook her head. "He was always so protective."

"He was bullying and possessive," Marta corrected. And if he had been so worried about Allison's safety, why hadn't he gone with her to the memorial?

"Yes, in some ways, he was. I see that now. But I let him be that way. He's not entirely to blame." Allison paused and Marta waited with trepidation for her friend to go on. "I'm ashamed to admit this, Marta, but there might have been a bit of defiance in my decision to finish that project I was working on before taking a few days of bed rest. You must think me an awful person."

"Nothing of the kind," Marta said firmly.

Allison shook her head. "Well, there's no way to change the past."

"Yes," Marta said softly, looking at the specks that were Chuck and Dean, at the gently rolling wavelets reaching shore. "There's no way to change the past."

"Well, I think I'll head back to the house," Allison announced, getting to her feet.

"I'm going to stay put," Marta said. Though being alone with her thoughts wasn't a particularly pleasant prospect, it was more appealing than spending another moment with the friend she had betrayed.

Chapter 39

Allison had looked for the big gray cat on her way back from the beach, but he was nowhere in sight. She hoped he would return. She had never felt such an affinity for an animal before. They had stared at each other for a long moment, during which Allison had felt that they were truly communicating. Suddenly, the cat had sprung off the branch on which he had been perched and raced off into a stand of bushes.

Now, a few hours later, Allison came down from her room, showered, and changed. Nathan and Mike were in the backyard grilling steaks; Chuck and Dean were supervising. From the backyard came cries of "Turn it, turn it!" and "How can you stand it so rare?" The women were lounging in the living area. Bess had put out cheese, crackers, olives, and wine.

"How many men does it take to grill seven steaks?" Marta asked.

Allison smiled as she took a seat in one of the many comfortable chairs. "Is there a punch line?"

Marta shrugged. "I'm too lazy to come up with one."

"Do you know if Chris is seeing someone?" Bess asked.

Marta sighed in exasperation. "Really, Bess?"

"It's okay," Allison said. "I have no idea. None of the people we know in common have said anything about Chris and other women and honestly, I'm grateful."

Marta frowned. "I understand what you're saying, what good would it do to know if Chris is dating or not, but it must feel horrible knowing that people are keeping things from you, even if their motives are good. I'd be tempted to shout, 'Just tell me already! I know you're dying to!' Of course," Marta went on, "that sort of behavior wouldn't leave me with many friends, would it?"

Allison smiled. "Probably not."

"So," Bess said, after taking a sip of her rosé, "have *you* thought about dating?"

"Absolutely not," Allison declared.

"It's too soon anyway," Marta added. "I'd think you'd want to wait at least until the divorce is final."

Allison shook her head. "It's not that," she said. "It's not about time, too soon, too late. It's that I can't imagine being with anyone but Chris. I don't think I'll ever be able to imagine that."

Bess smiled. "Never say never."

"Why? Why can't I know my own mind?" Allison demanded, leaning forward. "Why do people need to push optimism on others? That kind of thinking—'maybe I *will* meet someone great one day!'—isn't relevant for me. Maybe it is for other people, but not for *me*. Don't discount what I say because you don't like it or it's not the attitude you think you would adopt in my situation." Allison sat back in her chair and took a deep breath.

"I'm sorry," Bess said quietly. "I was just . . . I was just saying what you say when a person sounds defeated and hopeless."

"But I don't see myself as defeated and hopeless," Allison argued. "And even if I did, that's my business, if not necessarily my choice. Not everyone is fixable. Not everyone is going to have a happy life. That's reality."

"She's right, you know," Marta said, looking pointedly at Bess. "Life is nasty, brutish, and short, at least it often is. You just have to make the best of what you're given and shoulder on." After a moment, she added in a mutter: "Nice advice if you can take it."

"But you can change or refuse to accept what you're given," Bess protested. "You don't have to just sit back and accept that heartbreak is your lot in life."

"Not everything can be changed for the better, Bess," Allison said with a frown. "Don't be so naïve. I hate when you go on like that, it's so stupid!"

There was yet another moment of stunned silence. Allison sighed and pushed her hair back with both hands. "Look," she said, "I'm sorry I said that. If you need to be all Pollyanna-ish, fine, that's your right. Just don't try to foist that sort of soggy thinking onto everyone around you."

"I didn't mean to—"

"That's your problem, Bess," Marta interrupted. "You don't think before you speak. Not everyone wants to hear what it is you have to say. You need to learn when to keep quiet." Marta got up from her chair and excused herself to fetch a sweater.

"We sort of ganged up on you there," Allison said when Marta had gone. "I'm sorry. You do forgive me, Bess, don't you? I really didn't mean to sound so harsh."

Bess smiled a wobbly smile. "Of course, I forgive you," she said. She got up and headed toward the dining area. "Time to set the table."

Allison sat where she was, nursing a glass of wine. Poor Bess. She took so much on herself, with her inordinate sense of responsibility for other people's happiness. She deserved great happiness of her own. But that was the thing. Not everyone got what she deserved.

"Let me help," Allison called out to Bess as she rose from her chair.

Chapter 40

The steaks had been perfectly grilled to each person's specifications. There had been a slight tussle among the men about who was ultimately responsible for the success, with Mike and Chuck vying for supremacy. In the end, laughter had won the day with each of the men agreeing that together they had nailed not only the steaks, but the corn on the cob as well. If it was corn from New Jersey, the Maine season being later in the summer, it was no less delicious for that.

That afternoon Bess had dashed out to pick up two freshly baked raspberry pies from a local bakery. They had been immensely popular, though there were a few slices left over. A few small slices.

Dean had retired early with Thomas. Nathan was working in the den. Mike had gone down to the beach for a solitary nighttime stroll, leaving Chuck and the women lounging on the back porch. The air was clear and the stars bright. For the billionth time, Bess vowed to learn some basic astrology so that she could identify the popular constellations. Not that naming them would make the constellations any more beautiful.

Allison looked contemplative. Marta seemed miles away and that was unusual for Marta, Bess thought. She was most often hyperalert to the moment and ready to comment on it.

Bess had thought about what Allison and Marta had said to her before dinner. *You don't think before you speak. Don't be so naïve.* Did she really engage in soggy thinking? Well, maybe she did, but so what if she was optimistic and believed that what she had to say could be helpful to her friends? *Quand-même*, right? Onward and upward. Plus, there was leftover raspberry pie in the house. How low-spirited could a person remain with that sort of pleasure at hand?

"Listen to this." Chuck indicated the gossip magazine he had been reading. "It says here that there are more billionaires under the age of thirty now than ever before. I wonder if that's right. I'm not sure I trust a rag like this to be telling the truth."

"It's not a rag," Bess protested. "It's meant to be fun."

Chuck frowned and tossed the magazine onto a side table. "And vicious and poorly written. Still, I suppose the bit about the baby billionaires might be true."

"Who needs billions of dollars?" Bess said with a shrug. "I think we've all done remarkably well in achieving what we wanted to achieve in our lives and so what if we're not rolling in the dough."

Allison made no comment.

The subject of money seemed to have brought Marta back from wherever it is she had gone. "Speak for yourself," she said. "I've got college tuition to consider."

"Leaving college expenses out if it, I'm with Bess. In fact, there's been only one big disappointment in my professional life," Chuck said. "I'll never be entirely sure why I didn't get the position I went after at our rival hospital. Maybe I just wasn't considered good enough for the job."

"But that's the luck of the draw," Bess argued. "It doesn't mean you did anything wrong."

Chuck nodded. "You're right. I know I did my best. Not getting the job was a disappointment, that's all."

Bess smiled. "Not one of us is a failure in any way that I can see!"

"Mike could use some prodding when it comes to ambition. He does okay but . . ." Marta laughed harshly. "I'm one to talk. I don't have a career, floundering or otherwise."

Bess had never heard Marta criticize Mike's career. As far as she knew, he was very successful by anyone's standards. And there again was that note of discontent regarding Marta's own life path. . . .

"I'd say raising three kids is a career and a half," Chuck corrected. "Don't knock yourself, Marta. And you keep Mike in line, which is no small task. Do you remember that hideous sweatshirt he practically lived in? It went from bright green to olive to mud-colored and covered with stains before he gave up on it."

"He didn't give up on it," Marta remarked dryly. "I made it disappear. You'd think he'd care, the way he was attached to it, but he never said a word when it went missing. I don't think Mike has ever noticed what it is he's putting on."

"Don't tell me you lay out his clothes for him?" Chuck queried, a smile playing about his lips.

"What do you think?" Marta replied.

Until then Allison had been silent. "What about Chris?" she said now; the note of bitterness in her voice was unmistakable. "Isn't he a failure as a husband? Walking out without even an attempt at a genuine conversation that might lead to reconciliation?"

"I know what he did was painful," Bess said earnestly, "but the actions that result from emotional distress can't be classified as failures."

"How else can they be classified?" Allison demanded. "Chris left me when I was at my most vulnerable. He turned his back on me and on everything we had built together for over twenty years."

Marta nodded. "Amen."

Chuck shifted in his seat but was silent.

"But Chris did *try*, didn't he?" Bess asked. "Even if he failed in the end that doesn't mean all the earlier efforts he made to be a good husband are now meaningless."

"I don't know. Maybe it does. Maybe one spectacularly cruel action does cancel out all the kind actions that went before it." Allison laughed. "Of course, that means that my getting in the car that day in spite of Chris's asking me not to negates all the good things I did for him as a wife."

"You going to work that morning to complete an important assignment and Chris's filing for divorce are not at all equivalent," Chuck declared fiercely, leaning forward toward Allison.

"Chuck is right," Marta said.

"Well, I just can't accept that good deeds done out of love and kindness can ever be discounted. At the time, they mattered. They made a positive difference." Bess looked from one to the other of her friends. "Maybe I'm being naïve—I've been called that often enough by people who seem to think it's an insult—but I won't change my mind about this."

"Then we'll just have to agree to disagree," Allison said resignedly. "As far as I'm concerned, both Chris and I screwed up majorly."

Chuck rose suddenly. "I'm going to bed."

"A good idea," Marta said, getting up from her seat. "I hope Mike doesn't get lost out there or do something foolish like wander into the ocean and drown."

Bess saw Chuck give Marta a quizzical look. It had been an odd thing to say, and not a very complimentary one. If Allison heard Marta's remark, she chose to ignore it.

"I'm coming up, too," she said. "Good night, Bess."

Bess remained on the back porch after the others had gone. This most recent exchange with her friends had disturbed her. She had never heard Allison so bitter. She wouldn't have been surprised to hear such sentiments from Marta, but never from Allison. Where Marta could be quick to condemn, and Bess just as quick to acquit, Allison was usually the one to suggest a period of thoughtfulness before coming to a conclusion, and when she did reach a conclusion it most often involved a good deal of sympathetic feeling. Now she was as down on herself as she was with her soon-to-be former husband and that sort of attitude couldn't be healthy.

A sudden memory of that mysterious big wind that had arisen seemingly out of nowhere the first night they had all been gathered at Driftwood House came to Bess. It had seemed to presage a storm and in a way, it actually had. With a shiver that had nothing to do with the night air, Bess realized that starting her married life in such close proximity to a marriage at its end made her feel sick. Sick and determined. She would show her friends the right way to be married. She would never talk about Nathan in the critical way Marta had talked about Mike that evening. She would never abandon her vows as Chris had done. Even Chuck and Dean must have it wrong in some way. She would keep her eyes open, observe carefully and . . .

Bess dropped her head into her hands. She was ashamed of her descent into self-righteousness. And into cliché. She wondered if every bride-to-be felt the smug certitude that she and she alone knew what it would take to be the perfect wife. She owed it to her friends, to Nathan, and to herself to get over this dark and unpleasant mood.

Another slice of raspberry pie might help. Bess got up and went to the kitchen. Maybe, she thought, Nathan would like one, too.

Chapter 41

Marta had left the house that morning with no particular plan in mind other than to wander. She hadn't realized that proper sidewalks could be rare in some areas of this semirural neighborhood, but she had worn sturdy sneakers and given her habit of being alert to her surroundings, she wasn't particularly worried about being hit by a careless driver when she was forced to walk in the road. The sun was strong but the humidity low. Occasionally she passed another walker and they greeted each other with a nod and a smile or, more rarely, a verbal exchange. "Good morning." "Nice day." "Hello."

Mike had gotten back to Driftwood House the night before not long after Marta had retreated to their bedroom. He found her already tucked under the covers, reading a book on her Kindle. His hair was tousled from a day of ocean breeze and salty air; it made him look much younger than his forty-two years.

"What are you reading?" he had asked as he began to strip off his clothes and toss them into a corner.

It was a perfectly innocuous question, but it had struck Marta as annoying and interfering. She had bit back a snippy reply. "John McCain's last book," she said.

Mike had smiled. "I've been meaning to read that. What do you think of it?"

If I could be left alone to read it, Marta had thought, *I could form an intelligent opinion.* What she said was: "It's good."

Mike had gotten into bed, kissed her cheek, coughed a few times, and was asleep. But Marta's attention had been shattered. She abandoned the book and sat staring at the closed door, her mind racing with unhappy thoughts, until finally, more than an hour later, she had felt ready for sleep.

That morning Marta had woken with a dull headache. Mike was already up and whistling as he shrugged on his robe. "Another perfect day," he said brightly. He had gone off to shower and by the time he returned, Marta had left the house. She had not left a note saying where she had gone.

So, there she was, wandering along tree-lined roads, past quaint houses and stately homes and perfectly tended gardens but noting very little of the appealing scenery. Every so often a dog would bark from behind a fence; otherwise, the morning was quiet, allowing Marta to ponder the very reason for which the old friends had gathered this June. Marriage.

It was no great secret that marriage could be difficult to sustain. Each and every decision a husband or wife made, each and every word he or she said, affected the union. A person needed to know her own mind very, very clearly before participating with her partner in any decision more important than what to have for dinner. Wait, Marta thought. Even that decision should be made consciously. How many marriages had foundered on the rocks of faulty communication?

"You always order mushroom pizza. You know I don't really like mushrooms."

"Then why didn't you ever say anything?"

"I did! But you never listened, so I gave up."

"I'm not a mind reader, for God's sake!"

The sidewalk had ended again; with a glance over her shoulder, Marta stepped into the street. She knew she should have left Mike a note that morning. It was common courtesy. But communication in a marriage could so easily break down and when it did, it could be so difficult to get it going again. To reset the good dynamic took maturity, determination, and courage on the part of both partners.

A handsome older man lifted a hand in a wave from his front porch. Marta returned the greeting. She wondered if his wife was in their kitchen, sipping her morning coffee, waiting for her husband to return with the daily newspaper. She wondered if they were happy.

Marta and Mike had been happy. Until this pregnancy. No, Marta thought. Her dissatisfaction had begun before that, when she had looked around one day and realized that her own life—or what was left of it—was lacking. Could she possibly keep from Mike forever the dissatisfaction she felt about the negative turn her life had taken with this fourth pregnancy? And if she was able to stay silent, who would she be benefiting? Would she grow bitter and angry if she didn't speak what was in her heart? Would the marriage survive such deception?

The end of her marriage to Mike would mean the destruction of every aspect of the life they had built over the years, from the most minor bits like their shared preference for creamy over chunky peanut butter to the larger, more important matters like the charities they contributed to at the end of the year. It would mean irreparable damage to the children. It would mean major financial loss.

Suddenly, under the warm June sun, Marta shivered. She had known too many situations in which an otherwise rational husband or wife became brutally vindictive toward the soon-to-be ex-spouse. In spite of what she had implied to her friends, Mike was a powerful and well-connected lawyer. Would he attempt to punish her in a divorce settlement? Would she know how to fight back? But Mike would never be cruel. Or would he? Look at how Chris was treating Allison. Any of the friends would have said that Chris divorcing Allison for anything less than her taking to murder as a hobby was unthinkable.

Marta felt heartsick. How had it come to the point where she was imagining the end of the relationship that had meant more to her than any other? Maybe she was becoming clinically depressed. If she was still having such negative thoughts when she got back to New York after the wedding she would ask her PCP to prescribe an antidepressant that would be safe to take during a pregnancy. A pregnancy that was only one of the things that had triggered this unhappy mental and emotional state.

A young woman pushing a stroller was coming toward Marta. Marta didn't think she had it in her to greet this woman, to make a pleasant remark about her child. She would go back to the house, see what the others were up to, and have something to eat. Protein would be good. She could temporarily quell her sorrows with boiled eggs and turkey sausage. Marta made an about-face and at a faster pace began the walk back to Driftwood House. Of course, she had memorized the way.

Chapter 42

After a full hour at the beach, Allison decided to return to Driftwood House. She packed up her travel art kit and with one last appreciative look at the water, she set off. She would miss the Atlantic coastline when she returned to Chicago. The city that had become her home because of Chris. The city that might not remain her home. Chicago wasn't cheap. Her lawyer had been brutally honest about how a divorce would affect her economic status. In the marriage, Chris had handled the finances for the both of them. Allison was on a steep learning curve but with the help of a financial organizer recommended by her lawyer, she was slowly gaining confidence in her ability to live well on her own. Slowly. One step at a time.

"Successful expedition?" Marta asked when Allison came through the door that led from the back porch. She was sitting at the kitchen island with a cup of tea. Bess was with her, studying a series of paint chips. She had told Allison she was planning on doing some renovations to her condo in Portland.

"Yes. And guess who I saw again earlier? That big gray cat who mysteriously appeared in the dead tree. He was stalking something at the bottom of the yard by the azalea bushes but when he saw me he came trotting over, fell on his back, and demanded a belly rub! I really should try to find out if he has a home."

"And if he doesn't?" Marta queried.

Allison shrugged. "I don't know." She placed her sketchbook and kit on the dining table. "But I do know there's a reason art therapy exists. Flow activities can be hugely helpful in quieting a troubled mind. I feel downright positive at the moment."

"What's a flow activity?" Bess asked.

"I guess you could say it's something you're consciously doing," Allison said, "like playing a sport or planting a garden. It's something that challenges you, something that's rewarding in and of itself. Like drawing and painting is for me. I lose myself in the process. I'm concentrating, I'm enjoying what I'm doing, and the rest of the world just falls away for a while."

Bess nodded. "So, a flow activity is something that makes you happy."

"Right, but it's different from just leisure," Allison went on, "like watching TV or lying on a beach. Those things can make you feel good, but you're not the one producing the happiness. The TV show is making you laugh and the sun is making you feel warm and drowsy."

"I think athletes call it being 'in the zone,'" Marta explained. "Being so involved with running or swimming or skiing that absolutely nothing else exists but that moment and the challenges that moment brings."

"And I've heard some of my artist friends describe the state they get in when they're working as 'aesthetic rapture.'"

"Can I get that when I'm working?" Bess asked. "Because I totally love planning events." She smiled. "And picking paint colors."

Allison smiled. "Of course. You're lucky your work provides real happiness. I suppose pretty much any task might provide challenge and pleasure if you were inclined to find it."

"When you're shooting professionally," Bess asked, "do you lose yourself in the work?"

"Yes," Allison said, "but not to the extent I do when I'm creating images entirely on my own. I've got the client's vision to keep in mind. A well-informed client, one who knows his own mind, can be a joy to work with. On the other hand, a client who can't see past his own stubborn vision can be a nightmare."

"At least he's a client. And a nightmare client is better than no client." Bess laughed.

"I wouldn't know," Marta said.

The comment was made quietly, but Allison heard it.

"What do you do to get into the zone?" Bess asked Marta.

Marta laughed. "If I allowed myself to get into the zone I'd fall asleep for a week."

"No, really," Bess pressed. "Do you have a hobby?"

"I keep busy."

"You would have made a great lawyer, Marta," Bess commented. "You can be so evasive, saying something and saying nothing at the same time!"

"I didn't want to be a lawyer," Marta said dismissively. "I already told you I have no regrets about that. Regrets are foolish."

"They might be foolish," Allison said, "but they're universal. I doubt any human being over the age of ten is free of all regret."

"What's that old saying," Bess asked, "people rarely regret what they've done but often regret what they haven't done? Or is it the other way around?"

Allison smiled. "Whichever way it is, whenever I hear the word *regret* I immediately think of Édith Piaf singing that wonderful song, '*Non, Je Ne Regrette Rien.*' What a voice."

"What about you, Bess?" Marta asked. "Do you most regret things you've done or things you've left undone?"

"Me?" Bess's eyes widened. "Gosh, I don't know. I kind of regret having that second piece of pie last night because I had a sugar overload headache for a while. But it was awfully delicious so maybe I don't really regret it. And if I hadn't had that second piece of pie I probably would have been lying awake forever thinking about it so I probably would have regretted not having it."

"What I wouldn't give to live in your head, even for a day," Marta said musingly.

"I don't think anyone would survive five minutes in another person's head," Allison noted. "Assuming we retained our own consciousness for the duration. We'd be witnessing a completely different way of living a human life. We'd be so disoriented we'd— Well, it wouldn't be fun."

"Better the hell you know." Marta nodded.

Bess was frowning. "I don't understand. How, exactly, would that work, being in someone else's head?"

Marta rolled her eyes. Allison patted Bess's hand. "Don't worry about it," she said. "Is there any of that pie left or did you demolish it last night?"

Chapter 43

Dean and Mike had taken the baby to York's Wild Kingdom. Thomas was too young to appreciate the outing, which was clearly for the benefit of the men. Bumper cars. Butterfly exhibit. Merry-go-round. Greasy food. Chuck had asked Dean to bring him some fried dough.

Nathan was holed up in the den on the phone with his office. He had been very busy in the past few days and seemed a bit stressed, but when Bess had asked him if anything was amiss he had denied it. "The usual corporate craziness," he said. "Even those of us in communications get our wires crossed. Maybe especially those of us in communications."

The rest of the crowd was gathered once again on the back porch. It was perfect for lazing around, what with the shade provided by the roof, the spectacular views, and the comfortable furniture. Marta kept checking her phone; Bess assumed she was eager for word from her mother or from one of the kids. Chuck's legs were stretched out before him; his folded hands rested on his stomach. Allison, looking cool and collected in spite of the sultry weather, was sipping a glass of ice water and reading from one of the bridal magazines Bess had amassed.

"I've been meaning to ask what sort of wedding cake we have to look forward to," Chuck said.

"I couldn't decide on what kind of cake I wanted, so in the end I ordered three," Bess told him. "One classic vanilla cake with strawberry filling, one hazelnut, and one chocolate-chocolate mint."

Chuck grinned. "Mmmm. Three of my favorites," he said. "Something to dream about tonight."

"Speaking of weddings," Allison said, pointing to the magazine on her lap. "It says here that in general, more men than women want to be married. I wonder where the writer came up with that bit of information. This isn't a rag like that gossip magazine Chuck was reading, but it's not an academic journal, either."

Marta put her phone aside and laughed dryly. "I bet it's true. The benefits of marriage for a man are always larger than they are for a woman!"

"Oh, come on," Allison protested, "not always."

"Often, then. As late as the mid-nineteenth century in countries like England and the U.S. a married woman had no rights as an individual. The term used was *coverture*. Marriage voided a wife's separate legal identity." Marta shook her head. "And don't get me started on the practice of primogeniture, focusing all the family's money and property in the hands of the eldest son. Do you know how many mothers and daughters that nice little practice left in an economic mess?"

Bess opened her mouth to speak, but Marta went on, her voice more strident. "There are still countries where rape in marriage is legal! Where sattee, the burning of a widow on her husband's funeral pyre, is still seen as having significance!"

"Actually, I think sattee is illegal," Allison pointed out. "It still happens on occasion, but it's not a generally accepted practice."

Bess nodded. "Yeah, and that other stuff doesn't happen any longer, at least not here."

"It matters that it happens anywhere," Marta said forcefully. "Do you realize that in some cultures a married woman isn't allowed to leave the house without being accompanied by a male relation? What's the benefit of marriage for her? Security? More like prison!"

Bess frowned. "You're making me feel stupid for wanting to be married."

"Bess, you're too sensitive!" Chuck said. "Marta's just waxing political. By the way, does that article say anything about same-sex marriages? Or are those wedding magazines still skewed toward the heterosexual market?"

"Toward the heterosexual market mostly," Bess told him. "There are some publications, though, that cater to the homosexual market."

"How nice of them," Chuck commented dryly.

"I wonder if Chris will remarry," Allison said. "Surely every one of us has thought about that possibility."

"Unless he unloads the baggage he's carrying regarding his brother," Marta said, "that marriage would also be doomed to failure."

"We might never know if he remarries," Chuck said.

"What do you mean?" Bess asked.

"Chris has pretty much cut us out of his life already," Chuck noted. "After a trauma, it's not uncommon for people to turn their backs on those from their old life and try to begin anew. Whether that works or not I can't say—I guess it depends on lots of factors—but in Chris's case I wouldn't be surprised if we've heard the last of him." Chuck shook his head. "I can't believe those words just came out of my mouth."

"I never thought—" Bess realized she could not finish the statement aloud.

"That anything bad would happen to any of us?" Marta's tone was mocking.

"No," Bess replied stoutly, "that's not what I was going to say at all." But in fact, it had been what she was going to say.

Chuck rose from his seat. "I want to pop into that little bookstore in town, Fine Print Booksellers. Anyone want to come along?"

"I will," Allison said. "Maybe they have a title by Elizabeth J. Duncan I haven't read yet."

"Do you know that on average men grow more content in marriage while women grow less so?" Marta announced, the moment Chuck and Allison were gone, pointing to yet another of the magazines Bess had accumulated. "An article in that one says that a full two-thirds of divorces after the age of forty are initiated by women. Seems a bleak topic for a wedding magazine to talk about, but there it is in black and white."

Bess restrained a sigh. She had had enough talk about marriage, the good, the bad, and the ugly. Before she could say so, Marta received a text. She reached for her phone, read the text, and put the phone aside again.

"Nothing important?" Bess asked.

"Just a catty update on one of the women on the community board. She's been talking about leaving her husband."

"Was he unfaithful?" Bess asked. It seemed like a reasonable first question.

"No," Marta said. "He's fidelity personified."

"Did she fall in love with someone else?" A reasonable second question.

"Nope," Marta said. "And Ben isn't violent or a drinker or a gambler. He's a successful, well-adjusted, even-tempered guy."

Bess shook her head. "Then why does this woman want to leave her husband?"

"Because she's unhappy in the marriage."

"But why?" Bess pressed. "What's wrong with—"

"You were going to say what's wrong with her, weren't you?" Marta snapped.

Bess blushed. "Yeah, I guess I was."

"Nothing is wrong with Violet," Marta said forcefully. "She's unhappy in her marriage for reasons that are real to her if mysterious to her friends. Unhappiness, assuming it's genuine and not just a brief, irritating itch, is a valid reason for making a change."

"Still, her friends must be so confused," Bess pressed. "What can you say to help her?"

"You mean, to talk her out of a divorce?" Marta asked. "Pretty much every one of her friends think she's being incredibly stupid. They've told her that she and her son will suffer financially, no matter how good a settlement she gets. Some of them have decided that Violet's wanting to leave is just a whim. Her best friend, Rowan, reminded her that to some extent everyone is dissatisfied in their marriage and that she should just accept that fact and carry on. Of course," Marta pointed out, "Rowan is seriously miserable in her own marriage so I wouldn't trust any advice she's giving."

"And you?" Bess asked. "What do you say to Violet?"

Marta shrugged. "I support her. I believe she has the right to make her own decisions."

Bess wondered. Marta was often flippant and provocative, but at the moment she sounded downright cold. "Marta," she ventured, "is everything okay between you and Mike?"

"Of course," Marta replied quickly. "Why would you ask?"

Bess tried to choose her words carefully, something she often wasn't very good at doing. "It seems to me you're championing this woman's decision to leave her husband, so I can't help but think . . ."

"I'm not championing anything," Marta snapped. "All I'm saying is that everyone has a right to make her own choices. And no one needs to hear advice from people whose own lives aren't in perfect shape."

"But no one's life is in perfect shape," Bess exclaimed, "so that would mean that no one is equipped to give advice, but how could we live without it? How would children learn anything if someone wasn't suggesting they do A and not do B if they want to succeed and be well-liked?"

"Sometimes talking to you is like—" Marta laughed. "Forget it."

"Sorry," Bess mumbled. "I didn't mean to make you upset. I hope that your friend is okay, whatever happens."

"And I'm sorry if I sounded snappish." Marta rose from her seat. "I'm going to lie down for a while. I didn't sleep well last night."

"Is it the mattress?" Bess asked worriedly. "I could—"

Marta cut her off. "You could what? Buy a new mattress? Bess, don't be ridiculous. You're not responsible for everything. Besides, the mattress had nothing to do with it."

Alone on the back porch, Bess put her head in her hands and sighed. For the first time ever, the idea of elopement sounded wonderful.

Chapter 44

Marta hadn't entirely lied to Bess. Something did hurt but it was her head, not her back, and the pain wasn't physical. She had gone to her room to reset her attitude, but to no avail. Before half an hour had passed she was in the kitchen making a cup of tea.

Bess was nowhere to be seen. Marta felt bad for snapping at her. She just felt so smothered in Driftwood House. She wished she could run off to Portland for a night, but married women didn't just go off on their own, not without consequences. Some marriages might allow for solo overnights and even lengthy vacations, but not Mike and Marta's marriage. Besides, Marta knew that her own worst enemy would travel with her. Like Milton's Satan had so memorably said, "*Which way I fly is Hell; myself am Hell.*"

Marta heard footsteps on the stairs from the second floor and a moment later, Allison appeared, her travel art kit slung over her shoulder. She set the kit on the island counter and went to the fridge, where she retrieved a bottle of water.

"May I ask you a personal question?" she said. "I know this is out of the blue."

Marta's stomach dropped. *Did you sleep with Chris when we were in college?* "Yes," she said. "All right."

Allison tucked the bottle of water into a pocket of her bag. "Did you ever have a miscarriage?"

Marta breathed a silent sigh of relief. "No," she said. "My pregnancies were ridiculously trouble free."

But everything changed. Hadn't she said as much to Bess? Suddenly, Marta was seized by a feeling of panic. Why should this
fourth pregnancy necessarily come to an easy fruition like the first
three had? People's luck ran out. At some point in a person's life
things could go bad and they could continue to go bad. That's just
the way it was.

"Marta?" Allison said. "You okay?"

"Yeah, sorry. My mind went off there for a moment. . . ." Marta
managed a smile. "It's apt to do that a lot lately. Old age."

"Really, Marta," Allison scolded, "we're only a few months apart
and I certainly don't consider myself old."

"Sorry." Marta shrugged.

"Look," Allison went on, "I would never ask this in front of Bess,
but I've wondered if you had trouble bonding with your children
when they were born. I know it's not uncommon for a mother to have
some difficulty at first. I've read all about postpartum depression."

"With Sam," Marta told her, "it was just like it was supposed to
be. The second I saw her I was head over heels in love. Maybe it
was because she was my first child and I was so relieved the birth
had gone well. Then again I know women who had trouble connect-
ing with their first-born and chalked it up to outright terror at what
lay ahead."

Allison smiled. "I wouldn't be surprised if instant terror was far
more common than instant adoration."

"With Leo," Marta went on, "it was different. Remember how I
developed a fever right after he was born? That tiny hospital near
our ski lodge didn't have the greatest rating in the country. I hardly
knew who I was, let alone who the baby was. But once the fever
passed I was duly in love." Martha smiled. "And then there was
Troy. I admit that by baby number three much of the novelty had
worn off—do I sound like a terribly cold person for saying that?—
but I was smitten. Calmly, without obsessively cooing over his little
nose and his little toes."

Allison smiled briefly. "I was so looking forward to . . . to the
little nose and the little toes."

"I'm sorry," Marta said. "I really am. And I totally understand why you wouldn't want to talk about this in front of Bess. She'd be horrified to learn I didn't fall instantly in love with Leo in spite of my off-the-charts fever."

"I don't know how she maintains that innocence. Is it purposeful? Or is it, well, natural, for lack of a better word? You'd think that by this time in her life she wouldn't be so shocked by stuff the rest of us accept as part of the human condition." Allison shrugged. "Maybe Bess is the lucky one among us. It might be nice to have a seemingly never-ending ability to bounce back after adversity as hopeful and optimistic as ever."

"Has she ever experienced real adversity?" Marta wondered. "She was pretty broke for a few years after college, but none of us were making any real money."

"I don't know," Allison admitted. "Her parents and siblings are all alive and well. She never had her heart broken, not really. And she's always been perfectly healthy." Allison picked up her travel art kit and slung it over her shoulder. "I want to catch the light before it fades. Maybe my feline companion will make an appearance. I've decided he must belong to someone because he looks awfully well-fed. Maybe today I'll ask around the neighborhood."

When Allison had gone, Marta continued to sit alone in the kitchen. She suspected that Allison's questions about miscarriages and maternal love were part of the healing process and not just idle curiosity. And the questions had made her think. How *would* she feel about this baby when he or she was born? Would she love the child at first sight? At second or third? There were women whose postpartum depression was so bad it prevented them from thinking normally for months after the birth. Some women even experienced postpartum psychosis. Given her troubled feelings about the pregnancy, would she be more likely to suffer an emotional breakdown after the baby's birth?

Marta rubbed her temples. If only she could get away on her own for just one night without giving rise to outrageous speculation. It wouldn't necessarily solve anything, but it might help her achieve a calmer state of mind. Then again, she might return to Driftwood House more miserable than before.

"Marta?"

It was Mike. "Oh," she said. "Hi. I didn't hear you come in."

He came forward, a frown on his face. "Do you have a headache? I could rub your temples for you. Do you want a cold cloth?"

"No," Marta said, mustering a smile. "Thanks. I'm fine. Just fine."

Chapter 45

Allison was curled up in the living area, sipping a glass of wine. She had had a very productive afternoon sketching. Massive tangles of green and brown seaweed, glistening in the sun. Shifting clouds. Best, a strikingly beautiful woman with long silver hair, had obligingly agreed to let Allison make a quick character study of her as she sat perched on a particularly interesting rock formation at the top of the beach. Allison was looking forward to reviewing the sketches and working up one or more into a finished drawing.

Bess suddenly appeared from the direction of the den, dramatically wiping her forehead with the back of her hand. "I'm so relieved," she announced. "The children's performer just confirmed; she had a bad cold and was afraid she'd have to cancel the wedding. She's doing balloon animals and crowns, magic tricks, and face painting. The kids will love it."

"Why didn't you ask one of your nieces or nephews to be in the wedding party?" Marta asked. She had just strolled in from the direction of the stairs to the second floor.

Allison knew Marta was baiting Bess, who was not the warm and fuzzy person with children that she was with adults. "It's all right, Bess," Allison said stoutly. "No one is criticizing you. Besides, the kids will have a much better time if they don't have to worry about messing up fancy clothes."

"That's exactly what I thought," Bess said as she dropped into one of the cozy upholstered armchairs. Her face took on an expression Allison knew all too well. Bess was about to come out with a doozy of a comment or question.

"Allison," Bess began, "do you ever think that, I don't know, that maybe you weren't meant to have a baby? That maybe God decided it wouldn't be a good idea even if you and Chris thought it would be?"

Marta looked apoplectic. Allison shot her a look that told her to keep quiet.

"As much as I object to the idea of being a powerless plaything of the gods," Allison said to Bess, "yes, I did wonder if maybe . . ." She laughed a bit wildly. "I can hardly admit what I thought! After all, my infertility was officially unexplained." And that in itself had caused trouble. Weeks after the miscarriage, crazed with grief, Chris had accused Allison of never wanting to get pregnant in the first place. "All those years when no one could explain why you didn't get pregnant. It was *you*. You were the reason. You willed your infertility!"

Marta snorted in disgust. "The whole idea is ridiculous. And if a Higher Power did intervene to keep Allison from getting pregnant all those years, how do you explain the fact that she finally *did* get pregnant? The HP messed up? He—because it would have to be a He—looked away for a second and oops! Now Allison is pregnant so HP arranges for an accident to clean up his mess? That's utter nonsense."

Allison nodded. "Nevertheless, I can't help but think about the mind/body connection. You can't deny that the mind is powerful enough to cause a person to get sick or to get well. People talk themselves into and out of all sorts of situations in life, from falling in love with a totally inappropriate person like a convicted serial killer to achieving an amazing feat like lifting a car off a person pinned beneath it. Maybe my unconscious mind, knowing that Chris's obsession with his brother would interfere with our raising a healthy child, kept me from getting pregnant. Until it didn't. I know. It doesn't make sense and human beings hate when things don't make sense."

"So, they create entire systems of mythology and metaphysical nonsense and comfort themselves with outlandish notions of elaborate rewards after death." Marta frowned. "Too bad avoidance doesn't work for everyone."

"I believe in God," Bess said defiantly. "Even if the idea of Heaven is outlandish, I don't see what's wrong with believing in the outlandish. What better sort of thing to believe in? And I don't think I'm avoiding the bad stuff. I just don't think that bad stuff is all there is in the end."

Allison smiled kindly. "If believing in something outrageous brings you a degree of comfort in this difficult world, good for you."

"Just don't try to push your outrageous beliefs on others," Marta added. "Like me. I prefer to face life head-on with no illusions to lull me into a stupor of complacency."

"You know I would never try to make you think about life the way I think about it," Bess protested. "I respect your choices."

"I'm not sure belief is a choice," Marta said quietly.

But Allison heard her friend.

"I'd better start dinner," Bess announced. "Tonight, we're having chicken pot pies from Mainely Poultry. And a salad on the side for the healthy among us."

Marta rose to follow Bess. "I'll make the salad," she said. "One of my biggest successes as a mother has been getting my kids to enjoy eating salad."

When her friends had gone off, Allison wondered. Chris blaming her inability to get pregnant on the power of her will. His obsession with his brother. The way he had abandoned her in her time of need. All of these things and more gave weight to the argument that to reconcile with Chris under any circumstances would be crazy. But what if Chris was to conquer his demons and they *were* to reconcile, true loves reunited? Would she be able to sustain the relationship without slipping back into an attitude of resentment and anger? Would tension invariably creep in and spoil a pleasant meal in one of their favorite restaurants in Little Italy or a walk along the Lakefront Trail or even just an evening home watching a new favorite television show on Netflix? Any time Chris displayed concern for her safety or well-being, would she worry he was once again trying to control her in a misguided effort to assert mastery over the chaotic world that had snatched his little brother away so brutally? Whenever she displayed her independence, something Chris had fought against from the very start of their relationship—she knew that now—would he accuse her of betraying their bond? Would he walk away again or threaten to?

It seemed possible, maybe even probable. A reconciliation might have to exclude a revived romantic relationship.

Allison frowned. Why was she even thinking about reconciliation? In spite of the love she bore Chris, it wasn't what she wanted, not now.

It really wasn't.

Chapter 46

Bess was in the den the next morning after breakfast while the others were enjoying the good weather. She was due to FaceTime with Kara in a few minutes. Until then she was tapping a pencil against the edge of the desk in what was even to her an annoying tattoo.

Not much about this reunion was going as she had hoped it would, not with tempers flaring, people taking offense where none was meant, partners criticizing each other face-to-face. What must Nathan think of her friends? They certainly weren't matching the description Bess had painted for him. They were showing themselves not as a harmonious unit but as a divisive, bad-tempered lot. The charms Bess had selected to give to her friends the night of the wedding were decorated with the image of an anchor. The anchor symbolized stability, trust, and assurance. How did that symbol reflect some of the behavior she had witnessed these past few days?

Bess looked at her computer screen. Time for Kara. Bess was looking forward to getting her assistant's impression of the favors she had ordered for the wedding. Each guest would receive a small, rectangular box made of naturally weathered wood. Inside the box, he would find a bar of soap made by two sisters who worked from their home in nearby Biddeford. It was, Bess thought, a gift both practical and attractive.

"Your favors arrived," Kara informed her boss. Her tone was wry.

Kara showed Bess four glass coasters with the names BETTANY AND NED inscribed in red glitter across each.

"Have you ever seen anything so tacky and impractical?" she asked with a laugh. "How do you balance a glass on a lump of glitter? Good news is that the soaps you ordered from Reverie are here and they're lovely."

"Those aren't even our names!" Bess cried, horrified.

"It was obviously just a mix-up in mailing," Kara said easily. "Some spacey assistant put the wrong address on the wrong box, nothing more."

"But this is a disaster!" *A storm to shake up our complacency . . .*

"Look, Bess, relax." Kara spoke sharply. "It's just a mix-up. The wooden boxes are already on the way. Now, I'm ending the call and when I next touch base all will be well. Goodbye."

The screen went blank. Bess realized that she was breathing heavily. She knew she was overreacting—the problem really wasn't a problem at all—but . . .

Bess heard the front door open and footsteps cross the foyer. She wanted to see a friendly face. She hurried from the den to find that the friendly face belonged to Chuck. He was carrying a bag from the local bookstore.

"What's wrong?" he asked immediately. "You look agitated."

Bess told him about the glittery coasters. "Kara said she's handled it, but . . ."

"Pre-wedding jitters take all forms," Chuck said. "Come on, let's go sit out on the back porch. It's too nice a day to be inside."

When they were settled side by side in two of the white wicker chairs, Bess turned to her friend. "Chuck," she said, "are you happier being married to Dean than you were when you were an unmarried but committed couple? It's just that so many people say that marriage is just a piece of paper, a bit of legal mumbo jumbo no one really needs."

"What's going on, Bess?" Chuck asked with a frown. "Is it more than just pre-wedding jitters?"

Bess sighed. "A few days ago, I was fine with the idea of getting married," she said. "More than fine, I was elated. Now . . . It's not that I don't love Nathan, I do. Nothing about my feelings for him have changed. It's just . . ."

"It's just that ever since Allison told you the truth about her divorce you've been having second thoughts. And you're using her traumatic tale and the silly mix-up with the coasters as an excuse to consider canceling the wedding."

Bess felt a rush of relief. Chuck was so clear-sighted. "I guess you're right," she admitted, feeling a bit foolish. "I just wish Allison hadn't told us the whole awful story!"

Chuck smiled. "But curiosity was killing you, Bess. More than any of us you wanted to know."

"Yeah, so I could fix things for Allison and Chris." Bess laughed ruefully. "What arrogance! I can't believe I really thought I could bring about a miracle just by having them both at my wedding."

"In someone else's case, it would be arrogance, but not in yours, Bess."

"What then? Stupidity?"

"No," Chuck said firmly. "Good-heartedness. A genuine desire for your friends to reconcile." Chuck took Bess's hands in his and looked her square in the eye. "Bess, you're meant to be marrying Nathan. I know it. Don't let Allison's experience put you off living your own life. That would be—well, to be blunt, that *would* be stupid. Promise?"

Bess smiled gratefully. "Promise."

"Good. So, what tantalizing meal do you have planned for us tonight?"

"A simple pasta primavera with salad and bread."

Chuck frowned. "No dessert?"

Bess laughed. "Would I do that to you? Of course, there's dessert!"

Chapter 47

Marta shot awake. Her mother's ringtone. She threw off the sheet, leapt out of bed, and snatched the phone from the top of the dresser, where it was charging.

"What's wrong?" she asked, rubbing her temple.

"Don't panic, everyone's fine," her mother replied. "It's just that Troy had a nightmare around three and we had a devil of a time getting him back to sleep. He's been awake again since five—your father and I have been up with him—wanting to talk to his mother. I held off until a decent hour before calling."

"Put him on," Marta directed. "Troy? Tell Mommy what you saw in your dream."

"I saw a monster," he said. "It had all these eyes and they were red." There was a little catch in Troy's voice, but he soldiered on. "There were long things sticking out from him and they were waving at me, but not in a nice way."

"You know monsters can't hurt you," Marta said soothingly. "I know when they pop into your head at night they seem pretty scary and it's okay to wake up and yell at them to go away and leave you alone. And they will go away because in the end they're make-believe." Marta frowned. Or something like that. She was talking gibberish.

"Okay, Mommy," Troy said. "I'm going now."

Suddenly, Marta was back on the phone with her mother.

"He hasn't watched any TV he shouldn't have or seen any images on the computer that might have frightened him," Mrs. Kennedy assured her daughter. "At least, I don't think that he has."

"You can't police every moment. Does he want to talk to me again?"

"Troy?" her mother called. "Do you want to say goodbye to Mommy?"

Marta heard her younger son call, "Bye, Mommy!"

"Your father is making pancakes. I guess all is going to be well."

"Thanks, Mom," Marta said. "I'll check in later."

Marta turned toward the bed to see that Mike was just waking. "What's wrong?" he mumbled.

"Nothing. Troy had a bad dream, but he's fine now."

Mike raised himself against the pillows. "Leo better not have been showing him those creepy video games he plays, the ones with the mutant beasts with six eyeballs on stalks and claws like broadswords."

"That's it! It was Leo. Darn the kid."

Mike stretched his arms over his head. "I'm sure he didn't scare his brother on purpose. Well, almost sure. I'll have a talk with him when we get home."

Marta felt an unexpected and very pleasant surge of appreciation course through her. "You're a good dad," she said feelingly.

"You're a good mom. Hey, here's an idea. Let's spend the day on our own, drive somewhere pretty, have a lobster roll, hang out by the water."

Marta considered. Not once since they had arrived at Driftwood House had they taken time to be alone together. Maybe that was exactly what was needed. And maybe, just maybe, she would then find the courage to be honest about how finding herself pregnant again at the very time in her life she was needing to make a change was causing her to feel.

"Sounds like a plan," she said. "The others can do without us for a few hours."

"Good. We'll leave right after breakfast. Bess said she was making waffles this morning and I don't want to miss those."

* * *

To Marta's surprise, Mike was the one to suggest that for the duration of their date neither of them talk about the new baby or the kids. "Let's just focus on us," he suggested. Marta had felt an immediate loosening of the anger and tension that had been building up inside her. Maybe, she had thought, smiling at her husband and fastening her seat belt, maybe today they would turn a corner and head back in the direction of the contented marriage they had so recently left behind.

Things went well. They took back roads rather than the busy Route 1; they stopped at an antique shop that looked particularly promising (Mike collected old tools); they visited the famous Nubble Lighthouse in York; they decided to splurge on lunch at M.C. Perkins Cove in Ogunquit. Well, Mike decided. He had to persuade Marta, but she didn't really protest.

After a delightful meal of a watermelon salad with feta cheese and pickled red onions for Marta, and M.C.'s famous cheeseburger and fries for Mike, they picked their way to a spot on the rocks that tumbled into the rolling Atlantic.

"This is fantastic," Mike said. "We really should spend more time just you and me."

Marta smiled. "Like the good old days?" she said.

There was no one to demand their attention. For the time being, neither of them was needed by friends or family or colleagues. They sat side by side in comfortable silence. The sun was warm on their skin. Seagulls swooped overhead, cawing their raucous caws. The water glittered like a proverbial scattering of diamonds. And after a time, calmed by the beauty of a June day in southern Maine, Marta realized she was ready to tell Mike the truth. They had agreed not to talk about the pregnancy today, but this was different. This was something even bigger. She *knew* she could trust Mike with her feelings. She had always known that. He had never seriously disappointed her. Not since they had been married. He would help her as he always had.

"Mike," she began. "There's been something on my mind, something I think I need help with, and I—"

Mike turned abruptly to face her. "Sorry, Marta," he said. "Did you say something? I was distracted by that schooner. Do you see it? What a beauty!"

And as quickly as the impulse to speak had come, it left. The moment was lost. "Yes," Marta said carefully. "It's beautiful. Let's go back to Driftwood House now. I'm feeling tired. Maybe it was waking up to that call from my mother. I was in the middle of a dream."

"Of course," Mike said quickly. "You need your sleep."

Because you're pregnant. Again. It's what you do. Have babies.

They climbed to their feet. Mike took Marta's elbow as they made their way over the rocks toward the parking lot, though Marta, always sure-footed, was perfectly capable of managing on her own. Mike should know that, she thought. But she did not pull away.

Chapter 48

"It's me," Allison said.

Her assistant, Greg, laughed. "I assumed. How's it going?"

Allison spent the next few minutes giving Greg an edited rundown of the happenings at Driftwood House and then asked him for a detailed rundown of what was going on at the studio. After a moment or two Allison noted that life back in Chicago was chugging along very nicely without her, and suddenly she realized just how tired she had been for the past two years. Being on vacation was good.

Greg went on to outline a new project they had been offered; earlier Allison had read the job scope he had forwarded. The money was good and the client was one she had successfully worked with before. "Let's accept," she said when Greg had given his take on the work. "And why don't you take the lead on the project," she suggested. "You're more than ready and you'd be doing me a favor."

Greg was thrilled and grateful for the opportunity. "You won't regret your decision," he promised before they ended the call. Allison felt sure that she wouldn't. She wondered if she might like a partner in the business sooner rather than later. It was something to consider going forward, as was the possibility of leaving Chicago for good. She could, for instance, move back to the Boston area. She would be closer to Marta and Bess; she could visit either one whenever the impulse struck. It had been so long since she had been in charge of her own life. Since Chris's walking out she had been struggling to believe she had the competency to make decisions on her own, ones that benefited her before others.

But there was time later to think about such big changes. She decided to seek out Chuck, Dean, and the baby. She had noticed that Chuck and Dean were very affectionate toward each other and it pleased her. She wondered how the men would deal with a big crisis—and they would have to at some point, every couple did. She suspected they would stand or fall together.

After a brief search, she found the Fortunato-Williams family camped out near the bottom of the stairs that led down to the beach. Like any family that included a baby, they had brought with them an enormous amount of gear. Allison fought back a wave of sadness. She had once looked forward to happy days at the beach with Chris and their child.

"May I join you?" she asked brightly. If you acted happy, you might just become happy. Or so it was said.

"Of course!" the men chorused.

Allison sank onto the large blanket spread beneath a colorful sun umbrella. She noted the two diaper bags. A cooler. A stack of folded towels. A massive pile of toys. The baby was propped in a traveling seat of some sort, wearing a large sun hat and wee sunglasses. "How's Thomas today?" she asked.

"Chillin'," Chuck said. "I think he's going to be a beach bum when he grows up."

"What will you do when people start to call him Tom or Tommy?" Allison asked.

"Correct them," Dean said. "I hate when people assume a nickname."

"But if Thomas doesn't mind?" Allison asked.

"It's his life, or it will be," Chuck said firmly. "If he wants to be Tom or Tommy, that's his call."

Dean frowned, but let the matter drop and reached for one of the three tubes of sunblock by his feet.

"So, what have you been up to this morning?" Chuck asked, offering Allison a bottle of water.

"I've been thinking about my future," Allison replied. "For example, do I want to stay on in Chicago? Do I want to take on a partner in business?"

"Good questions," Chuck said. "Any answers?"

"Not yet. But at least I'm *asking* myself the questions."

Dean nodded. "Step one, often the most difficult."

"And you know what else?" Allison said suddenly. "If things continue to go well with the business, I could even take a leave of absence to work on a book project. I have a few in mind, as a matter of fact, all of which would require me to travel. I even know an editor who said she's eager to offer me a contract on delivery of a solid proposal."

Dean nodded. "That sounds awesome."

"Indeed, it does."

"You know, there are very few positive things about this divorce," Allison went on musingly. "Very few. But one positive thing might be the freedom it will afford me. An all-consuming thing like a book project would have been out of the question while I was married to Chris. I would never have left him for months on end. And Chris . . ."

"Say it, Allison," Chuck said gently.

Allison gave him a grateful smile. "Chris wouldn't have allowed it. He would have been nice about it; in fact, his forbidding me to go away on my own would have been neatly disguised as a very strong suggestion, one based in concern for my safety."

"It makes me angry to hear this." Dean frowned. "I'm sorry, Allison, but it does."

Chuck sighed. "Chris isn't a bad man, Dean. You have to understand that."

Allison laid a hand on Dean's arm. "I know hearing about his control over me is difficult, but I let him have that control. Even when I began to understand that the dynamic wasn't healthy, I didn't try to put a stop to it. Not really."

"Relationships," Dean said with a wry smile. "Can't live with 'em, can't live without 'em."

At that moment, Thomas let out a wail that caused all three of the adults to jump.

"Snack time!" Chuck announced.

Allison laughed and got to her feet. "I think I'll go back to the house for one myself. Thanks, guys. See you later."

Chapter 49

"Anyone for a glass of fresh brewed iced tea?" Nathan asked.

"Yes, please," Dean said, moving toward the kitchen. "It's about caffeine time."

"If you're tired," Chuck said, "you could join Thomas in a nap." He was sitting at the dining table, idly flipping through the local paper. "Nothing nastier in here than a drunk and disorderly tourist at one of the bed and breakfast places in town."

"That's Kennebunkport," Bess said with a smile. "Iced tea, Chuck?"

"Sure."

He rose from his chair and what happened next happened so quickly, Bess wasn't quite sure how to describe it afterward. One moment Chuck was firmly on his feet. The next he was hurtling in the direction of the occasional table that marked the edge of the living area.

"Chuck!" she cried as Dean dashed forward.

Somehow Chuck managed to stop his forward motion before he hit the floor, but not before his head made contact with the edge of the occasional table. Dean grabbed his arm and helped him to stand.

"I'm such a klutz," Chuck said with a weak laugh.

"You're bleeding." Dean's voice was tight.

"Head wounds bleed a lot, don't panic." Chuck leaned closer to the mirror over the offending table. "It's not too deep, but I probably should have it stitched."

"You might have a concussion!" Bess said worriedly. "Should I call an ambulance?"

"No need," Chuck replied, turning away from the mirror.

"This is all my fault," Bess went on. "I should have made sure the edges of that rug were properly held down. I know there's some two-sided tape somewhere in the den. I'll go look right now!"

"It was an accident, Bess," Chuck said firmly. "It was no one's fault, certainly not the rug's."

"Can we leave Thomas with you while we go to the local emergent care?" Dean asked, already moving toward the door.

"Of course, you can," Nathan said. "He's in good hands."

"We'll be back as soon as possible," Dean said unnecessarily as he and Chuck left the house, Dean still holding Chuck's arm.

"Have the chocolate ice cream ready," Chuck called over his shoulder. "My mom always brought out chocolate ice cream when one of us got a boo-boo."

Bess turned to Nathan. "Do you think he'll be okay?" Her heart was still pounding uncomfortably.

"He left under his own steam," Nathan said, giving her hand a reassuring squeeze. "He'll be fine."

Heavy footsteps on the stairs to the back porch announced that Mike had returned. "Where are Chuck and Dean off to?" he asked casually. "I just saw them driving off. I waved, but they didn't see me."

"Chuck stumbled and cut his head on that occasional table," Nathan explained. "He says it's nothing much but needed stitching."

"Yikes," Mike said. "Dean will take good care of him, I'm sure. They leave the baby here?"

"Yes," Bess told him. "Where's Marta?"

Mike shrugged. "No idea. The minute I turned off the engine she got out of the car and headed in the direction of the beach. We came home early because she said she was tired but . . ." Mike laughed. "Marta is her own woman. I gave up years ago trying to . . . Well, I never did try to keep track of her. I've always loved the fact that she's so independent. Anyway, see you guys later."

Mike lifted a hand in a wave and headed for the stairs.

"Do you think things are all right between Mike and Marta?" Bess whispered when he was out of sight.

Nathan sighed. "Now don't go imagining trouble, Bess."

"I'm not imagining anything," Bess protested. She felt anger course through her and she didn't like it. Chuck's fall; Marta's moods; Allison's unhappiness. "I just use my eyes and ears."

"I'm sorry," Nathan said. He reached for her and Bess hesitated for a moment before going to him. "Your intuition isn't to be questioned."

"It's okay," Bess murmured, her cheek pressed against Nathan's chest. "I know you just don't want me to worry unnecessarily."

"I don't, but it's wrong of me to tell you what to think or what to feel. Why do we men do that? It's a stupid knee-jerk thing. I'm sorry."

"You're forgiven." Bess pulled away from her fiancé. There was something she needed to know. "Nathan," she said. "What do you really think of my friends? Be honest. I can take it." At least, she thought that she could.

"I like them," Nathan said promptly. "They're proving human beings and that makes me more comfortable than if they were the paragons of virtue you'd made them out to be."

"I did?" Bess asked, eyes wide.

Nathan smiled. "I'm exaggerating. Don't worry, Bess. At least, not about me."

"Okay. But I'd better check the freezer for chocolate ice cream. I'd hate to disappoint Chuck."

Chapter 50

It was after three o'clock when Marta finally returned to Driftwood House. She had gone to the beach and tried to find some peace of mind after her failed date with Mike, but instead all she had found was a depression of spirits.

A stupid schooner.

The moment she came through the door of the back porch, Marta noted Chuck and Dean next to each other on the love seat and the others grouped around them. There was a small, neat bandage on Chuck's forehead.

"What happened to you?" Marta asked as she joined her friends.

Chuck explained his accident.

"Will there be a scar?" Bess asked worriedly.

Chuck gingerly touched his forehead. "I doubt it. The kid who did the stitching did a good job. I say 'kid' because he looked about twelve years old."

Marta looked toward Mike. He gave her a smile, but it didn't seem to reach his eyes. The room was heavy with a sense of tension. Or maybe, Marta thought, the tension was all hers.

"Dean and I have something to tell you. Now it's nothing tragic," Chuck went on quickly, looking specifically at Bess, "so don't freak out. It's just we'd rather you know the truth than have you waste time wondering if your old pal Chuck is getting clumsy for no good reason."

"If Chuck hadn't stumbled this afternoon," Dean went on, "we would have waited until after the wedding before telling you. Not that the fall was necessarily anything more than an accident . . ."

Chuck looked to Dean and the two men clasped hands. "About four months ago I was diagnosed with Parkinson's disease," Chuck said matter-of-factly. "There's no doubt about it; I had a second and a third opinion."

Bess immediately burst into tears. Nathan put his arm around her and murmured a soothing word. Marta's lips compressed into a frown. Allison sighed and put a hand to her mouth.

"What does this mean?" Mike demanded. "What can we expect?"

"Ever the fix-it guy," Chuck said brusquely. "You can expect the same old Chuck." Then he shook his head. "Sorry. I didn't mean to be short. Sometimes it gets the better of me, this new reality. . . ."

"Why don't you outline the basics for everyone," Dean suggested calmly. "How the disease was diagnosed, what to expect as it progresses, the common treatment options. Facts often help calm frayed nerves."

Chuck nodded and for the next fifteen minutes he spoke eloquently about his situation. "I've just about fully accepted this," he said finally. "It's the lot I've been given, but not the whole lot. I've also got a husband and a child who mean everything to me, and a career I love and dear friends and family to whom I'm devoted. No pity allowed, please."

"We're dealing with this as a team," Dean went on. "We told Chuck's family when we were all together last week on the Cape, we told my family before we left for the east coast, and we'll tell our friends in L.A. when we get home. We have a great support system. We'll be okay."

"Of course, we will," Chuck said brightly. "What I'm really worried about is ruining the wedding pictures what with this unsightly bandage on my forehead."

Bess's tears broke out anew. Nathan tightened his hold on her shoulders.

"Come on, Bess," Dean urged, "stop the waterworks. You'll give yourself a headache going on like that."

Until then Marta hadn't spoken. "I'm sorry, Chuck," she said now, her voice tight. "This sucks for the both of you. But of all the people I know, you two are probably the best equipped to handle the situation with grace." Marta smiled a pained smile. "No pressure there at all! Sorry."

"Grace under fire, isn't that the expression?" Chuck said, with a pained smile of his own. "Keep calm and carry on. And hide the messy breakdowns from the eyes of the world."

"Chris doesn't know, does he?" Allison asked. "It's just that . . ."

"He'd want to know." Bess's words came out muffled; at the same time as she was speaking she was busy blowing her nose and wiping her eyes.

"We haven't been in touch," Chuck said. "Well, you guys know that. I could let him know but honestly, if he's not interested in continuing the friendship it seems sort of harsh or at the very least odd just to drop the news on him. Hey, Chris, if you care, I've got this illness. Bye."

Allison nodded. "I see your point. Anyway, if he doesn't care enough to keep up with his friends he doesn't deserve to know about their lives."

"I wouldn't go that far," Chuck argued.

"Nor would I," Mike added.

"I'm with Allison," Marta said.

Nathan suddenly let go of Bess's shoulder and stood. "I don't know about you all, but I could use a drink."

"Make mine a neat whiskey," Chuck said. "It's not five o'clock but what the hell."

Marta briefly put a hand to her head; it was beginning to ache. No one got through life unscathed by nasty surprises. She looked at Mike; he was still wearing his determined, fix-it face, a face that masked the great love he had for his friends and family. Why couldn't she allow him to comfort and advise her at this difficult moment? She had never had trouble turning to him when in need—not that she was often in need of support—so what made this moment in time so different from all that had gone before?

Nathan returned with a large tray on which sat a bottle of good whiskey, a soda dispenser, a small bowl of ice, and several glasses.

"Better than a Saint Bernard," Dean pronounced.

Marta folded her hands in her lap so tightly that her fingers began to ache. She had never been much of a drinker, but at that moment she would have dearly loved to join her friends in a whiskey.

Chapter 51

The friends had eaten a meal of pasta with pesto sauce, bread baked locally, a caprese salad (with locally grown ingredients), and as no meal in Bess's home was complete without dessert, bowls of chocolate and butter pecan ice cream. Allison had consumed more than she had been wont to eat in the past months; her stomach felt uncomfortably full, but the meal had been delicious and she had no regrets.

They needed a cozy evening, Allison thought, after learning of Chuck and Dean's situation. The calm after the storm. Though that wasn't quite right. The skies had opened around seven and were still pouring at nine. Nathan had lit a fire in the living area, where the friends were gathered. The baby was safely in bed.

"A roaring fire in the middle of summer," Dean commented. "Who would have thought?"

Nathan laughed. "Anyone who's ever been to Maine!"

"I love the sound of a crackling fire and the fragrance of burning wood at any time of the year." Chuck looked down at the glass he held in his hand. "And the brandy doesn't hurt, either."

Bess nodded. "I love the sound of rain pattering on a roof. It's so romantic."

"Yeah," Marta said, "except when it's contributing to major flooding and the destruction of lives and property."

Bess frowned. "Spoilsport."

"Speaking of spoiling, what if it pours on your big day?" Dean asked. Once again, he and Chuck were on the love seat.

"Oh, I've got backup plans," Bess assured him. "In fact, my backup plans have backup plans."

"Isn't there some old wives' tale about rain on your wedding day bringing good luck?" Nathan asked. He was seated cross-legged on the floor; Bess was on his right side.

"There are a few tales, actually," Marta told them. "One says that rain on your wedding day symbolizes the last tears a bride will shed for the rest of her life."

Chuck laughed. "If only!"

"And there's another tale," Marta went on, "that claims the number of raindrops that fall on your wedding day symbolize the number of tears a bride will shed during the course of her marriage."

"That's more like it!" Allison winced. "Sorry. Just my opinion." In fact, her own wedding day had been beautifully sunny and the tears to come, far too many. So much for old wives' tales.

"Well, I don't believe in any of that nonsense," Bess stated.

Nathan grinned. "Yes, you do," he said. "You live and breathe folklore and fairy tales and wisdom passed down from mother to daughter."

"But I don't plan my life around superstitions," Bess argued. "I mean, I consult my horoscope and I use my crystals when I need . . . Don't laugh, Marta! None of that is the same as mere superstition, though small-minded people like to think so!"

"There's no need to defend your beliefs," Marta said. "You're among friends. Sensible, reasoning friends."

Allison refrained from mentioning the ghostly experience she and Bess had shared at The House of Seven Gables all those years ago. For all she knew Bess had kept that a secret from Nathan, though why she would have done so was anybody's guess. At any rate, she was glad the conversation was keeping its distance from Chuck's illness and her divorce.

Marta shifted in the armchair she had chosen; it was nowhere near where Mike was perched, on the arm of the love seat. "I was just thinking," she began, "how odd it was that you, Bess, the one who considers our reunions sacred, not to be intruded upon by passing boyfriends or girlfriends, were the one to bring along that weird guy you were dating one year, what was his name, Terry or—"

"Taryn," Mike blurted. "That was it."

"Oh, why are you bringing him up now!" Bess wailed, putting her hands over her face.

"He spoke with this obviously pseudo-British accent," Chuck told Nathan.

Bess dropped her hands. "It wasn't *obviously* pseudo," she argued. "I thought it was real."

"Then how did you reconcile the accent with the fact that he told us he grew up in Baltimore?" Mike asked.

"I don't know. He said he lived in lots of different places as a child. I guess I thought he just picked up an accent along the way."

"Yeah," Allison said. "From watching *Downton Abbey!*"

"I don't think I ever knew where you met this guy," Marta said.

Bess blushed. "Just around."

"Come on, where?" Dean prompted. "A nightclub? In the veggie section at the grocery store? At the gym? But you don't go to a gym, do you?"

"No," Bess said. "I don't go to a gym. Ugh. Okay, I met him in an old cemetery in the West End of Portland."

"What were you doing in a cemetery?" Allison asked. "Unless you were attending a funeral."

"There hasn't been a funeral there in ages," Bess explained, a bit grumpily. "It's a really old cemetery. I was just walking through. I'm interested in the symbols on old headstones and the written memorials can be very touching. Anyway, I was there with my camera and he was . . . He was doing yoga. Later he told me he liked to do yoga out of doors. He said it was freeing."

Mike frowned. "But why in a cemetery? Why not in a park? Isn't that kind of disrespectful of the dead?"

Chuck shrugged. "I don't see how. I mean, as long as he wasn't reciting the Black Mass while doing downward-facing dog. That would be disrespectful of the dead and of people who devote their lives to yoga."

"He wasn't naked, was he?" Dean asked. "There is such a thing as naked yoga. At least, I think there is."

"No!" Bess cried. "I'm not crazy enough to go up to a naked stranger in a deserted cemetery!"

"Okay, so he was wearing clothes. And you stopped to talk to him." A grin played around Nathan's lips.

Bess shrugged. "Yeah, he looked . . . nice."

Chuck cleared his throat and looked at Nathan. "None of us thought he was nice. Whenever the check arrived after dinner this guy would mysteriously disappear. Ditto when it came time to clean up after a meal at home. And I know I can't prove this, but I saw him cheat when we played Monopoly." Chuck shook his head. "I should have called him on it."

"So, how did this romance end?" Nathan asked.

"Can we just drop this, please?" Bess pleaded.

"Oh, come on," Allison said. "It was years ago. What does it matter now?"

"That's exactly my point!"

"It all came to a head when he made a pass at me early one morning before the others were up," Allison said. "Can you imagine the nerve? Telling Bess what had happened was the most difficult thing I'd ever had to do. It was far easier to tell Chris what had happened. He, at least, doesn't think that everyone is a saint until proven a sinner, unlike our innocent Bess."

"I still feel awful I didn't believe you at first," Bess admitted. "Is that what always happens when a person learns that her lover has hit on her good friend? Disbelief in spite of the fact that you know full well that your friend would never say or do anything to hurt you?" Bess shook her head, then turned to Nathan. "I confronted Taryn," she went on. "I asked him if he had tried to kiss Allison and his answer was to stare at me blankly. I knew then that he was guilty."

"He left that day and was never heard from again. Isn't that right, Bess?" Chuck asked.

"Yeah. Anyway, that's all in the past. I just want to forget about everything that went before and be happy with now." Once again Bess looked to Nathan. "I want to look to the future."

Nathan smiled and took her hand. "I'm glad. Because that's where I'm looking, too."

Chuck raised his glass. "A toast to the happy couple."

Allison raised her own glass. "To Bess and Nathan."

"Remember how the night before graduation we made a pact to remain friends forever?" Bess asked suddenly.

Mike laughed. "What I remember is that we were drunk," he said.

"Who knows what we said that night and why we said it." Chuck squinted. "I seem to recall—very vaguely mind you—quoting from Shakespeare's *Julius Caesar* while standing atop a table. Don't ask me why I was doing such a thing. I mean, I like the play, but it's not my favorite. And generally speaking, I prefer standing on a floor."

"It doesn't matter that we were drunk," Bess argued. "We pledged to be friends forever and that pledge was made in good faith."

"We were young and hopeful," Marta said, "and let's face it, we were ignorant."

"What do you mean ignorant!" Bess cried.

"She means ignorant of the challenges life would throw at us," Mike said hastily.

"Ignorant or not, we *are* still here together," Allison pointed out, with a smile for Bess. "So, the pledge meant something after all." To everyone but Chris, she thought.

"Why is it okay for people marrying to pledge to love each other until they die," Bess asked, "but not just as valid for friends to do the same?"

"It's just more difficult to pull off that sort of commitment outside of marriage," Marta said. "Let's face it, most people have several good friends. How do you make a serious pledge like the one you make in a marriage to a whole group of people? What if one friend feels closer to you than you do to her and wants a commitment you're not prepared to give? No, the whole thing would be way too messy and chaotic."

Allison laughed a bit grimly. "Ideally, your spouse is your best friend."

"Yes, but surely not the same sort of best friend as your best friend outside the marriage," Bess argued.

Nathan took Bess's hand again and kissed it.

"Sometimes I'm not sure there is much of a difference," Chuck said, "not once you remove the sexual and financial element, assuming of course you and your spouse share finances."

"But the sexual and the financial elements are huge," Marta said. "Those are probably the two most common reasons married couples stay together longer than they might want to. Aside from the issue of children, of course. The sex is good or at least it's available, and it would be too costly to split."

Suddenly, Dean took Chuck's arm and pulled him to his feet. "As fascinating as this conversation is," he said, "we're off. Chuck should have been in bed long ago."

"It's only a small cut," Chuck reminded him. "I'm not an invalid. Yet."

Bess flinched. Nathan put his arm around her. Mike pat Chuck on the shoulder. Marta gave Chuck a quick peck on the cheek. *I really do love my friends*, Allison thought as she followed the others from the room. *Flaws and weaknesses, skills and strengths.* Even when they were driving her crazy they were hers, and that was all that mattered.

Chapter 52

Bess was doing laundry. Nathan had gone to the grocery store. She had no idea where the others had gotten to. She wasn't entirely happy about their habit of going off without telling her where they were going and when they would be back. It wasn't a control issue, Bess told herself. It was more an issue of . . . an issue of feeling unnecessary. Bess needed to feel needed.

As she folded towels and sorted socks, Bess replayed part of last night's conversation. She was bothered by the others' feelings about the pact of forever friendship they had made so long ago. They seemed—with the possible exception of Allison—to take it so lightly and yet, as Allison had pointed out, here they were twenty some odd years later. So why did they feel the need to downplay the importance of their vow? Again, Bess thought of the symbol she had selected to represent her relationship to the others and theirs to her. The anchor. At the moment, it seemed to mock her idealism.

Her thoughts were interrupted by the sound of jaunty whistling coming from the direction of the yard. Bess hurried from the laundry room and out to the back porch. Chuck was striding toward her, a bunch of wildflowers in his hand. "Another perfect day," he said with a smile. He flopped into one of the wicker chairs on the porch and Bess sat next to him.

"Are you scared?" she blurted.

Chuck laughed. "Nice conversational intro!"

"Are you?" Bess pressed.

"Not so much for me, no," Chuck said easily. "I've got a good medical team and the accumulated experiences of other people with Parkinson's to help me face the future. But I am worried about what Dean will go through. We signed on for this marriage, in sickness and in health, but no one walks down the aisle—well, most people don't—anticipating life as a caregiver while their spouse is still a young person."

"But you," Bess pressed. "What about what *you'll* be going through?"

"You know me, Bess. I've always been a ridiculously resilient person. I seem to be able to just deal with whatever's being thrown at me. I'm like my father in that way. In fact, it's probably the greatest gift he ever gave me, his ability to take life as it comes."

"I don't know if I should mention this or not," Bess said. She really didn't.

"Whatever it is, you already have. Out with it, Bess."

"Well, last night I was reading medical sites on the Internet and—"

"A dangerous enterprise for the nonprofessional," Chuck interrupted. "But go on."

"And this one site talked about hallucinations. It said that sometimes the medicines that are used to treat the physical symptoms of Parkinson's can lead to auditory and visual hallucinations."

Chuck took Bess's hand in his. "First of all," he said with a smile, "hallucinations are only a possibility and if I do experience them, well, the key is information and awareness. I try not to anticipate every unhappy possibility, and definitely not at the same time. That old advice, to take things one day at a time, makes a lot of sense. When you can pull it off."

Bess sighed and looked out over the perfectly tended lawn. At the foot of the yard was the blighted tree, beautiful in its grotesqueness. Beyond that lay the pale sand and the shimmering sea. Why was life so fraught, she wondered? Why was the meaning of life— and it had to have a meaning—so incomprehensible? Way better minds than Bess's had wrestled with the big existential questions and as far as Bess knew, none of those minds had come up with any really satisfactory answers. There was no way *she*, whose idea of a brain teaser was a word search, was going to be able to do any better.

"Bess?" Chuck asked. "Where are you?"

She turned to him and smiled. "Nowhere. I mean, right here."

"It looked as if your head was in the clouds."

"Nope, I'm totally earthbound. Do you want some chocolate ice cream? There's plenty in the freezer."

Chuck laughed. "No, thanks. I had three bowls last night. But I should put these flowers in water." He rose and went inside.

Bess remained where she was seated. Maybe, she thought, if she stared at the shimmering sea, the cloudless sky, and the blighted tree long enough, the meaning of Life would come to her. She smiled at the notion.

Chapter 53

The call was from Sam. Marta frowned. It was likely Sam had gotten into another squabble with Leo and, unable to reach her father on the phone, had resorted to the lesser parent. Mom wouldn't be half as sympathetic as Dad would be, but she would do in a pinch.

"Hi," Marta said, leaning against the railing on the back porch. "What's wrong?"

"What makes you think something is wrong?" Sam said defensively.

"So, you've just called to chat?"

There was a moment of silence before Sam said, "Well, no. Actually, there's something I need your advice on."

Marta frowned. The last time her daughter had come to her for advice it had been about a pair of expensive sneakers her father had promised her. Should she pick the ones with the silver stripe or the ones with the purple stripe? Marta, annoyed that Mike had promised their daughter the ridiculously overpriced sneakers in the first place, had literally rolled her eyes. Sam had gone off in a huff.

"I'm not sure what to do," Sam went on. "You know Tara, right?"

Somewhere, in the deep recesses of her mind, Marta recalled Sam mentioning the name, but it had to have been at least a year ago. And then the memory surfaced. "The girl who meets her aunt in the city once a month to have lunch at a trendy restaurant and then go shopping," she said.

"I knew you'd remember. Anyway, at the start of the summer she got a job working the checkout at Target. And last week she told me that she's been stealing from her cash register! I don't know how she's gotten away with it so far. I mean, don't managers count the money at the end of the day or something?"

"They do," Marta confirmed. "But no one seems to have noticed any money missing?"

"I guess not. But Tara can't go on stealing forever. She's going to get caught and I told her that, but she just laughs it off like it's no big deal. I don't know what's going on, Mom. It's not like she needs the money; I don't even know why she's working when her allowance is so big. Do you think she wants to be found out or something? There's no way she can really think she's going to get away with taking such a big risk. It's crazy!"

"It's—" Before Marta could finish her comment, Sam was rushing on.

"Do I tell her parents? Not to rat her out but so that someone stops her before she gets in seriously big trouble. Do I warn her I'm going to tell on her if she doesn't promise to stop? But what if she lies to me and says she isn't stealing anymore, but she really is still stealing and I find out and then I actually *have* to tell someone about what's going on because I've already threatened I would? And why did she tell me this in the first place? Why not just keep it a secret?"

Sam was silent for a full thirty seconds; Marta assumed her daughter might have run out of steam and that it was safe for her to ask a few questions. Did Sam know if Tara had told anyone else about her stealing from her job? As far as Sam knew, had Tara ever stolen before now? Had something upsetting happened in Tara's family life? Was there a boy? Was there a girl? Had either broken her heart or was either a known bad influence? Did Sam know if Tara was involved in any other unsavory matters?

Sam answered these questions. She didn't know. No. Not that she knew of. There had been a boy, but that was over months ago. If by unsavory her mother meant drugs or drinking, no. Tara was a serious athlete, totally against putting anything unhealthy in her body.

Armed with this information—which didn't in fact tell her much—Marta thought hard for a moment and then formulated her next question. "Is it possible she's lying to you about her stealing?" she asked. "When you told me about the trips to the city with her aunt last year, didn't you also mention something someone had told you about Tara playing a practical joke on a girl back in middle school? Making the girl believe she was terminally ill and needing help doing her homework and carrying her books? And that when the truth finally came out Tara didn't even apologize? I'm not saying that once a liar always a liar, but maybe in this case . . ."

"OMG," Sam cried, "how could I have been so stupid? You're totally right, Tara did prank some poor girl back in middle school. So maybe she's been lying to me all along, just riling me up! But why me?"

"Don't waste time trying to guess her motives," Marta advised. "And we don't know for sure she is putting you on but given her past, I'd advise you to let the matter drop. Next time she brags about her criminal life, say something like, 'That's your choice, it has nothing to do with me,' and walk away. Okay?"

"Thanks, Mom," Sam said sincerely. "That's exactly what I'll do. You know," she went on, "I can't talk about this sort of stuff to anyone else but you. Dad's great, but he'd probably only see the facts and not all the emotional stuff that makes the facts not so straightforward. I know he'd tell me to go to Tara's boss because when you know someone is committing a crime you have a civic and an ethical obligation to report them. Which might be the right thing to do technically speaking and all, but it would never have occurred to Dad to ask all the questions you asked me." Sam laughed. "Why aren't you a criminal lawyer, Mom? Or an investigator or something."

Marta laughed, but the words hit a nerve. "In my next life," she said.

"I hope that when I have kids I can be half as good as you are at solving crises."

"When you have kids?" Marta blurted.

"Yeah. What?"

"It's just . . . Nothing." It was just that maybe she hadn't been do-ing such a bad job of parenting her daughter as she thought she had.

"Uh, it's totally normal for someone to want kids," Sam pointed out in a classic teenaged tone of patience sorely tried. "Wait. Are you guys having a good time?"

Marta was surprised Sam had thought to ask. "Yeah," she said. "The house is beautiful, the weather is great, and Bess is the per-fect hostess."

"Cool. I gotta go. Thanks again, Mom. Don't forget to take a lot of pictures at the wedding. I'm dying to see what Bess wears."

And she was gone.

Looking out over the blue Atlantic, Marta felt a glimmer of hope. Her daughter didn't see her as useless. She valued what strengths Marta could bring to making a difficult decision. There was a pos-sibility that Sam might turn out to be an ally of sorts through this upcoming adventure of the pregnancy, not against her father but for her mother. Only time would tell.

Chapter 54

Allison was sitting on the bed with her legs stretched out before her. She had just gotten off the phone with her assistant. Greg had reported that the first meeting with their latest client had gone well. He was sending Allison a detailed report of what had been discussed and decided at the meeting.

She was glad she had done that small service for Greg. It felt good to lend a hand to a young person, as several established professionals had done for her when she was starting out. Mentoring might be something she could begin to take seriously, and it might be something that could happen close to home.

For instance, why hadn't she gotten to know Marta's children better? Was it because she had been so focused on her own childless situation? She knew so little of Sam, Leo, and Troy. What sort of things made Sam laugh? Was Leo still competing in chess tournaments? What did Troy want to be when he grew up?

Allison vowed to make a change going forward. If Mike and Marta were okay with her reaching out to the children with gestures of friendship, then she would do exactly that. Maybe Sam would be interested in visiting her for a few days during a school break; she could show her the sights of Chicago, bring her along on one of her more interesting photo assignments, go shopping at some of the more exciting boutiques.

And she would make an effort to visit the MacIntosh family more often, something that would be easier if she moved back to the east coast, but not impossible to do from Chicago. She would make an effort to know Thomas, too, and if possible to offer concrete help should Chuck and Dean need it as the Parkinson's progressed.

Allison opened her laptop to check her e-mail. And there, at the top of the list, was a message from Agnes Montague. There was nothing in the subject line. Allison felt her stomach sink and realized she felt afraid. But what could Agnes possibly have to say in an e-mail that could be so horrible? If something terrible had happened to Chris she would have called.

With a deep breath, Allison opened the e-mail.

Allison—I thought you would want to see this. You were an integral part of supporting Chris in his career and I know he always appreciated your dedication. Agnes

Agnes had attached a link to an article from the *Chicago Tribune* about the firm of Montague and Montague having won a lucrative and prestigious design contest. Allison knew it was a goal Chris and his father had been actively pursuing for almost five years. There was a quote from Jonathan Montague; in it he praised his son for bringing a forward vision to the firm.

Allison startled as another e-mail from Agnes appeared in the in-box. Again, there was nothing in the subject line.

I'm sorry. I shouldn't have assumed you would be happy for Chris after what he put you through.

But there had been no need for Agnes to apologize. Allison realized that she was happy for Chris. Truly happy. And she hoped the losses in his personal life hadn't ruined the pleasure of a win in his professional life. Chris's demons had caused him to treat her badly, but that did not negate his value as a person with skills and talents. It did not.

Only days earlier she had spoken cruelly of Chris, mocked his excitement at being interviewed by the reporter all those years ago. It had been uncharitable and unproductive. She had no further need or desire to act so meanly.

Allison thought carefully for a few minutes; then she sent Agnes a reply.

Thank you for sharing the article with me and please don't apologize. I am happy for Chris; I know what winning that job meant to him and I hope he's able to truly enjoy this achievement. I also hope that you and Jonathan are well. I'm in Maine for the wedding of a dear friend from college days.

Allison hesitated. She didn't know if what she was about to say was the truth.

We all wish Chris was here to be part of the festivities.
Sincerely and with affection, Allison

Chapter 55

Bess was at her desk in the den, reading an online magazine. It wasn't a particularly good magazine but like most people, Bess occasionally found herself falling into the pit that was the Internet. Why? Because it was there.

Still, the interview she was reading wasn't too awful. She vaguely recognized the name of the actor who was currently making headlines because he and his wife had managed to stay married for twenty years.

Randy leans forward in his seat and folds his long, expressive hands on his knees. "Marriage is probably the most intricate of relationships," he says earnestly. "At the same time that it's about being totally comfortable with each other it's also about knowing how to tiptoe around the other's sensitivities." Randy pauses now and pushes his enviably wavy hair back from his forehead. "Put that way," he goes on, "it sounds exhausting, but it does become second nature. Mostly. For couples who are lucky, I suppose. I'm sure there are plenty of well-meaning, loving people who never manage to learn how to strike that balance, and all the other balances a good marriage demands. Merry and I have been blessed."

Bess turned off her computer. Randy Luther might be a fairly ob-noxious B-list celebrity, Bess thought, but he sounded like he knew what marriage was really about. Unless his publicist had given him a script to memorize. The point was that there were moments lately when Bess was frightened of discovering that she might not be one of those people who could be properly married. It had to be true that some people just weren't meant for marriage. Better for those people if they knew themselves well enough not to get married in the first place. But knowing oneself fully was a tall order, one no person (probably) ever got entirely right.

And mostly, Bess knew, a person only discovered her strengths and weaknesses through trial and error. You might think you were capable of climbing a particular mountain and only when you were halfway up and hanging on by one hand might you realize that you were patently *not* capable of climbing to the top of that mountain. Or, you might be absolutely sure that you could never, ever design an app that would make you millions, and then discover, when you had decided, what the heck, I'll give it a try, that you were suddenly able to retire at the age of thirty-one.

So, what would it be for her? Would she discover only months after the wedding that she made a lousy wife? Or would she realize that she could handle the role blindfolded and backward?

Abruptly, Bess got up from her desk and went in search of her friends. She found Marta and Allison on the back porch. The two women had just come from the beach.

"It's hot as Hades down there," Marta said, stretched out in a chair. "At least you can feel a breeze up here on the porch. Which is weird. You'd think the air would be warmer farther away from the water."

Allison produced a handheld fan from her beach bag. "One of the best purchases I ever made," she declared, waving it before her face. "And no batteries to replace. I got suckered into buying a battery-powered fan one of my Instagram peeps was touting. She swore it was the best thing since sliced bread, so silly me, I bought one, and it never worked. I got my money back but still. It just goes to show you can't necessarily trust your social media so-called friends."

"Which is why I don't have any," Marta remarked.

"I think," Bess said, "that we're unusual in this day and age of a 'surfeit of connectivity'—I came across that phrase recently—in the way we stick to a more old-fashioned standard of genuine closeness. Instead of having lots of friends we have a close bond with a select few who've seen us through thick and thin."

When neither Allison nor Marta commented, Bess went on. "What I mean is, each of us has a circle of colleagues and acquaintances we deal with on a daily basis, and even some people we might consider good friends, but when it comes to the people we *really* care about, it's the old college gang, isn't it? Okay, last year the reunion didn't come off because of too many scheduling conflicts, though I still don't understand how . . ." Bess shook her head. "Never mind. But in ordinary circumstances it would never occur to any of us to forgo a reunion for whatever reason, short of a life-threatening disaster."

"You were pretty upset about Chuck missing our reunion a few years back because it conflicted with a conference he wanted to attend," Allison said.

"I wasn't mad at him," Bess added quickly. "I was just disappointed. The reunion wasn't the same without Chuck, and the fact that he canceled at the last minute. . . . But you guys," she went on, "you and Allison, would never let anything not super important stand in the way of one of our reunions. I think women feel the bonds of friendships as more binding than men do."

Marta looked to Allison before she said, "That might or might not be true. Still, I'll admit that once or twice I've gone to a reunion reluctantly. There was this one summer our local community college was offering a three-week course on the art of block printing and I considered signing up. Okay, the reunion plans weren't the only thing that stopped me but . . ." Marta shrugged. "I love you guys, but sometimes I need more than what you can give me. But you must feel the same way, right?"

"I do," Allison admitted. "And I think it's perfectly normal. For instance, the year we all went to Puerto Rico, Chris and I had the opportunity to visit newer friends in London. Jeff and Amy had been given use of a lovely flat in Mayfair and there was plenty of room for two couples. We really wanted to join them, but we felt compelled to meet up with 'the old gang.' And we did have a good time in the end."

Bess took a deep and steadying breath. "I don't know what to say," she admitted. "I had no idea that . . . that you didn't care."

"It's not about not caring," Allison said quickly. "It's just about, well, about growth. Meeting new people and learning how to build new friendships."

"You haven't ever been tempted to skip our reunion?" Marta asked Bess.

"No," Bess said. "Never."

"Well," Allison said, her tone conciliatory, "every group needs an emotional focal point, someone to keep all the members connected. Bess is our emotional focal point. Our team captain. Our anchor."

Bess flinched. She had chosen the anchor as a symbol of the love that existed among the group, not as something referring only to herself. Bess wondered if her friends had lied about the scheduling conflicts of the year before. She couldn't bear to ask.

"I just realized something," Marta said. "Bess is probably the one who made us all swear the forever friendship pact the night before graduation."

Bess practically jumped from her seat. "I just remembered I need to check in with Kara," she said. She hurried to the den and closed the door behind her. Her heart was racing and her eyes were blurry with hot tears. She leaned back against the door. Marriage was an unknown. Her friends were proving not half as dedicated to the friendship as she had supposed them to be. Nothing felt certain— nothing but Nathan's love for her. At least she could trust *that* love.

Couldn't she?

Chapter 56

Allison frowned. "I feel bad I told Bess about that London vacation Chris and I missed out on. I shouldn't have said anything."

"I don't know about that," Marta countered. "It can't be good for Bess to go on believing that we're all exactly the same as we were back in college, with the same thoughts and feelings, untouched by everything that's happened in the past twenty years. That's dangerously naïve."

"Or," Allison said after a moment, "it's heroically brave, if that isn't redundant. 'However rare true love may be, it is less so than true friendship.' Supposedly de la Rochefoucauld said that. Whether he did or not, the message might be worth considering."

Marta considered. "What you said about Bess being our anchor. An anchor works both ways, doesn't it? It can keep you safe when times are tough, but it can also hold you back when you want to be moving on."

"Yes," Allison said, getting up from her seat. "I'm going for a drive. Some of the back roads around here are so charming it almost hurts. And my car has air-conditioning."

Leaving her beach bag and fan behind, Allison went on her way.

Marta remained in her seat and wondered. How could a friendship be expected to survive and continue to bring satisfaction when each party wanted or needed a different degree of closeness and support? Changing life circumstances changed friendships. The loss of a job. A change of location. A major illness. An unpopular marriage. Friendships were not immune to death from without.

Marta heard someone approaching and turned her head to see Chuck.

"What's up?" he asked, flopping down next to her.

"Nothing but my pondering questions too big for me."

"Pondering the imponderable. Not the best way to spend a hot summer afternoon."

"Why not now?" Marta countered. "The big questions never go away."

"Maybe life would be boring if they did," Chuck said.

"Does it ever get to you," Marta asked, "being confronted with so much human frailty, so much illness and sadness, watching the sick get sicker and their loved ones struggle not to fall apart as they stand by, helpless to stop the circle from turning?"

Chuck raised an eyebrow. "You're in a melancholy mood," he noted. "Yes, it does get to me. We're all so terribly fragile. Sometimes it amazes me we make it past the first day of our lives, just this little bundle of flesh and blood against such enormous odds." Chuck sighed. "Maybe I'm becoming too soft to be a good doctor. When does a healthy dose of compassion become something debilitating, something that gets in the way of facing cold, hard fact and the ability to ascertain when a patient is lying or even innocently neglecting to relate a bit of information that might be crucial to your making the right diagnosis or suggesting the best course of treatment?"

Marta sighed. "I can't answer that."

"No one can, at least in the broad sense. There's an answer in each particular situation, though. The trick is to find that answer quickly. And now that I'm more than just an occasional patient, as well as a doctor, I'll get to see it all from the other side. I wonder if I'll be a good, pleasant patient, always trying to make those around me feel good. What a lovely day it is, Dr. Black; oh, I love your necklace Nurse Brown! Or will I be a brutally honest patient. How are you feeling today, Mr. Fortunato? Awful, Technician White. Like crap. How do you think I feel?" Chuck raised an eyebrow. "Life is a Sisyphean task indeed."

"Especially when your friends turn on you. Allison and I made Bess feel bad a little while ago. We admitted we aren't always keen on showing up for the reunions."

Chuck frowned. "And she didn't take it well."

"I feel as if I'd kicked a defenseless kitten."

"Bess is tougher than she looks."

"Is she?" Marta said.

Chuck looked thoughtful. "I hope so."

Chapter 57

Allison had no destination in mind when she set out. She just wanted to be alone, away from Marta and her default negativity, Bess and her relentless optimism. It was enough to be going somewhere, anywhere.

She was only a few miles from Driftwood House when a strange grating noise caused Allison to pull to the side of the road. She got out of the car, cursing herself for not having taken the time to learn more about the workings of an engine. But she had let Chris handle that sort of thing, yet another habit that had contributed to her overall sense of helplessness.

Allison had pulled her phone from her bag and was about to call AAA when a dark blue pickup truck came cruising to a stop a few yards behind her car. The driver stepped out of the truck. His hair was bleached from the sun; his skin was tanned. He wore a plaid shirt with the sleeves rolled up. His jeans fit well. "Need any help?" he asked with a smile as he came toward her.

It didn't occur to Allison to be afraid. This was southern Maine after all, even the back roads were busy with summer traffic, and the sun was shining. "I was just about to call triple-A," she told him. "The engine was making a funny noise. Well, maybe not the engine. Something's wrong, anyway."

"I could take a look if you like," the man offered, "maybe save you some money."

"Okay," she said. "If you don't mind." She wasn't sure why she had accepted the man's offer. AAA was totally reliable; a mechanic would have been on the scene before long.

"You never really know what you're getting with a rental," he said, opening the hood.

"How do you know it's a rental?" Allison asked, suddenly wary.

"The license plates."

"Oh." Allison felt foolish. "Right."

"Where are you visiting from?" the man asked, his head bent over the car's engine.

"From Chicago. I'm here for a friend's wedding."

"We get a fair amount of summer weddings in these parts. Good for business. I'm Bill, by the way."

"Allison. Nice to meet you."

The man poked and prodded while Allison's thoughts took an interesting and an unprecedented turn. It would be nice, she thought, to enjoy attention from a person without overwhelming demons. Someone like Bill. But it was a silly assumption to make, that Bill whatever-his-name-was had no troubles of his own. Besides, changing people was only changing one set of problems for another. You could, however, consciously choose one set of problems over another set of problems. Nobody was perfect, but you *could* decide what level of imperfection you could live with without going mad.

"Nothing wrong with the engine as far as I can see," Bill reported. He began to circle the car, squatting to peer at the undercarriage.

There was no reason she couldn't have casual lovers, Allison thought as she watched her Knight in Shining Armor. It had been so long since sex had been uncomplicated; increasingly it had become about getting pregnant and not about enjoyment or intimacy. Always at the back of her mind—if not at the forefront—was the thought that "maybe this time" would be the magic time. The attempt to get pregnant had actually wedged its way between Allison and Chris so that what might have been the ultimate joint venture had become an uncomfortable three-party event.

"Here's your problem," Bill announced triumphantly. Allison came back to the moment with a start. "You've got a tree branch stuck pretty tight under here. Let me get a tool from my truck."

While Bill was focused on rescuing the car, Allison's mind continued to wander. If you loved someone, she thought, but chose not to be in a relationship with him because his troubles were hurting you too badly, was leaving a failure of your love? Until death do we part was a pretty tall order—some would say a cruel sentence—when one member of the couple was tormenting the other with his psychic pain or emotional immaturity. That said, love was eternal. At least for some people it was. *A name graven on a tablet.*

Suddenly, Allison shook her head. The topic of love was deep and complex, not one to be thoroughly plumbed in a few minutes while waiting for a particularly tenacious tree branch to be extricated from the undercarriage of your rental car.

"Bingo," Bill announced as he got to his feet holding the offending branch. He tossed it into the field at the side of the road. "You should be good to go. Drive carefully. Oh, and enjoy the wedding."

There was no doubt about it, Bill had a killer smile. For a split second Allison was tempted to give him her cell phone number. Instead what she gave him was her hand and a firm shake.

"Thank you," she said. "I really appreciate your help."

"My pleasure. Take care now."

Allison got into her car. She couldn't resist peeking in the rearview mirror to see if Bill was watching her drive away. When he lifted a hand in a final wave Allison bit her lip. The opportunity was gone, the moment had passed. But she didn't feel any real regret.

She really didn't.

Chapter 58

Bess was wiping the kitchen counters for the second time. She tended to go into housekeeping overkill when she was having trouble making a decision. The thing was she really wanted to tell Nathan that she was having second thoughts about giving her friends the charms she had bought for them. It wasn't as if she suddenly felt they didn't deserve the gift; at least, she didn't think that was what she felt. It was more like she felt the charms wouldn't be appreciated in the spirit with which she had intended them to be.

But she was hesitating. She didn't want to appear childish. Nathan was so steady and mature, not one to overreact as she had so often been accused of doing.

Bess put down the sponge, resisted the impulse to pick it up again to make one more swipe behind the sink, and dried her hands. She went out to the back porch, where she spied Dean on the lawn, stretched out on his side on a bright blue beach blanket, dangling a little floppy bunny for Thomas as if the baby were a lazy cat, content to take an occasional swipe with his paw, but not to make a real grab.

Bess hurried down to join them and dropped onto the blanket.

Dean smiled and adjusted Thomas's sun hat. "Hats are almost impossible to keep on little heads. I don't think he minds them, but they mind him. They keep inching off."

"I know," Bess blurted. "I never really talked about this, but I pretty much raised my sisters for the first few years of their lives. My mother was a full-time caregiver for two elderly relatives and needed my help at home."

Dean's eyes widened. "So, all this supposed fear of babies . . ."

"I'm not really afraid of them," Bess said with a small smile. "It's more like I've had my fill. That, and I'm way out of practice. Anyway, can I ask you something?"

"I don't know. Can you? Sorry. My father always used to correct me when I said 'can' instead of 'may.'"

Bess smiled. "It's about relationships. It's just that . . . There's something troubling me and I want to talk it over with Nathan, but . . . but what if he thinks I'm just being silly and selfish? And maybe I *am* just being silly and selfish, but I feel what I feel." Bess leaned beyond the edge of the blanket and plucked a blade of grass. "Do you understand?"

"I think I do," Dean said. "The prospect of total honesty and all that entails—like opening yourself to your partner's possible criticisms—feels really daunting."

"That's it," Bess admitted. "And what I want to talk with him about isn't even all that important. Well, it is to me but not in the scheme of things."

"Feelings are always important in the big picture, Bess. Don't discount them." Dean sat up. "Let me tell you a story. Chuck insisted he go to the doctor on his own to hear his diagnosis and nothing I said could change his mind. I was furious. I was hurt. Chuck was acting as if he were still single and not part of a unit, not a crime by any means, but not healthy for a marriage."

"Maybe he just thought it would be better if you heard bad news from him when you guys were home alone and not from a third party?" Bess suggested. "He is a thoughtful man."

"Yes, he's thoughtful, but what I could and could not handle was not his decision to make," Dean stated firmly. "If he was concerned about my hearing bad news in a clinical environment like a doctor's office he should have told me. Then I'd have had the opportunity to assure him that I wanted to be with him. I'm not someone who shirks responsibility or who's easily devastated by the slightest bit of difficult news. He should know that."

"I see," said Bess. At least, she thought that she did.

"The point is that particularly in the early days of a marriage it can be difficult to negotiate the boundaries between the individual self and the person who is an integral part of the couple. Hold nothing back from Nathan, ever," Dean went on. "It's all got to come out. Not necessarily in one big lump," he added with a smile. "Delivery is an art, as is timing."

Bess frowned. "You're saying I should share every little passing thought?"

"Maybe not every little one," Dean admitted. "He doesn't necessarily need to know that whenever you're in the bakery aisle in the supermarket you have a craving for a Twinkie. But you've definitely got to share the big stuff."

"How did you know I used to love Twinkies?"

Dean cringed. "You did? I was more of a Devil Dogs guy myself. Pop those suckers in the fridge for a while . . . heaven."

Bess laughed and gently touched the baby's cheek with her forefinger. "In some ways, we never really grow up, do we?"

"I guess. Though you couldn't pay me to eat a Devil Dog now, not with all the artificial stuff they're made of. In this case, memory will suffice."

"What happens when Thomas gets old enough to want a Devil Dog?" Bess asked.

"I'll deal with that issue when it arises. I'm not going to be one of those parents who force their child to eat only kale and tofu. An occasional cookie or soda isn't going to kill anyone, and allowing fun food here and there deprives it of glamour, making it no big deal and hence less of a temptation."

"You've got it all worked out," Bess said approvingly.

Dean raised an eyebrow. "Have I? We'll see."

"This is kind of out of the blue," Bess said after a moment, "but I read this very interesting quote somewhere, and I wrote it down because it really struck me. 'As one grows older, one becomes wiser and more foolish.' Supposedly it was said by François de La Roche-foucauld. Do you know him?"

"Not personally," Dean replied with a smile.

Bess herself didn't really know much about de La Rochefoucauld. She knew only that he lived in the seventeenth century, that he was French, and that he was famous for his maxims.

"Don't you think he's on to something?" she asked Dean.

Dean seemed to ponder for a moment before he said: "The expression that comes to mind is 'a fond old man,' meaning someone who's put aside all learned wisdom to allow foolish emotion to hold sway over him, lavishing his money on someone or some cause totally unworthy—at least, unworthy in the eyes of those who consider themselves the rightful heirs." Dean shrugged. "That's my take, anyway. But back to you and Nathan. Talk to him, Bess."

"Thank you, Dean," Bess said. "You've given me courage I didn't have a few minutes ago."

"You had the courage," Dean assured her. "You just needed reminding of it."

"What do you think, Thomas?" Bess asked the little one.

From under his white sun hat, Thomas burped and then smiled up at Bess.

Dean laughed. "See? He agrees with me."

Bess opened the bottom drawer of the tall dresser and removed from under a layer of neatly folded T-shirts the blue silk-covered case in which were stored the charms she had ordered for each of her old college friends, as well as for Dean. There was a special charm for Nathan, too, but that Bess kept separately. It was a surprise. She would give that to him on the eve of their wedding. About that gift, she had no doubt.

She sat on the edge of the bed, the case on her knees.

"What's wrong?" Nathan asked, sitting next to her. "You look so sad."

I am sad, Bess thought, placing both hands flat on the case containing the charms. She would risk appearing to Nathan as needy. She would risk total honesty.

"Nothing's the same as it was," she said quietly. "No one is the same, not Chuck or Mike or Marta or Allison. Certainly, not Chris. I don't know why I was kidding myself, thinking that our friendship hadn't changed since college, that everyone still feels as strongly about the friendship as I do. Maybe, if I was really honest with myself," she went on, "I'd realize that I, too, don't . . . don't care as much as I once cared."

Nathan put an arm around her shoulder. "Is that really true?" he asked. "Do you really care less for any of your friends than you did last week? Last year?"

Bess sighed. "No, it's not true. I love them all much as I ever did and I need them in my life as much as I ever did. But I seem to be the only one who feels that way. Everyone's moved on but me. I guess I feel a bit . . . betrayed. And more than a little foolish." A fond middle-aged woman, she added silently.

"I'm sorry," Nathan said gently. "I'm sorry this reunion isn't turning out to be as happy as you hoped it would be."

"Am I wrong to feel betrayed?" Bess asked, hearing the plaintive note in her voice. "Or am I just reacting like a spoiled child, upset that she didn't get exactly the right color pony she wanted for her birthday and overlooking all of the other lovely gifts she's been given?"

Bess lifted the lid of the blue silk case to reveal each of the charms laid out securely in a bed of cream-colored satin. "Maybe I should just forget about giving everyone his or her charms," she said, "donate them or sell them for the metal weight. No one's going to really appreciate them. I've been behaving as if I'm still in grade school when kids form these silly clubs and wear the same friendship bracelet woven in the same color threads and everyone thinks it's all so deadly important."

Nathan tightened his grip on her shoulders. "This is not the same thing as a grade school club and you know it," he said forcefully. "Come on, Bess, there's nothing wrong with your feeling so deeply about the old group, nothing at all. You're Bess Culpepper, and Bess Culpepper's heart is a big one. Loving unconditionally and forever is what you do. But if you really feel that giving the charms to your friends isn't what you want to do at this point," he went on, "there's no tragedy in that. But I suggest you hang on to them, at least for a while. You might change your mind."

Bess looked up at Nathan and attempted a wobbly smile. "I suppose you're right. I might change my mind . . ." Bess closed the case resting on her lap. "Thank you, Nathan," she said. "Thank you."

Chapter 59

Bess had served yet another excellent meal, though Marta's appetite hadn't been particularly stimulated by the pork roast and grilled vegetables. Everyone else had eaten heartily; even Allison had finished what she had put on her plate.

Now the three women were sitting on the back porch. Allison and Bess were sipping brandy; Marta was nursing a cup of herbal tea. It tasted vaguely oily. Why she was bothering to finish the drink escaped her.

With the exception of Chuck, who was having an early night, the men had gone off to play miniature golf; the baby was in bed. Marta wished she had gone with the guys. She was very good at miniature golf. Why was it that so often women got left behind with other women when what they really wanted to do was to hang with the men? It was her own fault, Marta thought. There had been nothing stopping her from going with Nathan and the others but her own knee-jerk sense of loyalty to her girlfriends.

"I've been thinking about divorce," Allison said suddenly. Then she laughed. "Well, I would be, wouldn't I? What I mean is, I wonder how many of the couples we knew in college are still together. I'm not sure it's the norm for our generation to choose a lifelong mate so young. Or is it?"

"I don't know," Marta admitted. "I'm sure there are studies that can provide us the answer."

"Maybe I'd rather not know." Allison turned to Bess. "Maybe the norm is for women to marry later, like you are, after their careers are established. Each generation must feel it needs to redefine how things should or shouldn't be done."

"And yet can anyone really say definitively this way or that way is best?" Marta shook her head. "I don't think so, not when it comes to matters of the heart like marriage and kids. In the end, it all comes down to individual choice."

"Did you know that you and Chuck were often mistaken for a couple?" she suddenly asked Bess.

"I knew and I didn't mind because I had a crush on Chuck for a while," Bess said. "But I never thought for one moment that anything would come of it. I'm sure he knew how I felt, too. You know me. I've never been good at hiding my feelings."

"Remember the girl with the frizzy blond hair who lived on the floor below us?" Allison asked. "She was head over heels in love with Chuck. She pursued him with a vengeance. Did she really think her charms—dubious though they were in my opinion—could override a basic truth of Chuck's nature?"

"She was stupid," Marta stated, "pure and simple. And I don't think that what she felt for Chuck was love. He was a challenge, that's all. If she had succeeded in seducing him you can be sure she would have dumped him the very next day."

"I don't know about that," Bess replied musingly. "I think she really was in love."

"She was in love with a phantom of her own imagination," Marta went on, "not the Chuck we knew, the real man. That kind of delusion is dangerous."

"Oh well," Bess said with a shrug. "People always pay for their bad behavior in some way."

"Do they?" Marta said. "I think plenty of people get away with murder or close to it." Look at how she had gotten away with her one-night stand with Chris, she thought, her stomach tensing. Look at how she had gotten away—at least so far—with her lie to

Mike. She had told him she was happy about the new baby. She was not.

"So, Bess," Allison asked teasingly, "are you sure you never had any romantic interest in Chris or Mike?"

Marta tightened her grip on her mug of tea and wondered where— if anywhere—Allison was going with this line of questioning.

Bess nodded firmly. "Totally sure. And not just because they were dating my friends. No offense, Marta, but Mike's habit of scratching his head when he's thinking about something serious would drive me nuts. And Chris, well, he looks too much like you, Allison, for me to have a crush on him. Ick."

"Ick?" Allison repeated with a laugh.

"I think Mike's habit of scratching his head is cute," Marta said a bit huffily. She didn't really think it was cute. But she felt the need to defend her husband. It was what a wife did.

"What?" Bess cried. "You asked me for the truth and I told you!"

"Be careful what you ask for . . ." Marta mumbled.

"Now it's time for me to put you on the hot seat," Bess announced. "Did either of you ever fancy the other's guy?"

Allison laughed. "As pathetic, or as grandly Romantic, as it might sound given what's happened, I never looked at—let alone thought about—another guy from the moment I met Chris."

"Me, neither. I mean, not Chris, Mike," Marta added hurriedly. "I never looked at another guy once I met Mike. Okay, for a brief time I had a crush on George Clooney, but a celebrity crush isn't the same and who didn't have a crush on George Clooney at one point in his or her life?"

Bess frowned. "But wasn't there a guy in our senior year that you liked for a while? He was a transfer student from—was it Bulgaria?"

"That was nothing," Marta said dismissively. "I was never interested in anyone but Mike." There was no way Bess could know about her one night with Chris, Marta told herself forcefully, willing herself to believe it. And Chris would never, ever have told Allison, no matter how angry he was with her.

Probably.

The trouble was that a guilty conscience needed no accuser.

"So, the kids are doing okay with your mom and dad?" Allison asked.

Marta was grateful for the change of topic. "According to my mother they're thriving." And how did she feel about that? Of course, she was glad her children were safe and secure. But she was also just a wee bit annoyed that they weren't missing her all that much.

"I've been feeling badly that I haven't spent much time with Sam, Leo, and Troy," Allison said. "I hope it's not too late to build a real relationship with them."

Marta was touched. She wondered what had prompted Allison's admission of benign neglect, as well as her desire for connection. Very likely both were related to the loss Allison had suffered. If she couldn't be a mother of her own children she could be a friend to the children of other women. And she would never want to be a friend to children of a woman who had betrayed her. Marta was in the clear. Allison did *not* know about the one-night stand.

"It's not too late at all," Marta assured her. "Thank you. I'd appreciate your getting to know my children better. And I know they'll love getting to know you."

Bess sat placidly sipping her brandy. Clearly, *she* had no desire to form a stronger relationship with the MacIntosh clan. Then again, Bess's nieces and nephews lived only a few hours away. If Bess were to suddenly develop an interest in anyone's kids, it probably would be Ann's and Mae's.

Still, Marta couldn't resist stirring the waters. "Maybe I could send one of the kids to stay with you and Nathan for a weekend this fall," she said brightly. "Not Troy, he's too young, but Sam or Leo might be up for the adventure. What do you say, Bess?"

Marta saw Allison put her head down in an attempt to hide a smile. And poor Bess! The color had drained from her face and though she opened her mouth as if to say something, no words came out.

"It's okay, Bess," Marta said with a laugh. "I was only teasing."

"Sam might not be so bad," Bess blurted. "I mean because she's almost an adult."

Might not be so bad? "Don't worry," Marta assured her friend. "I

won't be shipping my offspring to Maine anytime soon and that's a
promise."

Bess smiled. "Whew," she said. "Thanks."

The hostess with the most-est, Marta thought. Except when it
came to children.

Chapter 60

Allison was tucked into her bed. She had just finished another cozy mystery, which meant that a second visit to the local bookstore was in order, that is, if she couldn't find another favorite classic among the books in the living area. If reading was addictive, she was happy to proclaim herself an addict. She put the book on the bedside table, switched off the lamp, lay back on the pillows, and found herself rehearsing bits of the earlier conversation with Bess and Marta.

Why had Marta so adamantly denied having a crush on that Bulgarian exchange student twenty years ago? The guy was cute and the past was the past. Could Marta have a guilty conscience? Maybe she had cheated on Mike back in college. But Marta didn't seem the type to cheat, Allison thought. She was too rooted and clearheaded for something as crazy and dangerous as an affair, let alone a one-night stand.

Less puzzling had been Bess's comment about finding Chris too similar to Allison for her to see him in a romantic way. The resemblance between Chris and Allison *was* pretty obvious, if also fairly general. They were both tall, slim, blonde, and blue-eyed; most people stopped observing after noting those similarities. If they did look more closely they would see that Chris's features were large and angular; Allison had always thought his profile would look right at home on a coin. Her own features were petite and rounded. While Allison was all legs, Chris's body was more evenly proportioned between legs and torso. The way they moved differed, too. Chris did everything deliberately and slowly, while Allison moved with the energy of a hummingbird.

But physical similarities and differences mattered nothing in the end. What mattered were the internal demons that tore a husband from his wife. An image of the man who had come to her rescue on the road flashed across her mind. Handsome, friendly Bill. What if the unimaginable happened, Allison thought, and she did fall in love again? Would love transform her for a second time into a creature of utter devotion and passivity? A creature of acquiescence? Or would love find her a different person next time, one too strong to warp, one willing to give and to sacrifice, but not at the constant expense of her truest self?

It was interesting, Allison thought, that she hadn't mentioned to the others Chris's landing the big design gig. In the old days, she would have shared the news within minutes. But now? Now things were different. Anyway, Marta might dismiss the victory as meaningless; she wasn't Chris's biggest fan at the moment. But the others would be glad for Chris. Wouldn't they? Chuck certainly would give his old friend his due, and Dean would probably follow suit. Bess would be happy for Chris; it wasn't in her nature to be stingy with praise and like Dean, Nathan would likely side with his partner. As for Mike, well, he, too, would wish Chris and his father success, no matter his wife's views.

The sound of a car pulling into the drive caused Allison to check the time on her phone, charging by the bedside. It was after eleven. The guys must have stopped for a drink after their game of miniature golf. *I should go with them next time*, she thought, turning onto her side. She loved miniature golf but hadn't played since she was a little girl on vacation with her parents. *Yes*, she thought as she sank off to sleep. *I'll go with them next time.*

Chapter 61

"So, you guys had fun last night?" Bess asked with a smile. She and Nathan were in the den. "I can't believe I didn't hear you come in. It must have been the brandy."

Nathan laughed. "You were sawing wood, as the old saying goes."

"I was? But I never snore!"

"Yes, you do. It's not bad and it's not often."

"Why didn't you ever tell me?" Bess asked. She felt a bit distressed.

"I'm telling you now. Bess, it's no big deal."

Nathan turned away and began to leaf through a pile of papers.

"Are you okay?" she asked. "You seem a little, I don't know . . ." Distant. That's what Bess wanted to say but was afraid to. "You seem a little preoccupied."

Nathan turned back to her. "Do I?" he asked. "I'm sorry. I'm fine. Though I am a bit worried Simon's flight won't get in on time for him to make the wedding. I suppose if he's stuck in transit I can ask Howard to stand in for him. Ah, here's what I was looking for," Nathan announced. He sank onto the couch, immediately absorbed in what was printed on the document he had been seeking.

Bess left him alone and went to the kitchen. She wasn't quite sure she believed that Nathan was fine. Could he be getting cold feet? Was he hesitating about taking on the whole lot of them, which he would most certainly be required to do should he marry Bess Culpepper, the infamous anchor of the group? No. Bess knew she was being silly—she was, wasn't she?—worrying about Nathan suddenly changing his mind and leaving her. She knew she was cherished. And yet . . .

How could you ever be sure about anything? The answer was that you couldn't. Welcome to the adult world. This wasn't college, when life seemed pretty much eternal and everything and anything possible. People were always telling her as much. It was time she really heard them.

The front door opened and a moment later Dean appeared, a watermelon under each arm. "Break out the vodka!" he cried.

"I'm on it," she told him.

"I was thinking," Bess said as she laid her jeans over the back of the rocking chair. "You know that small writing desk in my bedroom? It might be a good idea to sell it and get a larger one and set it up by the window in the living room. My condo needs a few changes if it's going to be really comfortable for the both of us."

Nathan was leaning against the dresser, his arms folded across his chest. "Mmm," he said.

"Nathan?" Bess asked. "Did you hear what I said?"

"Yes, of course. The small writing desk." Then he shook his head. "I'm sorry, Bess. My mind was elsewhere. The thing is, there's something we need to talk about."

A storm to shake up our complacency. I was right, Bess thought. *There is something wrong. I knew it. He's calling off the wedding. He doesn't want to marry me after all.*

Of course. Allison and Chris were getting divorced. Chuck and Dean were battling an illness. Something was up with Marta, and that meant that something was up with Mike, too. And Bess was being left at the altar or almost. Her stomach began to lurch and her head to swim. She was going to faint in about thirty seconds. Maybe twenty. She knew it.

Vaguely, she was aware of a voice. "Bess, sit down!" it said.

"You've turned absolutely white." Vaguely, she was aware of hands taking her arms, of her feet shuffling backward, of her butt hitting a firm surface. "Let me get you some water. . . ."

"No," Bess croaked, her head clearing a wee bit. "Just tell me."

Nathan's face came into focus. It was below hers. He was on his knees, his hands resting on her knees. "Are you sure you're okay?" he asked, searching her face as if for clues. "You scared me, Bess."

"Tell me," she repeated. She swallowed hard. Even if Nathan was breaking up with her she had no desire to vomit on him.

"The thing is," Nathan began, taking her hands in his, "I've been offered a promotion. But it's not as simple as just a promotion. It requires a relocation to Stockholm. It would only be for two years, at the end of which time I'll have the option to extend the stay or come back to the States."

A wild laugh burst from Bess's lips. "Is that all?" she gasped.

Nathan, still on his knees, frowned. "I think you might still be light-headed. Why don't you put your head between your knees? Makes the blood rush to your brain or something. Maybe I should get Chuck."

"No!" Bess cried, snatching her hands from his and putting one hand on either side of his dear face. "I'm fine. I thought you were . . . I thought you were going to tell me you'd changed your mind about the wedding."

Nathan began to tumble off his knees. "What!" he cried, catching himself by grabbing the bed. "Why would you think something like that?"

"Never mind," Bess said hurriedly. "Nathan, this is huge! You're being transferred to Stockholm?"

"Not as huge as my calling off our wedding! But yeah, it's big." Nathan got to his feet and perched next to Bess on the edge of the bed. "A transfer means a major change in everything we planned in terms of our day-to-day lives for the next two years."

Bess felt a bit sick again. "Have you accepted yet?" she asked.

"Of course not, not without talking with you first."

Bess shook her head. "Give me a minute, okay?" she asked. "I need to think."

Nathan nodded.

A million questions flooded Bess's mind. What was she supposed to do? Close down her company for two years? Turn her back on her hard-won career? Could she and Nathan survive a long-distance marriage? But Bess didn't *want* to live apart from Nathan. It was tough enough negotiating the distance from Boston to Portland. They were on the cusp of promising to love each other in good times and in bad, till death did them part. Commitment was *not* about a Knight in Shining Armor and a Princess in a pretty dress. It was about the mundane. It was about putting up with a million little annoyances, as well as celebrating each other's million little successes.

Bess swallowed hard. Was she really equipped for a real-life romance?

"Look, Bess," Nathan ventured. "I'm willing to turn down the promotion if you're against it. To be honest, it would negatively affect my career, but our relationship is worth more to me. A lot more."

"I believe you," Bess said quietly. But could she ask Nathan to make such a sacrifice? One thing Bess knew for sure. One or the other of them was going to have to budge or the relationship would be over before it had really gotten started. Nathan was willing to give up the transfer and promotion. But was *she* as willing to make such a large a sacrifice for *him*? What would it say about their future as a married couple if she wasn't at least willing to give this unexpected adventure a try? Being willing didn't mean it would come to pass, Bess noted. She could say sure, I'll go with you to Stockholm and Nathan could decide the transfer wasn't worth the risks it involved, but if she *did* agree to the move she would have to mean what she said. There would be no going back on her word. None.

"How long have you known about the promotion and transfer?" she said finally.

"It became official only yesterday, but I got wind of the possibility a few weeks ago," Nathan admitted.

"Why didn't you tell me when you first heard the rumors?" Bess asked.

Nathan ran his hand through his hair. "I'm sorry," he said. "I didn't want to cause you anxiety over something that might not actually come to pass. Not with the wedding coming up."

Bess thought. What if Nathan had waited until they were married before telling her about Stockholm? That would have been underhanded. Nathan was not underhanded. "Okay," she said. "It's just . . . wow."

Quand-même. I was afraid, but I did it anyway. Courage was admitting to being afraid but doing what had to be done nonetheless. Courage sounded scary. Bess almost laughed at the inanity of that thought. Almost.

Nathan sighed and gathered Bess in his arms. She did not pull away.

Chapter 62

Dinner would be delayed that evening. Bess had seen a sign for a flash sale at one of the arty boutiques in Kennebunkport and was determined to—as Marta's mother might say—"do some damage." Marta had no desire to go along, but Bess had insisted and often it was easier to give in to Bess's enthusiasm than to fight it.

While Allison and Bess browsed, tried on hats and jewelry, exclaimed over expensively priced housewares, and chatted with other enthusiastic customers, Marta wandered, feeling very out of place in all sorts of ways she couldn't quite name. Okay. She could name one. Her mom jeans and oversized blouse were a far cry from the stylish summer outfits worn by the shop's staff and the potential buyers.

How many of those potential buyers—all women, as it happened—earned their own money? How many of them had careers, owned businesses, lived on the profits of their own smart investments or retirement savings?

Marta fought a sudden urge to dash from the shop. Only the knowledge that such behavior would put a damper on her friends' shopping expedition restrained her, so she wandered on, absorbed by thoughts of her sorry predicament. Here she was complaining that this fourth and unplanned pregnancy was interfering in her plans for a career, but in fact there *were* no plans. She had done little real thinking about what she might actually *do* with her life. She had not even begun to brainstorm. She had not sought out an organization that helped people reenter the workforce. She had done nothing but dream.

And now? Say she could somehow find the energy to build her own life while she was raising another child along with Sam, Leo, and Troy, she still had to find the *focus*. She might have to go back to school to earn a degree. She would need to learn how to interview; she would need to learn what clothes were appropriate for interviews. She would need to upgrade her computer skills and become more familiar with social media platforms. Platforms? She would need to learn a new language, if not several new languages, those of contemporary culture and gender equality and . . .

"See anything you like?" It was Bess.

"Not really," Marta lied. There was a silk tunic she had admired for about thirty seconds before moving on. It was handmade; the quality was extraordinary. As was the price.

"Oh, come on, Marta," Bess urged. "Splurge for once! You've always been so frugal. I remember back in college you used to get two or three cups out of a tea bag because you didn't want to be 'extravagant.'"

Marta remembered, too. The third cup was always tasteless.

Without waiting for a reply, Bess darted off toward a display of dangling earrings. Marta couldn't remember the last time she had worn dangling earrings. Maybe she never had.

She sighed and moved on through the beautifully curated shop. She knew there were small steps she could take to make starting out less daunting. She could read the better women's magazines; absorb the information on websites devoted to working mothers; read blogs written by women who had launched careers after years of being a stay-at-home parent. All Marta had to do was to take that first step. . . .

A burst of laughter caused Marta to turn in the direction of a display of mirrors in hand-painted frames. Bess was engaged in lively conversation with another customer. Marta might tease Bess for all sorts of behaviors, but she could never deny that her old friend was a successful, self-made businesswoman. Something Marta was not.

She wandered back toward the attractive tunic. She had never felt so aimless; maybe all she *was* good enough for was to have babies and raise kids. She knew she was being dramatic—she would die of shame should any of her friends discover her thoughts—and she knew that to underestimate the talents and skills required to be a good parent was foolish.

Marta gently touched the silk tunic. She was strongly tempted to buy it. It was so beautiful. She hadn't had anything so beautiful in years. *No,* she told herself automatically. *I don't need it. I don't deserve it. There are better ways to spend my money. The money Mike earned.*

"It would look lovely on you."

Marta turned to find Allison just behind her. And it wouldn't fit in a few months, Marta thought. And when it did fit again, if that time ever came, where would she wear it? To the playground? The grocery store? A PTA meeting?

"Maybe." Marta shrugged. "Getting anything?" she asked.

Allison indicated a small shopping bag in her left hand. "Already did."

Marta was relieved when fifteen minutes later she and her friends finally climbed into Bess's car and headed back to Driftwood House.

"Retail therapy," Bess proclaimed from behind the wheel. "There's nothing like it!"

From the backseat, Allison laughed. "You said it!"

Marta, in the front passenger seat, looked out the window and frowned.

Chapter 63

They didn't sit down to dinner until almost eight. Mike looked as if he were truly suffering, though Allison thought it just possible that he had fortified himself with a snack while the women were out. Men like Mike knew full well how to feed themselves when someone wasn't around to make them a balanced meal.

"What did you buy?" Dean asked, passing the bowl of green beans in a spicy sauce. Nathan had brought in food from a new Sichuan restaurant and it was proving a hit.

Bess regaled everyone with the story of her many purchases. "And I know I'll get a lot of wear out of the chandelier earrings with the polki diamonds," she said of her most expensive purchase. "They never go out of style."

"What about you, Allison?" Chuck asked.

Allison, mindful of her new financial situation, had exercised restraint. But she had treated herself to one special item. "I bought a blown-glass pendant in the shape of a cat. Okay, I know! I might be becoming a cat lady. It's all the doing of that big gray feline that's been hanging around."

"He's a beauty," Dean confirmed.

"And you, Marta?" Nathan asked. "What caught your eye?"

Marta shrugged. "Nothing," she said.

"I never have to worry about Marta spending money on herself,"

Mike announced. "She's the least wasteful person I know. And the most self-disciplined."

Marta did not respond to these compliments. Allison wondered if she had even heard them. Marta's expression was blank.

"My mother is the same way," Chuck said. "She considers money spent on herself foolish spending."

"Buying a gift for yourself isn't in the least bit foolish," Dean protested. "At least, that's what *my* mother taught me."

"We tried to persuade Marta to buy a lovely silk tunic she had her eye on," Bess informed the others, "but she refused."

Mike turned to his wife. "You should have bought it, if you really liked it," he said earnestly.

"I didn't like it enough to spend four hundred dollars," Marta said almost angrily.

"All this talk about money is reminding me of how much I hated economics in college." Chuck shook his head. "I barely passed the introductory course. I really tried, but something just didn't click for me."

"You loved economics, didn't you?" Bess asked Marta.

Marta nodded. "It came easily."

"Not to me," Allison added. "I'm with Chuck. Something just didn't click. I failed the mid-term exam miserably."

Mike laughed. "Marta never *didn't* ace a test! It was as if she couldn't do poorly on an exam if she tried."

Allison thought she saw Marta flinch at this praise.

"Marta, did you ever consider being a teacher?" Bess asked.

"Why?" Marta snapped.

"I don't know. Because you seemed to *get* school so easily. Like being a student was second nature. Maybe being a teacher would also have been easy for you."

"No," Marta stated. "I never considered it."

Dean frowned. "Teachers don't get the respect they deserve. I mean: Those who can't do, teach. Really? That sort of attitude is infuriatingly prevalent, even today."

"Marta could have been anything she wanted to be, a lawyer, a doctor, a Wall Street wizard." Mike looked proudly at his wife. "She's smart enough and once she sets her mind to something, look out!"

Allison took a sip of wine. Was it just her or did the others think Mike was being overly effusive in his praise of his wife? Not that Mike didn't take genuine pride in her accomplishments.

"Chris was good at economics, as well," Bess was saying. "And math. Well, he would have to be good at math to be a successful architect."

"At one point, he considered going on for an advanced degree in mathematics," Allison said with a smile. "But his creative side won out and architecture it was." It felt good, Allison realized, not to cringe at the mention of Chris's name or to feel compelled to insult the man she had once loved so dearly.

Once? The man she still loved. The man she would always love. That's just the way it was.

"I lived at home and commuted to campus," Nathan was saying. "That might have had something to do with my not forming as tightly knit a group of friends as you all did. I'm still in touch with two of my friends from college, but not very often."

"I did live on campus," Dean said, "but for some reason none of my college friendships lasted. I'm closest now to a kid I was friends with in grammar school. When Jason and I get together it's like no time has passed since we terrorized the neighborhood on our skateboards or copped ice-cream sandwiches from his mom's freezer."

"Ice-cream sandwiches!" Mike exclaimed. "I haven't had one of those in years."

Chuck nodded. "Simple pleasures."

"Ice-cream sandwiches," Bess said. "Noted. I'll get some tomorrow. They make them with different flavors of ice cream these days. When I was a kid it was just vanilla."

The conversation and the meal went on and Allison found that her appetite was particularly healthy that evening. So many things were different from what they had been when the group had first come together at Driftwood House. Some things were better. Were some things worse? Allison shot a glance at Marta. She didn't really know. Things were just different.

That was okay.

Chapter 64

Bess had seen Dean and the baby leave the house and head down to the beach. She waited a half an hour—she didn't want Dean to think she was stalking him, which she kind of was—and then followed. She hadn't promised Nathan she would keep the news of his promotion and transfer a secret, and she knew that unlike how Chris had acted with Allison, Nathan would never stand in the way of her reaching out to her friends for comfort and advice.

She found Dean and Thomas only a few yards from the stairs that led up to Driftwood House. "Care for some company?" she asked.

"Sure. Plenty of room on this massive blanket Chuck insisted on buying. He can never resist a sale. He winds up buying stuff we really don't need or stuff that's too big or too small, just because it's been discounted." Dean laughed. "It drives me nuts."

Bess sat crossed-legged on the blanket. It really was huge. She wondered if after a few years of marriage, she and Nathan would be good-naturedly complaining about each other to their friends. Probably. It was what everyone did.

"You put aside your career, at least for a time, to raise Thomas," Bess began. "How did you come to that decision? What convinced you to make that sacrifice?"

"I'm happy to talk about this, Bess, but why now?" Dean asked, adjusting Thomas's wide-brimmed sun hat. "What's going on?"

"Can you keep a secret? Okay, I know you have to tell Chuck, but can the two of you keep a secret for a few days? No more than that?"

Dean nodded and Bess told him about Nathan's promotion and the accompanying transfer to Stockholm. "He really wants to accept," she said finally, "but he says he'll turn it down if I'm not okay with it. And I believe him."

"Wow. That's big and what timing. So, what was your initial feeling about it? Yes or no?"

"I didn't have a yes or no feeling," Bess admitted. "I still don't, and I'm not sure if that's a good or a bad thing."

"Let's put a positive spin on your indecision," Dean said. "Let's say it means you're open to the idea of the move but that before you say yes you want to be thoroughly certain you're doing what's best for you." Dean nodded. "And for Nathan, too. For the both of you, never to be torn asunder and all that. At least, once the wedding ceremony is over."

"I guess that's it," Bess admitted, "except that I know accepting the promotion and transfer would be the best thing for Nathan."

"Not at the expense of your happiness," Dean pointed out, "which would negatively affect the happiness of the marriage and, subsequently, its chance of success."

Bess frowned. "Oh," she said. "Right. It's so complicated, Dean! Having to think for three! Me, Nathan, and the marriage."

"There's a reason marriage counseling is so popular and the divorce courts are so full."

The word *divorce* sent the usual shiver down Bess's spine. "So, how *did* you guys make the decision about who should stay home and who should continue to work?"

"First of all," Dean said, taking Thomas on his lap, "we were very lucky to have had a choice. We're financially secure enough for both of us to continue to work full-time and hire a full-time nanny, or to allow me to take a professional hiatus and be the stay-at-home parent. Our choice wasn't solely determined by economic matters."

Bess thought. *Her income. Her company. Her retirement savings. Her good name.* If the move to Stockholm went sour, if the marriage didn't survive, where would all that be? Where would *she* be?

"But why you and not Chuck?" Bess asked. "Isn't your career as important as his?"

"Sure. But it won't be as difficult for me to return to teaching one day as it would be for Chuck to get back into medicine. And don't forget, while he makes a lot more money than I do, his schooling cost a hell of a lot more than mine did. I'm not saying I'll be able to waltz into a good position once Thomas is in school full-time, but I should be able to build my way back up. I keep on top of the developments in educational theory. I have lots of friends in the teaching profession. I won't be left floundering."

Bess gazed out over the sparkling Atlantic. Maybe she could work in Stockholm. She just didn't know. There hadn't been time to do any research. There was certainly no way she could just show up in Sweden and announce herself as a professional party and event planner. For one thing, she didn't speak the language. For another thing, she had no idea at all about the country's employment laws. For yet another thing, she had no professional connections outside the United States. Of course, there was no reason she couldn't run Joie de Vivre from abroad, was there? Not if Kara was interested in accepting a larger role, and Bess had a pretty good idea that Kara would jump at the opportunity.

A blog. A Bride Abroad. That could be a fun project. Thousands of people made good money from their blogs; it shouldn't be difficult to learn how she could do the same.

"I can't deny how lucky we are," Dean was going on. "So many families in this country are destroyed by the cost of childcare or just don't have the option to stop working for a few years so they can raise their kids hands-on."

"That doesn't mean you and Chuck don't have difficulties of your own to face," Bess pointed out.

"Of course," Dean agreed. "But since when is anyone guaranteed a trouble-free life? Everyone has a cargo of woes, even those who look to be coasting along without a care. That's one of the reasons envy is so utterly stupid. We should be thankful that we have only the troubles we have and not the hidden tragedies of others."

Bess smiled. "My mom and dad used to remind us of that every time there was news of some celebrity in trouble. She might be dripping in diamonds, they'd say, or he might own a yacht the size of Cleveland, but Sally Starlet or Harry Handsome—I'm not making this up, Dean—is a human being just like we are, weak, flawed, subject to death and taxes just like the rest of us."

Dean raised an eyebrow. "Your parents never heard of tax evasion?"

"If they did they preferred not to know. Their point was that money didn't buy happiness."

"Maybe not, but it makes being unhappy a whole lot easier to bear." Dean shook his head. "But that's not what we should be talking about. Not that money isn't important; you'd have to be really simple-minded to deny that. Conflict over finances can tear a marriage apart as easily as conflict over infidelity can."

"Nathan and I haven't talked about how my moving to Stockholm with him is going to affect our joint income," Bess admitted. "I've been supporting myself since I was a teen. I'm not sure how comfortable I am being dependent on someone else, even just for a while."

"Look, Bess," Dean said, "relationships are about constant negotiation. What works one year might not work the next year. You have to be very honest with each other and learn how to balance your own happiness with the happiness of the union. But it's worth the effort, if you're with the right person. The question is: Is Nathan the right person? And if he is, he's the one you should be talking about this with, not me."

Bess nodded and climbed to her feet. "You're right," she said. "Thanks, Dean. I'll see you later."

Dean was right, Bess thought as she made her way back to Driftwood House. Nathan *was* the right person for her, she believed that wholeheartedly, and she needed to find the maturity and the courage to be a good life partner. It might be the most difficult task she ever had to undertake, but she believed—she did—that in the end it would prove to be the most worthwhile by far.

Suddenly, Bess thought of her sisters and had a sort of epiphany. Too often she had dismissed their marriages as merely unions of convenience between unambitious small-town people who were afraid of going through life alone. But what right had she to judge people about whom she really knew so little? None at all. Maybe Ann and Mae knew what marriage was truly all about. Love. Laughter. Sacrifice. Care. Maybe it was time she looked up to her younger sisters as examples of real maturity.

Bess climbed the stairs to the back porch. She felt she had learned more about life in the past two weeks than she had in the forty some odd years that had come before. She felt as if she had been enrolled in a crash course on love, its fragility as well as its strength, the false façades in which people tended to disguise it, as well as the grittier but far more beautiful reality underneath.

All this reflecting was well and good, Bess thought as she made her way to the kitchen, but there was another meal to prepare and laundry to do and details of a wedding to finalize. And Bess did love to get things done.

Chapter 65

Marta stood at the window of the room she shared with Mike. She could have been facing a blank wall for all she was aware of the view. She had been thinking nonstop of the conversation at dinner the previous night. The remarks about her intelligence; Bess's question about her wanting to teach; Mike's choice of the past tense: "Marta *could* have been anything." If she had had the courage. If she had had the determination. If she had had "what it took," whatever that nebulous quality consisted of.

In the past weeks, Mike's praise of her abilities had come to feel oddly like insults. How could he so admire and respect her and yet have no clue that she felt miserable and angry? Did he truly wear blinders when it came to observing his wife? What would he think if he knew that Marta deemed herself a failure?

Marta turned from the window. She decided to call her mother. She wasn't quite sure why. She had spoken to her only the day before. Did a child ever stop needing a parent, she wondered? Or maybe she just wanted to kill time. That couldn't be right. Marta never wasted a moment.

"Is Troy around?" she asked when she had exchanged a greeting with her mother.

"He's out with your father and Leo went with them. Sam is

working; she took on an extra shift. It seems there's a handbag she absolutely has to have."

"Oh," Marta said. She felt a stab of loneliness. She missed her children.

"I ran into Olivine Kaye again yesterday," her mother went on. "She really is amazing. Remember I told you she opened a classic English-style tea shop?"

"How could I forget?" Marta asked dully.

"And that she was planning to expand? Well, she got the space she was hoping for and the larger shop should be open by the new year."

Marta realized she was staring at the closet door. She blinked and looked away. "That's great for her," she said.

"What's going on, Marta?" Mrs. Kennedy asked shrewdly.

"Nothing," Marta said.

"You can lie if you like, but something's bothering you. Don't tell me you've found out some deep, dark secret about Bess's fiancé and are about to ruin her wedding for her own good?"

Marta laughed in spite of herself. "Nothing like that, Mom. Nathan's a gem. Bess couldn't be happier." *Except for when I'm being a jerk to her,* Marta added silently.

"Then is it Allison? Are you worried about how she's coping with this divorce?"

"I was," Marta admitted. "But not so much now. I think she's going to be okay."

It's me I'm worried about, Marta wanted to say. But she didn't. She couldn't.

"Is everything okay with you and Mike?" her mother asked. A dog with a bone. Marta had gotten the habit of persistence from her mother. How difficult would it be to answer honestly, to admit to her mother that she was unhappy and that it was largely her own doing?

Too difficult.

"Everything is fine, Mom, I told you," she said. "Maybe I'm just ready to come home. I miss the kids. I miss my own home." That was true enough.

"Well, if that's all, I perfectly understand. There is no place like home and a mother is never quite right when she's away from her children. At least, when they're young."

Never quite right when she's away from her children.

"Yes," she told her mother. "You're right about that."

"Did I tell you that your father is thinking of taking up tennis?"

Marta smiled. "He doesn't have enough hobbies already?"

"It doesn't bother me that he keeps so busy. It allows me more time on my own and with my girlfriends. Better than having him underfoot all the time. So many of my friends are saddled with these sad post-retirement husbands."

And what about the women who had retired from careers, she wondered? But Marta knew her mother's friends. None of them had worked full-time jobs outside of the home. Neither had her mother.

Neither had she.

The call ended soon after that. Suddenly, Marta had an urge to review the speech she had written for Bess's wedding. She pulled a file folder from one of her travel bags; the speech was tucked inside. In less than thirty seconds, Marta had balled up the paper and tossed it in the direction of the wastepaper can. The entire speech was wrong, full of clichéd sentiment, archly humorous, a show-offy piece less about the bride than it was about the intellect of the writer.

Why couldn't she say what she really wanted to say, which was that she wished for Bess a marriage filled with warmth and comfort and easy intimacy? A marriage like the one she shared with Mike.

The one she *had* shared.

The one she wanted back.

Chapter 66

Allison rejoined the others in the living area; she had gone to her room after dinner to get a sweater against the slight chill. Nathan and Dean were the only two missing. Nathan was in the den attending to a work matter. Dean, claiming an incipient migraine, had gone early to bed.

"What did everyone do today?" Chuck asked, his legs dangling over the arm of his chair.

"Not much of anything," Allison admitted. "It was wonderful. And my new feline friend hung out with me for a while."

"You've never had a pet, have you?" Bess asked.

"No, I've never even been particularly interested in animals, but there's something about this cat that compels me."

"Definitely a crazy cat lady in the making," Chuck said with a smile.

"There are far worse things to be!"

"What about you, Mike?" Chuck asked. "What did you get up to today?"

"I did have to take one call from the office but otherwise, I vegged," Mike said. "An hour or so snoozing on the beach, a leisurely stroll through town, an ice-cream cone to tide me over until dinner."

"Marta?" Chuck asked.

"Talked to my mother," she said flatly. There was an unopened book on her lap; Allison couldn't see the title.

"Are the kids surviving without you?" she asked.

Marta smiled weakly. "I seem to be surplus to requirements at the moment."

"And, Bess?" Chuck asked. "You're always a busy bee."

Bess was sitting on the area rug, her legs curled up under her. "True, but there's not much left to do regarding the wedding."

"Of course, there isn't," Mike said. "Planning events is what you do for a living!"

Suddenly, Chuck sat up properly in his seat. "I knew there was something I wanted to tell you guys," he said. "Remember Professor Kelly, the head of the classics department? Well, I got a text earlier from the alumni association. There's going to be a memorial in September for the old gent."

"Didn't he pass away last fall?" Allison asked.

"At the ripe old age of ninety-five," Chuck confirmed. "The college has set up a scholarship in his name to benefit one of those very rare things these days—a classics major."

Mike laughed. "Kelly was a real character! Do you remember that walking stick he carried, the one with the silver head in the shape of a particularly hideous gargoyle? Boy, did he wave that thing around when he'd catch a student misbehaving!"

"He never threatened a female student, though," Bess recalled. "He was a real old-fashioned gentleman."

"A bit of a Victorian if you ask me," Chuck said wryly. "He might not threaten a female with bodily harm, but he would give her a look of such severe disappointment she'd feel shame enough for an entire repentant church congregation."

Mike shuddered. "That sounds far worse than a knock on the head!"

"And he taught up until the very end of his life," Allison said. "Though I heard that in the last few years his lectures were far from coherent and that some students—or their parents, more like—demanded their money back."

"Poor guy," Bess murmured.

Marta made a dismissive sound. "I'd have done the same. If I'm paying good money for a service, I expect to receive the full service."

"Sadly," Chuck said, "I can't make the memorial. My fall is totally booked."

"I respected the man well enough," Allison said, "but I have no interest in attending the memorial."

"I doubt I'll be able to spare the time, either," Bess noted.

"As for me," Mike said, "I never even had a class with the guy. There's no reason for me to be there."

"Marta?" Chuck asked.

Marta tossed the book that was on her lap onto a side table. It landed with a slap. "The kids all have back-to-school events that require the participation of good old mom," she said. "Not that I'll get any thanks from any of them. No one ever tells you how utterly thankless a job motherhood is going to be. Good thing, too. No one in her right mind would have kids if she knew the truth behind the myths."

Allison saw Mike look questioningly at Marta. It had been a particularly bitter thing to say, and callous to boot, given what had happened to Allison two years earlier.

"What a shame one of us can't be there to represent the group," Bess said mournfully.

A harsh laugh escaped Marta's throat. "What does 'one of us' mean at this point in time?" she demanded. "Who is this 'us' you're always referring to?"

Bess looked puzzled, but before she could reply Chuck was going on. "Speaking of the old alma mater," he said smoothly, "a few weeks back I ran into Jon Wheeler. Remember him? The guy who graduated with a perfect 4.0 Anyway, he asked if I was still in touch with Chris. I didn't want to speak out of turn so I said yes, on occasion, and left it at that."

"I remember Jon," Bess said excitedly. "He always wore this ratty old scarf, even in the summer. At first I thought it was an affectation, then someone told me it was the last thing his grandmother had given him before she died. I felt so bad I'd misjudged him." Bess smiled. "Did he ask about the rest of us?"

"No, he didn't," Chuck admitted. "In fact, when I mentioned

your name, Bess, and the fact that I was attending your wedding this summer, he drew a blank. I'm sure he meant no offense by it. It has been over twenty years."

Bess frowned. "I find it odd he didn't remember me, not that *I'm* so special, but as a group we were pretty awesome. We were such a—"

"Such a what?" Marta asked harshly, cutting Bess off. "We're not a country, Bess. We're not required to send a deputation to important events like memorial services or ribbon cuttings. You've always thought of us as something we're not and never were, something larger and more significant than just an ordinary group of ordinary people. When are you going to grow up and face the truth? All of us—we mean nothing in the scheme of things."

Allison was shocked. She had never witnessed Marta acting so badly.

Mike shifted uncomfortably in his seat. "Marta, I don't think—"

"I'm sure most people we came across in college don't even remember we existed," Marta went on, ignoring her husband, "let alone recall our names. Why should they? What makes 'us' special? We were just a bunch of kids thrown together on a college campus. We were—we are—just like any random group of coworkers who become friendly over time, or travelers on a bus tour who are forced to make small talk and get along in close quarters. Nothing more."

Allison glanced at Chuck. He looked as uncomfortable as she felt.

Mike frowned. "That's not fair, Marta. We became friends. Real friends. And after graduation we remained friends. It's why we're here right now, twenty years on."

"And we did have a reputation for always being together," Allison pointed out. "Where there was one of us there was likely to be another."

"Mike and Allison are right," Chuck said forcefully. "And I'm with Bess. I think we are a special group of people. Why can't we be?"

Allison felt herself holding her breath in anticipation of Marta's response. Bess looked downright fearful.

Suddenly, Marta stood and headed briskly toward the stairs. "I'm going to bed," she announced. "I have a headache."

"There's aspirin and ibuprofen in the bathroom cabinet," Bess said to Marta's back.

Marta ignored Bess and continued on her way, her shoulders set.

"What the heck is up with her?" Chuck asked Mike when Marta was out of sight.

Mike looked supremely uncomfortable. "I don't know," he admitted. "She's been . . . I just don't know." Mike rose from his seat. "Maybe I should go up to her."

Brave man, Allison thought. If she were Mike she would let Marta calm down a bit first. But she wasn't Mike and Mike knew Marta best. Or did he?

"I think I'll turn in, too," Allison said. "See you in the morning. Thank you, Bess, for another lovely day."

Bess smiled vaguely.

On her way out of the room, Allison glanced at the book Marta had been holding. It was a collection of nineteenth-century nature poetry. No clue there as to what was bugging Marta. And, Allison thought as she climbed the stairs to her bedroom, she would put money on the fact that Mike wasn't lying when he said he didn't know what was bothering his wife.

She closed the door to her charming room and went to the window that faced the back of the house. She couldn't be sure, but she thought she saw the big gray cat sitting in the exact middle of the yard, staring at the house as if he was watching over her. "Good night, my Little Gray Ghost," she whispered.

Chapter 67

Bess straightened the sugar dispenser and the milk pitcher so that they stood perfectly side by side. She reorganized the bowl of oranges, larger ones on the bottom. She double-checked to be sure that both the Cheerios and the Kashi boxes were sufficiently full. And she waited for someone else to show up.

The night before she had tried to explain to Nathan what had happened while he had been in the den and how it had made her feel, but she had given up. It had been too difficult to put into words. And Nathan had seemed distracted. Of course. He was waiting for her answer to his bombshell of a question.

Later, lying in bed, unable to sleep, Bess had endlessly reviewed the confrontation. Marta had a right to her opinions and a right to express them when and how she wanted to express them. Didn't she? If she confronted Marta about her tirade (if that wasn't too strong a word for it), asked for an apology for Marta's rudeness, Marta might refuse and the result would be disastrous. Bess would lose her maid of honor and her dear friend, and for what?

Keeping the peace at all costs wasn't such a bad thing. It really wasn't.

Finally, Bess had fallen asleep but had slept badly and woke with a headache that not even two cups of very strong coffee could alleviate.

The sound of someone approaching the kitchen caused Bess to clear her throat and sit up straight in her chair. It was Marta.

"There's coffee," Bess said unnecessarily, gesturing toward the row of pots on the counter. She felt a bit fearful. What if Marta wanted to continue her critical rant?

Marta poured herself a cup of the decaf and joined Bess at the island. "I want to apologize for my bad behavior last night," she said promptly.

Bess noted how tired her friend looked. "Oh, it's all right," she said quickly.

Marta made a noise of impatience. "No, don't just dismiss it. I mean, I'd like to be forgiven but you have a right to feel pissed off at me and a right to be given a very sincere apology."

"Okay." Bess took a sip of coffee before going on. "What is it you want to say?"

"I was in a really lousy mood, but I was out of line. I should have just gone down to the beach and walked it off rather than hang around and subject you and the others to my nastiness."

"What was bothering you?" Bess asked, wondering if she really wanted to know. *Yes,* she thought. *I do. And I don't. Not if it's going to sour what's left of this reunion. . . .*

Marta turned slightly to face Bess. "Something back home was preying on my mind. One of my colleagues on the neighborhood watch committee seriously dropped the ball on hiring decent vendors for the end-of-summer party and now we're stuck hiring lousy vendors and for a price far above what their services are worth."

"Oh," Bess said. The situation sounded annoying but not annoying enough to cause such a foul mood. Could Marta be lying?

"Mike took me to task last night," Marta went on. "He was right, of course. I acted like an ass and I'm sorry. I don't know what I can do or say to make it up to you."

"It's okay," Bess said, with more conviction than she felt. "Really."

"But I'm your friend," Marta pressed. "I should have held my tongue. I probably shouldn't even have been annoyed in the first place." She laughed a bit shrilly. "I mean, why should I care about how strangers looked at our gang back in college?"

Or about how I see us now, Bess thought. "We can't help what we feel," she said automatically. And then she wondered how many times she had offered that clichéd sentiment as a way out to someone who had hurt or insulted her, when maybe what she should have said was, "You were wrong. I would like an apology."

"But we can help what we say," Marta pointed out. If she was stating the obvious Bess was still grateful for it. "Feelings come and go. Words tend to linger. I'm really sorry, Bess. And my timing couldn't have been worse."

The look of penitence on Marta's face, the tone of real regret in her voice, decided Bess. "You're forgiven," she said sincerely. "Really." Before she could offer to make Marta a hot breakfast, Nathan appeared in the entry to the kitchen. Marta shot to her feet as if she had been poked in the rear.

"I'm going to grab a shower," she said; then she was gone.

"You okay?" Nathan asked, coming into the room and pouring himself a cup of coffee.

Bess nodded. "I guess," she said quietly, concerned that Marta, possibly still in the hall, might overhear. "She apologized for her behavior last night and I believe she's sorry. I'm just not so sure I believe the reason she gave for her 'bad mood.'" Bess related the cause to Nathan; he didn't buy the story, either.

"Whatever was behind her saying what she did about your take on the old gang," Nathan went on, "at least she came to realize that it was unkind."

So, Nathan had been listening to her after all last night. "She said Mike took her to task." Bess smiled a bit. "I guess that's part of being a couple. Calling each other on bad behavior."

"Without being a scold or a cop," Nathan added. "It's one thing to offer constructive criticism, but it's another to set oneself up as a morally superior know-it-all."

Another thing to negotiate, Bess thought worriedly. Would she ever get marriage right?

"Want an English muffin?" Nathan asked. "There's a brand-new jar of blueberry jam just waiting to be popped open."

"Sure," she said with a smile. "I love blueberry jam."

Nathan plunked the new jar on the counter. "Have at it," he said with a smile. "You deserve to enjoy what you love."

Chapter 68

It was almost eleven o'clock. Marta and Mike were alone in their bedroom. Marta, already in her nightgown, was shaking out her T-shirts, refolding them, and laying them back in a drawer of the dresser. Mike was scrolling through his messages from the office.

Marta had spent the day largely on her own after apologizing to the others who had witnessed her bad behavior the night before. (She was particularly sorry that she had said what she had about motherhood being a thankless job, especially in front of Allison.) Hiding was in some ways easier than facing her friends, but in another way the isolation had only served to highlight her distress. And a million little things had gone wrong since morning, most of them while she had been doing something for someone else. No good deed ever went unpunished. Wasn't that the old saw?

While sewing a button on Mike's shirt she had stuck herself with the needle. She had thrown the shirt across the room before grudgingly retrieving it and completing the domestic task. Why couldn't Mike learn to replace the buttons on his shirts? If he was going to be rough enough on his clothing to damage it he should be adult enough to take responsibility for the repairs!

When she had wandered into the kitchen mid-morning for a bottle of water she found a jar of marmalade uncovered, a fly sitting on the jar's edge. The jar was sticky and when she went to the sink to wash her hands after cleaning the jar and putting it in the fridge, the water spurted out in a boiling torrent. Well, almost boiling. Marta had a red mark on her finger to prove it. The mark wouldn't be there if people learned to pick up after themselves.

Not long after that she had offered to watch Thomas so that Chuck and Dean could get a nap; the baby had cried most of the night, keeping both men awake and watchful. (Thomas's cries had woken Marta from a deep sleep, too. It had taken a fuzzy moment before she realized that the baby was not her responsibility.) The men had eagerly accepted Marta's offer. "No one else offered their babysitting services," Dean said. "Thanks, Marta."

Marta was a mother. This is what mothers did. They volunteered to watch their friends' baby and didn't complain when the child threw up all over them. No, she had thought, as she cleaned the baby and rinsed her blouse, it was Mike she was annoyed with. It was Mike and his resistance to the idea of a vasectomy that had landed her in her current situation, forty-two, pregnant, and facing another lifetime—okay, not a lifetime but years—of servitude.

Marta was tired. She closed the dresser drawer and gasped. Mike had come up behind her. He began to gently rub her shoulders. This was followed by a nuzzle and a kiss on her neck. His message was clear.

The very last thing Marta wanted at that moment was to have sex. The very last thing. Why were his needs always so important? Why was he so selfish? Didn't he even notice that she wasn't in the mood, or did all he see when he looked at her was his possession, his sidekick, his little woman?

"I'm not in the mood, Mike," she said flatly.

Mike did not reply; he was too busy kissing her, his hands holding her shoulders.

"Stop!" Marta cried, yanking out of his grasp and whirling to face him. "I said I don't want to!"

Mike stepped back and held his hands in the air. "Okay. Sorry. You don't have to yell."

"Yeah," Marta said raggedly. "Sometimes I *do* have to yell, otherwise no one hears me."

"What are you talking about?" Mike said.

"I can't take any more," Marta cried, heedless of her friends just down the hall.

"What do you mean?" Mike asked, his voice a deliberate whisper.

Marta sunk onto the edge of the bed and put her head in her hands. The truth was going to come out now, whether she wanted it to or not. She sighed, dropped her hands, and looked up at her husband. "I mean," she said, "that I don't want this baby."

If Mike recoiled—and he did—so did Marta. The words sounded so brutal when spoken aloud. But the words were out now. There was no taking them back. She didn't want to take them back.

The silence lengthened and grew heavy. "I don't understand," Mike said finally. "You've always loved being a mother. It's what you've always wanted to do."

"I do love it," Marta agreed. "But I've realized that being a mother can't be my forever-after. And by the time this baby is in middle school, and that's another ten years or so, I'll be in my fifties starting out."

"What do you mean, starting out? Starting out where?" Suddenly, Mike blanched. "You're not thinking of leaving me, are you?"

At that moment, Marta felt not an ounce of sympathy for her husband. "No, Mike," she said with a twinge of mockery in her voice. "I'm not leaving you. This is not *about* you. This is about *me*. This is about me wanting . . . wanting something new, an intellectual challenge, a career . . ." Marta shook her head. "There are times lately when I regret not having gone to law school."

"Do you want to go now?" Mike asked quickly. "It's not too late. I'll make it happen. Just say the word."

"I don't know," Marta replied testily. She didn't like it that Mike had co-opted her future. *He* would make it happen . . . Good old Mike, always trying to fix problems before taking the time to understand them! "Maybe. No, I *don't* want to go to law school, but I do want to do something worthwhile, something that has nothing to do with . . . nothing to do with you or the kids."

"I see," Mike said.

Marta wasn't at all sure he did see. To be fair, how could he?

"So," he went on, "where do we go from here? I guess I should have . . . I should have gone to the doctor. I'm sorry."

"Yes," Marta said fiercely. "You should have. This whole mess is your fault!"

"Wait a minute. Mine? You were the one who said we could have sex using some other birth control method until . . ." Mike rubbed his forehead. "Look, if you had said no, I might not have been happy about it, but I would have accepted your decision. And I . . . and I would have gotten a vasectomy."

Marta laughed. Would he have? "I wouldn't have had to make a bad compromise if you had been man enough in the first place to agree to the vasectomy! You're a selfish man, Mike. You always have been." Was that what she had really meant to say? Marta wondered. Maybe.

"Selfish?" Mike said, shaking his head. "Everything I do is for the sake of you and the kids. And I don't mind because I'm doing it so that my family is as safe and secure as I can make them in this insane world. Look, I'm not a saint. I make mistakes, lots of them. But I've never, not once, knowingly put my own needs before the needs of you and the kids."

Marta could not deny this. She had misspoken badly when she called Mike a selfish man. He might have selfish moments—what person didn't?—but he was fundamentally a selfless man. But an apology wouldn't come to her lips. She looked away from Mike.

After a moment, he knelt by her side and reached for her hands. Marta let him take them, but they lay lifeless in his grip. "Why didn't you tell me immediately that you were unhappy?" he asked. "Don't you trust me? Did you think I was going to be angry with you for not being totally thrilled? I know having another baby won't be easy for you. But did you expect me to be a mind reader?" Mike sighed. "So that's why you didn't want to tell the others about the pregnancy. You'd have to fake it with them, too."

Still Marta found that she couldn't speak. It was as if a perverse spirit was preventing her from communicating with her husband, from taking the all-important first step toward making things right again.

Suddenly, Mike let go of her hands and got to his feet. "Were you planning on keeping this a secret from me for the rest of your life?" he demanded, beginning to pace the room. "For the rest of

our lives? Do you have so little respect for me?" Suddenly, he came
to a stop and turned to face her. "Wait," he said. "*Have* you told the
others about the pregnancy, about how you're so unhappy? Am I the
topic of conversation in every other bedroom in this house tonight?"

"No one is talking about you, for God's sake!" Marta cried. With
effort, she took a deep breath and told herself to be calm, or at least
to appear that way. "Sorry. I can't seem to stop raising my voice. I've
been silent for so long."

"I haven't kept you silent, Marta," Mike protested. "I've never
wanted you to be some mindless little appendage who just sits in
the corner, nodding yes to whatever idiocy comes out of my mouth."

No, she thought. She had been the one to allow her situation to
render her silent.

"I haven't said anything to anyone about the pregnancy or about
what I've been feeling," she told him. "What with Allison's divorce
looming and Bess's wedding just around the corner, and Chuck
dealing with his diagnosis . . ." Marta shook her head. "I didn't want
to add to my friends' burdens."

"They're *our* friends, Marta. Not just yours. They mean as much
to me as they do to you."

Marta hadn't been aware of her choice of words. "Of course," she
amended. "Our friends. The point is I hate to appear needy."

"Even with me it seems." Mike's tone was bitter.

"I'm sorry," she said.

Mike made no reply. Marta realized she felt frightened. She had
never seen Mike so upset, not in this way. She had hurt him, badly.
It was not a nice feeling, to be guilty of hurting someone you loved.
Even if he had acted like a jerk. Even if . . .

Without another word, they both made their way into the bed.
Mike turned off his bedside lamp, flipped to his side so that his
back was facing Marta, and lay perfectly still. Even an hour later
Marta couldn't tell if he was asleep or awake. She lay there beside
the man she had loved unreservedly for so many years, feeling absolutely alone. Absolutely miserable. And terribly frightened.

Chapter 69

Allison felt very cozy tucked into her own bed in her own room. It had taken her a long time after Chris's desertion before she began to appreciate the pleasures of sleeping alone. There were moments now when she thought she might never allow anyone to spend the entire night next to her. Even in a queen bed like this one there was so much *space* in which to stretch out!

Sleep was rapidly approaching, but memories of the day just passed were still popping into her consciousness. Marta, for example, had apologized for her outburst the night before. It was a sincere apology. Allison had been tempted to ask Marta what was bothering her, but her gut told her that in Marta's current mood she would resent the question.

Otherwise Allison had spent a pleasant day sketching the magnificently gnarled tree and napping on the lawn, where her new feline friend had joined her. He had even curled against her leg and allowed her to rest a hand on his furry, muscular back.

Allison yawned and shifted to her side. And it was then that she heard raised voices. That was definitely Marta's voice and, yes, Mike's as well. Allison shut her eyes, as if that would help block out the sound of anger. It was deeply unpleasant to be privy to an argument between two people you cared about. Something very

unhappy was going on between Mike and Marta these days. Whatever it was, Allison sincerely hoped they could work it out before
there was another divorce for Bess to worry about.

Please, she prayed fervently to whomever or whatever might be
listening, *don't let Bess be hearing this fight.*

Chapter 70

Nathan was asleep. Bess was not. She was thinking hard about the decision she had to make. To go with Nathan to Stockholm. To tell Nathan he would have to turn down the promotion and transfer. To let Nathan go to Stockholm on his own, and to spend the first two years of their marriage as a long-distance commuter couple. No. Not that.

Earlier, Bess had considered calling her mother to seek her advice. The idea had surprised her. Bess never turned to her mother for anything. In the end, she decided against making the call. She knew what her mother would say. "Do what makes you happy." But would Mrs. Culpepper say that? Or would she say: "Your duty is to your husband."

Bess sighed quietly. And that was when she heard the raised voices coming from down the hall. Allison was on her own, so it had to be Mike and Marta. Bess put her hands over her ears as the voices became louder and angrier. What could they be fighting about? What was so important that it couldn't wait until they were in the privacy of their own home?

Please, Bess prayed fervently. *Please, God, don't let anything else bad happen to my friends.*

Chapter 71

The sun was warm; the breeze slight but fresh; the stretch of beach spread out before her largely empty. Marta sat perched on a large rock at the top of the sand; it wasn't the most comfortable seat, but it was solitary. Besides, Marta wasn't sure she deserved comfort at the moment.

She and Mike had barely spoken to each other that morning and what they had said had been delivered in polite and measured tones. "You can use the bathroom first." "Did you sleep all right?" "Fine, thanks. You?" "Fine." Marta knew that Mike was hurt and she hated herself for having hurt him. She had underestimated him badly. She should have told him her true feelings about the pregnancy immediately. Not to have done so was an insult. And it was cowardly. Maybe together they could have tackled the situation and come to a happier state than that in which they found themselves now. When you were married—legally or not—two minds and hearts were always better than one. They had to be.

"Mind if I join you?"

Marta startled, looked up, and managed a smile. "Of course not."

Chuck lowered himself to the rock next to the one on which Marta was perched. "Another beautiful day," he commented.

"Yes," Marta agreed.

"You're pregnant, aren't you?"

Marta looked at her friend with wide eyes. "How did you know?" she demanded. "I'm not showing yet."

"You are," he said, "but not in the way you think."

"That's the problem with doctors. You can't hide anything from them."

"It's not the doctor in me that saw," Chuck pointed out. "It's the friend."

Suddenly, Marta found herself confessing all, from how she felt about the unwanted pregnancy to the awful scene with Mike the night before.

"I really screwed up by keeping my unhappiness to myself for so long and then by springing it on Mike the way I did," she said when she had finished. "It's going to cost him to keep a smile on his face for the rest of the week. He's not like me. He's not able to dissemble when it comes to his feelings."

"Don't take this as an insult, because that's not how it's meant, but I've always felt that women are better dissemblers than men. They've been trained from an early age not to make trouble and to get what they want in roundabout ways, the more direct ways available to men not being available to them. Not that every woman paid attention to those lessons," Chuck added, "and good for those who didn't or who had the luck not to be bound by them."

Marta thought about that for a moment. When did a girl—or a woman—finally realize that she had the right to be angry and to tell the world about it? Too late. Too late.

"Maybe I shouldn't have said anything to Mike," she went on archly. "Maybe I just should have sucked up my unhappiness like I've always been able to do when times are tough and just got on with things."

"Don't be silly," Chuck said. "You were right to tell Mike how you feel, though it would have been wiser to do so before now. But when are human beings ever wise? Anyway, things will probably be awkward between you two for a while. No doubt you'll both have to put in some hard labor. Pardon the pun."

"I know," Marta said. "The really scary thing is we've never been in this sort of a situation before. Compared to this our conflicts have always been of an insignificant nature. I just hope . . . I just hope we can work through this."

"Do you still love Mike?" Chuck asked after a moment.

"Yes," Marta said unhesitatingly. "But is love always enough?"

"It had better be," he answered wryly, "or we're all in trouble."

"How are you doing?" Marta asked. "You told us that you're handling the diagnosis well, and I'm sure you are, but . . ."

Chuck smiled. "But yeah, in spite of being Mr. Resilient there are moments when I think I'm going to collapse in sheer despair and never get up. Those moments pass but while they're happening, they have the feeling of an eternity."

"I've always hated that old saying, 'This too shall pass.' And then what? Maybe something worse will come in its place. And even if something good is to come, how do I survive the here and now? How exactly do I *do* that?"

"Giving real comfort to someone in distress is pretty much impossible, which doesn't mean we shouldn't try. Of course, we should," Chuck said firmly. "It's our duty."

Marta sighed. "But most times it might be better to keep our mouths shut when we go about offering comfort. A gesture, a small gift, a favor, or even a touch might be all that's required, rather than platitudes and ill-judged advice."

"I'll take a handful of Necco wafers over a bit of clichéd advice any day."

Marta shuddered. "I seriously don't know how you can eat those things!"

A family group appeared not far to the left of where Chuck and Marta sat. They began to settle down, the father spreading out the blanket and opening a chair for the mother, who had a baby strapped to her chest. A girl of about eight helped smooth out wrinkles in the blanket and busily arranged the family's beach bags to her liking. A boy of about five dashed off toward the water's edge. His mother, baby in tow, hurried after him.

"You know," Chuck said, his gaze turned out over the water, "when Dean and I got engaged we had a grand plan for our lives. We'd get married. We'd have two, maybe three kids. We'd fill the house with love and laughter. Our kids would grow into caring, intelligent, and successful adults, and Dean and I would grow old together, surrounded by the younger generations we had helped along the way. Picture-perfect. No crisis larger than the grocery store being out of someone's favorite yogurt or the neighbor's dog throwing up in the pool." Chuck turned briefly to Marta and smiled. "That happened a few weeks ago."

"Your plan sounds like a good one," Marta said. And she thought: *Just like what Mike and I planned. Just like what we did. And now we'll be adding another element to that love and laughter . . . Why can't I see the situation as a positive?* "And now?" she asked her friend.

Chuck sighed. "Since my diagnosis neither of us has mentioned having another child. It's as if the ideal life we planned to build has just slipped away into memory. All we seem to talk about now is how to prepare for the future of my illness. It's as if this disease has stepped in the way of everything else and I understand that's probably normal. But how long will this way of thinking go on?"

Marta honestly didn't know what to say, but she didn't think that Chuck expected she would have an answer to his question.

"More kids means more work for Dean," he went on, "and that seemed okay when I was in robust health and could be of help at nights and on weekends. But if Dean has to care for me as well . . . I'm saddling him with caretaking responsibilities he never anticipated he'd have to deal with, at least not for a very long time."

"I don't know Dean all that well," Marta said, "but I strongly suspect he's up to the challenges your illness will present."

"But what about children?" Chuck pressed. "Is it fair to bring more children into a home with one parent losing his grip?"

Marta put her hand on Chuck's knee. "You're not losing your grip, Chuck, don't say that. And you and Dean are fantastic people. Any child would be seriously lucky to be included in your family, illness or no illness."

Chuck smiled. "Old friends never really see the truth about each other, the pedestrian truth those who only know us in the here and now are aware of. You and I remember each other as youths, and all young people are innocents, guiltless, wonderful. Even know-it-all, starry-eyed eighteen-year-old youths are lovely."

"You're right, of course," Marta agreed. "We were youths judging youths. The inexperienced encountering the inexperienced. Of course, we all fell in love with one another. How could it have been otherwise?"

Marta thought for a moment before going on. "Remember what you said to me a few minutes ago about being right to have told Mike exactly how I feel? And how I should have told him sooner? Chuck, you need to talk to Dean. Now that the families and your close friends know about the Parkinson's—or will know soon—there's no reason to tiptoe around any aspect of what might lie ahead. And the key word there is *might*. None of us know exactly what will happen, good or bad." Marta wondered. Maybe this fourth child would turn out to be a blessing in disguise. She had to keep an open mind about this baby. She had to.

Chuck grimaced. "The last time I tried to talk about more kids I broke down crying. I think I really scared Dean. Crying is so downright ugly."

"Even when babies do it?"

"Then it's just heartbreaking." Chuck shook his head. "Seriously, every time Thomas cries I feel as if I'd do anything, *anything* to make things better for him. The last thing I want is to rush through these early months, but in some ways I can't wait until he can tell us with words just what it is he needs and wants."

"He'll be telling you long before the words come," Marta promised. "Just keep paying attention. For the moment, you have to remember that babies have so few ways of communicating. Crying is easy and available. Most times they're not in pain or even any real discomfort, just trying to say, hey, I'm here."

"I know that intellectually, but my heart refuses to accept that Thomas's tears are anything other than sheer existential angst and unbearable physical pain wrapped up in one unendurable bundle." Chuck sighed. "Thank God for Dean. Where's my professional distance when it comes to my son?"

"Don't worry about it, Chuck," Marta said. "You're doing a fine job as a father. No one would think otherwise."

The two friends sat in companionable silence, listening to the happy cries of the brother and sister racing to and from the ocean's edge with pails of water; watching the small group of surfers in the distance; enjoying in spite of their personal troubles the warmth of the June sun.

"You know," Chuck said after a while, "all my life I wanted to be a doctor. When I was a kid I had one of those old doctor bags filled with plastic instruments and pill cases. I loved giving our dogs checkups, though my sisters weren't always thrilled when I came at them with the stethoscope!" Chuck shrugged. "At some point my career is going to have to take a different shape, thanks to the Parkinson's. I don't want to be self-pitying, but sometimes I do want to stamp my feet and ask, Why me? And the answer to that is: Why not me? Am I so special I should live a charmed life? And the answer to that is no, I'm no more special than the next person." Chuck turned to Marta and smiled. "In spite of what my mother always told me."

Marta laughed. "How did she take the news of your illness? And your father?"

"Mom assured me that I only had to say the word and she would move in with me and Dean and take care of everything. Dad grumbled and patted my shoulder and nodded. In short, each acted in typical fashion. For which I was hugely grateful, by the way."

"And your sisters?" Marta asked.

Chuck winced. "They wept and wailed and then proceeded to smother me with hugs and kisses and to stuff me with food. According to my family, food and plenty of it cures all that ails you. They think bad cholesterol is a myth and low-fat anything the work of the Devil. So do I, but don't tell my patients."

"Sounds nice in a way, all that being fussed over." Marta knew that her parents loved her, but they had never been particularly demonstrative people. Neither had Marta.

Chuck nodded. "Nice and suffocating. But I shouldn't complain. One should never complain about being loved, even if the manner in which one is loved is at times, well, suffocating."

Or not quite what you need when you need it, Marta thought. But human beings did their best. At least, the best of them did and Mike was indeed one of the best. She believed that Mike loved her. More, she *felt* that Mike loved her. "I really do love that man," she said suddenly.

"I know you do. And he loves you. Thanks for listening to my stuff," Chuck added. "Especially with all you have on your mind."

"You too," Marta said. "You won't say anything to the others about my being pregnant, will you?"

"Of course not. But I don't like to keep secrets from Dean."

Marta smiled. "You can tell Dean. I'll have to come clean with the others before long, but not before the wedding. I don't want anything else getting in the way of Bess's focus. I've never seen a bride-to-be more invested in everything going right without becoming a Bridezilla in the process."

"Bess is far too sweet-natured to become a monster of any sort," Chuck stated. "I hope that's one of the things Nathan loves and respects about her. Too many men in the past have taken advantage of that sweet nature. Anyway, I should get back to the house. Dean will be worrying."

"I'll come with you," Marta said. She doubted Mike would be worrying. Not this morning.

Marta and Chuck each rose from their perch and turned back toward Driftwood House.

"Maybe Bess is on to something by taking that drunken pact we made in college so seriously," Chuck said. "Best friends forever. Where would I be without you guys?"

Marta smiled. "Ditto."

Chapter 72

"Pass me that knife, Bess?"

Bess did so and was rewarded with a kiss on the cheek and a word of thanks.

Allison was in the kitchen with the bride and groom, perched on a stool at the island, sipping a cup of tea, but mostly watching Bess and Nathan interact. There was no doubt about it. The pair was in love. But while being in their presence might have sent Allison spiraling into depression only a month ago, now it only produced a twinge of discomfort and a much larger sense of good and sympathetic feeling.

"Anyone know where Marta has got to?" Bess asked. She was slicing tomatoes while Nathan was expertly chopping celery.

"No," Allison replied. She wondered if Marta had guessed that she and Mike had been overheard. And if Allison had heard them, it was likely that Bess had as well, Nathan, too. Chuck and Dean had probably been spared. Lucky them. Allison had decided not to mention what she had heard to Bess. And when Bess said nothing more on the subject, Allison assumed that she, too, had decided to stay out of Mike and Marta's private affairs.

Nathan scooped the mound of finely chopped celery into a stainless-steel bowl. "Ready to be added to the chicken salad," he said. "I'm going to run to the farm stand out on Beach Plum Lane. They have the homemade gingerbread Bess likes so much."

After another kiss, Nathan was gone and Bess now turned to shredding the poached chicken. She claimed not to be a good cook, but Allison thought she did just fine. Her own culinary skills had lain dormant for so long. She didn't like to make a meal for one. Would she ever again enjoy cooking for another person?

Allison thought again of the pact they had all sworn the night before graduation and of how so often through the years she had forgotten about it, at least consciously. She wondered what Chris would say about the pact now if one of them were to remind him. Was he still suffering all on his own? Had he finally turned to friends of the more recent past for comfort? Allison truly hoped that Chris would reach out to Chuck at some point. That friendship, at least, should not be left to die.

"Penny for your thoughts?" Bess asked, wiping her hands on a towel.

"You might not be glad you asked," Allison told her. "The truth is, I had mixed feelings about coming to this reunion—and to your wedding. I wasn't sure I could face everyone's pity and questions. I wanted to celebrate your happiness, but I wasn't sure I had the generosity of spirit not to be a drag."

Bess shook her head. "You shouldn't have worried. None of us expected you to be jolly."

"Still, I want to thank you for being so unfailingly kind. I know I haven't always been the most pleasant houseguest—or the best of friends—but you've been the most generous hostess—and friend— there could be. You raise the art of loyalty to a new level, Bess. You always have."

Bess wiped tears from her cheeks and came around the island to hug Allison. "Thank you," she said. "I'm so very glad you're here."

When Bess had released her (and what a grip she had!), Allison went on. "I called you our anchor the other day and I mean that. You have our backs, even when we're not sensitive enough to know you're there. Bess, please believe that you can rely on my friendship more than ever as you enter this next exciting phase of your life."

Bess laughed. "By exciting do you mean tumultuous?"

"Challenging. But also wonderful." Allison grinned. "By the way, what's your stand on Miracle Whip in chicken salad?"

Bess shuddered. "No, thanks. It's mayonnaise or nothing!"

Chapter 73

The house was empty but for Bess, who was putting the finishing touches on a fresh pitcher of lemonade. It was a mindless task, though pleasant enough, and while she measured and stirred she thought about the raised voices she had heard the night before.

Neither Mike nor Marta had said a word about what had gone on between them all day, and Allison had given no indication that she had heard anything unusual, so Bess had kept her own mouth closed. She did, however, tell Nathan, who, typically and probably wisely, had advised her to let the matter alone. "Husbands and wives argue," he said. "It doesn't mean the end of the world—or of the marriage."

Her cell phone alerted Bess to a call. Bess put down the long-handled spoon she had been using to mix the sugar into the lemonade. For a moment, she didn't recognize the number on the phone's screen. And then she did. It was Chris's number. She stared at the screen for another second before accepting the call.

"Hello?" she said.

"Bess."

"Where are you?"

Chris laughed nervously. "I'm not sure how you'll feel about this, but I'm at a bed and breakfast in Kennebunkport."

Bess felt her head swim. As much as she had wanted to hear

something like this from Chris, she had given up on the possibility entirely. "Oh," she said. "Since when?"

"Since last night. Look, I know this might sound . . . The thing is I was hoping it would still be okay if I come to the wedding. I understand if you'd rather I not," he added quickly.

He sounded sad and hesitant, as if he really didn't have any idea of what Bess would say to his request. And for a moment, neither did Bess. Then she said, "Of course you're still invited. Of course." And then she wondered if she should have consulted the others first, especially Allison, who had so recently praised her loyalty. But she hadn't. Too late.

"Thank you," Chris said feelingly. "It means a lot to me."

"Look," Bess said, "why don't you join us for dinner tomorrow evening. We're having a fondue feast, sort of a reprise of the one we had back in college but without the disasters."

"Thanks, Bess," Chris said quickly, "but it's probably better that I don't."

"But what are you going to do with yourself until the wedding? You can't sit around all on your own."

"I'll be fine," Chris told her. "I've got my computer with me; I'm not on vacation."

Then, before she could stop herself, Bess blurted: "Allison told us about the accident and the miscarriage. She told us everything."

There was a long silence during which Bess wondered if she had lost her mind. Allison had specifically asked her friends not to tell Chris she had come clean. "Chris?" she asked, with a bit of trepidation. "Are you still there?"

When Chris spoke, his voice was unsteady. "She swore she wouldn't tell anyone," he said.

"Don't be mad at her, Chris. She had to tell us. She's suffering." Bess flinched. "Sorry. That sounds like blame. Blame shouldn't be a part of this. But you should know that Allison is terribly unhappy."

"And you still think that my being at your wedding is a good thing?" Chris sighed. "I think I should just go back to Chicago. I'm sorry, Bess. This was a very bad idea on my part. At the very least I should have called before I left for the east coast."

"No," Bess said firmly. "I want you to be part of my celebration. Please say you'll come for dinner tomorrow. Please. We need to be together again." *Why*, Bess asked herself suddenly, her hand tightening on the phone. *Why do we need to be together? Why do I still need this to happen, after all this time and all I've learned these past days about the inevitability of change, about impermanence, about loss?*

"I'll think about it," Chris promised. "I'll let you know by tomorrow afternoon."

"All right," she said. "In the meantime, I'll tell the others you're in town."

"They might not be so welcoming," Chris pointed out. "If everyone thinks it best I leave, you'll be honest with me?"

"I will," Bess promised.

"Thanks. Until tomorrow, then."

Phone still in her hand, Bess leaned back against the counter. It was what she had wanted, Chris to be there with them, the whole gang together to help her celebrate the most important day of her life.

Be careful what you wish for . . . Her dour great aunt Mercy had loved to intone that grim old warning and others like it. It had driven Bess mad at times, all that doom and gloom, but now she wondered if Great Aunt Mercy hadn't been on to something after all. *Look before you leap.* That was something else she used to say.

Bess put a hand to her forehead. She thought of Chuck and Dean, of Mike and Marta, of Nathan, and especially of Allison, the one who had so recently praised Bess's sense of loyalty. What had she gotten them all into?

Chapter 74

Marta was straightening the clothes that hung in the bedroom closet. The pants and shirts and sundresses didn't need straightening, but Marta needed something to keep her hands busy. Busy work. It was something at which women were meant to be good. She wished that Mike was not with her in the room. She wished that he would envelope her in his arms.

"Do you love me?"

Marta jumped at the sound of Mike's voice and turned from the closet. "Of course, I love you," she said. He was standing by the dresser, hands in the front pockets of his jeans.

"Why of course?" he said in that logical, lawyer-like way he rarely used outside of the office or courtroom.

Marta tried to smile. "Mike, nothing's changed between us."

"Yes, it has," he said simply. "Of course, it has."

"What is it that you most object to?" she asked. "Me being unhappy about having another child, or me not having told you the truth right away?"

"Both upset me," Mike admitted, "but I can get my head around you not being thrilled to have to go through another pregnancy and childbirth. All the stuff I can't help you with. I wish you were happy about it, but I'd be totally callous and stupid if I couldn't understand your frustration."

Marta swallowed hard. He was a good man. One of the best. "So," she said, fighting tears, "it's my not having been honest up front that really hurts."

"Yeah."

"I tried to tell you how I felt but—" Marta realized she didn't know how to go on.

"But what?" Mike asked.

"But you didn't listen! The other day, when we were at the Cove, I said I needed to talk to you about something important, but you were too busy watching a schooner to hear me! I needed help, but you . . ." Again, Marta struggled to find the right words. "You really had no suspicion that I was unhappy," she asked, "even when I kept refusing to share the news with the others?"

"No." Mike laughed bitterly. "Silly me, I thought it was a hormone thing. A mood that would pass."

A mood that would pass. Was that all it had been, Marta wondered? Had her desire for a career, a fresh start, been but a passing mood?

"Dean and I are going for a drive," Mike said, grabbing a baseball cap from the top of the dresser. "I'll see you later."

And then he was gone.

Marta sank onto the bed and dropped her head into her hands. She should have kept her mouth shut. She should have lived with the solitary consequences of her silence. This is what honesty had wrought, a disaster, and in spite of what Mike claimed, even if she had told him the truth about her feelings immediately upon learning about the pregnancy, he still would have been hurt. And Marta would have been to blame.

Finally, the tears came.

Chapter 75

Bess had asked them all to gather in the kitchen. Allison's curiosity was aroused but not piqued. Everyone knew that Bess liked dramatics.

"So, why have we been summoned?" Dean asked, shifting the baby from one hip to the other. He and Mike had returned from a road trip with a box of a dozen donuts from a local bakery. They seemed very proud of the fact that they hadn't eaten any of the dozen on the way home.

"How many did you have at the bakery?" Chuck had asked, lips twitching.

"None," Dean said at the same time Mike was saying, "Only one."

"Actually," Dean added, with a hangdog expression. "We each had two."

Allison suddenly noticed that Mike and Marta were standing at opposite ends of the group. That was unusual. They always seemed to gravitate to each other's side. But she was more interested in what Bess had to say than what might or might not be going on between Mike and Marta after last night's argument.

Bess looked nervously from one to the other of the group and, finally, to Nathan, who stood at her side. "I got a call from Chris earlier," she said quickly. "He's here, in Kennebunkport."

Allison felt a tingling course through her arms and legs. "Did you know that he was coming?" she asked sharply.

"Gosh, no!" Bess cried. "I was totally surprised when he told me he was in town. He asked if he could still come to the wedding."

"I hope you told him that the answer was no!" Marta's expression, already grim, grew darker.

Nathan put an arm around Bess's shoulders. "It's Bess's decision to make," he said quietly but firmly.

"I told him that he was still invited. But—"

"But nothing," Nathan said. "Don't apologize."

Mike shook his head. "I can't believe he just showed up. What nerve."

"Nathan is right. The decision to invite him was and still is Bess's decision to make," Chuck pointed out, not without a sympathetic look for Allison. "Of course, it would have been better if he had called from Chicago and asked if the invitation was still open, rather than putting her on the spot like this."

"There's something else," Bess went on. "I told him that we know the truth about the accident and the miscarriage and about his being the one to want a divorce."

Allison flinched and sank onto the nearest stool at the island. Chuck put a hand on her shoulder. So much for Bess's exalted sense of loyalty, Allison thought. She had *promised* not to tell Chris that Allison had broken her word to him.

"I'm sorry, Allison," Bess added quickly. "Really. But I thought it best that he know, especially as he still wants to be a part of the celebrations."

"How did he take the news?" Dean asked.

"Fine. I mean, he wasn't angry, just surprised."

Marta frowned. "He has no right to be angry. It was a ridiculous thing to ask from Allison, her silence. It's not a good idea for him to be here. At the very least things are going to be awkward."

"Allison?" Chuck asked quietly.

"I haven't seen him in so long," she said, her voice low. *And I've been doing so well these past few days,* she told herself. She had been feeling calm and strong, able to think about Chris without bitterness or anger.

Chuck cleared his throat. "If Bess says it's okay for Chris to be here for the wedding I know we'll all welcome him with open arms. Or at the very least with an open mind. After all, it's brave of him to stick around now that he knows we're aware of what happened. He could have chosen to fly right back to Chicago rather than face us."

"He might still decide to run off," Marta said.

"There's something else," Bess blurted. "I asked him to come to dinner tomorrow night. For the fondue party. But we agreed that if everyone else objects he won't come."

A slightly hysterical laugh burst from Allison. "In for a penny, in for a pound," she said, rising from the stool onto which she had collapsed. "If you'll excuse me," she said, "I need some air."

With rapid strides, she passed through the living room, grabbing her bag from where it sat on an end table, and out to her car parked in the drive. Damn him, she thought. Just when she was on the verge of finding peace and forgiveness so that she could move on into a postmarital world . . .

Determinedly, Allison steered the car out of the drive and onto the road. She was not going to let Chris ruin everything for her, the progress she had made these past two years, the progress she had made these past days here in Kennebunkport. Sure, she was mad at Bess; Bess had betrayed a trust. But it was Chris who was responsible for the wreck her life had become.

Correction. The wreck her life might have become if she had let it.

Chapter 76

The only people left in the kitchen were Bess and Marta. Bess wasn't sure exactly when or where the others had gone. Except for Allison. She had made it clear that being far away from Driftwood House was where she wanted to be.

"I wish this whole mess hadn't happened!" Bess wailed.

"I'm sure Allison and Chris do, too," Marta said dryly. She was sitting at the island, stirring a cup of tea from which she had yet to take a sip.

"I wanted Chris to be with us and now that he's going to be I'm a wreck. I should have told him no, but I just couldn't bring myself to say the words." No was not a word she used with frequency, not when it came to the wishes of other people.

"You could still tell him no," Marta pointed out. "You could call him right now and tell him you've reconsidered and that his being here for the wedding wouldn't be right. Look, things are bad enough between Chris and Allison. How much worse could they get by telling Chris to go home?"

"It probably wouldn't affect anything between Chris and Allison at this point," Bess admitted. "But I could forfeit Chris's friendship."

"Do you still really consider him a friend?" Marta asked thoughtfully. "I mean, a close friend? When was the last time you had a heart-to-heart with Chris?"

Bess considered that question for a long moment. "Never, not really," she said finally. "Chris is in my life because of Allison. I doubt we would have become friends otherwise. Chris and I never had much in common."

"If that's the case," Marta said, "then do you really miss Chris as Chris or do you miss the easy, reliable way things were, with Chris as Allison's husband and Chuck's BFF?"

Bess sighed. "I primarily miss Chris as part of the group, I suppose. But that doesn't mean I don't care for him! Look, would you do it for me, Marta? Would you call and tell him not to join us tomorrow night?"

"No," Marta said. "Absolutely not. You need to take responsibility for this, Bess."

Bess put her hands to her head and groaned. "What have I done?"

"Nothing that requires such dramatics."

"Did I hear someone groan?"

Bess was startled to see that Chuck, Dean, and Mike were back. She hadn't heard them.

"Bess is agonizing over the situation," Marta explained. "Someone talk her down. She's not listening to me."

"I still say we give Chris a chance," Chuck said.

Mike nodded. "He was badly hurt, too," he said. "Not that I'm letting him entirely off the hook, but . . . Men need compassion as well."

Mike was right, Bess thought. Poor Chris.

"Is it fair to put Allison in this situation?" Dean asked. "I mean, she's here because she believed Chris wouldn't be."

Marta nodded. "Good point."

"Look," Mike said. "I could call Chris, tell him it's not a good idea that he join us tomorrow."

"You'll fall on your sword for the crew?" Chuck asked.

"A phone call isn't as dramatic as all that, but yeah. Bess?"

Bess sighed. "I think I should let the invitation stand. Chris said he'll call tomorrow to see what the consensus is. When he does, Allison can make the final decision about both dinner and the wedding and I'll abide by it."

"That's putting a lot of pressure on Allison," Mike said quietly.

"She can handle it," Marta said sharply.

Bess looked to Chuck. "It's a good idea," he said. "Don't worry, Bess. Everything will be all right."

Bess was arranging the breakfast things for the following morning. She liked to get at least part of the meal in readiness the night before—the coffee beans ground; cereal boxes lined up on the counter; a note if there was something special to be found in the fridge. That way, if someone came down to the kitchen before she did, they wouldn't have to start from scratch.

Usually, Bess enjoyed the task of preparation. But not that night. Dinner had been tense. Mike and Marta were clearly still at odds. Allison hadn't said much, not after having confronted Bess upon her return from wherever it was she had gone earlier. The conversation kept playing itself in Bess's head.

"You should have had the courtesy to check with me before telling Chris it was okay to join us," Allison had said angrily. "Why is it so important to you that we all be one big, happy family? Why can't you accept that sometimes life is awful and that people do stupid and hurtful things?"

Bess had felt shame rush through her. "I've asked myself the same question over and over," she admitted. "I'm sorry, Allison."

"Well," Allison had gone on, her tone sarcastically bright, "you know what they say. What doesn't kill you makes you stronger."

For the first time, Bess had realized the absurdity of that remark. Stronger? No. Plenty of people lived broken lives with broken hearts. Some even died of their heartache, no matter what dry and factual explanation scientists gave to such deaths. Those people had to be accounted for. They had to be respected. And they had to be left alone at some point to live their lives the way in which they were best able to. Sugarcoating trauma didn't help anyone. Pretending that every person was strong enough to conquer any conceivable obstacle was more than wrong. It was insulting.

Still she hadn't been able to resist voicing the idea that had been tickling at the corner of her mind since Chris's call earlier that day.

"Maybe he wants to be at the wedding because he wants to see you," she had ventured. "Maybe—" The look on Allison's face brought Bess to a halt.

"I won't make a scene," Allison had said without expression. "But don't expect me to go out of my way to welcome him. Just don't."

Bess continued to lay out fresh napkins and coffee mugs. She checked that the bowls of raw and of white sugar were filled and free of alien bits of food (sometimes Mike forgot to use the spoon designated for the sugar and stuck his cereal spoon into the bowl) and peeked through the little plastic window on the pepper grinder to be sure it was filled with enough peppercorns to last another few meals. She went to the fridge. They were low on grapefruit juice. She wondered if she should buy another container; who among them was drinking it? Not Nathan. His cholesterol medicine prevented him from overdoing his consumption of grapefruit. And Dean didn't like tart things, so that left . . .

Bess slammed the door of the fridge. Suddenly, it all seemed so stupid and futile. Why did she bother? Who really appreciated all of her efforts to be a good hostess? It was ridiculous to have put faith in a pact of friendship made by a bunch of drunk kids. Bess sank onto a stool at the island and put her head in her hands.

Maybe her compulsive need to play hostess was masking some big insecurity or character deficiency. She had always enjoyed catering to people, so much so that she had built a career around the art of caring. Why? Was it some sort of hangover from the years she had spent taking care of her baby sisters? Did she need the thanks so badly? Did she crave attention and praise, even adulation, to an unhealthy extent?

Bess dropped her hands and sighed. Why now? Why on the cusp of the most important day of her life was she plagued by these annoying and possibly darkly important questions? Her obsession that everyone around her be happy. Her compulsion to make it so.

Obsession. Compulsion. Where were these words coming from?

Suddenly, she couldn't wait until this whole wedding business was done and dusted. She couldn't wait until she could be alone with Nathan, living their own life, here or in Stockholm, away from . . . away from her friends, the people who looked to her for spoiling and special treatment.

The house was so awfully quiet. Everyone but Bess had retired for the night. Suddenly, she felt frightened, but of what she could not have said. She got up, turned off the lights, and hurried upstairs in the dark.

Chapter 77

Marta opened the door to the dryer and began to unload the clothes. Mike's jeans and shorts. His T-shirts and socks and underwear. Most of her own stuff she washed in the delicate cycle and hung to dry. As she folded and smoothed her husband's clothing, she felt a stab of sorrow so sharp it was physical. One could die of a broken heart. That was something Bess was sure to believe, but not Marta. Not until now.

Mike had been his usual pleasant self at dinner, if a bit less animated. Marta suspected no one but she—not even Chuck and Dean, who knew the truth—were aware of what it was costing him to act as if nothing earth-shattering had happened in his marriage. They had gone to bed at different times. Mike was up before she was that morning; she wondered if he had slept well or at all. At one point that morning Marta had attempted to engage him in more than a cursory word.

"Do you want to talk?' she asked quietly, passing him in the living area.

To which he had replied, "Marta, you're not the only one who needs time alone."

The words—and coming from Mike—had stunned her. Mike had never, ever wanted time alone. Time away from her. Occasionally, his devotion had annoyed her. More often she had taken it for granted. Now . . .

I've ruined everything, Marta thought, then immediately scolded herself for being so dramatic. But she felt so bad. Scared. Full of regret for so many words both said and unsaid. And she realized how very, very good her marriage had been until now. Was this state of dreadful miscommunication and misunderstanding common to most marriages? She felt sick to her stomach and knew the feeling had nothing to do with the pregnancy.

Marta gathered the folded laundry in her arms and headed for the stairs to the second floor. It would have to wait until they were back home—or at least until they were alone in the car on the long drive to New York. Whatever "it" would be. A détente, a reconciliation, a deal, a truce.

When she had stowed Mike's clothes in drawers and closet, she came back downstairs to find Allison alone on the back porch.

"Where is everyone?" Marta asked as she joined her friend. She didn't really care to know the answer. It was just something to say.

Allison shrugged. "Not sure," she admitted.

Marta hesitated a moment before she said, "Bess has decided to give you the final decision regarding Chris's joining us tonight and at the wedding."

Allison laughed a bit wildly. "How generous of her!"

"What will you say?" Marta asked.

"I don't know. She's either put me in a position of power or handed down a punishment. I can't decide which."

Marta wondered as well. Was Bess simply passing the buck to avoid a responsibility that was rightly hers?

"I got an e-mail the other day from Chris's mother," Allison went on. "She attached an article from the *Chicago Tribune* detailing Montague and Montague's landing a highly coveted project."

"Huh," Marta said. So, Chris was moving along nicely with his life. Bully for him. "How did that make you feel?"

"I realized that I felt genuinely glad for Chris. It felt like a breakthrough. I'd finally achieved some distance from the pain, enough to feel happy that Chris had achieved something for which he'd worked so hard."

"And now?" Marta asked.

Allison frowned. "And now he just shows up . . . Was he considering my feelings at all? Then again, I did tell Bess months ago that I was okay with her having Chris at the wedding. What a mess."

"It doesn't have to be," Marta pointed out. "You have control over how you handle this. Though I am on record as being furious with Chris for putting you in this situation."

"*Do* I have control?" Allison laughed. She thought of a line from *Jane Eyre*, one she had read just the night before. *Surely,* Jane says, anticipating her reunion with Mr. Rochester, *I should not be so mad as to run to him? * Jane went on: *And if I did—what then? Who would be hurt by my once more tasting the life his glance can give me . . .*

"I have this awful fear," Allison said, "that the moment I see Chris I'll do something completely stupid like beg him to take me back. And that's not even what I want."

"You won't do anything of the sort," Marta said firmly. "I know you won't. You've come too far, farther than you think. You won't betray yourself."

Allison smiled. "Thanks, Marta. Sometimes a gal just needs to spill. And I've been keeping things bottled up for so long."

"You're welcome," Marta said.

"I think I'll try to take a nap," Allison said, rising from her chair. "Once I'm back in Chicago it'll be all systems go again. I might as well take advantage of enforced laziness while I can."

Marta remained where she was. She spotted a baby's plush toy out on the lawn. Thomas's. She watched as a dragonfly made its crazy beautiful flight across the length of the porch. And she admitted to herself that while she was genuinely sorry for Allison's current distress, she had felt a degree of satisfaction in having been trusted as a confidante. She thought of how she had been able to advise and to comfort Sam recently. The maternal faculty. Clearly her wifely skills weren't what they had been, though her skills as a mother and a friend were still somewhat intact.

And for that Marta was grateful.

Chapter 78

Dean was on the rug before the unlit fireplace, playing with Thomas. Chuck was stretched out on the love seat, reading a medical journal. Allison wondered how he could concentrate with the background noise of a blender (Nathan was making a smoothie), baby babble, and music. Mike had put on a CD of pop hits from the early nineties and was singing along as best he could, which wasn't very well. The poor Counting Crows, Allison thought. They were being butchered.

Marta was staring at her phone, occasionally scrolling. Allison had a suspicion that she wasn't actually reading anything; she had the air of someone largely occupied with her own thoughts. *As am I*, Allison noted. She felt real regret about having spoken so harshly to Bess about her inviting Chris to join them. At the same time, she was not prepared to apologize for speaking her mind. For too many years she had kept quiet when she should not have.

"Everyone?" Bess said suddenly. She was perched on a stool at the kitchen island. "Chris just sent me a text. He'll join us tonight for dinner if it's okay."

Marta looked up from her phone and shrugged. "You know my view."

Mike simply nodded. Chuck looked to Dean and said, "We're okay with it."

"Allison?" Bess said. "You're the deciding vote."

Allison remembered what she had talked about earlier with Marta. A position of power or a punishment? What if she allowed herself a moment of perversity and said no, Chris cannot join us, to punish Bess for her failure of loyalty?

"It's fine with me," she said, "if he's here tonight and for the wedding."

"Thank you." Bess tapped away at her phone. "He says he'll see us at seven."

Mike looked to Allison. "If you need anything tonight," he said, "just come to me."

Marta laughed. "What could she possibly need from you?" She put a hand to her head. "Sorry," she said. "The whole thing is just . . ."

"Yeah," Mike said, turning away. "It is."

Allison tried to catch Marta's eye, but once again Marta was staring down at her phone. Allison frowned. *Things just keep getting better and better.*

Chapter 79

The table had been set since three o'clock. The canned heat under the fondue pots was ready to be lit. Bess had turned the lights low enough to soften the atmosphere. The wine was chilled. All was in readiness, but Bess was more nervous about this evening than she had been since, well, since she couldn't remember when.

Allison came slowly down the stairs and joined the others. She was wearing an apricot-colored sheath dress. Her wedding ring was in place. Her face looked strained. Bess could only hope that by allowing Chris to join them that evening she wasn't setting back the process of Allison's healing in any significant way.

"Where's your camera?" she asked. "Aren't you going to take pictures of tonight's dinner?"

"No," Allison said firmly. "I'm not. Sorry, Bess. I'm okay with Chris's being here, but it isn't in me to turn the camera on him smiling along with the rest of the gang."

Bess felt her cheeks flush. "Of course," she said.

The baby was in bed. The men were milling around the room aimlessly, looking decidedly uncomfortable. Marta was checking the glasses on the table for water spots.

The doorbell rang. Bess glanced at her friends. The way Allison was holding her body—rigid—revealed all too clearly the emotional strain this evening was causing her. The faces of the others were carefully bland. Even Marta, for whatever reason not great at masking her emotions these days, looked calm and cool.

With a silent prayer for something on the order of peace and forgiveness, Bess opened the door. And there was Chris, the same and patently not the same as he had been when Bess had last seen him two years earlier, at Chuck and Dean's wedding.

"Welcome," she said. She reached out and hugged him; Chris returned the embrace but awkwardly.

Chuck was the first of the others to step forward and greet Chris. Dean joined him, followed by Nathan. "It's good to finally meet you," Nathan said, extending his hand for Chris to shake. "Now I've met the whole crew."

Chris managed a smile. "Brave of you," he said.

It was a fairly meaningless thing to say, Bess knew, words to fill a space that might quickly become awkward. Before she could add her own meaningless words to the silence, Chris handed her the bottle of wine he had been holding by the neck. "I hope you still like Pinot Gris."

Mike then mumbled something that might have been "hey" or "hi." Chris nodded in response. Somewhat to Bess's surprise, Marta greeted Chris with a degree of welcome her recent remarks about him would not have led Bess to believe possible. And Marta wasn't play-acting. She wasn't capable of it. Or was she?

Lastly, it was time for Allison and Chris to greet each other. Bess held her breath but did not lower her eyes as the others did.

"Hello, Chris," Allison said evenly. She managed a brief smile but did not extend her hand or move forward.

Chris nodded and cleared his throat before he said, "Hello, Allison."

"Can I get you a drink?" Nathan asked, putting a friendly hand on Chris's shoulder. Bess was aware of the others dispersing, moving slowly in the direction of the dining area, gathering around the table. She had thought it best to dispense with a cocktail period and keep the pace of the evening brisk.

To avoid a potentially awkward seating situation, Bess had set out place cards. She and Nathan were seated at the two heads of the table. Allison was on Bess's right; Mike on her left. Next to Allison sat Marta; across from Marta sat Chuck. Dean was on Marta's right; across from him was Chris. Allison and Chris need not even look directly at each other if they chose not to.

Nathan raised his glass and proposed a toast to his bride. Chuck then raised his glass and said: "To old friends and new."

The experience of cooking one's own food as one ate seemed to help ease tensions; pieces of meat falling off forks and into the boiling oil and bread getting lost in the bubbling cheese caused shouts of laughter and a few colorful expletives. Mike swore he was not going to get burned like he had the last time they had been silly enough to sit around a pot of burning oil; Dean admitted he had never had fondue until this evening. The wine flowed freely; Bess suspected they were all drinking a bit more than usual in a determined effort to keep spirits from sagging.

Still, Bess found herself praying that no one would mention the miscarriage or the impending divorce. She doubted that any of her friends would be so cruel or so careless, but you never knew what a person might say or do when under stressful conditions. "Remember, don't mention the time Aunt Clara was in jail," her mother would warn her children before Uncle Albert's arrival on Thanksgiving. Invariably, one or more of the Culpeppers would mention the word *prison* or the phrase *breaking the law*, which was followed by a long moment of embarrassment, which was in turn followed by a few frantic moments of someone desperately attempting to change the subject.

There was one painful subject that did come to light during the course of this meal and that was Chuck's Parkinson's. "Might not be wise for me to be trying to negotiate around a vat of boiling oil before long," he said at one point, sotto voce but loud enough for Chris to hear and to ask why.

Chuck explained. Chris's face drained of color. "My God, Chuck," he said, his voice low. "I . . . I don't know what to say. I'm sorry. I should have kept in touch these past months. I—"

For a moment, Bess thought Chris was going to cry; she had never seen Chris in tears. Christopher Montague did not make free with his more troubling emotions. But that Chris might not be the man sitting at her table this evening. Surreptitiously, Bess glanced at Allison. She was staring down at her plate; Bess could not read her expression.

"You're here now," Chuck said firmly. "That's what's important."

"Hey, Chris," Mike said heartily. "Remember that time you tried to teach me how to play racquet ball? What a disaster! I was so full of myself going in. I thought, this will be a breeze. I'm powerful. I'll annihilate this skinny guy!"

Chris smiled. "You had that lump on your head for weeks."

"Served me right for bragging before I could prove myself."

Bess speared a slice of apple, dipped it into the bubbling cheese, and silently thanked Mike for saving the moment. He was one of the good guys.

Chapter 80

Bess and Nathan had brought dessert and coffee to the table. Marta found that in spite of her discomfort in anticipation of the evening, her appetite had been hearty. She considered a second small helping of pie, but rejected it.

Mike had eaten two large pieces of pie and now he groaned. "I couldn't eat another bite. Well, maybe one more mini-cupcake."

Conversation went on around her, but Marta had no real interest in joining in. It felt surreal to be sitting around a table, talking and laughing, acting as if nothing monumental was in the works. The sundering of a marriage. She wondered if Bess was as aware of the strangeness as she was, as she was sure the others were, or if her eternal optimism allowed her to put a normalized spin on the evening.

"To the past," Nathan was saying, raising his glass again. "It made us who we are."

Chuck laughed. "Let's hope that's a good thing. Personally, there are several moments of my past I wouldn't mind being erased."

Dean sighed. "If only. In my case, everything from a series of really awful hairstyles to—Well, never mind the other stuff."

Marta saw Allison smile quickly and it seemed, automatically. Allison hadn't uttered more than a word or two since they had come to the table. Well, Marta thought, that was understandable.

"If we've learned something helpful from our past mistakes, those mistakes are as valuable as the good things we did." Bess smiled.

"On a lighter note," Mike said suddenly, raising his coffee cup. "To melted cheese."

Amid general laughter the others, including Marta, raised their glasses and cups. She watched Chris take a small sip of water before setting his glass carefully next to his untouched piece of pie. A good deal of the harsh attitude Marta had taken toward her old friend in the recent past seemed to have fallen away, leaving in its place a curious, almost maternal fondness.

What was that about? she wondered. And then she decided simply to accept it.

Chapter 81

For the duration of the meal Allison had studiously avoided looking directly at her soon-to-be ex-husband, though she could not block out the too-familiar voice. She heard Chris ask Marta about the children; heard him recall a funny moment he had shared with Leo when the boy was about five. She heard the tone of his voice, shock combined with grief, when he responded to the news of Chuck's illness. His laugh, a bit strained this evening, was, nevertheless, musical.

She thought she had never lived through a more difficult meal than this one, but living through it she was. She ate and drank automatically, unaware of flavor or texture, careful not to reveal the depth of her roiling emotions, smiling when the others did.

Thank God for Nathan, she thought, sending a quick glance his way. He was a good host. He kept the conversation flowing, deftly turning it away from potentially painful subjects whenever possible, making sure everyone had what drink he or she needed. For all of his efforts, Allison was grateful.

Now all that remained was her getaway. She was determined to avoid an awkward farewell with Chris; their greeting had been painful enough. At just the right moment she would disappear.

She had always been good at disappearing.

Chapter 82

It wasn't long after Nathan's next toast that things wound down the way they often did at dinner parties, when an unspoken but universal decision was made to end the festivities and toddle off to bed or one's car.

"No one, and I mean no one, is to stick around to clear up tonight," Bess announced. "I'm on it."

"For once I won't argue," Marta said. "I'm groggy with food. Not a complaint."

Suddenly, Bess noted that Allison was no longer with them.

Everyone rose from their seats and began the round of farewells.

"We'll see you tomorrow for breakfast?" Bess asked Chris.

"I'll see what the morning brings," he replied noncommittally.

Chuck reached out and hugged Chris. "I'm glad you came tonight," he said. "Really glad."

"Be careful getting back," Nathan told him. "There can be an occasional drunken reveler on the road, even in a place as civilized as Kennebunkport."

Bess watched as Chris rapidly scanned the room, no doubt for a sign of Allison. She couldn't tell if he was disappointed or relieved by her absence. She alone watched as his car left the driveway and turned onto the road toward town.

She turned back to the room and was aware of murmurings among the friends.

"It went okay, don't you think?"

"Yeah, sure."

"You really think so?"

"Nobody shouted or stomped off. That's usually a sign that things went well."

"I still wish he hadn't come."

"Too late now. He's here."

"I hope Allison is okay. She slipped away pretty quickly the moment we all got up from the table."

"Can you blame her? She probably didn't want to have to say goodbye to Chris."

"Yeah. Damn, I'm tired."

"All that cheese."

"I was thinking it's more from witnessing all that pent-up emotion."

"Possibly."

"Good night."

When Bess was alone she began to clear the table. Darn that Annie, she thought, that Scarlett O'Hara, that Rebecca of Sunnybrook Farm, and every other fictional heroine who turned her back on an unhappy present and set her face toward what she believed would be a better tomorrow. And darn Sarah Bernhardt, too, going onstage with her one leg! They had set the standards for optimism and a can-do attitude pretty high for people like Bess, who trusted in a world that was welcoming and nurturing and full of joy.

Wearily, Bess loaded the dishwasher. She wished she had asked someone to help her clean up. Too late now.

Chapter 83

"Do you think things will be all right?" Marta asked. Mike was lying beside her in their bed.

"With us?" he asked quietly.

Marta's stomach dropped. That either of them could be in doubt for even a moment as to the health of their marriage sickened her. "No," she managed to say. "I meant with Allison and Chris."

"I have no idea. It will be if they want things to be. And if they don't . . ." Mike turned on his side, his back to her. His aborted comment lingered in Marta's head long after he had fallen asleep and she lay there staring into nothingness.

Chapter 84

The evening had been a weirdly disorientating experience. At one point, Allison had felt an almost overwhelming desire to laugh. There they were, all sitting around the table pretending that nothing was wrong and yet all knowing that something *was* wrong. The sense of dislocation, of brokenness had been palpable; she was sure each and every one of them felt it.

She had said very little; had she said anything at all? Chris had offered nothing new. He had replied to general questions; no one had asked him anything about his personal life. How was the business? (Chris had not mentioned his recent professional coup.) How were his parents? Had his flight been without incident? Was the B and B comfortable? Where is your wedding ring? That was one question no one had asked. Allison looked down at hers, still on her finger.

The moment the first person had begun to get up from his seat, Allison had successfully slipped out of the room unnoticed. She could be forgiven for rudeness. The wine might have mellowed Chris; he might have reached out to hug her. Chris wasn't particularly demonstrative, but this was such a strange situation that one couldn't be sure what anyone would do. A touch would have been disastrous. Absolutely disastrous.

"Surely . . . I should not be so mad as to run to him?"

She was not sorry she had disappeared.

She was not sorry.

Chapter 85

At seven thirty that morning Bess received a text from Chris, crying off breakfast. As it happened none of the others seemed interested in breakfast. Of the dozen fresh bagels she had put out, only two had been eaten. The new box of cereal remained unopened. Last night's meal must have been more filling than Bess had realized.

After her own meager breakfast of coffee and an orange, Bess had busied herself with chores pertaining to the wedding. Guests were arriving in town; Bess had called the hotels where they would be staying to be sure her welcome baskets had arrived. Her dress was hung on the closet door of a small, otherwise unoccupied bedroom. The bouquets would be delivered early the next morning; Bess had confirmed the delivery with the florist. The band was a go; the caterer was ready; the bakery was set to drop off the various wedding cakes and other sweet treats.

Momentarily without anything in particular to do, Bess went to the back porch. The atmosphere was dense with fog; she could barely see the water. Suddenly, a figure appeared at the bottom of the garden. Bess blinked. It was Chris. She was reminded of the day that large gray cat, the one who had subsequently befriended Allison, first appeared in the gnarled branches of the tree as if by magic. Chris waved to her and Bess went to join him.

"Do you know where Allison is?" he asked.

Bess hesitated. She wasn't sure it would be right to tell Chris where he could find her. She could suggest he text Allison. Allison could respond or not, as she saw fit. But the look of weariness on Chris's drawn face got to her.

"Probably on the beach," she blurted. "She goes there a lot on her own. And, Chris?"

"Yes?"

"I'm really sorry about the baby."

Chris swallowed hard and then headed for the wooden stairs that led to the sand.

Alone, Bess tried to convince herself that she hadn't done wrong in telling Chris where Allison could be found. But she couldn't quite pull it off. Allison had a right to her privacy. She had a right to make the decision to meet with Chris or not to meet with him.

Then again, she argued, she could be excused for allowing her emotions to make a decision rather than her brain. In little more than twenty-four hours she would be getting married. She was under a lot of pressure.

But that wasn't a very good excuse. Bess turned back toward the house. She hoped Allison would forgive her.

Chapter 86

Mike was not in their bed when Marta woke the next morning, dripping with sweat.

She had been dreaming about her children. Sam had announced she was leaving forever and never coming back. Marta had watched from a window as her daughter went running down a dirt road, her hair streaming behind her. Marta had tried to shout, but only a croak emerged from her throat.

Leo kept changing form. One minute he was twelve-year-old Leo and then he was ancient, barely alive, hideous; then he was his namesake lion, blood dripping from his jaws.

Troy had no eyes. While his siblings went wild and ran off, he sat silently in a corner, the upper half of his face a blank.

Marta sat on the edge of the bed and tried to forget the horrible images that had plagued her sleeping mind. The dream had been a warning, it had to have been. How could they bring a child into a home where the parents were estranged? Chaos would ensue. Misery. Loss.

Ordinarily, Marta was not prone to panic. But this was no ordinary situation. She would *have* to make Mike forgive her. She would forget her ambitions, at least for a few more years. She would have this baby, be happy about it, do anything it took to restore what had been. The status quo of the MacIntosh household.

Briskly, Marta rose, grabbed her robe, and headed for the bathroom down the hall. She couldn't wait for the wedding to be over. She couldn't wait to get home and make things right with Mike. Her beloved Mike.

Chapter 87

It seemed the others had already eaten; the dish drainer held several cups and plates, as well as two of the coffeepots. Bess had left a note for her—*I hope you slept well*, it said. *There's a box of waffles in the freezer and fresh bagels*. Allison could hear Mike's voice in the direction of the back porch, and someone was using a lawn mower around the side of the house; probably Nathan. Allison didn't want to run into anyone so she quickly drank a cup of coffee and left the house by the front door, eager to get to the beach.

It was a foggy morning. The sun was struggling to be seen through a heavy haze, but already beach enthusiasts had set up camp. Still, Allison found the sense of healthy aloneness she so cherished.

She had been there for twenty minutes or so when something made her turn her head in the direction of the house. Walking toward her over the soft, pale sand was Chris. This morning he was wearing a pair of chinos that hung loose from his thin frame; an open-necked linen shirt remained untucked.

She had thought he might seek her out, especially after she had slipped away the night before without a farewell. She had determined to be kind, to rely on the love she had born him from almost the moment they had met, to respond to his words with sympathy. She was also determined to remember what Marta had said about her, that she had come too far to betray herself.

"Can we talk?" Chris asked, when he was only a few feet away. He removed his sunglasses. There were more wrinkles around his eyes than Allison had remembered.

"Did you come after me?" she asked. "Or is this an accidental meeting?"

Allison's direct question seemed to surprise Chris. He wouldn't be used to her being blunt. "No," he said. "I mean, yes, I came looking for you. I went to the house and Bess told me that you were probably here."

Allison frowned. So much for loyalty. Why had Bess betrayed her again? Why hadn't Chris called or texted her directly, asking to meet? Did no one respect that she had agency, that she had a mind of her own?

"We didn't get to say goodbye last night," Chris went on.

"I know," Allison said flatly.

Suddenly, face-to-face with the man who was still legally her husband, Allison felt all of her resolve to be kind and sympathetic take flight, to be swiftly replaced by a blazing anger. For the past two years, she had been living in misery, tormented by guilt and grief, isolated from her dearest friends by a promise extracted from her in a moment of supreme weakness. Right then, she hated Chris for having coerced her into that final round of IVF therapy when he knew she was exhausted and depressed. She hated him for having punished her so badly when their child had died. She hated him for having tracked her down this morning, for forcing his presence upon her. She wanted to see him suffer more than he might already have suffered. She didn't care if that desire made her a bad person. She didn't care.

The power of her emotions shocked her. How tightly had she been keeping herself under control? Too tightly.

"What do you want, Chris?" she asked. "You've got me here now, so tell me what it is that you want."

Chris swallowed hard. "I wanted to . . . to see you. To ask if you're well. To—"

"Ask if I'm well?" Allison interrupted. "Of course, I'm not well. I haven't been well for a very long time, Chris. Or can't you tell? What do you see when you look at me? Tell me what you see."

"I—"

Allison cut him off again. "What you should see—if you had any heart left in you at all—is a wreck of a woman. But I'm coming alive again, Chris. I'm coming back to myself."

"I'm glad. I mean . . ."

"You suggested I was hoping for a miscarriage to end the pregnancy," Allison went on. "Do you have any idea what that accusation did to me?"

Chris flinched. "That was cruel. I'll never forgive myself for saying that, or for thinking it. I was crazy with grief. Maybe just plain crazy. Allison, I wish I could take back every hurtful, mean, horrible thing I said, erase it from memory, yours as well as mine. But I can't. What I can do, what I have been doing, is figure out why I said such things, why I suspected you of terrible thoughts and behaviors, and promise never, ever again to be the person I was back then."

"That's a tall order," Allison said dryly.

"I know," Chris admitted. "But I mean to keep at it for however long it takes."

Allison turned to the horizon. It spoke to her of possibility. It gave her hope. She turned back to Chris. "I don't want to be with someone who's always struggling to believe the best of me," she said calmly, evenly. "So, I don't think there's any point in continuing this conversation."

Chris looked as if he was going to be physically ill. "I'm sorry," he said. His voice was barely audible. "I can't tell you how sorry I am. I'm asking for your forgiveness but . . . but I don't believe I deserve it."

She watched for a moment as he turned away and began to walk, head bowed, hands hanging at his sides. She did not allow his forlorn figure to touch those old wellsprings of kindness and concern.

She felt no regret for what she had said.

She looked down at her left hand, the one that wore the ring Chris had given her so long ago. *Always mine.* The ring slipped off easily and for a moment, but only a moment, Allison saw herself stride down to the water's edge and throw the ring as far she could into the blue waters of the Atlantic. Instead, she stowed the ring in a zippered compartment of her camera bag. She had stood up to Chris; she was finally ready to move on with her life.

But she still loved him. She still loved him. That was okay.

Allison straightened her shoulders and realized she was alone on the stretch of sand but for the strutting seagulls and the tiny little birds scurrying along the water's edge.

It felt okay, being alone. Maybe not as okay as it had felt standing side by side with Chris all those years.

But it felt okay.

Chapter 88

"Have you given the idea of Stockholm any thought?" Nathan asked. He and Bess were in the den. Nathan had made the small couch his workstation, leaving Bess the desk at which to sit with her laptop.

"No," Bess admitted, turning to face him. "I haven't. I've been focusing on the last-minute wedding details and worrying about Chris and Allison and—"

"There's no need to explain or to apologize," Nathan said, firmly. "We'll talk seriously after the wedding, once everyone has gone home. I'm sorry I brought it up, really."

"I love you so very much," Bess told him.

"I know." Nathan smiled. "And I'm very grateful for it."

Bess sighed, got up from her desk chair, and went to sit next to Nathan on the couch. "I might have done something stupid again," she admitted.

"You never do anything stupid," Nathan protested.

"Be that as it may, I sent Chris after Allison this morning. He came by the house and asked if I knew where she was and I told him."

"And do you know if he found her?" Nathan asked.

"Not for sure, but I suspect he did."

"Don't beat yourself up. Allison and Chris's future is up to them,

not you. Right now, *you* are the most important person in your life."
Nathan grinned. "Along with me, I hope."

"It feels weird to put myself before others," Bess admitted. "I'm
not sure I'm any good at it."

Nathan put his arm around Bess and she nestled into him. How
good it felt to have someone with whom she could share the good
and the not-so-good parts of her. "This is a happy moment," she
said.

"There'll be many more like it," Nathan assured her. "I promise."

Chapter 89

A depression of spirits had given way to an unpleasant bout of nervous energy. Marta had used that energy to walk the few miles into downtown Kennebunkport. The streets were busy, but she was only vaguely aware of her fellow tourists, from the well-heeled men and women wearing yellow slacks printed with tiny pink fish and the women carrying designer handbags, to the more casual tourists sporting baseball caps and T-shirts declaring their allegiance to the Boston Red Sox.

She was, however, acutely aware of the children. So many young women pushing strollers containing infants! So many young men holding the hands of toddlers! What did a good stroller cost these days? They had been expensive enough seven years ago when she had needed one for Troy.

Marta was already considering heading back to Driftwood House when she saw Chris standing on the dock across the way, looking out over the leisure boats at rest in the water. There was something about the set of his shoulders, something sad that made her go to him without hesitation. That powerful maternal instinct, the impulse to offer comfort to someone in distress.

"Hi," she said.

"Hi," he said, managing a smile.

"Been standing here long?"

Chris shrugged. "A while I guess."

"You spoke with Allison this morning, didn't you?" Marta asked shrewdly.

If Chris was surprised by her question he hid that surprise. "Yes, Bess told me she had gone down to the beach. I wanted to talk. I wanted to apologize." Chris looked out again over the water. "She was so angry. I'd never seen her so angry."

Marta noted again the lines around Chris's mouth, the pronounced cheekbones, the dark hollows under his eyes. The divorce was draining him badly.

"I've let her down twice now," he said suddenly, fiercely.

Marta sighed. "Chris, forget that night. It's in the long-distant past. It has no bearing on the present moment, and the present moment is what you need to focus on."

Chris raised an eyebrow. "My therapist tells me the same thing. Right after he tells me the root of my issues lies in the past."

Marta smiled wryly. "Your brother?"

Chris nodded and Marta was overcome by a deep compassion for her old friend. Life wasn't easy and no one acted perfectly at all times. Judgment should be reserved for only the most horrible cases of misbehavior, rapes and murders and child abuse. What did she really know about Chris's struggles after the death of his younger brother?

"Would you go back if she'd have you?" she asked.

"Yes," he said promptly. "I would. But I don't know why she would have me back, not after what I've done to her. And she's so, so angry. I don't know how to defend against anger that intense."

Marta put her hand on Chris's arm for a moment. "Don't defend against her anger," she advised. "Just accept it. It's real, it's powerful, and it's justified. Look, Chris, you've dominated Allison all along, and I'm not saying you did it intentionally or with any evil purpose in mind. But you've been selfish, and Allison was so head over heels in love with you she allowed her life to take the form you chose for it. But now Allison is well on her way to becoming her own woman, and if you want her back in your life you're going to have to accept her terms. Let her talk. Just listen. Don't make assumptions about what she does or does not feel, about what she will or will not do. Just. Listen."

Chris looked at the ground. For a moment, Marta wondered if she had said too much. She really had no idea what Chris could tolerate hearing at this point. She looked toward the beautifully tended boats for a moment and then back to her friend, but still Chris said nothing. Finally, he nodded.

"I'll try," he said, his voice raspy with emotion. "I really will try. If she'll let me. To be honest, I don't have much hope for a future together. So often life doesn't give you a second chance, especially not when you've blown the first run-through so spectacularly."

"I don't think life works that way," Marta argued. "I don't think you're necessarily punished for having screwed up—or necessarily rewarded for doing things right, for that matter—and though yeah, you might have screwed up in your marriage, there was no maliciousness in your behavior or your motives. Just . . . just pain."

"And fear," Chris said quietly. "A very ignoble motive if ever there was one."

Marta sighed. "Oh, Chris. I wish I knew what to say to make a real difference for you. Look, I'm going to head back to the house. Are you coming?"

"Why should I?" he asked. "I'm not sure anyone there would be glad to see me."

Marta didn't argue this statement. She wasn't sure, either. "Okay," she said. "Your call. Get yourself something to eat," she advised before turning to walk away. "You look a little peckish."

Chris smiled. "Peckish? I haven't heard anyone use that word in ages."

"Hungry, then. Have a lobster roll or an ice-cream cone. And, Chris? I'm sorry for the loss of your child. I really am."

Chris bowed his head. Marta turned and walked away. It might have been better if she had left Chris alone in the first place. But she had said what she had said genuinely and maybe some of her advice would prove helpful to her old friend. She could only hope.

Chapter 90

Allison had settled on the back porch with a cozy mystery—the sixth or was it the seventh she had read since coming to Maine?—and a glass of iced tea. She had decided not to tell the others what happened between her and Chris. Something still felt unfinished between them. She was sure of it. To speak now would be to speak precipitously.

Bess, she was sure, was dying to know what had happened but probably just as eager to avoid asking. She had looked downright hangdog earlier, but Allison had been in no mood to scold. In fact, Bess's sending Chris in pursuit might have been the best thing that could have happened. Without being put on the spot like she had been, Allison might not have had the courage to seek Chris out and speak her mind.

The screen door behind her opened and Chuck appeared, Thomas against his hip.

"Allison, could you keep an eye on Thomas while I pop in the shower?" he asked.

Allison put aside her glass and gladly accepted the baby. He sat upright on her lap, his slim neck miraculously supporting his big baby head. Allison gently brushed his cheek with her fingertip and Thomas smiled his gummy smile. She hoped Chuck would take his time showering. It felt very pleasant to be sitting there with a little one on her lap.

And in that moment Allison knew something for sure. Crystal clear. As much as she had wanted the baby she had lost—and she had—she knew now that if she never became a mother she would be all right. It wasn't that her maternal instincts had died with the child, though in fact they had mellowed in intensity over the years of dashed expectations and shattered hopes. It was more that her instincts of self-preservation had come into their own at long last.

Holding wee Thomas, with his lovely long eyelashes and his bow-shaped mouth, Allison knew as sure as she knew her own name that motherhood was no longer necessary for a complete life. In fact, she might have ceased to need or even to want a child years ago, but she had gone on with the pursuit in order to please Chris and to fulfill a promise she had made to them both, to have a family. Until the end, the sacrifice had largely been worth it.

Thomas pointed his wee chubby forefinger at a little bird that had alighted on the porch railing. "What a pretty birdie!" Allison said. She smiled. She was closer now than ever to making peace with the reality that was her new life.

Sitting on the back porch with Thomas, Allison realized something else. The pity and softness she had felt for Chris almost from the moment they had first met was in fact an almost maternal instinct, an instinct that somehow went hand in hand with an attitude of subservience. Maybe that was the norm; maybe maternal love was fundamentally a love of service, the most unconditional love there could be. But maternal love for a fellow adult was not a great idea. She knew that now and she would never forget it.

The sound of the screen door alerted Allison to Chuck's return. "Daddy's squeaky clean," he announced. "And Thomas looks very contented sitting on your lap."

Allison smiled. "I think he is. And I'm very contented to have him here."

Chapter 91

Bess was startled for the second time that day by Chris's sudden presence.

"You're back," she stated. She had seen no one on her way from the house down to the gnarled and blasted tree where she now stood.

Chris nodded. "Yeah, I'm back."

Bess did not ask if he had found Allison that morning. If Allison had wanted her to know she would have told her earlier.

"When I first saw this tree," she said to Chris, "I couldn't imagine why the owners of the house had left it here. It seemed an eyesore. But now . . ." Bess shrugged. "Now I like it. It seems necessary." She did not tell Chris how many hours Allison had spent sketching the tree, enthralled by its odd beauty. In a way, maybe the tree had kept Allison better company than her friends had been able to. The tree and that big gray cat.

Suddenly, Bess felt uncomfortable. And angry. Why hadn't Chris stayed back in Chicago? He was going to ruin everything now. She had seen the strain poor Allison was under at dinner the night before. And as for what Bess herself was going through, trying to manage everyone's moods and needs and . . .

"You shouldn't have asked me where to find Allison this morning," she blurted.

"You didn't have to tell me," Chris countered.

Bess flinched but went on. "It was awful, your leaving Allison. I don't know how you could have done it, Chris, I really don't."

"You weren't there," he said mildly. "You don't know all the details."

"I know enough. I know that you promised to love and cherish Allison forever and you broke that promise."

Suddenly, the expression on Chris's worn face turned dark. "My God, you can be self-righteous!" he said.

Bess felt a flicker of conscience but only a flicker. "I'm not being self-righteous," she argued.

Chris ran a hand through his hair and sighed. "Look, I know you feel bad for Allison—and maybe even in a stray moment you've felt bad for me, too—but please, Bess, stay out of it. You're not helping anything by reading me the riot act."

But Bess could not seem to stop. "It was really terrible of you to make Allison promise she wouldn't tell any of us what happened. When she first came here she was a wreck. I could hardly look at her without wanting to cry."

"Wait a minute," Chris said with a short laugh. "Are you mad at me for hurting Allison or for ruining your fairy-tale wedding and reunion?"

"Both! Your silly behavior has made a mess of everything, Chris."

Chris laughed harshly. "Silly? I'd hardly call what I've been through these past two years silly!"

"I didn't say that what happened was silly. I said your actions have been—okay, silly is the wrong word. Let's call them petulant and self-serving." The moment the words were out of Bess's mouth she regretted them. She wanted to apologize. But she didn't.

"It's not too late for me to leave," Chris said flatly. "Your big day doesn't have to be spoiled by my presence."

"Don't get all martyr with me," Bess cried. "I'm not the one who's done anything wrong!"

"Perfect Bess. She never says or does anything to hurt anyone."

"Well, I don't! At least, not intentionally. I mean—" Bess couldn't go on. She felt sick.

Chris shook his head. "Look," he said, "let's just forget we had this conversation. This is your special time and I've already screwed it up enough. I'll show up for the wedding if you still want me to and then I'll be on my way."

"Of course, I want you to be there," Bess said wearily, but she wasn't sure she meant it. To say yes seemed the easier thing to do. Maybe not the wisest thing.

Chris nodded and walked toward the house and the road beyond. She guessed he was heading back to town. And maybe to the airport from there.

Bess moved closer to the shattered tree and leaned against it. She had never, ever had an exchange like the one she and Chris had just engaged in. She felt ashamed. How could she have said the awful things she said? She had been downright mean and absolutely nothing was made better by being mean. Ever. And Chris was right. Even though Allison had shared a lot of what had led to the split, she hadn't shared all. No one ever did.

Suddenly, Bess cringed. Had she transferred the anger she felt toward herself for having betrayed Allison twice in as many days onto Chris, an easy target? It was possible. But was it likely?

No. She was a self-aware person. She made it a point to know her own mind. She never took out on others her own frustrations and . . . Bess cringed again. Yes, she thought. She did. Everyone did.

It was called being human.

Chapter 92

Marta was within yards of Driftwood House when she suddenly saw Chris walking swiftly toward a blue rental car parked at the curb. She called out. He turned but looked reluctant to speak to her.

"Why did you come back to the house after all?" she asked when she reached him.

Chris swallowed hard. "I don't know. It was stupid. I . . . I had a fight with Bess. It was bad."

Damn, Marta thought. "Are you all right to drive?" she asked.

"Yeah," he said. "I'm fine. Thanks, Marta."

He hurriedly got behind the wheel and she watched him drive away. She realized she didn't want to face any of the others, not at the moment. She turned toward the beach. It was crowded with people, not wonderful for solitary contemplation, but then again maybe she had indulged in enough solitary contemplation for the moment. Marta went halfway to the water's edge; the sand there was dry and slightly packed, making walking easier than it was closer to the small dunes and large rocks at the top of the beach.

Marta must have walked close to half a mile when she came upon a young woman holding an infant against her chest. The woman was wearing a diaphanous dress in a particularly pretty shade of pale yellow. Marta stopped. She wasn't sure why she did.

"How old?" she asked.

"Two months," the young woman said proudly. "He's my first."

"What a head of hair," Marta said with a laugh.

"Can you believe he was born with it? You know, until I finally saw little Joey for the first time I never realized just how amazingly powerful women are." The young woman shook her head. "Men have nothing on us, I mean nothing! They can't give birth to and then feed another human being!"

Marta smiled. Mike would agree. It was one of the reasons she had always loved him. His respect for women was real. "I have three kids," Marta told her. "Seventeen, twelve, and seven."

"Awesome! My husband and I hope to have at least three."

Awesome. Marta smiled. "I wish you the best," she said feelingly. "Cherish every moment with your son. It's all worth it."

Marta moved on, leaving the young woman gently stroking her baby's hair. She hadn't gone more than ten feet or so when it hit her. It finally hit her. She felt a surge of strength and joy, a physical and emotional rush of power and glee. Marta laughed out loud.

"I am having another baby," she said to the sky, sand, and sea— and to whomever happened to be within hearing distance. "Awesome, indeed."

Marta's pace became jaunty. Would it be tempting fate, she wondered, to admit that she felt proud of herself? Proud that her body was still capable of this amazing feat, proud that it had already brought three wonderful human beings into this world? To hell with it! She would feel proud! And she would do everything in her power to protect and nurture this wee life inside her and then to deliver that life safely into this big, beautiful world!

"I rock," she said to the blue waves, to the white clouds, to the gray beady-eyed seagull stalking her footsteps in hopes of a scrap of food. "I seriously rock."

A middle-aged woman came striding toward Marta, one of those frighteningly intense power walkers.

"I'm having a baby," she announced to this stranger. "Isn't that great?"

The woman averted her eyes and stepped up her pace. Marta laughed. So what if the world thought she was nutty or unhinged? She was *happy* and happiness was so rare that it could appear to others as nuttiness, naïveté, or even, in extreme cases, as pitiful. Marta knew she was eminently sane, the antithesis of naïve, and the furthest thing away from pitiful there could be.

There was no time to waste. Marta reversed direction and ran—as best she could—back toward the house Bess had so thoughtfully rented for her friends. Within less than fifteen minutes she was charging through the door. She found Mike in the kitchen, a small lamp and a pile of wire and tools spread out on a counter.

"Mike," she announced, "I've got to talk to you."

"Can't it wait?" he asked, looking up with a frown. "I promised Bess I'd take a look at this lamp. It keeps shorting and—"

"No," Marta interrupted. "It most certainly cannot wait. Come on." She grabbed his arm and marched him out to the backyard. Mike went along unprotestingly, probably in shock. She brought them to a halt beneath the leafy maple tree and let go of his arm. Mike's expression was wary. *Poor Mike*, Marta thought. *What I've put him through!*

"What is it?" he asked.

Marta took a deep breath and felt a smile spread across her face. "Don't interrupt me. Let me say it all. I'm glad we're having this baby. I love you and I love Sam and Leo and Troy and I love little Boy or Girl as-yet-unnamed. I'm going to be a mother again and you're going to be a father again and it's great! In fact, it's awesome!"

Mike's expression grew even more wary before outright suspicion began to take its place. Finally, he said, "But what about a career?"

"I'll make a career for myself," Marta said. "I know I can do it. Well? What do you have to say?"

"I'm happy, of course," Mike said readily. "As long as you really mean what you say, that you're happy, too."

"I do mean it." Marta felt a tear come to her eye and she reached for her husband's hands. "I'm so sorry, Mike. I should have trusted you with my feelings right from the start. I don't know why I couldn't."

"I'm still kind of shaken by what you said the other night," Mike admitted. "I felt that maybe the real reason you were unhappy was because the baby was mine. That maybe you no longer loved me."

Marta released Mike's hands and threw her arms around him. He held her tightly. "I'm sorry I accused you of being selfish," she whispered fiercely. "It's not true and it never was. You're the most generous man I've ever known and if my sincere flattery goes to your head so much the better. You deserve to be praised for all you've sacrificed for me and the kids."

"That may or may not be, but I do apologize for my complacency," he said. "I guess I have a lazy streak that's gotten a bit out of hand. You've spoiled me, Marta, but you're not the one at fault. In the future, I swear I'll pay more attention to what you're saying and not take for granted that you're always going to be content with the current status quo."

"Thank you," Marta said, her words choked with tears. Without releasing her hold on him she stepped back in order to look him in the eye. Her dear husband.

"I asked Bess a while back to define 'soul mate' for me," he said. "I guess I felt that I was losing you in some way. Maybe I was picking up on your unhappiness about the baby, but I saw it as unhappiness with us. The thing is, I know that you're my soul mate. Am I yours, Marta, or is that too much to ask?"

"No," she assured him. "It's not too much to ask."

"Answer me this," Mike said suddenly. "Why were you thinking it has to be one way or the other, a baby or a career? We've done babies before. We're pros. Together we can define what it means for us both to be working parents. You're not alone, Marta."

"I won't forget that ever again," she promised.

Suddenly, Mike's face took on a look Marta knew all too well. It was a look that meant a trip to Home Depot was in order. "You might want a home office," he said, excitement tingeing his voice. "We could possibly build onto the garage, maybe put a second story. Or, and I'd have to check the zoning codes, we might build a new structure in the backyard. We could make it look like a cute little cottage! Another option might be to—"

Marta cut him off. "Now is not the time to make those decisions. But thank you."

"I really do apologize for not having taken my responsibility as your husband more seriously," Mike went on. "It's my job to help you protect your health and emotional well-being. I should have gotten a vasectomy immediately. I promise to make an appointment with my doctor the very day we get home."

Marta smiled. "You had better. Because otherwise I'm shutting down business for good."

Mike pulled her closer. "I don't want that to happen," he said very sincerely.

"Neither do I, Mike," Marta said. "Neither do I."

Chapter 93

Allison had spent an hour or so that afternoon asking around about the big gray cat. No one knew where he had come from. One neighbor thought he had been around for a month or so. Another swore he had only appeared in the past weeks. No one had seen signs about a missing cat. One woman had suggested Allison check with the police. She did. Nothing.

Then an idea had formed in Allison's mind. What if she took the cat back home with her to Chicago? It was a slightly terrifying notion, to kidnap—because that was a better word in the circumstances than adopt—a strange cat and transport him halfway across the country. Would he hate living in an apartment? (She might be able to train him to walk on a leash. Or maybe she would move to the suburbs, where he would have the run of a small backyard.) Was he ill? (He certainly didn't look sick.) Would his original caretaker suddenly come forward, heartbroken at the loss of her kitty, having no idea that he was living comfortably in the state of Illinois? (Possible, though what kind of pet parent let her cat go missing for weeks before sounding the alarm?)

Chris didn't particularly like cats, or dogs for that matter, Allison thought. But what did that matter? In spite of her feeling there was still something unfinished between them, she wasn't at all sure she would ever see Chris again. She would be okay with that. She would have to be okay.

Allison carefully lifted the painting she had made for Bess; it was still packed in bubble wrapping and brown paper, though Allison had discarded the outer cardboard box. She made her way downstairs. She had heard Bess rattling around in the kitchen.

"Hi," Bess said brightly. A platter of freshly baked cupcakes sat on the counter, along with a can of white icing and small bottles of colored sprinkles.

"I want to give you my present now if that's okay," Allison said. She didn't want Bess to feel bad for one more second about having sent Chris after her, and Allison knew that Bess was feeling bad in spite of her cheery tone. In fact, the cupcakes might be a peace offering of sorts. Allison had always liked cupcakes with vanilla icing.

"Oh, goody!" Bess clapped her hands like an excited child and came around the island.

Allison watched with some amusement as Bess tore off the brown paper only to be confronted by layers and layers of sealed bubble wrap. "You'll need a knife," she pointed out, "but be very careful."

Bess worked slowly and methodically until the painting was released from its cocoon. She gasped and looked up at Allison with tears in her eyes.

"The subject is a little dark for a wedding present," Allison said hastily, "but we did have quite a memorable experience that afternoon."

"I love it," Bess said. "It's just perfect. Thank you, Allison. You know, maybe we should go back to Salem one day, visit The House of Seven Gables, and see if we're affected the way we were all those years ago."

"That would be interesting," Allison admitted. "Why not? Anyway, I'm sure the work I'll put together for you from these past two weeks will be a lot jollier. Though I did get some wonderfully thoughtful shots of each of us. Well, of me excepted."

"And the dead tree?" Bess asked. "I've come to love it, you know."

"Oh yes. There's beauty in ruins for sure."

A thud caught the women's attention. They turned to see the large gray cat sitting on the back porch, staring at them. Allison's heart quickened. He had come to find her!

"That's the first time he's come so close to the house," Bess noted. "I'm not sure I should let him in. The owners didn't say anything about no pets but . . ."

"I'll go out to him," Allison said. She thought she might put to her Little Gray Ghost the idea of coming to live with her. But not until she had given him all the belly rubs he demanded.

Chapter 94

Bess had decided not to mention her encounter with Chris to any of her friends, only to Nathan from whom she would keep no secrets. They had found a few moments alone together later that afternoon in the sanctuary of their room. They were sitting on the bed, their legs stretched out before them. Bess was holding a pillow to her chest as she might hold a teddy bear for comfort.

"Chris accused me of being self-righteous and he was right," she said.

"I'm sorry things got heated between you," Nathan said sincerely.

"So am I. I felt physically ill by the time we parted. And then I started to remember some of the really nice things about Chris, things I shouldn't have forgotten, like how ever since college he's done all sorts of volunteer work for the homeless and how when I was just starting out in Portland and was kind of overwhelmed by living in a city for the first time he sent me a cookie-of-the-month subscription." Bess smiled. "Little did he know that at times those cookies were pretty much all I had to eat."

The two sat quietly for a few long moments. Bess's mind roamed. Earlier she had caught a glimpse of Mike and Marta walking hand in hand toward the beach. Whatever had been troubling them seemed to have been resolved, at least for the moment. She thought of Chris and Allison and of the joy that might have been in store for them. She recalled the words of wisdom her friends had shared with her in the past days. Chuck had told her he believed she was meant to be married to Nathan. Dean had said that the effort of balancing one's own happiness against the happiness of the thing called marriage was worth the effort if you were with the right person. She thought of her own revelation, that real commitment was not about a Knight in Shining Armor and a Princess in a pretty dress. It was something far grander and yet more down-to-earth. And suddenly Bess knew for certain that she wanted to make a challenging sacrifice for the sake of her marriage.

"Nathan," she began, tossing the pillow aside and turning on the bed to face him. "I've made a decision. I don't care where we live or what we do as long as we're together. You're accepting the promotion and we're moving to Stockholm."

Nathan took her hands. "But what about your business? I know you haven't had time to think through a game plan yet."

"I'm still young," Bess said with a shrug. "Young-ish. If I don't take a risk now, when will I ever? Carpe diem and all that." Bess thought for a moment before going on. "I have events booked through the middle of January. I'll talk to Kara about a new role in the business; I can follow you in a few months if I'm forced to stay until a smooth transition regarding the day-to-day running of the company is made."

"Thank you, Bess," Nathan said earnestly. "I promise to do everything in my power to support your adjustment to our new life. I know Stockholm well. I can introduce you to people and show you around the city." Nathan touched her face gently. "We're so very lucky, Bess. If I weren't constitutionally opposed to pain I'd pinch myself to be sure this is real and not a dream. When should we tell the others?"

"After the wedding," Bess said. "We'll tell them when I give everyone his or her charm. Yes, I've decided to go ahead with my gift. I love long and I love deeply and I take chances for the sake of love and . . . And I love that about myself!"

Nathan smiled. "And I love that about you, as well."

Chapter 95

The friends were gathered around the dinner table. Chris was a no-show. Marta wasn't surprised, not after what he had experienced with Allison and Bess earlier. Neither woman had mentioned her encounter to Marta; Marta, of course, only knew because Chris had confided in her. And in that spirit, she had decided to keep her conversation with Chris from the others unless she felt it absolutely essential to share with Allison Chris's hopes for a reunion.

Surreptitiously, or so she thought, Marta sent Chris a text. *Thinking of you. Don't give up hope.*

"Ahem," Mike said. "Good thing our children aren't here to see this."

Marta quickly put her phone in her pocket. "I tell my kids no texting at the table. Sorry. By the way, Bess, it was great to meet Kara after all we've heard about her."

Kara had stopped by earlier to deliver the favors and had stayed for a cocktail. Marta had found Kara to be just as Bess had described her—competent, energetic, and organized. And a new thought had struck her. Maybe she could team up with another woman looking to build a business. Why had she been imagining only a solitary venture? There was power in numbers; women working together could accomplish miracles. Mike was right. Why had she been thinking she would have to fly solo, without the support of her husband and other women?

"Bess, this roast chicken is perfection," Dean said. "I don't know why you say you can't cook."

Bess shrugged. "Anyone can roast a chicken. Just follow the *Barefoot Contessa*'s recipe and you're golden!"

Allison smiled and reached for a bottle of seltzer. "I adore the episodes that feature Jeffrey as well. The cutest married couple ever."

The cutest married couple ever. Suddenly, Marta noted that Allison's wedding ring was missing from her finger. Bess must have noted it as well. It certainly didn't bode well for Chris. Maybe, she thought, she shouldn't have advised him not to give up hope of a reconciliation.

"So where is your family staying?" Chuck asked Bess.

"They're driving down tomorrow morning," Bess explained. "And tomorrow night they'll stay in a motor lodge not far outside Kennebunkport and drive back to Green Lakes the following morning."

"It's too bad they can't be here for longer," Mike said.

For once, Marta didn't feel the impulse to tease Bess about her attitude toward the other Culpeppers. After all, only Bess knew her family experience; only Bess had the right to manage it to her advantage.

"There are jobs to get back to," Bess said with a shrug. "Though in truth maybe I should have asked my sisters to stay on for a day or two with the kids. They would have enjoyed a vacation at the beach."

"It's not too late, is it?" Nathan asked gently.

"Maybe next year," Bess said quickly. "Chuck, would you pass the butter?"

Still, Marta held her tongue.

Chapter 96

Allison wasn't surprised that Chris hadn't joined them for dinner. He would have to be in a very strange frame of mind indeed to show up for dinner after their confrontation that morning. She felt a bit sorry for Chris now. She hoped he would get himself a healthy dinner. She hoped he would have a good night's sleep. She thought about all those nights he had helped her recover from nightmares, even if it meant sitting up with her for hours.

As if he was reading her mind, Mike said, "It was good to see Chris again." He turned to Allison. "I hope you don't mind my saying that."

Allison shook her head. "Not at all," she assured him.

"I was thinking about the time he offered to take me shopping when I needed something decent to wear for an interview. It was for a summer internship in a pretty staid law office, real old-school Bostonian." Mike laughed. "I don't know how he didn't kill me that day. I was miserable trying on jackets and ties. He finally made a selection for me and when the bill came to about forty dollars more than I could afford he floated me the cash."

"Did you get the job?" Allison asked with a smile.

"Of course! Looking as good as I did I was a shoo-in!"

"Do you think any of us will ever see him again after the wedding tomorrow?" Dean asked. "Maybe I shouldn't have said that out loud."

"Why not?" Allison said. "It's what we're all thinking, even me."

Chuck shrugged. "Impossible to say. Life is long, things change all the time." Then he smiled at Allison. "People might not change all that much but circumstances do and circumstances can force you into behavior you once thought impossible. Anyway, that's my take on things."

Allison took a sip of her coffee. Her left hand lay flat on the table next to her dessert plate. She wondered how many of her friends had noted that she wasn't wearing her wedding ring. Certainly, the women had, but neither had mentioned it. For that she was grateful. She had no idea what she would say to a direct question regarding her reasons for taking it off.

"This time tomorrow you'll be a married woman," Marta was saying. Allison thought she looked less tense than she had in the past days. Good. "Nothing will ever be the same as it was. Well, not that it ever is; every day is brand new in some way, but you know what I mean."

Bess smiled. "For better or worse. I know. And I'm ready."

Allison glanced around the table. "In spite of what happened to me—or, what I got myself into—I'm still a great proponent of marriage. I really am. It's a wondrous, beautiful thing, even in its less glamorous moments. Maybe especially then."

"Hear, hear," Chuck said.

"There's a section in C. S. Lewis's book *Mere Christianity*," Allison went on, "where he talks about how being in love comes before real love, which he says is a quieter but stronger thing that keeps a married couple together." Allison smiled. "Excuse my rough translation. He puts it beautifully."

"That's awesome," Bess said, wiping a tear from her eye. "I'm going to be a weeping mess tomorrow, I just know it!"

"Waterproof mascara," Marta said with a firm nod.

"You could go without any makeup," Dean suggested.

The look of sheer horror on Bess's face caused everyone else at the table to laugh.

"Dean," Allison said with a shake of her head. "You have a lot to learn about our Bess."

Chapter 97

Bess had drawn a chair close to the window in the bedroom. She could see nothing much from where she sat, but she could hear the ocean lapping gently on the shore. Time spent at the seaside was such a soothing and yet such a vitalizing experience. She would always cherish it.

Still, Bess wasn't entirely happy at that moment. It was her fault that Chris hadn't joined them at Driftwood House for dinner. She had been beastly to him. A part of her didn't expect him to show up tomorrow. But maybe she wasn't the only one responsible for Chris's absence that night. Allison had not been wearing her wedding ring. Maybe they had fought that morning. She might never know.

Where, Bess wondered, would the friends go from here? Would their bond ever be as strong as it used to be? Would it be so terrible if it wasn't? It was unrealistic to expect things to stay the same and maybe, just maybe the big shake-ups each of the old friends was experiencing might turn out to be beneficial to the entire group. Complacency led to staleness. But what was wrong with a bit of complacency in an old and established friendship? Why did relationships need to be shaken up? Well, maybe they didn't need to be, but they often were and the sooner you accepted that the better.

The door opened quietly and Nathan stepped inside.

"What are you up to?" he asked.

Bess smiled. "Thinking. And dreaming." She got up and went to the dresser. From her own traveling jewelry case, she removed a velvet pouch. "Here," she said, extending it toward Nathan. "This is for you."

Nathan accepted the pouch and shook the contents into the palm of his hand. "You didn't say you'd gotten a charm for me," he said softly. "Thank you, Bess. I'll wear it with pride."

"Of course, I got you a charm," she said. "My best friend forever."

Nathan drew her to him. "This adventure we're embarking on. It's going to be wonderful. I know it is."

"Me too," Bess said. "I know it. And I hope this adventure includes hiking in the Swedish Lapland and canoeing in the Gothenburg archipelagos."

"You've done your homework. Sure, hiking and canoeing and skiing if you want."

Bess smiled. "And dog sledding. A lot of snow parks offer dog sledding with those gorgeous blue-eyed Siberian huskies!"

"And we could go to Abisko National Park to see the aurora borealis. We'll have to bundle up really well as the cold is pretty brutal in the mountains."

"Speaking of cold," Bess said excitedly, "I read about the *Lakrits glass*. I'm probably saying it wrong, but it means 'black liquorice ice cream.' It sounds awesome!"

Nathan shuddered. "I've tried it. Not so awesome, but hey, that's just me."

"Whatever we do," Bess said, holding Nathan even closer, "even if it's staying at home with our feet up watching TV, will be lovely because we'll be together." *The quieter love that Allison talked about,* Bess thought. *The stronger love.*

"It will indeed," Nathan agreed. "It will indeed."

Chapter 98

Marta sat propped against the pillows, a satisfied smile on her face. She and Mike had made love the night before at Marta's instigation. Her motives had been mixed. Love and affection had played their parts, as had downright lust. The intensity of her passion had taken her by surprise. Could the fact of this fourth child actually be proving a catalyst in bringing his parents closer than ever before? Marta wondered. Far stranger things had happened.

The door to the bedroom opened and Mike came in bearing two cups of coffee. He closed the door behind him with his foot and joined his wife in bed. At home, coffee in bed was pretty much never possible, what with the demands of jobs, kids, and domestic duties.

"Do you remember our wedding day?" she asked when Mike was settled beside her.

"Of course! How could I forget the cheese ball your mother insisted on having at the cocktail hour!"

"Not exactly the classiest touch," Marta pointed out.

"I thought it was awesome," Mike said. "It was when I realized how much I liked your mother. And I remember how touched I was watching you dance with your father. Touched and scared out of my mind. I thought, this man will pulverize me if I screw up this marriage."

"Dad wouldn't hurt a fly," Marta protested.

"Yeah, well, I wasn't taking any chances." Mike turned to her, spilling a drop of coffee on Bess's expensive sheets. He didn't notice and Marta said nothing. "I'm still not," he went on. "I don't know where or who or what I would have been if I hadn't married you, Marta. I really don't."

"The same goes for me," Marta said earnestly, "so let's not even think about it." And then she laughed. "You know what I just remembered? That poor old couple who wandered into our reception thinking it was their great-nephew's wedding. They couldn't find their place cards and they were so agitated until you got wind of what was going on and came to their rescue."

Mike shrugged. "All I did was bring them some champagne and when we'd had a good laugh about the mix-up I walked them down the hall to where their family had been going crazy with worry."

"You were very kind," Marta said. "You always were. It's one of the things I love best about you, Mike."

Mike put his coffee cup on the bedside table. "No one will miss us if we aren't down right away," he said.

Marta put her own cup on her bedside table. "You're right," she said, sliding closer to her husband. "No one will miss us."

Chapter 99

Allison slipped back into her room, bathrobe belted tightly around her. She had encountered no one in the hall on her way to and from the bathroom. She thought she heard the murmur of voices as she passed Mike and Marta's room, but she couldn't be sure. She had no doubt that Bess, if not Nathan, had been up for hours already, eager to greet the day.

It was a bittersweet morning for Allison, though, as memories of her own wedding day insisted on making themselves noticed. The Longfellows, the Montagues, and Chris and Allison had booked into a high-end hotel in downtown Chicago the day before. The three couples had celebrated that evening with a dinner of prime rib, chocolate soufflé, and plenty of champagne. Chris had accompanied his parents back to their suite for the night, leaving Allison alone in theirs. She had barely been able to stand being without him; she had listened to the maddeningly slow ticking of the clock, counting the hours until she would become Chris's wife.

Allison and her mother had started the big day with a light breakfast followed by a mani-pedi in the hotel's salon. Later they were joined by Agnes Montague for lunch. And all that day Allison had longed to be only with Chris. It had been his choice, in a nod to tradition, not to see his bride until she appeared at the foot of the aisle, dressed in her finest.

The ceremony had taken place at three o'clock in the afternoon at a church chosen by Agnes Montague more for its stunning architecture than its homey familiarity. It was a traditional service, serious in tone, with appropriately soaring music. Allison was magnificent in a Candlelight Ivory peau de soie gown. Chris was desperately handsome in a bespoke tuxedo.

The reception, an elegant affair, had ended at midnight, after which Allison and Chris had changed into comfortable clothing and joined up with Chuck, Bess, Mike, and Marta, who had done the same. Together they descended on a late-night jazz venue, where they spent hours listening to the music and dancing. At six in the morning they piled into an old-fashioned diner for a breakfast of eggs, bacon, toast, and for Mike, an additional pastry. It had been, Allison thought, the best twenty-four hours of her life.

But that was then. This was now. This was Bess's wedding day. Allison found her friend in the kitchen, full of nervous energy.

"Come with me to the nail salon," Bess begged. "I don't know why, but I don't want to be alone for one minute today."

"Sure," Allison said, hurrying after Bess, who was already at the front door.

"What color are you going to get?" Bess asked as they got into her car.

"You know I only wear pale neutrals. Probably Ballet Slipper."

"Why not get something different?" Bess suggested. "Just for the fun of it."

It was difficult to hold out against Bess's enthusiasm and Allison found herself choosing a gray-tinted lilac she thought would work well with her dress. Bess was disappointed Allison hadn't chosen something bright, like one of the neon colors new to the salon that summer, but she hadn't pressed her point. Allison was sure Bess had more important things on her mind. Like her own manicure, for which she had selected—yes, Ballet Slipper.

On the drive back to Driftwood House, Bess fretted about the details of the day. Would the bakery deliver the right order? The weather forecast was clear, but would a freak rain shower send everyone running into the house? (Bess had bought plastic mats to cover the better rugs against that possibility.)

"I wonder if the florist has been to the house yet," she said, tapping her newly manicured fingers against the steering wheel. "I know Kara is on top of things and Marta said she would triple-check the delivery but . . ."

"But it's your job to worry," Allison said soothingly. "I'm sure everything will be fine."

Indeed, the florist had been to the house in their absence. Marta had inspected the flowers according to Bess's instructions and found everything perfect. Kara had directed the florist's delivery people as to where garlands were to be draped and vases set out.

The bouquet Bess was to carry was a fairly simple one consisting of three sunflowers—one a traditional sunny yellow, the other a sunset orange, and the third, a bronze. Small yellow flowers and green-and-white leaves completed the outstanding look.

"What flower says Bess Culpepper better than a sunflower?" Allison asked. She took Bess's hand in hers. "Bright. Cheery. And unashamed to be so!"

"It's not sunflower season here," Bess explained. "The florist had to hunt them down, but the added expense didn't bother me. There was no way I was going to get married without sunflowers!"

Allison smiled. "I hope you remember today as truly the happiest day of your life," she said earnestly. *As I still remember my wedding day as the happiest day of mine.*

Chapter 100

Bess and Allison had been back at the house for about half an hour when the sound of a car in the drive caused Bess to hurry to the door. But it wasn't another delivery. It was her brother-in-law's old station wagon that had pulled up to the house. Bess could make out Gus behind the wheel with her father beside him. In the backseat were her sister Mae and her mother. Behind them were crammed the kids. Ann, Walt, and their kids would, of course, have come in their own vehicle.

Bess ran out to greet her family. She hadn't expected to see any of them before one o'clock, the time the celebration officially began. She hoped none of them had taken ill or . . .

Mrs. Culpepper was climbing out of the car. Bess embraced her warmly. "Mom," she said, "I'm so glad you're here. Is everything all right?"

Mrs. Culpepper, dressed in her usual summer attire of mid-calf cotton skirt and a short-sleeved blouse, laughed. "Everything is fine and I'm sorry to be disturbing you before we're expected." She handed Bess a shoe box Bess hadn't noticed until that moment. "Your bag is inside," Mrs. Culpepper explained. "It's wrapped in tissue to protect the beading. I hope it's what you wanted."

Bess felt tears come to her eyes. "I'm sure it's perfect," she told her mother. And she believed now that it would be.

Mrs. Culpepper nodded and stepped back toward the car. "Well," she said briskly, "we'll be off to the motor lodge."

"Don't you want to come in for breakfast," Bess offered. She didn't really want them to go.

But her mother was already in the backseat. Mae waved excitedly at Bess. "You don't need us underfoot," Mrs. Culpepper called.

Bess watched as Gus maneuvered the wagon back onto the road. She thought about what she had said at dinner the other night, that maybe she should have invited her sisters and their children to stay at Driftwood House for a few days. And she realized now why she hadn't. She had been afraid they would say no.

Slowly, Bess went inside the house, where she found Marta and Allison at the island in the kitchen.

"Who was that?" Allison asked.

"My mom," Bess explained. She put the shoe box on the counter and opened it. In the midst of the pristine white tissue paper was her wedding bag, a small drawstring confection made of pure white satin with an artful sprinkling of pale yellow and orange crystals to work with the colors of the flowers in Bess's bouquet. It was simple and elegant and, Bess thought, absolutely perfect.

"Wow," Marta said. "It's stunning."

"The workmanship is superb," Allison noted. "I had no idea your mother was so talented."

"Neither did I," Bess admitted. "She paid attention to every idea I provided, but then made the bag something far better. She made it her own." Bess hesitated but only for a moment. "And you know what?" she said. "I'm going to wear the garter Mae lent me as my something borrowed. I know, I didn't tell you guys about it because frankly, it's horrid. But it was given in a spirit of love and that means a lot."

Marta nodded. "And she doesn't need to know about the bracelet Kara lent you."

"Speaking of what you'll be wearing," Allison said, pointing to the clock over the sink, "it's about time you started getting dressed and thought about doing your hair."

Bess looked at the clock, as well. "You're right. I've brought my dress into our room and Nathan's going to use the small spare room at the end of the hall to get ready so I can freak out to my heart's content on my own. You know, if a zipper gets stuck or something."

"I'm packing a needle and thread," Marta said. "Now, let's get you ready."

Chapter 101

Once Bess was dressed and Allison was dealing with the bride's hair, Marta went to her own room to prepare. Bess had given her carte blanche regarding her dress—a very generous gesture, Marta thought. Surprisingly, Marta had found just the thing in her closet. Tiny sprays of green and yellow flowers were scattered across the cream-colored background of the dress, which came to just above her ankles. Long, billowy sleeves and a high neck with the tiniest bit of lace made the dress a more romantic style than Marta usually wore; she must have been in a strange mood the day she bought it, but there was no denying it looked good on her. Mike definitely thought so. And it had been on sale.

Marta took more than usual care with her appearance. She used product and a blow-dryer on her hair and while she hadn't gone with the others to the salon that morning, she had painted her own nails neatly with a pale-pink polish. Her maid of honor speech was tucked into her bag, which she had borrowed from Sam for the occasion. Sam had worn the Art Deco, spring-green Lucite bag with clear Lucite handles to her prom a few weeks back; it had been a gift from her father. At the time, Marta hadn't been happy about the expenditure, but now she was glad to have the opportunity to wear something that worked so well with her dress.

With a little advice from his wife, Mike had chosen to wear an impeccable lightweight navy suit with a sky-blue shirt and a slightly darker blue tie. Marta was pretty sure the tie would disappear soon after the ceremony. She just hoped Mike would remember where he had tossed the tie. She expected he wouldn't and she would spend some time checking under tables and behind bushes before it came to light.

As she put on her jewelry—her modest and much-beloved wedding and engagement rings; her trusty Fossil watch; simple gold stud earrings—Marta thought about the call she had made to her mother and the kids earlier that morning.

"Please wish Bess the best from your father and me," Mrs. Kennedy had said. "I sent a card to her Portland address. It should be waiting when she gets back."

Sam had sighed. "Weddings are so romantic! Be sure to get a picture of the first kiss!"

"What does this guy do, the one Bess is marrying?" Leo asked. Marta imagined the frown of assumed maturity on his twelve-year-old face.

"He's some bigwig in communications with Winter International."

"Never heard of it," Leo said dismissively.

Troy didn't want to know anything about the wedding. He wanted to know if they could get a puppy like his grandfather's Dachsund. Wanting at all costs to avoid a meltdown over the phone, Marta had relied on the "we'll talk about it when Mommy and Daddy get home" put-off.

Marta gave her reflection one last approving look and went downstairs to join the others. Guests had begun arriving twenty minutes earlier. Marta scanned the back porch and yard. There was no sign of Chris so far, and Marta had heard nothing from him. She decided not to send an inquiring text. Chris might interpret it as pressure, and he had enough on his plate without Marta hounding him.

Suddenly, Marta felt overcome with emotion. The day Bess had been dreaming about for most of her life. Marta, who did not believe in God, nevertheless sent a prayer into the universe for her dear friend and the man she loved so completely. *Let Bess and Nathan appreciate the love they've been given to share,* she thought. *There is no greater gift.*

Then Marta went in search of Mike.

Chapter 102

Guests had been arriving for some time, many carrying gaily wrapped boxes and gift bags in spite of Bess's request for no presents other than a donation to one of her favorite charities. The need for celebration, Allison thought, was very strong. A wedding was not only cause for the couple to cheer, it was an opportunity for an entire community of friends and family to break out of the day-to-day and to consciously remember that life was grand. At least, that it could be grand.

The majority of the guests were strangers to Allison. She guessed the average age to be forty-five, and the average income healthy. The Culpepper clan—all thirteen of them—stood out, but not as outrageously as Bess had hinted they would. Allison noted that Bess's mother was a natural beauty, one of those lucky women with bone structure that didn't quit.

Allison was dressed in a slim, mid-calf length slip dress in a soft minty green. She wore her long blond hair loose, and her only jewelry was a simple diamond pendant on a white gold chain her parents had given her on her graduation from college. She had managed to pin her nosegay—a miniature version of the bouquet Marta carried—onto the strap of her camera so that she could be hands-free to document the more casual and intimate moments of the day. Flat sandals completed her outfit.

Chuck and Dean had beautifully coordinated their outfits. No surprise there, Allison thought. Each man wore a linen suit in a shade of beige. Chuck's shirt was pale yellow and his pocket handkerchief was lilac. Dean's shirt was the exact same shade of lilac and his pocket handkerchief the same shade of pale yellow. The baby wore a pale blue romper with a short-sleeved white shirt underneath accented by a teeny lilac bow tie and yellow socks. One of Bess's nieces, the nine-year-old Tildy, was hovering around the Fortunato-Williams family, entranced by little Thomas.

Allison couldn't help but see that Chris had not yet arrived. Maybe he had decided not to come after all. For a moment, Allison felt real disappointment at the possibility of Chris's deciding not to show. But only for a moment.

Before any more time passed, Allison made it a point to introduce herself to the photographer Bess had hired for the event and to explain why he would see her taking so many photographs. It was a stroke of luck that Allison and the photographer's head assistant knew someone in common, so that her promise to stay well out of the way was taken seriously.

When that task had been accomplished, Allison made a visual search for her feline friend, but he was nowhere to be seen. It was probably wise of him to stay far away from a bunch of shouting children and adults drinking more than they ordinarily did, Allison decided. A tail might get stepped on.

Indeed, the crowd was growing by the minute—and enjoying itself. For the thirsty, there was red, white, and rosé wine in addition to Prosecco. For those who preferred nonalcoholic drinks, there was fizzy water, pomegranate juice, and iced tea. Several people had already made a foray into the buffet. Allison wasn't surprised. Lobster dumplings. Crab quiche. Pigs in a blanket. Cold shrimp. Roast beef. Tiny peanut butter and jelly sandwiches. There was something to tempt every appetite.

Bess had chosen to use restraint in terms of decoration. The tablecloths and napkins were snowy white against the green of the grass. Simple greenery garlands were strung along the buffet tables. The backs of the wooden folding chairs were decorated with a swath of shiny ivy leaves and a small white papery flower. Big bunches of sunflowers in various colors stood tall in old milk cans on either side of the stairs that led to and from the back porch, as well as at the corners of the temporary bandstand. It all made for a great background against which to capture the all-important human exchanges to come.

Or the ones that were happening right now, Allison thought, spying an older couple sharing a sweet kiss. She raised her camera to her eye and began to shoot.

Chapter 103

Earlier, Bess had stood before the full-length mirror in the room she was sharing with Nathan, and smiled. The dress she had chosen was a simple, strapless A-line gown rendered in pure white with a tasteful amount of white beadwork for visual interest. Her hair was done in a loose, tousled braid worn down her back; Allison had helped with the styling. On her feet, she wore custom satin flats with enough structure to prevent her from turning an ankle on the sand. To complete the look, she wore the Victorian filigree bracelet borrowed from Kara; her engagement ring; the aquamarine ring from Market Square Jewelers; and vintage clip-on earrings in gold and crystal. To the ribbon around her bouquet she had pinned the brooch that had belonged to Nathan's grandmother. The wedding rings she and Nathan had chosen were simple gold bands.

"If I do say so myself," Bess had whispered to her reflection, "I am a very pretty bride!"

When Nathan had at last seen Bess descending the stairs to the first floor of the house he had put his hands to his face as tears sprang to his eyes. Bess had rushed across the room to him.

"You love it, don't you?" she asked.

Wiping the tears from his eyes, Nathan laughed. "I love *you*," he said. "You look so beautiful."

Now Nathan was busy greeting guests and in his navy suit with a bright white shirt, Bess thought he was by far the most handsome man she had ever seen. With reluctance, she tore her eyes away from Nathan and located her family. They were gathered together not far from the table on which the favors were laid out. As far as Bess knew, none of them had yet ventured to speak to the other guests—and neither had those guests approached the Culpepper family. But it was early and no doubt as time passed, music was played, and wine was drunk, the mingling would take place in earnest. Bess knew how these things worked.

Her mother, Bess thought, looked beautiful. She was wearing a mauve linen dress of her own creation. In both cut and color it suited her perfectly. Though she wore a crystal necklace and earrings that had once belonged to her own mother, her best accessory was her genuinely happy smile.

Mr. Culpepper was wearing his one suit. The suit itself was like a photograph album of the family's past; Owen Culpepper had worn it to Cousin Todd's high school graduation; the funerals of the grandparents; the weddings of both of Bess's sisters; countless christenings; and now, Bess's own wedding.

Today the suit was fitting very snugly. The fabric was so worn that it was shiny in parts, though the suit was nicely pressed and it was clear to Bess that her mother had replaced the buttons recently. The tie was one Bess recognized as well. She had given it to him on a Father's Day when she was about ten or eleven. Her dear father.

Ann looked charming in a dress Bess recognized from her sister's previous pregnancies. It was a blousy midi with long, loose sleeves and a bit of lace at the modest neckline. The pale-green and blue pattern was summery and brought out the startling green of Ann's eyes.

Mae's outfit was far less outrageous than the one she had worn to Bess's shower. Once again, the ensemble was too short for attractiveness, but the overall pattern of cherries against a white background made the dress appropriately festive.

Ann's husband Walt's suit was clearly an off-the-rack affair, a dark, muddy blue worn with a maroon shirt and a tie of indeterminate hue. Gus's suit had a bit more style. Bess recognized it as an Armani from about 1990; he must have purchased it in a decent resale shop. It didn't fit properly, but Gus looked proud to be wearing it and pride in one's appearance could go a long way.

As for Bess's nieces and nephews, they seemed thrilled with the amount of yummy food available; they were all munching mini-cupcakes and tiny peanut butter and jelly sandwiches, food especially provided for young palettes. A memory of Ann and Mae as toddlers flashed across Bess's mind, Ann with her tiny blond pony-tail, Mae clutching her favorite stuffed toy, a very battered giraffe. The memory made her smile.

Bess stepped forward to the porch stairs and no sooner had she done so than her sisters spotted her and came hurrying to her side.

"I never thought I'd see the day!" Ann exclaimed.

Mae nodded. "Me, neither. I had you down for an old maid, Bessie. Not that there's anything wrong with that," she added hastily.

Bess ignored the tactlessness of the remark. "I'm wearing the garter you lent to me," she told Mae.

"You are!" Mae exclaimed. "You know, I really wasn't sure you would. Your style is so much more, well, it's so much better than mine."

"Not better," Bess said, taking Mae's hand. "Just different."

"I missed you when you went away to college," Ann suddenly blurted. "Not at first, but when you couldn't come home until Christmas that first year it was like, wow, she's really gone."

Bess thought her heart would break. In some way, she thought, she had been waiting most of her life to hear this admission of love.

"I missed you, too," Mae added. "Sometimes I slept in your room so I could be closer to you." Then she shrugged. "But everyone moves on, I guess. You graduated and went to Portland and Ann and I got married. That's just the way it is."

Bess smiled through tears. "But we're all here together now," she said feelingly.

Suddenly, Ann put a hand to her mouth. "Uh-oh, Little Owen is crying! I'd better go."

"I'll come too," Mae said, the two women already hurrying off. "Once Little Owen starts my Dennis won't be far behind."

It was at that moment that Bess spotted a tall, thin man coming into the yard from around the side of the house. Chris. He wore a cream-colored linen suit with a pale peach, open-necked shirt. He stopped when he spotted Bess, clearly hesitant to continue.

Bess walked toward him, her hands outstretched.

"I'm really glad you came today," she said. And she meant it.

Chris nodded. "Me too. And I'm sorry our conversation got out of hand yesterday," he said.

"That's okay," Bess said. "I'm sorry, too. I know I can be too pie in the sky. Enough people have told me that."

"Don't apologize," Chris said firmly. "Idealism is a fine quality. I once heard someone say that a cynic is a disappointed romantic. I would hate to see you become a cynic, especially as a result of something I said or did."

"That will never happen," Bess assured him. "I think I came closer to cynicism these past weeks than I ever want to be again. It doesn't suit me. Neither does being mean. I do love you, Chris."

"And I love you, Bess. You look gorgeous. You make a lovely bride."

"As long as Nathan thinks so."

"I'm sure he does." Chris smiled and moved off. Before he had gone far one of Bess's nephews approached him; ten-year-old Gus Jr. was holding up a balsa wood plane that was one of the little toys Bess had provided in a large basket set up next to the children's performer. Chris squatted and took the plane in his hand. Poor Chris, Bess thought. He *would* have made a good father, in spite of his demons.

"Bess?" It was the minister. She smiled and tapped her watch. "It's time. You'd better find your groom."

The minister turned away and began to herd the guests in the direction of the beach.

This is it, Bess thought, her heart fluttering. *This is the start of it all.*

Chapter 104

Of course, the weather was perfect, Marta thought. Bess Culpepper would have it no other way, in spite of her backup plans that had backup plans. The sun was warm but not uncomfortably so; the air was fresh; the sky cloudless. Wedding weather if Marta had ever seen it.

Marta stood to one side of the minister; Simon, Nathan's best man, stood to the minister's other side. Nathan, looking nervous in the time-honored fashion of grooms everywhere, stood just in front of the minister, fiddling with his cuffs and collar, waiting for the arrival of his bride.

There was no seating. Bess had wanted her friends and family to cluster loosely around the bride and groom. Bess had also nixed the idea of writing personalized vows; Nathan, she said, had been pleased, as the idea of committing his feelings to paper was too daunting. All in all, Marta thought, Bess had created a beautifully low-key event that was nonetheless very special.

A small crowd of onlookers was gathering in addition to the invited guests. Marta smiled to herself. In spite of so much evidence that marriage was no bed of roses or a guarantee of a happy-ever-after, people continued to love weddings, even those of total strangers. That said something good about human nature.

A murmuring and a series of "Ohhs!" and "Ahhs!" announced the appearance of the bride at the foot of the stairs that led from Driftwood House. Marta felt tears spring to her eyes. Bess looked beautiful. Innocent and yet wise. Natural and yet poised.

With a trembling smile, Bess walked slowly toward the minister, Nathan, Marta, and Simon. The crowd of guests and onlookers parted to let her through and then joined again when she had gone by. When she reached her destination, she handed her bouquet to Marta. Marta held Bess's hand for a moment at the exchange.

"Mommy, why is Aunt Bess so pretty today?"

The crowd laughed at this delightfully innocent question loudly posed by Mae's five-year-old son, Alan. Bess turned to her nephew and waved. Then she and Nathan joined hands. Marta glanced toward Mike, who stood with Allison, Chuck, Dean, and Thomas at the front of the crowd. Mike gave his wife a look that melted her already tender heart. Reluctantly, Marta looked away to see if she could spot Chris among the crowd. He was there, but at the very back. Marta wondered if he would disappear the moment the ceremony was over, never to return.

The Universalist Unitarian minister, who had married several of Bess's colleagues and Portland friends, welcomed the bride and groom and Marta turned her attention to where it rightly belonged. The service was simple. In less than five minutes, the minister was pronouncing Bess and Nathan husband and wife and giving them permission to share a first kiss as a married couple.

Guests and onlookers burst into applause. There was some hooting and hollering as well. Several people wiped tears from smiling faces. Cell phones were held aloft. The children ran in circles or kicked sand into the air or screamed with glee. Some did all three.

After a few minutes, when the initial excitement had died down, the guests were asked to return to Driftwood House for the speeches and the cutting of the cake—or in this case, the cakes. While Bess and Nathan received congratulations, Marta made her way to the bandstand. She realized she still held Bess's bouquet and absentmindedly shoved it toward the band's guitarist. He took it, shrugged, and placed it atop an amp. Marta reached into the vintage Lucite bag and withdrew the paper on which her speech—in its latest iteration—was written. The band's front man handed her a glass of champagne.

She felt more nervous than she ever had when about to address a crowd. Nervous and emotional. Valiantly she fought back tears—Marta MacIntosh did not cry in public; well, not often—and once the band's front man had called for attention, she scanned the crowd to locate her support system—Mike and her friends—and then, looking directly at the newlyweds, she began to speak. *Short and sweet. Keep their attention.*

"I am honored to have been chosen to stand here before you to say a few words about my dear friend Bess. Thank you, Bess, for keeping me—for keeping all of your friends—honest by continually reminding us of the importance of friendship. You truly are our anchor in this world so fraught with challenges.

"But to something even more important," Marta went on. "Bess never stopped believing that one day she would find her soul mate. I admit there were times in the past when I thought she was being naïve. But I was wrong. Bess did find her soul mate and I think she—and Nathan—would agree with Rumi, the mystic and poet, when he says: '*Lovers don't finally meet somewhere. They're in each other all along.*'" Marta raised her glass. "To Bess and Nathan!"

Amidst cheers and shouts, Marta left the bandstand and joined Mike, who enveloped her in a hug. Simon took Marta's place on the bandstand. Briefly, he recounted an amusing incident from his boyhood spent with Nathan, then a slightly embarrassing incident from their college days. That was followed by a discreet mention of Nathan's becoming a widow in his early thirties and of the many years he spent, as Simon put it, waiting for Bess to walk into his life and make it whole once again.

"Everybody," Simon said at the end of his heartfelt speech, "have fun!"

Marta smiled at her husband. "You heard what he said. Now, let's get to it!"

Chapter 105

Allison took a sip of the excellent Prosecco Nathan had chosen for the celebration. She was resting, but only for a moment or two. There were plenty more photographs to be taken before her work for Bess was done, though she would not take a photo of Chris. That she would leave to the pro Bess had hired.

Allison was surprised that Chris had shown up for the wedding. He had seemed so defeated when they had parted the day before. But from somewhere he had found the strength to return. She was glad. She wondered if she owed him a greeting; she wondered if a greeting might wound him. She doubted he would approach her. Indeed, not once throughout the speeches had he tried to catch her attention, though she had found herself sneaking glances at him. Twice she saw him wipe tears from his eyes with his handkerchief. Chris always carried a nice handkerchief.

Suddenly, one of Bess's nieces—Allison wasn't quite sure of her name or if she belonged to Ann or to Mae—careened into the table on which were laid out the wedding favors. Several of the boxes containing the handmade soaps toppled to the ground. For a moment, the poor girl looked distraught but then, Chris was at her side, replacing the boxes on the table and speaking to the child with a smile. The little girl's expression of guilt and fear lifted, and she laughed. Chris placed a gentle hand on her head and then off she ran.

Allison felt her heart break just a little and she looked away from the man who was soon to be her ex-husband. *A quieter love* . . . In another moment, Chuck and Dean were at her side. Thomas, in Dean's arms, reached out toward Allison's neck and grasped her diamond pendant.

"They do that at this age," Dean explained, gently extricating the diamond from his son's chubby fingers. "Start to get focused on details."

Allison knew this bit of fact. She had read so much about a baby's development. "He's got good taste," she said. "Going for diamonds."

"I spoke with Chris," Chuck told her. "Rather, I spoke to him. He was too choked up to say much of anything other than hello."

Allison shook her head. "Why is he doing this to himself? Why doesn't he go home now?"

Chuck sighed. "I don't know. I'm trying not to dwell on that question."

Mike and Marta joined their little group. Mike's tie was gone, his collar was opened, and his sleeves rolled up.

"Have you talked to Chris?" Marta asked immediately.

"No." The big question on everyone's mind, Allison thought.

Mike cleared his throat. "I did," he said. "Just hello. And I told him it was good to see him again. I meant it."

Marta asked to hold Thomas. "How much does he weigh?" she asked when Dean had handed him over.

"Pretty much right on target," Dean said. "A little under eighteen pounds."

"Good job, Thomas," Marta told the little boy, planting a kiss on his smooth cheek.

The band's front man suddenly announced that it was time for the bride and groom's first dance. Bess had kept to herself the song she had chosen for this special moment, but Allison was not at all surprised when the band played the opening notes of "What a Wonderful World," a song made popular by the late great Louis Armstrong.

Allison watched fondly as Nathan held out his hand and Bess joined him. Allison wasn't the only one of the guests who sang along to the beloved standard and who watched with tears in their eyes as husband and wife held each other.

When the song was over the wild applause began, and went on for some time.

What heartbreakingly beautiful lyrics, Allison thought, casting her eye about for Chris. But he was nowhere to be found.

Chapter 106

The formal portraits had been taken after the speeches and cutting of the cakes. Bess and Nathan with Marta and Simon; Bess and Nathan with the Culpepper clan; Bess and Nathan on their own. The first dance as a married couple had been danced. Now Bess and her husband were once again free to mingle among the guests. They received congratulations as they wandered hand in hand across the lawn. They shared observations—Kara looked as if she had stepped out of the pages of a high-fashion magazine; people seemed to be enjoying the band; the lobster dumplings were a hit.

"We've been fighting the crowd to get to you!"

It was Lisa Fanshaw. She looked fantastic as always, Bess thought, in a classic, cornflower-blue wrap dress. Howard wore a pale gray suit with a white shirt opened at the neck and a pink silky handkerchief in the breast pocket of his jacket.

"I've told everyone that I'm responsible for bringing the two of you together!" Lisa declared with a laugh. "I hope you don't mind my claiming the fame. I just love weddings! And happy endings."

"This is a happy beginning, I'd say," Nathan opined.

"True," Lisa said with a firm nod. "The wedding is only the start of wonderful things."

"Not always wonderful." Howard put his arm around his wife's waist. "But I think what Lisa means is that it's a heck of a lot easier to face life's challenges with a partner. At least it has been for us."

"That's exactly what I meant," Lisa confirmed, beaming at her husband.

Arm in arm, they walked off in the direction of the open bar.

"Are they always so happy and in concert with each other?" Bess asked.

Nathan smiled. "Not always. I think a few glasses of champagne are behind their current state of bliss. Still, they are one of the most well-matched couples I've ever known."

"Like we are," Bess said earnestly.

Nathan smiled down at his wife. "Yes," he said. "Like we are."

"I'm so happy Chris came after all," Bess said as she took Nathan's arm and they continued to stroll among the guests.

"Has he talked to Allison?" Nathan asked.

"I don't know. Poor Chris. Poor Allison! Today must be so hard on them."

"Hey." Nathan gently tugged Bess to a halt. "Remember who this day is about."

Bess smiled up at her husband. "You and me. Me and you."

Nathan had gone off with Simon for a catch-up conversation. They managed to see each other only once or twice a year, though Bess imagined that with her and Nathan living in Stockholm the men might be able to spend more time together. Bess liked Simon and she wondered why he wasn't yet married. Hmm, she thought. Maybe she could find someone for him!

Somehow Chuck had located a softball and was playing catch with Chris. Like they had in college, Bess thought. Teammates. Roommates. Friends.

The children's performer was a huge hit, and not only with the kids. Dean was sporting a purple balloon crown on his head. "I am Dean, Duke of Driftwood House," he announced as he paraded the lawn with his son, who clutched a small balloon dog in his fat fist. Bess's brothers-in-law also wore crowns, as did several of Bess's colleagues.

Shoes and sandals had been abandoned as people danced on the grass to the jazz and blues tunes being performed by the band. Marta had been commandeered by Bess's brother-in-law Gus, who, Bess was surprised to learn, could really dance. Allison was busy circling the yard, taking pictures but staying well out of the way of the hired photographic team.

Suddenly, Bess spied her mother making her way toward her. Mr. Culpepper, Bess saw, was deep in conversation with Howard Fanshaw. Bess wondered what the two men could possibly have in common. Her mother told her. "They're talking mulch."

Bess nodded. "A topic that unites all homeowners. Are you getting enough to eat, Mom? Have you tried the lobster dumplings? The tomato tartlets are awfully good, too."

"Bess, don't worry about me, I'm fine." Mrs. Culpepper smiled. "Though I think your father has had enough of those little pancake thingies topped with caviar and cream for three people. Well, he works hard. And this is a lovely chance for the family to be together and celebrate."

And we should do that more often, Bess thought. *It's up to me to make that happen and I'm ready to do it.* "I can't tell you how much I love the bag, Mom," she said. It hung from Bess's right wrist; the beads sparkled in the sun. "I'll treasure it always."

"It was my pleasure to make it. You're a lovely bride."

"All mothers must say that to their daughters."

"And all mothers mean it."

Bess hesitated. There had been something on her mind these past few days, but she wasn't sure if now was the right time to mention it. But there was no time like the present. "Mom," she said, "I have to ask you something. Last year, when you refused the money I offered to repair the roof. Why didn't you accept my help?"

Mrs. Culpepper folded her hands before her. "Your father and I weren't raised to take money from our children."

Bess sighed. "But, Mom, it wasn't as if you wanted money to take a luxury cruise. You needed a new roof. It was a necessity. Which is not to say I wouldn't do my best to send you and Dad on a cruise if you wanted," she added hurriedly. "The point is, what is family for if not to be there in the tough times?"

"We didn't mean to make you feel bad," her mother said quickly. "And the bank was willing to lend us what we needed. Well, most of it."

"Okay, but next time, if you and Dad need a new boiler or if you just want a nice long weekend away, just the two of you, promise that you'll come to Nathan and me. Please."

Her mother nodded. "All right. I promise."

"Good." Bess felt herself beaming. "Now, have you had a piece of cake yet?"

Mrs. Culpepper laughed. "I'll have one right now if it will stop you worrying about me."

Bess watched her mother approach the dessert table and select a slice of the vanilla cake with strawberry filling. And as she did she was overcome by a feeling of deep gratitude for all her mother had done for her. Bess had been a shy kid, not bullied as much as ignored because she confused most of the other kids in tiny rural Green Lakes, with her quirky clothing and her nose always in a book that most certainly hadn't been assigned at school. Whenever she was left off the guest list for a classmate's birthday party or excluded from schoolyard games, it was her mother who would assure Bess that her time of inclusion would come when she left Green Lakes for college and met people from other places and walks of life. Matilda Culpepper had known that true happiness for her oldest daughter lay elsewhere, far from the ancestral home. She had probably known that even before Bess herself had, as far back as when she had been forced to rely on her oldest daughter to help care for her younger two.

How could she have forgotten that her mother had always been her champion? If Mrs. Culpepper had at times suggested that Bess give up her quest for a professional life in Portland and move home to Green Lakes, it was not because she didn't understand that Bess was different from her younger sisters or because Mrs. Culpepper was trying to control her oldest child. It was because like any doting mother she was concerned for her child's safety and security.

And her sisters. They were pretty great, too. Bess vowed to really get to know Mae and Ann, the siblings who had missed her when she had gone off to college, even though they had later chosen not to visit her in Portland. And she vowed to get to know their children, as well. Well, maybe once the children were grown. Watching all seven of them swarming across the lawn, stuffing their mouths with cake, shouting for no apparent reason other than the fact that they had lungs and could shout, dodging adult guests with only inches to spare, and shedding clip-on ties and patent leather Mary Janes as they went . . . Well, it was all making Bess feel a bit queasy. And her blood pressure might just have jumped into an unhealthy range watching Gus Jr. fling a Frisbee in the general direction of the house for which she had paid so much money. Ann's oldest daughter, Lily, caught the Frisbee and Bess's blood pressure returned to a healthy level.

A quick glance around at the adult guests confirmed the fact that the party had achieved its own momentum. If Bess Culpepper knew how to do one thing, it was to throw a party. Just as she was congratulating herself on this latest success, however, she spotted the founding member of her book group, looking overwhelmed. In one hand, Barbara held an empty plate on which rested a fork and a spoon. In the other she was juggling a glass of wine and her purse. Barbara would be eighty-five come autumn, and Bess had noted that she had become the tiniest bit frail and mildly confused at times.

"Let me take that empty plate for you," Bess said, striding over to her.

"Thank you, dear," Barbara said with obvious relief. "This is such a wonderful event! I expect we'll be talking about your wedding at our next meeting rather than the book we're supposed to be discussing!"

Barbara moved off toward another member of their book group.

"You're not supposed to be on duty," a voice said.

Bess turned to find her assistant, Kara. She looked smashing in a periwinkle silk sheath dress and her hair worn up in a neat French twist. Diamond studs twinkled on her earlobes. "I can't turn it off," Bess said with a laugh. "I need to be sure that everyone is enjoying himself."

Kara smiled fondly. "I know. It's what makes Joie de Vivre the success it is. And it's also what makes you such a good boss."

Bess hesitated but only for a moment. "How would you feel about sharing that responsibility?"

"What do you mean?" Kara asked, her expression keen.

"I'll fill you in on the details when I get back to Portland, but let's just say there's going to be a change at Joie de Vivre and I'm going to need you more than ever before."

Kara beamed. "Count me in!"

Another guest called out to Kara and she moved off to join her.

Bess remembered how badly she had felt the other night, insulting herself for her love of being a hostess, for caring so much about every little detail meant to make a person happy. Accusing herself of being obsessed, of having compulsive needs.

The thing was, she didn't want to change. She didn't want to become someone who didn't care so very much. What else might she lose if she lost her porous nature, the very thing that allowed her to feel such immense sympathy for and empathy with others? Would she lose her sensitivity to beauty and her appreciation of art and nature?

It didn't bear thinking about. Bess wanted people to be happy and while in the future she would keep in mind what both Allison and Marta had said about her tendency to "interfere," as well as about her not having the power to compel happiness and not always knowing what it was that would make a person happy—she would also joyfully continue to provide bowls of favorite candies in bedrooms and scented candles in bathrooms and to perform the small, thoughtful gestures that could make such a positive difference in a person's daily life.

Bess thought once again of that strange wind that had come out of nowhere one night two weeks ago as she and her friends were gathered around the dinner table. Allison had surmised it was a conspiracy of moon and sea to create a storm to disturb their complacency—such as it was.

Ha! Bess laughed. Sometimes a gust of wind was just a gust of wind.

Chapter 107

Ann and Mae zoomed in on Marta as she stood on the periphery of the dance area, watching Bess and Nathan's friends Lisa and Howard Fanshaw do a unique version of The Twist.

Bess's sisters wanted to know about Marta's children. Was Sam seriously dating anyone? Was she planning to go to college or to settle down and get married after graduation? Did Leo play sports? Did he have a little girlfriend? What was Troy's favorite television show?

Marta answered their questions. Yes, Sam was seeing someone, but not seriously, and most certainly she was going to college and maybe to law school after that. No, Leo did not play sports. (He thought ball sports were stupid, but Marta kept that bit of information to herself.) He did not have a girlfriend. He did not want a girlfriend; he was only twelve and had better things to do with his time than date. (That was a direct quote.) And Troy didn't have a favorite television show because he didn't watch television. He wasn't allowed to. He loved to read, though. He had been reading since he was five.

Ann shook her head. "My Lily is boy crazy, has been all her life. I just hope she doesn't get herself in trouble. Tildy doesn't care one way or the other about boys and I hope it stays that way for a good

long while. But she does love babies. Jacob's a little ladies' man—
he's seven. He'll have the girls lined up around the block waiting for
a date! As for Little Owen, well, at three all he's interested in is that
cartoon, what's it called, the one with the pink chicken."

"What about your children?" Marta asked Mae.

Mae chuckled. "I can't get my Gus, he's ten, to sit still long
enough to finish his homework. He never had much interest in
school. His daddy is pretty sure he can get him a job at the hard-
ware store once he graduates high school, if he doesn't quit when he
turns sixteen, and it's my bet that he will. Alan, he's five, he does
all right in school, though the teacher says he's bored and maybe
should be in a private school. How we could afford that is anyone's
guess! Dennis, of course, is only two. He and Little Owen are an-
gels once you put them in front of the TV. You can walk away and
get all sorts of things done and they won't even know you're gone!"

Marta nodded. She didn't know what to say to the women regarding the brief picture they had painted of their families. Both
were so different from her own. She had, however, noted that all of
Bess's nieces and nephews were clean, happy, and decently dressed.
"They all look very healthy and festive," she said, hoping the words
sounded appropriately complimentary.

The sisters thanked Marta and went off in search of their husbands. Ann was worried that Walt hadn't gotten enough to eat, and
Mae was worried that Gus had eaten too many sweets. "I don't want
him to get the diabetes," she said. "It runs in his family."

Bess really was cut from a different cloth, Marta thought when
Ann and Mae had gone. No wonder she had difficulty bonding with
her sisters. Still, blood was thicker than water (not always but often
a good thing) and Marta hoped that over time Bess would grow to
feel more united with the other members of her family. They were
good people. Bess was a good person.

A shout of laughter caused Marta to look in the direction of the
bandstand. A very dapper man was leading Mrs. Culpepper in a
rather wild two-step. But Marta was more interested in who was
standing a few yards beyond the dance area. Chris. Marta sighed. It
was impossible to miss the look of despair on his face as he watched

Simon, Nathan's friend, in animated discussion with Allison. There was no denying that Simon was an attractive man. He was tall and well-built. His hair was thick and silver and swept back off a strong, tanned face in which dark eyes sparkled.

It was good for Allison, Marta thought, to be reminded that she was a young, attractive woman, soon to be single—if Chris couldn't work a miracle and get Allison to reconsider the marriage—and that she had a long life ahead of her. As for Chris, Simon's attentions to his soon-to-be-former wife might just spur him on to attempt that miracle. But that was not Marta's concern any longer. She had said what she could say.

Marta made her way toward the bottom of the yard, where Mike was having a grand old time playing with Bess's nieces and nephews. The sight warmed her heart. She knew that if she could do it all again she would do exactly the same as she had done. She would never trade all she had—Mike and the children and the life they shared together—for any other scenario. And there was no point in feeling ashamed that for a brief period of time she had felt a yearning for a life she might have had if she had made different choices. That was part of being human, having to negotiate curiosity, the thirst for the "what if," the temptation of the foreign, the lure of fantasy. There was nothing to be proud of in behaving well in a cozy, nonthreatening atmosphere, but you could feel proud of having resisted temptation or despair when confronted with it, no matter its source.

Marta shook her head fondly as Mike threw himself onto the ground and the kids piled on top of him, laughing and squealing. She hoped he hadn't hurt his back taking that fall; he wasn't as young as he used to be—none of them were—and . . . Marta caught herself and smiled. If he pulled a muscle during the horseplay she would nurse him back to health. Still, she was glad he had shed his suit jacket and his tie. The pants were going to need immediate dry cleaning, and the shirt would need a presoak if it had picked up grass stains.

Marta let her gaze wander. Ann Culpepper—Marta realized she had never bothered to learn Ann's married name—was making her way toward her husband with two cups of coffee. She handed one of the cups to Walt and he leaned down and kissed her cheek. Marta saw Ann put a hand to her pregnant belly and smile. A good mother, Marta noted. Kind and loving.

Raising children, Marta knew, was a very special task. Lots of people with advanced degrees and significant careers were appallingly bad at it; being a successful parent took talents and strengths not taught in schools or rewarded with money or public acclaim. Besides, there was not enough money in the world to properly compensate a parent for doing a good job of being a mother or a father. But it would be nice, Marta thought, if the stay-at-homes got a healthy stipend for their pains!

"Marta!" It was Mike calling from under the pile of children. "Help! I'm being devoured by tickle monsters!"

Marta laughed. "You're on your own," she called back. She thought of Sam, and Leo, and Troy, and of this new baby, and she recalled a few lines from the song Bess had chosen to mark her special day.

"It really is a wonderful world," Marta whispered feelingly.

Chapter 108

"I'm so glad Nathan and Bess found each other. It's been so long since I saw him smile this way, as if happiness was truly his once again."

Allison nodded. "I'm glad, too," she said to Simon. "I have a good feeling about this marriage."

She liked Simon. He was intelligent and amusing and undoubtedly good-looking. If he had time before his return to England and wanted to see her again she might very well say yes. She could always postpone her flight to Chicago. Greg could handle the business on his own for a few more days. He might actually welcome the opportunity.

Suddenly, Allison caught sight of Chris looking at her and was almost amused—almost—to realize that he might be a bit jealous. Simon, too, had become aware they had an audience. "I think your ex-husband wants a word with you. Sorry. Soon-to-be ex-husband."

"You don't have to go," Allison said earnestly. She didn't owe Chris anything beyond common courtesy. Not really. Not much, anyway.

Simon smiled. "That's all right. I'll see you later."

The moment Simon began to walk away, Chris started toward her.

"Do you think we could take a walk along the beach?" he asked when he was close enough to be heard without shouting.

Allison didn't hesitate. There was nothing to be gained by being rude or even politely dismissive. For all she knew this might be the last time she and Chris would come face-to-face. Better to make a neutral memory than a hostile one. Besides, she still had a feeling that they had left something unfinished the morning before.

"For a few minutes," she said. "I don't want to miss anything important." Allison indicated the camera slung around her neck.

Chris nodded and side by side they walked down the lawn to the stairs that led to the sand and then to the water's edge. Allison wondered who among their friends had watched them go.

When they reached the water's edge, Allison turned to face the man she had married so joyfully so many years ago. She noted the familiar curl of hair around his ear; his beautifully shaped hands; his eyes more violet than true blue. A surge of fondness tinged liberally with passion swept through her. She hadn't noticed these beloved things about Chris at dinner the other evening or the following morning on the beach. Both times she had been so tightly wrapped in her own anger and efforts at self-preservation.

"I'm listening," she said. *I am an independent woman*, she added silently, *and I am choosing to listen.*

Chris sighed. "I don't know where to start," he began. "It all goes so far back . . . Back to my childhood if that doesn't sound like too much of a cliché. Back to what happened to me when Robby was sick."

"Yes," Allison said. "I know."

"I've had so much time to think about how I acted after the miscarriage. I'm ashamed I put my own emotional needs before yours. I should have been more understanding and supportive. You were suffering, too. I should have been able to see that and to feel empathy for you. But I wasn't able to. It was as if a part of me had died along with the child. I . . . For a time, I thought I was going mad. That's not an excuse for my behavior," he added hastily. "Just the truth."

Allison felt her heart wrench with pity. "Thank you for sharing that," she said after a moment. "It means a lot."

Chris looked out over the water. "Your ring," he said. "You were wearing it yesterday."

"I was. I took it off after we talked. I was upset." She didn't tell him that her finger felt odd without it.

"I see."

"Do you still have yours?" she asked.

"Of course," Chris said, turning back to her. "There have been times when I've wanted to put it on again, but I felt I had no right to wear it. *Always yours.* I forfeited that gift two years ago."

Had he really? Allison wondered. "What did you hope to accomplish by coming here to Maine?" she asked. She did not mean the question as a challenge. But she did want an answer.

"I hoped to see if you would agree to give us another chance," Chris said without hesitation. "You're all I need in this life, Allison. If you'll have me back I'll be the happiest, most grateful man alive. And I'll do everything in my power to make you the happiest woman alive."

"My happiness is ultimately my responsibility," Allison said evenly. "But I appreciate your intent."

Chris nodded and said nothing more. That was all right. Sometimes, Allison knew, silence was enough. She looked into the eyes of the man she had married with such hope in her heart. He returned her steady gaze. And she realized as the moments passed that that man, her husband, was still there before her. He was. He had gone through a dark passage and had taken his wife along with him on that journey. She had gone willingly, mostly. The journey had ended badly. But the marriage—their love—didn't have to do the same. It just didn't.

"Yes," Allison said, her voice strong. "Yes, I'll have you back. Because I still love you." Maybe not in quite the same manner as she once did, she realized. But she did still love him. And in the end, love was what mattered most.

Chris looked as if he might faint. He stumbled a bit before reaching for her hand. "Allison," he said, his voice raspy with emotion, "thank you. I still love you, too, and I've come to realize that I never did stop loving you, not even when my selfish grief was trying to mask every ounce of affection I had ever felt for you."

"I believe you," Allison said. "But there are some things you need to know." The feel of Chris's hand around hers made Allison weak in the knees, but she soldiered on. "I won't go through ART again."

Chris nodded. "I thought as much. It's okay."

"In the future, assuming there is a future for us," Allison went on, "I might like to consider adoption."

"Yes," Chris said. "All right."

"Also," Allison went on, "I'm considering seeking out my birth parents and if I go ahead with that I'm going to need your support. In the past, you were adamantly against the idea, and maybe for the best of reasons, but it's not your decision to make."

"You're right," Chris agreed. "It isn't my decision."

"And we should see a counselor together, in addition to seeing our own therapists," Allison went on. *Boy*, she thought. *I could get to enjoy this laying down of the law!* A line from her beloved *Jane Eyre* came to her then: *"Where there is energy to command well enough, obedience never fails.*

"I'll be keeping my own place," she went on, "until we can reestablish an emotional intimacy and trust."

Still, Chris did not object.

"We're going to have to work hard, Chris, and even that won't necessarily be enough to bring us together again for the long run. I've come to believe in luck playing a part in our lives. Call it fate if you'd prefer."

Chris nodded. "I finally understand that we can't control our lives, not entirely. We can't keep our little brothers alive and we can't bring them back to life, either, no matter how hard we try. It's unfair to ourselves and to the ones we love to persist in such an impossible pursuit."

Suddenly, Allison was seized with a fit of laughter. "I'm sorry," she gasped after a moment. "I don't know why I'm laughing. None of this is funny. It's just that I've laid down so many rules and regulations . . . How can you bear to take me on?"

"How can I bear not to?" Chris countered with a laugh of his own. He reached out to hug her and Allison welcomed his arms around her. She felt herself sag into him; the sense of relief was enormous. *Welcome home*, she told him silently. *We do not belong apart.*

"Should we tell the others, or keep this to ourselves until we know we'll be okay?" she whispered. And that might not ever happen. She would need to be prepared for that eventuality, as well as for a happier one.

"This is your call," Chris said. "I've proved I'm not always so great at making smart decisions for the both of us."

"All right," she said, stepping back from their embrace. "We'll tell them."

"I'm so sorry I demanded your silence about what happened between us," Chris said. "It was wrong in so many ways."

"It was. But that was then." A shred of laughter caused Allison to look back toward Driftwood House. "I really should be getting back," she said. "Who knows what funny snaps I'm missing. You know," she said as they began to walk, "your mother sent me the article from the *Chicago Tribune* announcing your big win. Congratulations. I know how hard and for how long you worked to land that assignment. But you didn't even mention it the other night at dinner when Chuck asked how the business was going."

"The victory didn't feel like much of a victory without you to share it with me," Chris admitted. "So, my mother contacted you?"

"I was glad. She wasn't sure I'd want to celebrate your win, but I did. I was happy for you and I told her so."

"She's a good person, my mother. Both of my parents. They've been incredibly supportive." Chris smiled. "And always hopeful that one day we would reunite." Chris reached for her hand and Allison gave it to him. "I've never seen you wear color on your nails," he said with a smile. "It looks pretty."

Allison laughed. "Bess made me do it. Actually, she wanted me to go with neon green, but I said absolutely not."

They walked side by side, hands clasped, back to the party. *It is indeed a wonderful world*, Allison thought. *Bess could not have chosen a more appropriate song for this day.*

Chapter 109

The sun had finally set after a glorious display of color. Stars were visible in the velvety blue-black sky. The gentle swoosh of the water lapping at the shore could be heard from the house. The air smelled cool and sweet. Each person had changed out of his or her fancy clothes and was wearing comfortable clothing like sweatpants and hoodies, T-shirts and jeans, and in Bess's case, a lightweight flannel nightgown imprinted with a pattern of neon daisies. When Chris, who had removed his suit jacket, asked where in the world she had found such a thing, Bess had shrugged and replied, "Online, of course. All I did was type in 'daisies' and 'neon' and voilà!"

"As long as she doesn't buy a pair of matching pajamas for me," Nathan said with an exaggerated shudder. "Those things burn my retinas."

"So, I see you have a new friend," Mike commented, nodding at the large gray cat that sat curled up against Allison's left side. Chris, on Allison's right, kept shooting anxious glances at the beast.

Bess had been pleasantly surprised when Chris had stayed around after the other guests had gone off. Pleasantly surprised and hopeful. She was sure the others felt the same. And if no one came right out and asked what was going on between Allison and Chris, Bess decided, then she would. She was the bride. She could do what she wanted.

"I ascertained he's a stray," Allison explained, "and that no one has advertised for him, so I asked what he thought about coming home with me and he agreed. And don't ask how I know he agreed because I just do. His name is Gray, aka Little Gray Ghost, and he's come into my life for a reason."

"He's hardly, um, little," Marta pointed out. "And he's obviously young. He could still be growing."

"I know." Allison laid a hand on the cat's back and a loud purr erupted into the room. "Isn't he gorgeous?"

"Hey, where's your bandage?" Mike suddenly asked Chuck.

Chuck put a hand to his forehead.

"It probably fell off when you were dancing wildly with Bess's mother," Dean noted. "But no worries. The wound looks clean and the stitches seem to be undisturbed."

"I thought I was the doctor in this relationship," Chuck said with a smile.

"Your friend Inez really seemed to enjoy herself," Allison said to Bess. "One of the women from your reading group. I swear she consumed two bottles of champagne all on her own."

Bess laughed. "At least she's not belligerent when she drinks."

"As far as I could tell," Chuck noted, "no one misbehaved. No messy middle-aged 'lady' trying to seduce every male over the age of fifteen, no creepy old 'gentleman' putting his hands where he shouldn't. There was one of those at our wedding, remember, Dean, some distant cousin of yours. I don't even know how he got on the guest list."

Dean grimaced. "I'm afraid that was my aunt's doing. Wally's mother. Sorry."

"Well," Allison said earnestly, "*this* wedding was an unqualified success. Tell us you think so, Bess."

"I do. I don't have one complaint. There wasn't even a pesky seagull to deal with! Okay, maybe the lobster might have been a little more tender and the—"

Nathan raised his hand above his head. "Stop! Don't ruin the perfection for us."

Bess smiled. "Sorry. It's hard to keep my professional head from butting in."

"Now that the wedding is behind you," Marta said, "you can give that professional head a much-deserved rest."

She might be willing to give her professional head a rest, Bess thought, but not her curious personal one. She was just about to open her mouth and ask Allison and Chris what exactly was going on between them and why they were suddenly holding hands when only two days ago they couldn't even look directly at each other when Dean launched into a tale involving Ann's nine-year-old daughter, Tildy, and her fascination with Thomas. That was all right, Bess thought. The night was young and before it was over she would have her answer.

Chapter 110

Marta rested her hand on her belly. It was as flat as it had been the day before, but now she imagined she could feel the tiny contours of the new life growing inside her. The notion made her smile. One day she would tell the child about this moment and if he or she was anywhere close to being a teen, Marta would be met with an eye roll and a comment on the order of "Mom, that's so silly." That was okay.

Suddenly, Allison cleared her throat. "Chris and I have something to tell you all," she said.

Marta noticed that Allison's hand clutched in Chris's was white-knuckled. She felt a tingling run down her spine. She had been waiting not so patiently for one of the pair to speak and explain this newfound coziness.

"Yes?" Bess prompted.

"We've decided to give our marriage another try," Allison announced. "There's a long road ahead with a lot of challenges, but we each want this and we know we have your support."

There were shouts of "hurrah" and "woohoo!" and a chorus of congratulations. Gray, awakened by the noise, stepped onto Allison's lap and settled himself again, eyes warily on Chris.

"I knew it would work!" Bess cried.

"Knew what would work?" Mike asked.

"Never mind." Bess smiled. "I'm so happy for you guys," she told Chris and Allison. "I really am."

Marta gave her friends a smile. "Well done," she said. "The both of you."

When the excitement had died down, Allison looked to Chris. "I'm going to put you on the spot," she said. "Will you promise, in front of all our friends, to bake me a German chocolate cake for my birthday each year, like you used to?"

"I'll bake you one every day of the week if you'd like!" Chris said firmly. "It would be my pleasure."

Allison laughed and kissed her husband's cheek. "There's no need for that."

"And I'm going to have to get into this guy's good graces," Chris added, nodding at the feline on Allison's lap.

Marta noted that Bess's expression could only be described as smug. Clearly, she thought that bringing Allison and Chris together at her wedding *had* worked some magic, and Marta would like to think that her pep talk had helped bring Chris and Allison together, but in reality, they had done—and would continue to do—the real work of reconciliation. What Marta and the others could do now was lend what support Chris and Allison required—and to respect their need for privacy.

She glanced at Mike. He nodded. Now was the perfect time to share their own secret with those still not in the know.

Chapter 111

In one hand Allison held Chris's; the other rested on Gray. Sitting there surrounded by her dearest friends, she felt grounded in a way she hadn't felt in a very long time. Well, maybe never. This was a new life she was creating, a different one, with a fresh perspective on what it meant to be her own person before she was anyone else's.

"Mike and I have our own surprise to share with you," Marta announced.

A thought flickered across Allison's brain. How could she not have guessed?

"We're all ears," Bess said. "What an odd expression!"

Marta looked to Mike and took his hand. "I'm pregnant," she said. "And yes, it was a surprise, but sometimes surprises are what you really wanted after all."

Marta's oddly negative comments about motherhood. Her veiled complaints about the lack of a career. Her general testiness. Poor Marta, Allison thought. She must have been struggling with this new fact of her life. "Congratulations," she said. "You're right. Sometimes surprises really are gifts in disguise."

"Four kids!" Bess exclaimed. "Wow!"

"She'll be great," Mike said enthusiastically. "She's the best mom ever!"

Dean and Nathan offered their best wishes.

"And we haven't told our families yet, so mum's the word. Pardon the pun." Marta cringed. "I'm not sure how the kids will take the news."

"They'll deal with it," Chuck pronounced. "Kids are resilient and they're often better equipped to handle life's disruptions than adults are."

"This explains why you were so on edge these past two weeks," Bess said, nodding like a sage.

"Was I really horrible?" Marta asked.

"Not entirely," Allison teased. "Just here and there."

"And that's why you weren't eating oysters!" Bess cried. "No raw seafood!"

Marta laughed. "Yeah, and it's been killing me! Chuck guessed my secret."

Chuck shrugged again. "I have a gift for knowing these things. It comes from having three sisters and about a thousand female cousins."

"I have something to say and I think I speak for Marta as well." Mike smiled. "In fact, I know that I do! Allison and Chris, we'd like you to be the godparents of this new baby."

"Good idea, Mike," Marta said, giving him a kiss on his cheek.

Allison tensed. How would Chris respond to this offer? It was well intentioned, but it might also cause a degree of pain. It would compel Chris to become closely involved with a child.

"I don't know what to say," Chris admitted after a moment, his voice thick. "Thank you. The world is already full of children to love and to nurture. I realize that now."

Allison felt a surge of relief. "Remember what I said the other day, about wanting to get to know your children better," she said to Marta. "This honor will certainly help. Thank you."

"Any ideas about names?" Dean asked.

"Yes," Marta said at the same time that Mike was saying, "No."

"It won't be anything crazy, will it?" Dean asked. "Like Suburb or Cantaloupe?"

The others shouted with laughter.

"I can assure you," Marta said, "that no child of ours will be burdened with an outlandish moniker."

Allison looked to Chris; he smiled at her. It was a bittersweet moment for them both, but what really mattered was that they would soon be welcoming a new life. Together.

Chapter 112

Bess thought she would burst with happiness. Another odd expression. And kind of a gross idea, too!

Still, this day could not have been any better than it was turning out to be, not in her wildest dreams. The ceremony had been lovely, the reception a big success, her dear family had thoroughly enjoyed themselves, and now . . . Allison and Chris reunited, Mike and Marta having another child!

Bess cleared her throat dramatically. "Nathan and I have an announcement to make, too, though our news isn't half as exciting as everyone else's." She looked to Nathan and he smiled. "Nathan got a promotion and we're moving to Stockholm for two years."

Dean winked at Bess. "Congratulations," he said.

"Wow. When did this happen?" Allison asked.

"Just a few days ago," Nathan told them. "It was a bit of a trauma to spring on Bess so soon before the wedding but . . ."

Bess laughed. "But that's life, messy, too late, too early, never what or where you expect it to be."

"So," Marta asked, "how will it all work? I mean, your company, Bess?"

"I'm not sure yet," Bess admitted. "Right now, I'm thinking I'll keep the business up and running, with Kara the on-hand person and me doing the behind-the-scenes work. And I might start a blog about my adventures. And when we get back to the States," Bess went on, "well, who knows what will happen then? Chances are I'll have benefited from new experiences that will allow me to expand Joie de Vivre or even to forge a brand-new career if I want to. I did it once; I'm sure I can do it again!"

Allison smiled. "I was afraid, but I did it anyway!"

"Congratulations are due to Nathan," Chuck said.

"Thank you. I wasn't really expecting this promotion, but I'd be lying if I said I'm not excited about it."

"There's one more important thing that has to take place before this day can be truly deemed perfect," Bess announced. "I have something for you all." She reached into a large lavender-colored bag slouched at her side and took out a blue silk-covered box.

"As long as it's not more food!" Mike laid a hand gingerly on his stomach. "I had to loosen my belt to the last notch before giving up entirely and changing into my sweats."

"I'm going to join you on your morning constitutional," Marta said. "I might not be up to running, but I'll stagger along."

"I've been wondering what you had stashed in that sack," Allison noted. "You look like a summer Santa."

Bess got up from her seat, opened the box, and began to move from one of her friends to the next, handing each a charm as she went. "I had these made for you," she explained, "as a token of our friendship. The anchor is necessary for navigation over unknown waters. It provides hope when the sea is raging and the wind is bellowing and you think that's it, this is the end. And then you remember that something is tethering you to the solid ground and you go on and face the next minute and the one after that with more courage than you thought possible in the first terrified moments when you forgot you were not alone. You guys keep me hopeful and facing forward. You always have and I believe you always will. Okay, things change, for better and for worse, as most of you are fond of pointing out to me! But I choose to believe that our friendship—my love for you and yours for me—is eternal. Everlasting. As secure as a ship firmly anchored to the bottom of the sea."

"Hear, hear!" The cry was unanimous as Bess sat back next to Nathan.

Dean unabashedly wiped a tear from his eye. "I'm honored to be included in this tribute," he said. "Thank you, Bess."

Chuck, clutching his charm, put his arm around Dean's shoulder and planted a kiss on his cheek.

"I figured out that when marriage is at its best," Bess said, "the two people involved really do become united as one being in a very important sense. You're a part of Chuck now, Dean," Bess went on, "and he's part of you. For better or worse."

"And worse would be those Necco wafers he's so fond of. Ugh." Dean turned to Nathan. "So, did you get a charm, too?"

Nathan dug under his shirt and pulled out a chain on which hung his charm. "Of course!"

"With the way I've been acting," Marta said quietly, "I'm not sure I deserve this from you, Bess."

"Stop it," Bess said. "These gifts have been given freely."

Marta smiled gratefully. "It seems we've all been on your wavelength, Bess, even if we didn't know it at first. I used the image of the anchor in my speech today. Allison referred to you as our anchor days ago."

"I'll add mine to my keychain," Mike announced.

Allison smiled. "I know the perfect antique silver chain for mine."

Chris shook his head. "I can't believe you had one made for me," he said softly, "not after what happened . . ."

Bess smiled at her friend. "When I ordered the charms," she said, "I had no idea what had gone on between you and Allison to cause the split. To be honest, when I learned the whole truth I hesitated to include you in my gift. I felt so angry with you for . . ." Bess felt herself blush as she recalled the terrible encounter she and Chris had shared. "But I've learned a lot about love these past two weeks," she went on. "I'm not happy being a judgmental or a self-righteousness person. It makes me feel ugly."

"That's our Bess," Chuck said feelingly. "She loves one and all equally!"

"With one exception," Bess said, linking her arm through her husband's. "I'm sorry, but I do love Nathan best!"

Chapter 113

Nathan realized that he had left a few cases of Prosecco at the foot of the back porch. "We don't want any tipsy wildlife waking us up in the middle of the night," he said, hurrying toward the door. Chuck, Dean, Mike, and Chris had gone along to help—and maybe to drink a bottle with Nathan. With the men temporarily out of the room, Marta knew what was coming. Her girlfriends would want to know the important details. That was okay.

"We were wondering," Bess said, "if you're really happy with the pregnancy."

"It's just that you've been in such a strange mood these past two weeks," Allison added.

Marta smiled ruefully. "You mean a mad, bad, and dangerous mood. The fact is, I wasn't happy. It's a long story, but like I said, the pregnancy came as a total surprise. I'd begun to imagine the next phase of my life and it included a career, anything but another baby."

"So, what changed your mind about the pregnancy?" Bess asked.

"Aside from the fact that it's *your* baby," Allison guessed.

"Yes, maternal instinct kicked in," Marta admitted, "wide-eyed astonishment that somehow this body that I often take for granted is growing another life. That sense of awe is something I hadn't yet felt with this baby, not until yesterday when suddenly it struck me that I was a walking miracle. But that's not all. These two weeks here with you all has helped me come to grips with what I'd been battling in terms of not having pursued a career and now wanting to do just that." Marta paused. "A fourth child adds another challenge but doesn't render a career impossible. I have to believe that."

"Did Mike know about your fraught feelings?" Allison asked gently.

Marta frowned. "That was part of the problem. I couldn't seem to tell him. He was so totally into the idea of another child . . . I know it was wrong to keep my feelings from him. A few days ago, I finally broke down and admitted my unhappiness. It was an ugly scene followed by an ugly few days and I'm afraid it was all my doing. It seems you're never too old to be stupid."

"Not stupid," Allison corrected. "Human."

"Mike will forgive you," Bess said quickly.

"He already has. But I still feel bad about hurting him."

Allison nodded. "Marriage is a minefield, Bess. You never stop having to step carefully, not really."

"Gee, thanks. Now I feel so much more enthusiastic about my future!"

"Hey," Marta said, "no one ever said life was going to be a bed of roses."

"Don't worry, Bess," Allison said. "You and Nathan will be fine. The benefits of marriage outweigh the challenges. Don't let anyone try to convince you otherwise."

"I won't," Bess assured her. "You know, I think we've all grown up—or at least, we've been bumped sideways!—these past two weeks. Summer vacation as boot camp for adulthood. Who would have thought?"

"Now it's your turn on the hot seat," Marta said, turning to Allison. "I'm a bit surprised that you agreed to try and rebuild things with Chris. Pleasantly surprised—I believe Chris really and truly wants to be your husband—but also—"

"Concerned," Allison said with a nod.

"Me too," Bess said.

"Honestly, I wasn't sure until the moment the words were out of my mouth what I was going to say when he asked me to take him back. But suddenly, everything became clear. I never stopped loving him. And love goes a long way toward making peace in a relationship."

Marta nodded. "That it does."

"And in some ways, love is so much easier than liking. I don't like some of the things Chris said or did, but I *love* him and I'm willing to give him another chance. And I'm willing to give myself another chance with him, to be stronger and more of my own person. To know the difference between service and servitude. If Chris really loves me for me, and not for the version he—we both—created all those years ago, we'll be all right."

"You're brave, Allison," Bess said. "I really admire this decision."

Allison smiled. "You guys deserve admiration, too," she said. "You helped bring me to this point. Being here these past two weeks was worth more in the end than the two years I'd been try- ing to get through on my own. Something very healing happened for me here in Maine and I'm grateful."

"And only days ago you were so sure that your life wasn't going to turn out to be a happy one," Bess said. "You were so sure that not everything can change for the better."

"I'm still a realist, Bess. As for my life turning out to be a happy one—we'll see. But I feel a lot more optimistic now than I did when I got off the plane in Boston two weeks ago." Allison smiled and nodded toward the feline, who was at this moment stalking toward the kitchen. "And now I've got Gray on my side! My familiar as Marta suggested a few days ago."

"I wouldn't mess with that cat," Marta remarked. "Chris had bet- ter watch his step."

Allison laughed. "He will," she said. "I really believe he will."

So did Marta.

Chapter 114

The men had rejoined the women in the kitchen. Allison noted that one of the cases of Prosecco they piled up on the island counter was not quite full. Well, it was a celebration.

She reached for Chris's hand and he took it warmly. Nathan put his arm around Bess's shoulder. Marta leaned into Mike. Chuck and Dean were holding hands, as well.

"Look," Bess said suddenly, "I promise I won't be upset, but I need to know the truth. Were you guys lying about not being able to get your schedules in sync last year when I was trying to plan the reunion? If you were, I get it, but there's no need to lie in the future. If you just need a break from the old gang, I'm fine with that. Really."

"Mike and I weren't lying, Bess, honest," Marta assured her.

"Same here," Dean said. "Chuck's schedule was a nightmare and I was knee-deep in adoption paperwork."

"My schedule wasn't much lighter," Allison told her. "And Greg was taking a long overdue vacation, so I was on my own for almost a month."

"I'm afraid you know my excuse," Chris said.

Bess smiled. "All right then, where should the next reunion take place?"

"As long as there's a hospital nearby," Marta said. "I'm not giving birth to my next child in a snowbank."

"Maybe we should wait until this baby is here safe and sound," Mike suggested.

Marta nodded. "Agreed."

"We could visit Bess and Nathan in Stockholm," Chris suggested.

"That would be fantastic," Nathan said enthusiastically.

"I've always wanted to go to Sweden," Allison said happily. "My mom believed I have Swedish blood in me."

"How would everyone feel about the kids coming along, all four of them?" Mike asked with a smile.

Dean nodded. "Thomas needs to meet his de facto cousins. I think it would be great."

"I agree," Bess said, with a bit of an impish look. "I'm not as hopeless with children as I might have led you to believe."

Allison saw Dean give Bess a wink and wondered what secret they shared.

"You know," Chuck remarked, "Bess couldn't have chosen a more appropriate wedding song. The world truly is a wonderful place as long as your friends are at your side."

"Bess?" Allison asked. Bess's expression had gone dreamy. "Are you hearing any of this?"

Bess startled. "What?" she said. "Yeah, I mean no. See, I was just thinking—what if when Thomas grows up he marries Marta's next baby? Wouldn't that be awesome? We'd all be officially family then. Well, not all of us but most of us and—"

A collective groan rose from the others.

"Bess," Allison said, shaking her head, "you are absolutely the worst case of an incurable romantic I've ever encountered!"

"Guilty as charged," Bess said. "And proud of it."

"Is there any cake left?" Mike asked suddenly.

Marta raised an eyebrow. Mike shrugged. "What can I say? It was really good cake, especially that chocolate-chocolate mint."

"My appetite's come back, too," Chris admitted.

While Mike and Chris descended on the fridge, Chuck and Dean went in search of forks and plates. Nathan decided to pop open yet another bottle of Prosecco.

Allison, after pouring a small bowl of half-and-half for Gray, watched the proceedings with a light heart. Marta, usually so cautious about her diet, eagerly accepted a piece of cake from her husband. Bess and Nathan shared a slice of the hazelnut. Chuck shoveled cake into his mouth in his usual manner, while Dean savored his more slowly.

"For you," Chris said, as he handed Allison a glass of Prosecco and raised his own. "To my wife."

Allison raised her glass in return. "To my husband," she said. She was so very happy.

Please turn the page
for a very special Q&A
with Holly Chamberlin!

Q. So, did your wedding take place on the beach?

A. No, my wedding, both the ceremony and the reception, was held at the InterContinental in my hometown of New York City. It was partly a practical decision as my husband's family was coming from out of town; this way they wouldn't have to be dealing with NYC traffic while trying to get from church to reception venue. The decision was also partly a nod to my parents' wedding reception that took place at a gorgeous hotel on the West Side of Manhattan in 1961. I wore my mother's dress, slightly altered to accommodate our different waistlines and the fact that the material in a few places hadn't worn very well.

Q. Have you ever attended a beachside wedding?

A. No! I think it would be really lovely. In fact, all of the weddings I've attended or been part of have taken place indoors. Hmm. Maybe I could crash a wedding on the beach one day, like onlookers crashed Bess's ceremony.

Q. Speaking of those onlookers, you have Marta comment that people's fascination with weddings says something good about human nature.

A. Absolutely. Anytime I've seen a bride having her picture taken or emerging from a church hand in hand with her groom, or with her bride, as the case may be, I become a weepy mess. The fact that we keep trying to love and commit to each other is pretty amazing, especially when we witness so much strife on a daily basis. I have a few friends who haven't tied the knot with their longtime loves and if they ever decide to marry I think I might pass out with happiness.

Q. Do you have a favorite character, or put another way, is there a particular character with whom you closely identify?

A. It's odd, but in this story I pretty much like every one of the main characters equally. And I realized at one point that the unlikable things about each of them—and we're all unlikable at some moments—are often drawn from what I perceive to be my own flaws and failures. I'm not sure how that happened, but it did. I won't tell you what bits of me are to be found in Bess, Allison, and Marta, though! I will say that Chuck is the character who speaks most about certain issues that have been on my mind a lot in the past year, so in a way I feel closest to him.

Q. What's your next book going to be about?
A. Well, all I can say at this point—and not because I'm being coy; because I've barely begun to think the story through!—is that it will feature two sisters in their sixties. They've been estranged for a number of years due to a number of circumstances, but something happens to force them to face each other and to lay to rest—if they can!—their demons. It should be exciting to write for a number of reasons, one of which is that with very few exceptions, I haven't focused on characters this age. It won't be too many years before I celebrate my sixtieth birthday so it's about time I write about my peeps!

A WEDDING
ON THE
BEACH

Holly Chamberlin

ABOUT THIS GUIDE

The suggested questions are included
to enhance your group's reading of
Holly Chamberlin's *A Wedding on the Beach*!

DISCUSSION QUESTIONS

1. Bess is the only one of the friends without real regrets in terms of her career or her love life. Then, on the eve of their wedding, Nathan announces he has received a promotion that will require a two-year stint in Stockholm. Bess is forced to make a decision that will affect the career she built with such passion and hard work. How do you feel about the decision she makes?

2. Marta is currently doubting the wisdom of her decision to forgo a career outside of the home. She recalls that when she made the decision not to go on to law school, she felt too embarrassed to admit to anyone but Mike that what she wanted more than anything was to be a full-time, stay-at-home mother. Now, just as she had begun to consider how she might build a life for herself outside of the home, she is faced with another pregnancy. Why do you think she experiences such terrible dismay and self-doubt regarding her ability to handle the arrival of another child along with the challenges of a nascent career?

3. Allison has come to see that her behavior in her marriage, i.e., her constant willingness to adopt Chris's needs and desires as her own, was a big mistake. While her career doesn't seem to have suffered due to this dynamic, she now considers how far she might grow her business without the restrictions of marriage to Chris. For example, she considers taking time off to travel and shoot a book of photographs. How might her reuniting with Chris impact her implementing these ideas?

4. At one point Marta mentions that women can be harshest with other women. Has this been your experience? If so, how have you encountered prejudicial judgment or unhelpful criticism from other women? When have other

women—friends, colleagues, family members—offered support and understanding of your choices?

5. The theme of friendships over time is one of the most important in this book. The characters discuss what exactly holds long-term friendships together—love, habit, laziness, a desire to maintain the status quo, nostalgia. Old friends are compared to new friends, i.e., those with whom we share current circumstances and not the past. How does our need for old friends change over time? How important are our circumstantial friends? Is Bess naïve in her belief that friendships can last forever, and that old friends—the ones we make when young—are more valuable than friends we make later on in life? Do you think that marriage will alter Bess's need for her old friends in any appreciable way?

6. Chuck says to Bess: "Your life is your own. But being married complicates that truth. By taking that pledge of love and commitment, you've created a third being, the union, to which you each have a duty to contribute the best person you can be." Do you think a person can ever be truly independent while in a committed relationship? Do you think that Dean is correct when he tells Bess that constant negotiation—talking and tweaking—is key to a good marriage?

7. Talk about Bess and her awkward relationship with her family. For example, for most of her adult life, and for reasons that are understandable, Bess has felt isolated from her sisters. Do you think Bess can follow through with her resolve to get to know her sisters and their children more thoroughly?

8. Talk about Allison's struggle with adoration versus a healthier sort of romantic love. When is sacrifice for a

loved one damaging to oneself? Chris, too, has his difficulties in this regard, viewing Allison as more saint than flawed human being. How is this unfair to both members of the relationship? When Chris tells Allison that he wants a divorce, he extracts a promise of silence from her regarding the circumstances that led to this moment. Later, Allison feels that guilt and shame have become her jailors, keeping her from reaching out for support. How is this situation typical or illustrative of their relationship?

9. Marta, while reflecting on her one-night stand with Chris, realizes that: "To a young person, the future didn't really exist; long-term consequences were insignificant; trouble could be dealt with in a mythical 'later'; there was always time to give up the bad habit, start over, change direction. Until there wasn't." At another point, the women talk about the universality of regret. Discuss these ideas in relation to each of the friends.

10. If you were writing the sequel to this novel, what would the future hold for the characters? Do you think Allison and Chris will make it as a couple? Do you think Allison will one day search for her birth parents? What do you foresee for Marta in terms of forging a career alongside the demands of her family? How do you think Bess will fare, both with Nathan and in her career? Will she make the effort to spend more time with her family? Do you think Chuck and Dean will adopt more children?

Connect with Us

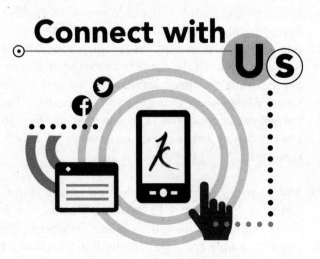

Visit us online at
KensingtonBooks.com
to read more from your favorite authors, see books
by series, view reading group guides, and more.

for sneak peeks, chances to win books and prize packs,
and to share your thoughts with other readers.

facebook.com/kensingtonpublishing
twitter.com/kensingtonbooks

Tell us what you think!

To share your thoughts, submit a review,
or sign up for our eNewsletters, please visit:
KensingtonBooks.com/TellUs.